BLOOD IN THE LAKE

BLOOD IN THE LAKE

by ANNE L. SIMON

Sewanee, Tennessee

Also by Anne L. Simon:
Blood in the Cane Field

Copyright © 2015 by Anne L. Simon
Border Press
PO Box 3124
Sewanee, Tennessee 37375
www.borderpressbooks.com

Blood in the Lake is a work of fiction. Although loosely based upon actual events, details of location and characters are the product of the author's imagination. Any resemblance to persons living or dead is accidental and unintended.

Library of Congress Control Number: 2015933852

ISBN-978-0-9862801-2-2

Cover art by Nan M. Landry

Dedicated to everyone who works in the American system of justice —a flawed system, but the best as yet devised by man.

And to Maggie—lawyer, editor, the voice of Mandy, beloved granddaughter.

PART I

MISSING

PawPaw went missing on Monday, the last day of August. I didn't know that day. No one did. The next day, Tuesday, just back after my early morning class, I'd made a cup of tea and settled in to read the five cases I needed to master before my evening seminar. My cell phone buzzed in the pocket of my jeans.

"Mandy? How are you, Mandy?" My Mom's voice.

"Fine, Mom. What's up?"

"Nothing to be alarmed about. Nothing serious. But I thought you should know we have a little problem here."

Mom didn't need to tell me she had a problem. I knew as soon as I heard the strain in her voice. She sounds like that when she's stressed.

"So what's happened?"

"PawPaw isn't home this morning, and he didn't tell us where he was going."

"So? PawPaw's always out at this time of day. He goes to Thib's for coffee with the boys."

"No-o." Mom spoke slowly. "He's not at Thib's. I called."

"Maybe he stopped by Aunt Tut's? Did you check with her?"

"Sure did." Mom's false breezy tone returned. "But not to worry, dear. I'm sure he's somewhere around. We just don't know where he is right now. I just thought you should know."

"Is his truck at his house?"

My question went right past her. "I've made a lot of calls, so someone will be calling back soon with news, but... It kind of looks like he wasn't home last night."

"What do you mean, not home last night?"

"Nothing to be alarmed about. I'll call back when he turns up."

This was not like Mom, repeating herself and making non-responsive answers. Now I repeated myself. "Wait, what do you mean he wasn't home last night? How do you know that?"

"Well, I just think maybe he wasn't home. I'll be in touch."

I didn't want to let her end the call, leaving me hanging, but the line went dead.

What the heck was going on? Why wouldn't Mom talk? Was there someone close by who shouldn't hear what she had to say?

I'm a deliberate sort, not one to jump into action. I usually take time to process information and think through the options, but the strain in Mom's voice had me worried. I checked the caller ID and saw she'd phoned from PawPaw's house. I pressed the talk button to call her back. Busy. I waited a few minutes and tried again. Busy again. I called our house, next door to PawPaw's. No answer. That did it.

I snapped my law book shut, grabbed my wallet, and headed for my little Corolla. Not yet eleven o'clock, I'd have time for the trip home, check on things, and be back for my seminar at six. I threaded through the early lunch crowd on Dalrymple Drive and merged into I-10 to cross the Mississippi River. I tried the calls again. No luck.

Once on the calmer twenty-eight-mile stretch over the Atchafalaya Basin, thoughts of PawPaw came back into my head. Where could he be? We'd been noticing a few dents and scrapes on the bumpers and fenders of his truck, but he'd never driven somewhere and not known how to get home. An eighty-year-old out alone? Anything could have happened.

Damnit! I'd completely forgotten my afternoon appointment at Career Services. As a 3L, third year law student, midway through my last semester at LSU Law School, I was finally looking at the end of years of non-stop study. I could almost feel the diploma in my hand. But then what? I needed to sign up for interviews and focus on finding a job.

I didn't have top grades that brought forth bids from the major firms, so what were my options? During my first law school summer, in addition to classes, I'd worked at a Lafayette firm doing insurance defense. Summarizing depositions bored me batty. My second summer, I worked as a research assistant in the DA's office in Baton Rouge. Much better, actually exciting, but I didn't have the political connections to snag a permanent job in that office. Stay local? We had a large family, but no lawyers who might take on an associate. I didn't have the money to set up my own office and accept whatever came in the door. I'd probably get only divorces, and be totally on my own. Did I want to clerk for a judge? If so, where did I want to do that? Indecision.

I called and cancelled my Career Services appointment—for the third time. And I made a resolution. As soon as this distraction passed, I'd make some decisions.

A flashing sign on the shoulder snapped me back to the present. *Atchafalaya Basin Speed Limit. Cars 60, Trucks 55.* My speedometer read well past seventy-five. I slowed down and turned on the cruise control. I didn't need the financial hit—and delay—of dealing with a ticket. There's a good reason for reduced speed up here, especially on the high bridge over the Whiskey River. No place for refuge in case of a sudden emergency. I took a few deep breaths and pulled up a pleasant memory to pass the time as I drove over the cypress studded swamp toward home.

I thought of Sunday afternoon, just two days ago, the last time I'd seen my PawPaw. After noon dinner, my brother Taddy had jumped up from the table and run next door to PawPaw's for his favorite pastime, fishing in Lake Peigneur. I helped Mom clean up the kitchen and spent a couple of hours reviewing my cases for the next day. About five o'clock, at my mom's urging, I had crossed over to PawPaw's to summon Taddy home.

Shouting a supper call seemed totally out of harmony with the tranquil lakeside scene. I walked down the slope to the water's edge to call him within a closer range. Cypress and oak trees canopied the shoreline, shading my brother's perch on the bulkhead. Memories had come flooding back. Fishing at PawPaw's had been my favorite pastime when I was Taddy's age. To my left, a Great Egret strolled through the muddy shallows. He stopped. Drawing up one twig-thin leg, he dangled his skinny, three-inch long, coal-black toes above the mirrored surface of the lake. Stretching his neck, he rotated slowly to survey the scene. Satisfied to find everything in order, he tipped his head ten degrees and pointed one beady eye downward into the murky water covering his feet. Could he spot a tasty morsel stirred up by his toes? Not this time. He drew his neck back into a pleasing curve, carefully reset his long toes on the lake bottom, and resumed his stately promenade.

Until he spied a minnow who swam too close. With the speed of a dagger thrust, his neck uncurled. His bright yellow beak plunged downward to pierce the surface. The bill rose again, now flaunting a squirming flash of silver. He raised his bill skyward, yawned, and flipped the minnow into his open mouth where it slipped, still squirming, into the maw. The quivering bump traveled down the chute and vanished into the body of the bird. After a mere two seconds dealing with the mundane business of digesting his dinner, the egret had raised one thin leg and then the other, resuming his majestic stroll. He dared anyone to take note that his imperial highness, the Great Egret, had interrupted a survey of his realm to satisfy a mere commoner's need for food.

The Great Egret and Taddy had taken no notice of one another. The process of impaling a fat brown worm on a fishhook commanded the boy's full attention, and the bird felt no threat from what for him was an everyday sight. A flock of peeps needled the shallow water off to the right, and a dozen shiny green-headed mallards drifting a little farther out from shore found tasty duckweed to pass through their wide bills. For this country boy and his bird, both totally at home in the shallows at the edge of their lake, not even an alligator would be worthy of anything more than a mental note to maintain respectful distance.

"Taddy, you need to be getting on home. Tomorrow's a school day."

Intent on the process of baiting his hook, Taddy hadn't heard me coming.

"What? Not now. I'm just gettin' this wiggler on my hook."

"OK. I'll wait a bit, but we've got to go soon."

I took a seat on the bulkhead next to my little brother. To pass the time, I began mentally packing my car for the trip back across the Basin to return to law school for the coming week of classes. I remember deciding to ask Mom if I could take a few packages of shrimp from her freezer. And maybe some filleted reds. I missed the local food when I was at school, and I missed these quiet afternoons at the lake.

After he had baited his hook, Taddy stepped up on a weathered board that led from the bulkhead down into the dark water, spreading his bare feet wide for balance. Oh, those feet were grimy! With practiced ease, Taddy swung his rod back and then forward. The line whirred as it spun twenty feet out over the water. Taddy stood still, hands relaxed, fingers waiting to feel the slightest pull on the line. Before him, the sun sliding down the western sky painted a palette of rosy hues on the shining surface of the lake.

On the porch of a white frame house set some distance above the water's edge, our PawPaw bobbed slowly to and fro in a weathered rocker. Occasionally, he had glanced out to check on Taddy. Quiet, a touch of cool in the air, a visit from a grandson who loved his lake, many times PawPaw had told us Sundays in the fall were the best.

Back to reality. PawPaw missing now? Oh, God. Where could he have gone? Mom didn't sound right. Why wouldn't she answer my questions? After trying the calls one more time, I pushed those worries out of my mind and returned to memories of last Sunday at the lake.

I recall I glanced now and then toward the black and white TV screen flickering on the end of PawPaw's porch. Child of the Depression, PawPaw hated to throw out anything that still functioned. When we bought him a new TV for the central hall, he insisted we put the old one on the porch. Sitting with Taddy down by the lake, I was too far away to hear the sound, but I could guess what was on the screen: an aerial photograph showing white bands swirling over the island of Cuba, a bent funnel reaching from the western shore into the Gulf of Mexico. A tropical storm. A hurricane tracking chart of the Caribbean is familiar to anyone who lives in south Louisiana in the late summer and early fall.

I remembered something else. On the far shore of the lake, where a two-lane blacktop road leading from the bridge over the Delcambre Canal crumbled into a shell-covered turnaround at the water's edge, movement caught my eye. A battered white pickup truck had pulled up and parked. As I watched, the driver stepped out and came around to the front of the truck. He wore faded jeans and white rubber shrimper's boots, an everyday sight in these parts. A white pickup truck is probably the most common vehicle you find in rural south Louisiana.

I didn't think a thing about the scene until, after a check in all directions, the man leaned back against the front bumper, pulled a package of papers from his shirt pocket, and drew a plastic baggie out of his pants. He had rolled a joint expertly—using only one hand—and placed the white cylinder between his lips. He reached back into his shirt pocket for a lighter. He inhaled the smoke, held it for a few moments, tipped up his chin, and exhaled toward the sky. Damn! That stuff is everywhere. The man had watched the smoke waft upward and then vanish, carried away by the slight breeze blowing across the water.

Attention back to the lake, I remember a bustle of activity in the flock of mallards forty feet from shore. Nervous green-heads quivered from side to side, picking up glints of light from the lowering sun. Accompanied by splashing and a crescendo of honks, the mallards rose together, pawing their wide webbed feet in a clumsy effort to find traction on the surface of the water. One shiny green-head took the lead, drawing the flock skyward across the lake until they all vanished behind the cypress treetops on the far side.

The peeps—we call all the little shore birds peeps because only real bird nuts can tell one kind from another—needed only a second to process the flight of the mallards. Cued by the splashy departure of the ducks, the head of every little bird twitched. Then, following the baton of an invisible conductor, they lifted in a cloud, banked, turned, and resettled in the shallows below the big white house commanding a rise above the northern shore of the lake.

At the departure of the mallards and the relocation of the flock of peeps, the Great Egret halted his leisurely stroll. Again, he haughtily stretched out his magnificent neck. What had caused the change of mood in his dining room? He looked skyward and sighted the source of the disturbance. A grand armada had materialized over the treetops in the southern sky, silent at first, then emitting a low thrum.

The flight of the mallards and peeps had not interrupted Taddy's concentration on his fishing, but then, his attention drawn by the unfamiliar sound, he looked at the sky. Scores of huge brown birds with long heavy beaks and five-foot feathered wings flew straight in his direction. Taddy froze. The huge birds kept coming. When they were directly in front of him, they tucked their heads, aimed their bills downward, and plunged into the lake. Their front ends disappeared beneath the surface of the water not more than twenty feet past Taddy's fishing line. Perhaps ten seconds later, each bird rose from the splash he had created, awkwardly righting himself, and settled on the surface of the water, rocking on his own wake.

Taddy didn't see the last scene of this play. Startled, and probably frightened by the assault he thought targeted directly at himself, he had hastily pulled in his line, dropped his rod on the bulkhead, and hightailed it up the bank toward PawPaw. I had followed him halfway.

"PawPaw," he called out to his grandfather. "Come see! Come see, PawPaw!"

Taddy tore up the wooden porch steps, pulled open the screen door, and let it slam behind him. Bam! The old man started from a doze. Taddy stood panting before his grandfather. I was equally startled to see pelicans on Lake Peigneur, but Taddy wouldn't turn to me for information on this topic. Man stuff.

"PawPaw! Dinosaur birds! A whole flock of dinosaur birds just crashed into the lake!"

"What you say there, son?" PawPaw shook himself awake. PawPaw called all his grandsons "son" and the girls he called by a half dozen names like honey, sugar, and most often, *chère*. When you have eight grown children, most with families of their own, the names of the third generation become far too numerous for an eighty-year-old to remember—especially in a family that likes to recycle the old names. Soon PawPaw would have great-grandchildren old enough to come to play at the old homestead on the lake. He'd never keep them all straight.

"I'm not makin' it up, PawPaw. I saw 'em. Honest, honest I did. There must be a hundred of 'em. They just came flappin' in like crazy, headed straight across the lake toward Davy's house. Then they dove, swoosh, down into the water." The boy's right arm swept the air, miming the birds' maneuver.

PawPaw had punched the off button on the remote control on his lap. Steadying himself on the door frame, he stood up, pausing a moment. He nodded his head when assured that all body parts were responding to instructions from his brain.

Taddy continued to sputter. "We got to call Jay. We just got to call Jay. He'll go crazy to see dinosaur birds."

"Jay?" PawPaw tipped his head.

"Cousin Jay, PawPaw. You know, Uncle J. Allen's boy. He's got a thing about dinosaurs. He even likes to act like he's a dinosaur himself, curling his hands and making those grunts. Grumph, grumph. Let's go, PawPaw. Before they fly away." Taddy had reached for his grandfather's hand.

"Sure, son. Let's go have a look at 'em."

Taddy helped PawPaw down the porch steps. PawPaw's touch banished the boy's fear, and his steady young arm replaced the old man's need for a walking cane, a fine arrangement for both the boy and his beloved grandfather as they made their way down the slope to the bulkhead.

Remembering that scene tightened my throat. Where could

PawPaw be now? Again I tried to reach Mom. Still no response.

Back down at the water's edge, we three had watched the big birds rocking slowly on the surface of the lake.

"There, PawPaw. You see 'em? Dinosaur birds. They're dinosaur birds."

"Uh, hum," PawPaw said slowly. "I see 'em all right, son. A magnificent sight!" The old man shaded his eyes with his hand and peered across the lake into low sun. "A magnificent sight indeed, son." PawPaw had then added a gentle suggestion. "I do believe those birds are pelicans, my boy. Louisiana Brown Pelicans. And you're right, a crowd. There're at least fifty out there, maybe more. I'm proud of my little birder. You made a great sighting."

Taddy's head turned upward. "You say they're pelicans?"

PawPaw placed his hand on Taddy's shoulder, softening the words that might disparage the boy's achievement. "Right, son. Pelicans. I don't ever before remember seeing pelicans this far inland. Really a marvelous sight to see."

"You're saying they're not dinosaur birds, PawPaw? They sure look like the dinosaur birds in my book."

"I'm pretty sure about that, son. They're not dinosaurs, but they're wondrous all the same. These big birds have quite a story. A few years back they were just about wiped out by the DDT—some chemical that made their eggs so brittle they cracked in the nest. No chicks made it. Then the birds came back, just about all the way, only to be hit again by the big oil spill that darn near sank every one of 'em. Now my fishermen friends tell me we got bunches of pelicans in the Gulf, back roosting on the oil rigs and nesting out there on what's left of the barrier islands. But not like before the spill. But here? On our lake? That's news. Quite a discovery, all right. You've made a real discovery."

"But PawPaw—"

PawPaw kept talking. "How about you go get me that lawn chair over there, son. Then cast your line again. I'll sit here with you and your sister for a while."

The old man, the boy, and I had settled in to watch the bobbing birds. Taddy pointed to the Great Egret who had now resumed his stately stroll.

"PawPaw, look at that big bird. He's my friend, you know. He's not a bit worried about those dino—pelican birds."

"No, son. Not a bit. The Great Egret knows pelicans want deep water, not his shallow fishing spot. They dive for big fish, not sweep for minnows or forage for crawfish burrowing in the mud close to shore."

The sun moved lower in the rosy sky, spreading a blood-red shimmer on the surface of the lake. I remember thinking bad weather wouldn't come the next day. *Red sky at night, travelers delight.* The glowing orb dropped behind the tops of the cypress trees, stenciling their limbs against the evening sky. Watching the rocking pelicans, PawPaw slumped and his eyelids drooped.

I stood up. "Come along, Taddy. It's past time. Tomorrow's a school day. You need a good shower."

"Could I call Jay tonight? I know it's too late for him to come today, but I could ask him over tomorrow afternoon. Could I? Please? Could I?"

"I'll be back at school. We'll ask Mom. Come on home now."

"If we can't call Jay, could we call Davy? Those birds were heading right for his house. Maybe he saw 'em. He could have looked at 'em straight out of his bedroom window." Taddy wanted to show off his discovery to one of his buddies and maybe get someone to agree that PawPaw was wrong.

The Victorian mansion known as Jefferson House, Davy's summer home, dominated a gentle rise on the northern shore of Lake Peigneur. The cupola or the upper windows would both have been great vantage points from which to view the scene.

Paw-Paw had turned aside Taddy's request. "Davy's back in Tennessee, son. There's no one over there now. His dad came by the house last week to drop off the key and said he wouldn't be back until duck season, around Thanksgiving. Davy had to go back to school. Just like you."

I was always glad when the Alexanders were at the lake. From the time they bought the Jefferson House and spent their first summer in Louisiana, PawPaw had enjoyed their company. Before the Alexanders had children of their own, Mom told me

PawPaw taught the nephews and their visiting friends how to cast a line, and PawPaw continued to be a fishing guide to the three Alexander sons who followed. I knew Jack Alexander was trying to sell the place, and that made me uneasy. What would happen to it? I hoped the man who ran the nursery down the shore would take on the house as well. He would do a magnificent job.

We had tried to convince Taddy he couldn't have seen anyone over there. He wouldn't listen.

"No, PawPaw. I saw someone on the dock. Right when I first got here."

"You're imagining things, son."

I remember wondering if Taddy had seen the same man I'd spotted across the lake. I checked the shell turn-around; the pot smoker had gone.

"Go put up your rod, Taddy, and let's get going," I told him.

I took Taddy's arm and shot him a look of reprimand that said *stop arguing with your grandfather.* Taddy sensed I had little patience left and followed my instruction, but first he looked over to the lake and dipped his head to his friend, the Great Egret. PawPaw rubbed a gnarled hand on the boy's shoulder. "I swear that bird bowed his head to you, Taddy. Haughty thing never even acknowledges the rest of us are around."

Nostalgia. Remembering the many Sunday afternoons I'd spent at the lake when I was a young girl made me sad. How many times had my mother come down to the water to call me in for supper? I couldn't guess. At Taddy's age, more than a dozen years ago now, I'd been as fond of the lakeside as Taddy. PawPaw used to call me his Lady of the Lake. I had a favorite spot on the bank right where our yard met PawPaw's. Beneath a canopy of live oaks, two-foot high cypress knees trapped still ponds teeming with aquatic life. That corner became my secret hideout, tree house, fairyland, or whatever imaginary kingdom I visited at the time. That's where I had found Yellow Puff, a little mallard unable to keep up as her mother led newly hatched chicks onto the lake. I took Yellow Puff home to raise. When she had her coat of feathers, her beak long and looking around for mischief, I returned her to the lake. She swam away, but for almost a year afterward, whenever I called her name, Yellow Puff came to my little corner to take bread straight from my fingers. Maybe *she* was a *he*. I never knew.

We walked the old man back up to the porch. When we were out of earshot, Taddy started in on me again.

"PawPaw says they're pelicans, but they sure look like dinosaur birds to me. We got to call Jay, Mandy. He's *really* into dinosaurs you know."

"Oh, yes. I know. Please, Taddy. Aunt Mathilde will kill us if we do anything to encourage Jay's dinosaur fixation."

Taddy had said good-bye to his PawPaw just two days ago. "I'll see you next Saturday for sure," PawPaw had said. "Maybe sooner, son."

"Do you think the big birds will still be out there?" Taddy had asked.

"Could be."

I remember thinking: *if the tropical disturbance doesn't turn into a hurricane.* When the outer bands enter the Gulf of Mexico, birds sense the drop in atmospheric pressure well before scientific instruments tell the onshore weathermen there's a serious storm ahead. Were the pelicans telling us we had a hurricane coming our way? I bet PawPaw had the same thoughts, but neither one of us wanted to say the words aloud. Mentioning the possibility of a hurricane might bring bad karma. Like the old days when people didn't utter the word *Cancer.*

Worry crept back into my head, pulling me into the present. Where could PawPaw have gone?

THE SEARCH BEGINS

Taking the first exit at the end of the Atchafalaya Basin, I turned south onto Grande Point Highway to a shortcut through St. Martin Parish. Not really *grand* or a *highway*. Just another blacktop country road. I had to watch out for hazards—overhanging mailboxes, loose dogs, slow moving carts stuffed with cut cane stalks ready to be planted. No longer soothed by the peaceful swamp, anxiety about PawPaw kicked in hard. Why on earth didn't anyone know where he'd gone? PawPaw lived alone in the old house, but Mom, Dad, my brother Taddy, and Uncle Bub were right next door. Bub had coffee with PawPaw every morning, and a child or a grandchild checked in on him at least once a day. PawPaw never stayed away overnight. He never drove farther than the parish line, and he never drove at all after dark.

Then I remembered the damned tropical storm. Sunday night the National Weather Service had posted a hurricane watch along the entire Gulf coast, from Galveston to Tampa Bay, and predicted drift to open water within the next two days, intensification probable.

I played with the radio knobs until I picked up a weather report. The storm hung around and now had a name—Hannah. No one knew how Hannah might develop, or if, where, when, or with what force she might come onshore. Unpredictable like a woman, the reporter quipped. A male reporter, of course.

Yesterday, when I got up early and drove back to school for class, the storm had vanished from my brain. Not the case for the family at the lake. When you live twenty-five miles from open water, at this time of year you always keep a little piece of your mind tuned for the possibility of a hurricane. Four years had passed since the last serious storm, but my family, just like every family, probably woke up on Monday thinking about dead flashlight batteries, loose yard furniture, the need to board up the windows. And emergency power. The summer haul of shrimp and crabmeat in the freezers would spoil without a generator to keep the electricity humming.

PawPaw was a strong man, but a life of physical labor takes a toll on the body. Even with only himself to worry about, he had more than enough to do for an eighty-year-old. He'd have made a shopping list: duct tape, a loaf of bread, maybe a jar of peanut butter. Now *there* was a thought. Could he have had a heart attack on the way to the grocery store? Or an accident? No. Someone would've found his truck. What if he'd gotten distracted and slipped off the road into a ditch? So many times I'd heard Mom fuss at him for driving onto a headland to check on someone's cane fields or crawfish ponds.

With a storm brewing, Mom and her siblings would have had lots to do. My aunts would have thought first of food. What could they have on hand that didn't need refrigeration or cooking? My dad, a firefighter, would've been called to the station to organize an emergency protocol and an overtime schedule for his crew. Uncle J. Allen and Uncle Etienne, who ran the family sugarcane farm across the road from PawPaw, would've had to make plans to shelter the equipment and the animals. And they'd have been worried sick about what the winds might do to their crop, grown tall and green, so close to harvest. My Uncle Ti Pierre would be sure all his trucks had plenty of gas and air in the tires. Even Uncle Bub would've been busy. He'd probably been called in for extra duty at the sheriff's office in New Iberia.

Uncle Bub loved his job, and even more the idea that he

could have one. He stationed his wheelchair at the front desk where he answered the telephone and greeted visitors as they came in the door. The sheriff knew what he was doing when he put Uncle Bub on his payroll. The path to PawPaw's heart lay through his youngest child, and with the children, in-laws, and a collection of lifetime friends, my family could be counted on to deliver a couple hundred votes at every election. Nothing happened out at Lake Peigneur that our PawPaw, Pierre Boudreaux Sr., didn't know about. PawPaw and Uncle Bub were the sheriff's eyes and ears for our corner of Iberia Parish.

Trouble brewing in the Gulf meant the sheriff's office would be humming with activity. Many of the callers would need to hear Bub's soothing voice giving them the latest coordinates of the storm, recommended evacuation routes, where to pick up sandbags, which buildings would become emergency shelters. Uncle Bub would've been crazy busy all day Monday.

I had a catch in my throat thinking about my Uncle Bub. Whatever would he do if something had happened to PawPaw? They were so close.

With the threat of a storm, the roads out of town would be crowded, but I could be pretty sure no one in my family would be packing up to flee. The Boudreaux clan never evacuated unless the State Police issued a mandatory order. Not even Aunt Mazie down in Houma. If a storm did come, I, for one, would be happy if she took her bundle of nerves to another location for the duration, but she never did.

The gradual loss of barrier islands and protective marshes had made us more and more vulnerable. If tropical storm Hannah became a hurricane and headed for shore directly to the west of Iberia Parish, a mandatory evacuation order would be a real possibility. We'd be on the eastern side, the wet side, we called it, where the circulating force might bring water surging through Vermilion Bay, up the bayous and the Delcambre Canal, straight into the area surrounding our Lake Peigneur. I had never heard of a hurricane taking that course, but I'd been told the probabilities had increased.

I smiled thinking of PawPaw's take on the threat of a storm in the Gulf. His clear blue eyes would twinkle and he'd say, "It's hard to be a Christian when there's a hurricane out there. The crazy lady has to go somewhere, but you can't help wanting her to choose someone else's backyard."

The family probably had the usual argument about the safest place for PawPaw to wait out the storm. Mom and Dad thought our one-story brick house, built in the seventies, was the best structure to withstand high winds. Not PawPaw. He insisted the old homestead next door had stood the test of time. My uncle Ti Pierre always voted for his own house across the road, but then Uncle Ti always thought everything he had was the best.

The threat of a storm no doubt captured everyone's attention and probably explained why no one had checked on PawPaw yesterday, Monday, the last day of August.

After the half-hour drive through St. Martin Parish and around the city of New Iberia, I reached Lake Road, the two-lane blacktop on the east side of Lake Peigneur. When I rounded the first bend, I could see a cluster of cars in front of PawPaw's house. Enough for a Sunday Saints football party, or—I gulped—a wake.

Blocking one lane of travel, the grill of Uncle Ti Pierre's green panel truck, *Big Beeline Trucking* emblazoned in two foot high letters on the cab doors, nudged the back bumper of a sheriff's black and white cruiser pulled up in front of PawPaw's house. At the sight of two fresh-faced young deputies stepping out onto the narrow concrete walk leading to the front porch, Uncle Ti lowered his car window, leaned out, and bellowed in their direction.

"Get on the horn to your friggin' boss, guys. Tell him to get his fat ass right over here. And make it damn quick!"

Oh my God. Uncle Ti was acting up again. Ti, or Petit Pierre to give him his full nickname, the oldest of PawPaw's eight children, could be counted on to embarrass us all. But he had his good side as well. A can-do sort of guy, the family relied on Uncle Ti for action. When your car, your truck, or your tractor for that matter, was stuck in mud, or when a tree had blown down on your shed, you called Uncle Ti. He came in a flash, with a truck and a towline. Maybe today was one of those times we were going to need Uncle Ti. I shuddered at the thought.

Ti owned a fleet of six trucks. He and two of his own sons made *hot-shot* deliveries of tools and other supplies to oil rigs and offshore loading areas all over south Louisiana. Uncle Ti liked this work much better than his first job farming sugarcane under PawPaw's critical eye. Now his own boss, he could leave his crew in charge when he wanted to crawfish, troll for shrimp, or shoot a turkey, a deer, or a few ducks. Off-season in the cane fields, his brothers Uncle J. Allen and Uncle Etienne, who still worked on the family farm, only occasionally risked PawPaw's disapproval to join a hunt or a fishing trip. Ti always gave his brothers a hard time about having to sneak around their father like teenagers hot after a new girlfriend.

Hearing the foul-mouthed demands, the younger of the two deputy sheriffs stiffened. His right hand dropped instinctively to his holster, and he opened his mouth to snap a response. The older deputy put out a settling hand. The younger deputy returned to his unit, and I heard him on the radio making a business-like request for the sheriff to come out to the Boudreaux farm on Lake Road.

I bypassed the crowd on the front porch of the old house and went around to the kitchen door. I saw Aunt Tut first, dripping boiling water by the tablespoon into PawPaw's white enamel coffeepot. Tut was the aunt closest to my mom. I wasn't surprised to see her pitching in. The sight of me brought tears to Tut's eyes and she held me in a long, hard hug. I knew immediately I'd done the right thing by coming home. Mom's hug was even longer.

"So, what's going on?" I asked.

Mom spoke in a whisper, keeping one eye on the door to the central hall. "Like usual, this morning Bub went to PawPaw's for his biscuits and coffee. He couldn't get in. The back door was locked, and PawPaw didn't come answer his knock."

Uncle Bub lived in the barbecue cabin in our back yard. He'd probably used his crutches to cross the little bridge over the ditch between our house and PawPaw's. One leg was a good four inches shorter than the other. He bumped up the sidewalk, jerked up the new concrete steps to the back porch, and grasped the special handle that permitted him to open the screen door with two fingers. Last year Mom had insisted on these little home improvements. She feared one day Uncle Bub's crutches would catch on a loose board in the old wooden steps and he'd go crashing to the ground. He didn't need to have one more problem with his legs.

Another glance to the hall, and Mom continued.

"PawPaw always let Bub know ahead of time if he had to leave home early, but at first Bub wasn't worried. He thought he'd just missed a message. He came across to our house to see if I had a cup of coffee for him. I hadn't heard about PawPaw having to go somewhere so I thought I'd better check it out. I grabbed the key off the hook. Bub and I crossed over to PawPaw's kitchen door."

Mom looked around again. No one in earshot.

"Mandy, I was scared the minute I walked in. The old coffee pot stood upside down on the drain-board. There were no biscuits on the table."

The mention of biscuits brought back memories of Mama B. My grandmother always made her biscuits from scratch, her flour-covered hands kneading the dough on the metal kitchen table. Now that she was gone, PawPaw's biscuits came out of a plastic bag from the freezer.

"And then I noticed the drain board. A zip-lock bag of pork roast and gravy lay limp and warm in a puddle of water. The sight of that thawed meat stabbed me in the gut. I knew right then something was terribly wrong. PawPaw would never leave food out overnight."

Mom saved leftovers so PawPaw wouldn't have to cook for himself. He always had a supply of those little zip-lock bags in his freezer. Every morning he'd take out one for his dinner, which he ate at noon. Tuesday's meal would've still been icy if it had come out of the freezer that morning.

"And so you figured he hadn't been home since after breakfast the morning before?" I asked.

"Right. My first thought, but I didn't let on to Bub. I'm sure I was chattering like a fool, telling him PawPaw would have some simple explanation, that he'd probably changed his plans and spent a night with one of his other children. I told Bub we just had to check with the family to see where he went. I picked up the telephone and began to call your aunts and uncles." Mom smiled and tipped her head to a list taped under the calendar from Our Lady of the Sea. "I just read the inch-high telephone numbers PawPaw keeps on the wall right above the phone. I called all the family—except Dora of course."

When my Aunt Dora married, she and her husband moved to a suburb outside Atlanta. Dora was the only one of PawPaw's children to graduate from college. I remember PawPaw saying you end up leaving home if you get a lot of education. Would I leave? Maybe, if I ever figured out what I wanted to do with my life.

"Then I checked with PawPaw's buddy, Thib Thibodeaux. Thib said PawPaw hadn't shown up for morning coffee, and they all wondered if he was sick or somethin'. Thib expected the boys to start gathering again pretty soon. He'd ask them if anyone had seen PawPaw around. I probably sounded crazy, trying to keep a smile in my voice so Bub wouldn't get worried."

Her strained, *oh, everything is all right* voice had gotten a workout.

PawPaw loved his coffee hour with the boys. Every morning, around eleven o'clock, he and a half-dozen of his buddies gathered at Thibodeaux's Grocery in Coteau—not another town, just the settlement to the northwest. They tipped back in wooden chairs and propped their boots up on an old pot-bellied stove. The stove would've been cold in the late summer, but it crackled with fire in the winter. The boys at Thib's had very little concern for national or international affairs. Once they'd exchanged information about the height of the sugarcane and the going price for sugar and rice, they moved on to the political maneuvering for the next election. PawPaw would say it used to be so simple to know how everyone stood on the issues and to keep track of who supported who when everyone was either Long or an Anti-Long. Now things were all mixed up. You couldn't predict how a politician would turn out. They'd tell you one thing and do another.

Right then, I had a wave of dread. I'd begun to think of PawPaw in the past tense.

Mom again glanced at the door to the hall. No one in earshot. She kept going.

"A half hour later, calls began to come back in. One family member after another asked me if I'd heard anything. Not yet, I told them. And then they started coming to the house." Mom sighed. "My cheeriness wasn't fooling Uncle Bub. He went out on the porch and propped himself on the railing, his face pale. I made another pot of coffee and convinced him to come back inside. I pulled out a kitchen chair and got him to sit down. His cup rattled in the saucer. The lower half of his face looked funny, drawn to one side, and his fingers did little dance steps on the tabletop. He gave me the telephone number of the radio room at the sheriff's office—six twenty-one, twenty-one hundred—and told me to call and tell them PawPaw had gone missing. His voice crackled as he spoke."

At this point, my Aunt Mazie came from the central hall into the kitchen.

"Any coffee, Mandy? Did your Mom make any coffee for us? Did she?"

Damn Aunt Mazie. The most aggravating member of the family. She said everything twice.

"Over on the counter, Mazie," Mom said through tight lips. She took my arm and drew me with her out to the back porch so she could continue her report out of Mazie's presence.

"Elnora on the sheriff's switchboard said she'd notify her boss and radio the deputies who were patrolling in our area of the parish. They'd make a pass by the house. Bub then insisted we get Ti to come over. I didn't know Ti's cell phone number so I called his wife Nell."

"She must have found him. He just pulled up outside," I told Mom.

"Good. Anyway, I guess that's good. Then I called you."

"I'm glad you did, Mom," I told her, circling her shoulders with another hug.

Then my Dad came out onto the back porch. He went right to

Mom and kissed her on the cheek.

"I swear, Mimi, Mandy can get all the way here from Baton Rouge in the time it takes me to escape from the boys at the firehouse. The chief made us go through the hurricane protocol for the tenth time!"

"I told you not to come, Emile. We're fine here. We're just waiting for the sheriff."

Of course Dad had come. He wouldn't let any of us be in trouble without trying to help.

"Let's go back inside, Mimi. We've got quite a crowd in there now."

Within a half hour after I arrived at PawPaw's house, the law appeared. Chief Deputy "Big" Theriot pulled the sheriff's customized Jeep onto the scruffy growth that passed for the front lawn. Without Mama B to nag him, PawPaw hadn't kept the place up the way he had in the past. Anyway, we can't make our yards look like the ones we see in magazines. In Louisiana, a fifth column of squirrels works 'round the clock burying acorns in the damp earth, and birds scatter seeds of every known variety of weeds. Trees and weeds. If we don't stay on top of the growth, in three months we have ourselves a jungle like the one that awaited the Spanish conquistadors and Acadian settlers two hundred years ago.

Sheriff Septimus Landry, a bulldozer of a man, slid down from the passenger seat of his jeep. He paused to tug his pants into place, and motioned to one of his deputies to get back in the unit and lower the window. Although the sheriff had a cell phone and a walkie-talkie strapped on his body, he wanted to stay in touch with the police scanner as well. He strode up the front walk to the house. Boots give a man a walk that says *don't give me no trouble*; the sheriff's stride broadcast the message loud and clear.

The sheriff greeted the family and friends assembled on the front porch, and they fell on him. Led by Uncle Ti, they asked and then demanded action. Filling his ample chest with air, the sheriff squared his shoulders and took command of the situation. "OK, men, let's go on inside and get to work."

Men, he said.

The sheriff instructed Big to go back out to the car to give the OK for a missing person alert. Out on the wire went a BOLO. *Be on the lookout for Pierre Boudreaux, WM, 80, 6', 200 pounds, driving white Ford pickup, LA DES 062.*

Once in the central hall of the old house, the sheriff pulled Ti Pierre to his side, threw his burly arm around Ti's shoulders in a man-hug, and faced the assemblage. So transparent. He wanted to make Uncle Ti think he was second in command of this situation. The truth? The sheriff held on to Ti to keep the family hothead on a short leash.

The sheriff drew from his shirt pocket a topographical map of the area surrounding Lake Peigneur and asked Ti to hold the corners while he taped the map to the back wall. Then the sheriff pulled over an antique marble-topped table, placed it under the map, and laid out a stack of colored markers. He picked up the red marker and drew a circle, Lake Peigneur at the midpoint. Then he drew spokes leading from the center of the lake to the edges of the map.

"See these pie-shaped areas, men? I'll assign a team to each section. Each team will be headed by a member of the family and accompanied by one of my deputies."

Reverse the instruction and you have a true translation of his order. *Each team will be headed by one of my deputies and accompanied by a member of the family.*

"We're gonna scour every damn inch in every damn section, one after the other," the sheriff said.

With about twenty men now antsy to take to their trucks, the sheriff again put his arm around Uncle Ti. "Ti Pierre, I'm gonna need you to get this search organized. Work with Big to make up the teams." Sheriff Landry turned to me. "Mandy, you write down these assignments so we have a record of who is on which team and where they go. Clock the times in and out."

The sheriff was oblivious to my raised eyebrows. I was to be the secretary of the operation. OK. No need to make trouble. For a greater cause, I could handle the role. I shrugged my acceptance —but I wasn't about to say 'yes sir.' I got a legal pad and pen from my car and prepared to take down the plan for the search.

The sheriff continued booming out his instructions. "Ti Pierre, take your big truck home and come back in your 4X4. I'm goin' out to my unit to make radio contact with the office. With that storm out there, I've got a shitload of work to do. We've got a few days leeway until it could come onshore, but it's easier to get everything ready before the rain. You know the drill. We've gotta touch base with all the shelters. We gotta make sure the barns have what they need for sandbag distribution. We gotta put the National Guard on alert. But rest assured, we're on top of the search for your PawPaw. Major Theriot here will be making calls to all the places the family thinks he might have gone, and I'll be back within the hour to see you off on the search. Big, get goin' on those calls."

I caught sight of Bub sitting by himself on the sofa by the front door. I put my hand on Mom's arm. "Bub looks so lost. I think I'll go talk to him a bit."

"Do that, Mandy. He probably cares for you as much as anyone in this world, with the exception of PawPaw." I was glad to hear her use the present tense.

I sat down next to my youngest uncle, moving his crutches aside. "Feel like talking?" I asked.

"That'd be OK," Bub answered softly.

"You're the last one to see PawPaw, Uncle Bub. Tell me about it."

Bub swallowed hard.

"Yesterday we had our coffee and biscuits at the table in the kitchen, like always, and we talked about the storm. I guess that's *all* we talked about. Around eight o'clock I went out onto the front porch to wait for the patrol car. PawPaw walked out with me. Deputy Green pulled up, I got into the unit and waved. That's it Mandy, the last time I waved him good-bye." Bub squeezed out the word good-bye as slowly as toothpaste from a tube. "The last time I saw him."

"Did you notice anything unusual about PawPaw? Like did he seem sick or anything?"

Bub shook his head. "Everything was just like usual. What could've happened to him? I know he would've told me if he was going somewhere."

"I don't know what happened, but we're gonna find out. For sure."

Bub slumped down into the sofa pillows and muttered to himself.

"Why in Jesus' name didn't I look over here when I finished supper last night? Just a glance would've done it. I'd have noticed his truck was gone. We could've started looking for him right then."

We were all blaming ourselves. I was wondering if we should've let PawPaw live alone. Or drive. Mom said she'd put off an appointment with PawPaw's cardiologist in Lafayette. Now she felt that if they'd gone, maybe a doctor would've detected some problem with his heart.

"Don't beat yourself up about what might have been, Bub. Anyway, we're gonna find him. It's just a matter of time."

True. We would find PawPaw, all right. But in what condition?

Bub dropped his head and stopped talking. I put my hand on his thigh.

After a few minutes of quiet, Uncle Bub sat up straight, or at least as straight as he could. I saw the first smile on his face since I'd come home.

"I'm remembering something else PawPaw and I talked about yesterday morning. He said he was on his way to town to cash his Social Security check so he'd have some money for the storm. Yesterday I saw the check under the sugar bowl, but it isn't there now."

"Good thinking, Bub!" I gave him a high five. "We'll get in touch with the bank to see if anyone remembers him coming by. They'll have a record if he cashed his check."

"Yeah, and something else." Bub's eyes opened wider. "PawPaw said he had to pay his water bill. Maybe he went by LAWCO after the bank."

Another high five.

Big Theriot interrupted us. "I need you over here, Mandy."

Shit. I was being summoned to resume my duties as madam

secretary.

"Keep on thinking, Bub. I'll get Big on this right away."

* * *

Unknown to all of us, something else was taking place that morning, not very far away—a bad house fire, with serious injury, on Captain Cade Road. Sometime in the afternoon the Boudreaux family heard news of the fire and of a woman who had been seriously hurt. But none of us knew for days that the event had any connection to PawPaw's disappearance.

THE FIND

My evening seminar vanished from my mind.

I set up my legal pad on another of one of Mama B's little marble-top tables. Chief Theriot stood by the phone punching in the numbers I found for him. He made his first call to Thib's Grocery. Thib said he'd questioned the boys when they came for the morning coffee hour, but none of them remembered seeing their good buddy Pierre.

I made a note of the conversation.

Next, Big called the branch of the Farmers' and Seamen's Bank where PawPaw always cashed his checks. The manager took a while to locate the teller who had been on duty at the drive-in window on Monday morning. When he found her, she recalled the transaction and remembered PawPaw stuffing the cash—a little over $400—into his shirt pocket. She didn't think the money would be secure, but perhaps the old man, who was a bit wide in the girth, couldn't maneuver his wallet out of his pants while seated in his truck. No, she hadn't noticed anyone suspicious in the area. I wrote all that down.

The clerk at the water company found the record of bill payment at 9:30 a.m., but she had no memory of PawPaw. She didn't think anything unusual had happened all day. No, she said, she didn't make a practice of conversing with the customers. She just took the money, punched the amount into the computer, and handed the customer a receipt.

All day, every day. What a dull job that must be. I didn't know what kind of work I'd find after graduation, but I hoped I wouldn't be stuck doing anything like that.

Calls went out to the hospitals, the used car lots, the bus station, even to the mall in Houma, where Aunt Mazie lived. Nothing. Yesterday, at 9:30 a.m., Monday, the thirty-first of August, when I was back at school getting ready for my first class of the day and the rest of the family was worrying about a hurricane, the trail went cold.

I drew a copy of the sheriff's map on my legal pad. Uncle Ti claimed leadership of the search party assigned to the pie-shaped segment stretching from the west side of Lake Peigneur toward Vermilion Bay. As a life-long hunter, he knew the land out there. Anyone unfamiliar with the area could get lost in the thick woods for days. I took down Uncle Ti's assignment with care. He'd give me a piece of his mind if I got it wrong.

Uncle J. Allen claimed another isolated area, the segment that included the shoreline of Lake Tasse, teacup in English, a smaller body of water closer to town. In the early spring—off-season on the sugarcane farm—my uncles leased a couple of acres of fallow rice fields to flood for their crawfish traps. PawPaw often took a ride out there to see if nutria had dug breaches in any of the little levees controlling the flow of water into the ponds, and he'd check the locks on the metal shed where they stored their pirogues and stacks of wire traps. Maybe PawPaw had gone over there yesterday and run into a problem. Major Theriot signed himself on as the deputy for J. Allen's segment of the pie.

"Take Bub along with you," Uncle Ti instructed. "He knows that area like the back of his hand. And Chief, when you get there, you be sure you get down from your truck—all the way down—to look for tire tracks, trampled scrub, anything unusual."

Chief Deputy Major Theriot wasn't called Big Boy for nothing. His muffin-top belly hung over his belt, and he got short of breath just getting in and out of his unit. Uncle Ti thought Big needed reminding you can't do much detecting sitting on your rump.

Uncle Ti allotted the remaining segments to his brothers, his brothers-in-law, and the older grandsons. The sheriff assigned an experienced deputy as the so-called assistant to each search group. I noted every assignment.

Sheriff Landry instructed a deputy to man the radio in the jeep in front of the house, take the calls, and send messages inside to be posted in my notes. He ordered one of the patrol deputies to stand by the map ready to yellow-highlight each area searched.

Uncle Ti was loving this. He strutted around like a rooster, bellowing instructions to every crew. "Check every friggin' road, every ditch beside every friggin' road. Call in your reports."

Faces stiff with resolve, one by one the men of the family climbed into their off-road vehicles and pulled away from the house. That was how the search began.

By dusk, I had almost filled my legal pad with handwritten notes. Yellow highlight covered large portions of the sheriff's map. The search parties returned one by one, shut down by darkness, scheduled to crank up again at first light. What a different picture. Now shoulders sagged; steps slowed. Discouragement breeds exhaustion. No one had seen any trace of an old man or a white pickup, license number DES 062.

Women had been coming in all afternoon carrying covered dishes and staying to help my aunts pass the anxious hours. Word spreads quickly through the countryside around the lake.

I was raised saying the rosary, and I love my Aunt Tut, but when she pulled those beads out of her purse and summoned her daughters to the front room, the sing-song mumble got on my nerves. *Holy Mary, Mother of God. The Lord is with you. Blessed art thou among women, and blessed is the fruit of thy womb, Jesus.* The litany droned into the night. When I could, I hid out in the kitchen.

And that was the first day. On Wednesday, the second day of the search, probably one hundred people had volunteered to help in any way they could. A diving crew from St. Martin Parish arrived to start an underwater operation in Lake Peigneur. The

State Police helicopter crisscrossed miles of swamp in the four-parish area of Iberia, St. Mary, St. Martin, and Vermilion. Air boats borrowed from their assignments with seismic crews in the Atchafalaya Basin scoured the honeycomb of canals and bayous draining into Vermilion Bay and the Gulf of Mexico. Still, no sign of PawPaw or his truck. Nothing. By night, the ache in my stomach told me we weren't searching for PawPaw. We were searching for his body.

Thursday, still nothing. The tropical storm remained in the lower Gulf and had reached hurricane strength. A system of low pressure was scheduled to move into south Louisiana by the weekend. If so, the storm would be sucked northward and onshore over the vulnerable marshes and lowlands along the coast. Our coast. Everyone got testy.

After three days without results, we stopped telling each other there could be any good explanation for PawPaw's disappearance. I no longer recorded the details of each search operation. The sheriff, if he noticed, didn't ask me why. With no other subject on anyone's mind, and nothing more to say, everyone just stopped talking.

I'd already missed two days of class and we were only allowed three cuts. If I wanted to stay on track to finish in December, I couldn't let attendance cause me to fail a course. I slipped away and drove to Baton Rouge and back, telling only Mom and Aunt Tut. Mom had her hands full, especially chasing after what seemed like an unlimited supply of kids produced by the prolific Boudreaux family. Why the hell didn't they keep them at home? This was no family party. It was serious.

In a house full of long faces, Uncle Bub was the exception. His devotion to the operation never lessened. He bumped himself over to the big house first thing each morning and climbed into the vehicle with anyone who had a new idea about where to look next. He was always the last person to leave at night. I tried to sit with him as much as I could. "I know my daddy would never, ever leave me without saying goodbye," Bub must have told me a dozen times.

Uncle Bub's story had become part of the family lore. Now,

watching Bub struggle to keep control of his emotion, it came back to me.

When Bub was born, a curve in his spine twisted his tiny body to the left. His right leg bent in at the knee, and then out again to the right. His right arm had a bend also, and his right hand had only three fingers, no thumb or little finger. In her five-year-old innocence, Aunt Dora said her baby brother looked like a "broke puppet." The family doctor sent him to New Orleans to see the specialists at Big Charity. They operated on Bub twice before he was five years old, then said more surgeries would have to wait until he stopped growing. For now, he said, Bub would have to use a wheelchair. PawPaw and Mama B feared he'd never walk.

PawPaw built special ramps so Bub could get around the house and yard, even down to the dock so he could fish like his brothers and sisters had before him. In the summertime, Mickey Brown, the nephew the Alexanders had taken in for vacations after the boy's dad walked out on Mr. Alexander's sister, came over a lot, at least until an unfortunate incident with a litter of kittens made PawPaw ban Mickey from his yard. Thinking back now, I suppose the kittens met some catastrophe, but I never heard the details.

When Uncle Bub was six, PawPaw and Mama B enrolled him in first grade. They expected him to go to Coteau Elementary where all the others in the family had gone, but when the first day of school came, the bus took Bub to the special building the school board had fixed up for the handicapped at the old air base. PawPaw waited out the first six weeks. He and Mama B had only been through the eighth grade and were no experts in education, but it seemed to them all the school did for Uncle Bub was teach him how to pledge the flag, take his shoes and socks off and on, and color pictures of balloons. They weren't even trying to teach him to read. One night PawPaw, sputtering mad, pounded the kitchen table and told Mama B he'd had enough of that special school. The next day he went to see the principal, who blew him off.

PawPaw climbed back into his truck and drove straight to

town. He pulled up at the School Board office in the old Texaco building on the highway to St. Martinville and barged into the office of the Superintendent of Education, steaming. So say, or *on dit que* to use PawPaw's expression, PawPaw said, "maybe my boy can't walk, sir, but he sure enough can think. You have him stuck in there with all those retards. It ain't right!"

The school bus wasn't set up to handle a wheelchair, and the handicap van went only to the special school at the base, but the superintendent offered a compromise. If PawPaw could get Bub to the regular school, have someone there at lunchtime to take care of his needs, and pick him up again when school was over, he could go to Coteau Elementary right close to the farm.

And that's what they did. PawPaw taught Bub to pull himself into and out of the truck, and he and the boys drove him to school every day until the end of May. Mama B had never driven a car before, but PawPaw put her behind the wheel of his truck and gave her lessons. She passed the test and got her license. When school opened again in the fall, and PawPaw was busy in the fields, Mama B took over the job of delivering Bub to school. For the next eleven years she drove Bub there and back from August planting time, through grinding, and until the mills shut down in late January. Then PawPaw and the boys took over again.

Eventually, Bub had more surgeries and traded the wheelchair for crutches. He was never the best student in the class, but he did just fine. When Uncle Bub bumped down the aisle to receive his high school diploma, the whole family was there, most of them in tears. I was just a little girl, but I remember it well. Uncle Bub knew how different his life would have been if it hadn't been for PawPaw's persistence.

By Friday afternoon we had received one bit of good news. Tropical storm Hannah was a *shoo-shoo*. The winds had decreased to seventy-five miles per hour. The National Weather Service downgraded the hurricane watch to a warning, predicted a path straight north across the Gulf, and narrowed the point of projected landfall to Marsh Island due south of Iberia Parish. Lake Peigneur faced a weekend of drenching rain, but, barring some drastic change in the upper wind patterns, we wouldn't be battered by a storm surge bringing floodwaters to our doorsteps.

But still no sign of PawPaw.

Mom, who'd always been the assistant mother for this family, had the lion's share of the work operating the big house for all the people who kept coming by. When day was done, she collapsed from exhaustion. One night I met Dad in the kitchen warming two cups of milk. "Mom can't sleep, Mandy," he said. "Nightmares."

Dad carried the milk back to the bedroom and placed the cups on the nightstand. I left him stroking Mom's back to soothe away her shudders.

Saturday night the tropical storm swept in on schedule, pounding the rooftops with punishing rain. Wind bent the live oak branches down to the ground, toying with the hundred pound limbs like they were twigs. Pecans tap-danced on the rooftops. Windows creaked. That night I woke with a start and sat straight up. "Where are you, sweet PawPaw?" I whispered into the darkness. For the first time since he went missing, I hoped my dear grandfather was at peace with the Lord and not stranded on some side road with only his old truck for shelter. Or worse yet, out wandering through a fog-bound swamp. I hoped that my dad, who was spending a lot of time with Taddy, had prepared my little brother for the prospect of bad news.

On Sunday afternoon, just short of a week after PawPaw disappeared, Uncle Ti took a call from the sheriff. I watched him reach out his left arm to steady himself on the back of a chair. His face reddened and then sagged like a jack-o-lantern in the October sun. A family crabbing in Delcambre Canal, just down from the far side of Lake Peigneur, had sighted a large metal shape under twenty feet of water just this side of the drawbridge linking Iberia to Vermilion Parish. The object could be a truck.

The sheriff called in a favor from a supporter conducting a dredging operation in the Basin. He agreed to move some equipment over to the canal and attempt to bring up the submerged object. The sheriff asked if a couple of the family members, not the whole clan, please, could come on out to the canal, just in case. Uncle Ti and Mom knew the job was theirs.

My dad had been called back to the firehouse to relieve one of the men who had been on duty all through the storm watch, so Mom gave me the high sign to come along as their driver. Uncle Ti, Mom, and I slipped out of the house. We didn't want Uncle Bub to know where we were going.

We stood on the bank of the Delcambre Canal, arms entwined, watching muscular men in black T-shirts handle ropes and pulleys on the deck of the work barge they had moored some thirty feet up from the bridge. Between the shoreline and the barge, the massive form of the sheriff commanded the bow of a sleek rescue vessel, one boot up on the gunwale like George Washington crossing the Delaware. Near the barge, glistening black wetsuits broke through the surface of the water and back-pedaled away from the operation. With gloved hands, they signaled a *come on* to the crew on the barge.

"Pull her up, men!"

The awkward shape of a pickup truck rose up from the muck, a grinding, sucking, splashing gorgon, dripping muddy ribbons of marsh weed. The sheriff's rescue boat nudged closer. Leaning from the deck, a deputy extended a crowbar and pried open the passenger door of what now clearly appeared—a white truck. The deputy drove the instrument into the suspended wreck and pulled a long, heavy bundle through the opening.

Mom gasped at the sight. "That's PawPaw's jacket!" A hoarse whisper.

The deputies lowered the sodden load onto the deck of the sheriff's boat, and the sheriff gave a quiet order to return to shore. The crew didn't hurry. They offloaded the package onto the dock and closed ranks, shielding the body from our eyes.

The sheriff caught sight of a photographer in the wings: Dee Hall from *The Daily Iberian*. Dee received a dagger look from the sheriff that said *don't you dare put this in the paper*. From the pockets of the light khaki pants hanging from the body, the deputies pulled out a quarter, two pennies, and a medal of the Blessed Mother on a silver chain.

"No wallet," the sheriff mumbled to the deputy by his side.

Behind him, Mom and Uncle Ti clung to each other. The

sheriff turned around. "I hate to ask you to do this, but if you could identify..." He didn't finish the sentence, thank God.

I stepped in front of Mom to do the job for her. Uncle Ti pushed me aside, but not before I saw where a ragged stab wound had sliced through the center of the shirt, exposing pulpy, peach-colored flesh.

Underneath tattered rags hanging from steel grey skin, I recognized our PawPaw. Not his twinkling blue eyes but grey-white stones. Not lips parted to tell again a story I'd already heard scores of times. Thin blue lines pulled apart to reveal a gaping hole. No teeth.

A scream pierced the hush. Ti Pierre raised his arms and cried to the heavens.

"In the name of God, who could do such a thing?"

I reached to support my mother so she wouldn't fall to the deck. She sank onto my shoulder and sobbed until the ambulance took the body away.

Sheriff Landry touched Mom on the back.

"We'll get whoever did this, Mimi. I promise you. And I promise you, for this he's gonna die."

A CELEBRATION OF A LIFE

Mom sat next to me on the worn sofa in the central hall of the old house. Aunt Tut, Mom's favorite sibling and my favorite aunt, sat in a rocker at her side. Mom tossed her head in the direction of a large poster-sized photo, angling slightly off-kilter on the opposite wall. She spoke to her sister, barely above a whisper. "We were all there with PawPaw for his birthday celebration, just a month ago, Tut. The whole Boudreaux clan."

"I'm so glad we did that. Look at your granddaughter Sophie-Claire. Barely two years old and her deep curtsy is worthy of a presentation at the Sugarcane Farmers' Ball."

Mom looked older these days, her eyelids darker, new wrinkles played around her mouth. But the pinch of her eyebrows eased at the mention of my older brother's little girl. The first grandchild is special.

"And look at your Taddy, Mimi. The little trouble maker!" Aunt Tut continued. Bless her for turning Mom's thoughts to her precious little ones.

In the picture, my brother Taddy had made bunny ears over the head of Uncle J. Allen's boy, little Jay.

"There's Taddy's best fishing buddy, Aunt Tut," I said. "Right after Dee took the picture, Jay started hopping around the yard with his arms drawn up like a T-Rex. Remember the sound effects?"

A smile cracked through Mom's melancholy expression. "Little Jay's non-stop grunting was about to drive your Aunt Mathilde crazy. Jay knows a heck of a lot about dinosaurs; I'll give him that. But tell me this, who could know whether those animals growled, barked, or roared like a lion?"

"Jay's guess is as good as anyone's," I said.

The photographer from *The Daily Iberian* had come out to Lake Peigneur to cover the event. He arranged the family members in front of the old cistern. My Dad wore his firefighter uniform, a rare treat for his admiring nephews. Dee Hall's camera caught Billy Boy Bienvenu, Aunt Tut's ten-year-old, as he raised his arms in the air like Rocky Balboa. Aunt Tut's daughter Eula Mae gazed lovingly at her boyfriend, the one who would soon break her heart. I could study the family picture many times and still find details I hadn't noticed before.

The newspaper ran the photograph on the front cover of the Sunday supplement. Dee then blew it up to poster size and presented a copy to PawPaw as a gift. PawPaw hung it in the hall where he could look at his family every day.

"Mimi, I do believe I see a little of that blackberry wine sparkling in PawPaw's eyes," Aunt Tut said.

Mom broached a delicate subject, which only a dear sister could do. "It was really good to see Burt, Jr., Tut. He's looking great."

"Yes. Six months working on the farm with J. Allen put color in his face and, I pray to God, took the craving for drugs out of his system. He leaves tomorrow for a landscaping job Dora found for him in Atlanta. Pray for him, Mimi."

"We all do, Tut."

No one counted the number of people that day, but we'd all tapped an index finger on the faces in the photograph many times since. We were sixty-two, not counting the three grandchildren in the oven, as we say. Not everyone was family. A few of my cousins brought girlfriends and boyfriends to meet the relatives who were swept into the crowd. PawPaw enjoyed the toddlers most of all. He laughed aloud as they chased each other around the yard, trampling through mounds of clover. Like a litter of three-month-old kittens, he said.

After the picture taking, Uncle Ti pulled out the family treasure map. Every family around here has one, and every family thinks theirs is truly authentic and will one day make them rich. Almost two hundred years ago, the pirate Jean LaFitte made the lake his winter headquarters and, legend has it, buried his plunder on the shores. When the site of Jefferson House was known as Orange Island, fortune hunters digging for pirate gold found salt, a valuable commodity for the Confederacy. Even now, every few years someone uncovers a round piece of metal, sets off a flurry of rumors, and the treasure hunters arrive. They've never found anything except broken pots and animal bones.

At PawPaw's birthday celebration Uncle Ti tried his best to interest Uncle J. in a Saturday treasure hunting excursion into the swamp on the other side of the lake, but Uncle J. didn't bite. He said he wasn't about to waste his time trying to locate a stake in the ground twenty arpents from a big oak that had probably died of old age a hundred years ago. And anyway, since the catastrophe when Texaco drilled into the salt mine, the lake had an entirely different shape.

"You're missing your best chance to be a millionaire," Uncle Ti told his brother. Uncle J. Allen said he'd settle out his part of the claim for one souvenir doubloon.

PawPaw beamed at all the teasing, and then fell asleep on his lawn chair. I remember Uncle Ti and Aunt Tut's husband Burt had a time lifting him up, carrying him into the house, and settling him in bed. Way too much blackberry wine for an old man who probably could count on one hand the number of drinks he'd had in the past decade.

Memories of that day sent floods of emotion through all three of us. Mom and Aunt Tut sniffled, but I was angry. What monster would hurt this dear old man? And why? For his few dollars of Social Security?

About four o'clock the sheriff's unit pulled up at the end of PawPaw's front walk. Sheriff Landry had changed out of his camo jumpsuit and tall black rubber boots and into a crisp khaki uniform that stretched tight across his belly. He had dressed for a formal sympathy call on the family. No one recognized the younger man in street clothes who walked at his side. The sheriff came in the front door and greeted PawPaw's children and many of his grandchildren by name. He introduced the man with him as Ted D'Aquin, a detective on loan from St. Martin Parish.

"I need to explain a few things to y'all," the sheriff said to us. "Our top detectives, Buddy Aymond and Deuce Washington, are out of town on another case and won't be back for a couple days. We can't wait for them to start this investigation so we've called in reinforcements. Ted D'Aquin from St. Martin is very good. He'll be lead investigator until our boys get back, and I promise you he'll do it all right. What D'Aquin does holds up in court. You know we don't want any mistakes that will scr—mess us up."

We listened politely, all but Uncle Ti, that is. Ti scowled in the sheriff's direction and bellowed out his gripes.

"Look, Sheriff. You'd better get your friggin' detectives back here right away. We've already lost a whole week. When your boys don't find a guy right away, most times they never find him at all. We gotta start right now turnin' this whole area upside down."

"Easy there, Ti Pierre. I talked with Detective Aymond just a few minutes ago. He and Deuce will be back in town tomorrow. And believe me, we're already at work."

Uncle Ti stomped a boot on the floor, rattling Mama B's little coffee cups displayed on a mini-shelf directly behind him.

"I bet I know who did it. One of them slit-eyes that hangs around the docks on the road to Intracoastal City waitin' to sign onto a shrimp boat. You know, the trash that lives in the bunkhouses when they're onshore between jobs. You talked to them yet? You need to go door to door out there and turn the screws until you find that fu—g guy, or someone who'll rat him out. That scum goes on those boats and stays on the water for a month at a time. Our guy could even jump off on some island full of spics and never be seen again."

The sheriff raised his eyebrows but kept silent. Uncle Ti's

prejudice made me cringe, but I thought for once he had a good idea. Someone should go check the docks right away. Uncle Ti continued his rant.

"You got a snitch in there? You sure should."

More of his venom. I bit the inside of my cheek to keep from saying something. Thank God we were just family here. Except for the sheriff and Detective D'Aquin, of course.

The sheriff didn't react. He'd had plenty of experience dealing with hot heads. When Uncle Ti saw his words weren't having any effect, he didn't stop his rant, he just spoke louder.

"You got nothin' yet? I thought as much. Damnit, man! You better get out there right quick before I do, or you won't have any so-called investigation. I'll find the bastard and take care of things myself."

Over the years, Uncle Ti looked more and more like PawPaw. His thick hair glowed white, his stomach bulged over his belt. His temperament did not take the same track. PawPaw became a sweet old man; Uncle Ti got more and more obnoxious.

Aunt Nell stood up and put her hand on her husband's arm. "Ti, let the sheriff get on with his job."

Aunt Nell turned to the sheriff and invited him to have a seat. Bless her. No one else had thought to extend the usual courtesies of a host. The sheriff nodded his thanks but remained standing. He probably wanted to keep a position of control.

"I assure you we *are* on the job, Ti Pierre. We sent the missing person report out days ago, and as we drove over here, Detective D'Aquin put more information on the wire. Our investigation is in full flower."

"Full flower? What the hell else are you doing?"

"Well, today we want to take some detailed statements. We'll start with you Mimi, and Bub too, since you were the ones who began the search. We'll trace every step your father took, and we'll uncover every connection he made until we get a lead. We'll find our man, I assure you."

Aunt Tut broke in. "Sheriff, may I ask you something?"

"Yes indeed, Mrs. Bienvenu," the sheriff said quickly, relieved to have reason to turn away from Uncle Ti.

"As you know, Mimi's husband Emile is a firefighter. He says his crew answered the call last week on that horrible house fire back on Captain Cade Road, the same day PawPaw disappeared. Could there be any connection to PawPaw's disappearance? That woman was so badly beaten."

The sheriff turned to Detective D'Aquin. "Now Ted, wouldn't Mrs. Bienvenu make a good addition to CID!"

"CID?" The acronym puzzled Aunt Tut.

"That's the Criminal Investigation Department, ma'am. Our detectives. No, we have no evidence of a connection between the two events, nor that they might have been caused by the same person. I'll admit it's unusual to have two violent incidents a day apart in our peace-loving parish, but looks like we'll probably have to find *two* dangerous persons out there."

He should have said in *our part* of the parish. The sheriff wasn't including the area known as back-a-town where a couple of stabbings—or stobbins as they call them—occurred every Saturday night. He knew the people in this room rarely thought much about what happened there.

"Of course, we don't rule out a tie-in between the two events, ma'am," the sheriff continued. "Right now, we don't rule anything out."

The sheriff had left the door open for the possibility the crimes were committed by the same person, which turned on my "what ifs." Perhaps the motive was the same—robbery to find money for drugs. No one would target PawPaw for any other reason I could think of.

Aunt Tut had another suggestion. "I saw on the paper that the lady on Captain Cade Road knew the person who did that to her."

The sheriff raised his right thumb. "More good thinking, ma'am. We're working on that."

"How's the lady doing? That must have been horrendous, what happened to her."

"Name's Lydia Falgout. She's beat up so bad she's been off limits to us since the trooper found her almost a week ago. But the doctors say she'll make it. When she's been cleared to talk to us, our detectives will be right there. Incredible guts, that lady."

Aunt Tut's husband, Burt, entered the exchange. "I heard she gave a name. Who did she say did it?"

The sheriff hesitated just a moment before he answered. Seemed to me he wanted to put an end to the questions.

"We have some information, but I can't go any further right now. Maybe we'll have more to tell you after we're able to have a real conversation with her. We'll see what our detectives have to allow when they get back in town."

The sheriff slipped smoothly into political mode. He scanned the room like an airport searchlight, casting his condolences on each pair of eyes turned in his direction.

"I hope y'all know that you have my deepest sympathy for your loss. What happened to your PawPaw shouldn't happen to anyone. I promise you, every one of you, that our whole department will not rest until we've solved this terrible crime, until we send that mean bastard for an appointment in that very special room at Angola. The table is waiting, and that's exactly what he deserves."

The sheriff's glance skipped around the room. Through one of the tall windows he caught sight of Father Martin on the front walk—and sensed opportunity.

"I see Father coming up right now. Y'all have business to tend to. I'll leave you alone to make your arrangements."

The sheriff appeared visibly relieved. Smiling to the right and left, he strode through the front door. He paused, very briefly, to shake Father Martin's hand as they passed on the walk.

Mom and Uncle Bub led Detective D'Aquin into one of the large bedrooms off the center hall of the old house. Mom signaled me to come along. The detective asked Mom's permission to turn on a little tape recorder to take down the conversation. Her eyebrows asked for my guidance; I nodded approval.

"Mrs. Aguillard—"

"Call me Mimi, detective."

"And you call me Ted. All three of you."

Uncle Bub didn't call him anything. He didn't speak.

Answering the detective's questions, Mom began at the

beginning of PawPaw's last day. Again. How many times did they want her to go over this? Mom filled the detective in on some of her father's routines. Ted told her he'd write what she told him into an affidavit and come by for her to sign.

Really? Was that how it was done? Seemed to me an affidavit should be in someone's own words. But I guess if Mom wrote the story on her own she'd leave out details. And she'd make a lot of extraneous comments.

Detective D'Aquin had some more questions for Mom.

"Can you think of anyone who might have had a grudge against your father? Any reason to do him harm?"

The question surprised me. Mild mannered, easygoing PawPaw? It aggravated Mom.

"Absolutely not. PawPaw got along with everyone," Mom snapped.

Detective D'Aquin dug deeper.

"Maybe a problem with a neighbor? The family owns quite a few acres and they farm even more on a share. With property, there can be boundary issues, rotten tree branches dropping on a neighbor, blocked water flow, or a rut from heavy equipment turning over the line."

Damn. Did he really have to ask these questions? Preposterous! People don't kill over that stuff. Well, maybe. Detective D'Aquin had more experience than I did, and I don't remember learning anything about investigations in law school.

"No problems I ever heard about." Mom cocked her head. "Long ago, I do remember hearing something about a little tiff PawPaw had with his neighbor Jack Alexander. Mr. Alexander owns Jefferson House next door, you know. Something about Alexander's nephew who spent the summer here and played with Bub when they were both little boys. That was years ago, and PawPaw and Mr. Alexander patched it all up quickly and became pretty close friends. Alexander leaves his key with PawPaw when he goes north."

The detective's questions gave me an idea. Maybe my law student status allowed me some leave to butt in.

"Detective, if there was no particular motive, does that tell us these crimes were just random, someone looking for money? Or was PawPaw a particular target? What I mean is, do the rest of us have reason to fear anything from this person?"

"Random robbery is our working theory, Miss Aguillard. You have no more reason to be fearful than anyone else out there in this troublesome world."

But the idea that PawPaw might have been a target, and that another member of our family might be as well, found space in some corner of my brain. I resolved to check out Dad's flip phone and see about updating Mom's old cell. We needed to keep track of each other—and of Taddy and Uncle Bub.

Turning away from Mom, Detective D'Aquin tried to speak with Uncle Bub, but Bub scrunched his fists into the sockets of his eyes and mumbled words I couldn't understand. The detective didn't make any suggestions, seeming to hope Bub would say things his own way. But Bub couldn't put his sentences together. He mumbled something unintelligible and didn't protest when Mom told the detective her brother needed to lie down awhile. I suggested to Ted that he come back another day.

Relieved from the questioning, Uncle Bub paused in the doorway of what had been the room he'd shared with his brothers when they were boys. He didn't go in. He turned and limped back into the hall, bumped on to PawPaw's room, and threw himself on top of the big bed close to the door. He buried his face in the pillow and breathed deeply, drawing in the lingering smells of his father. Mom went to a tall armoire and pulled out a hand-stitched quilt. Uncle Bub didn't stir when she tossed it over his crooked back. Her hand lingered a few moments on her brother's shoulder.

Mom and I returned to the center hall to find Father Martin talking to the family. He had made an offer to have PawPaw's wake inside the church, PawPaw's church, Our Lady of the Sea in Delcambre. He expected a crowd would be coming to pay their respects.

"But I think we'll have to wait a few days before they release the body," Father Martin said.

"No way. We're not going to sit still for *that*." Uncle Ti again.

"The coroner tells me they'll be getting in someone special to do the autopsy. We have to wait."

Mom's face pinched in pain at the word autopsy. Uncle Ti went into another rant.

* * *

Father Martin scheduled the Requiem Mass for Friday afternoon, five days after the body had been raised from the Delcambre Canal. Although Mom protested, the priest insisted on displaying the old-time funeral banners, black teardrops on stark white background, hung high on the pillars in the nave. Only this deep country parish still went for trappings like that. I told Mom I didn't like them either but had to say PawPaw would've thought they were fine.

Mom added a few other touches more in keeping for what they now call *A Celebration of Life*. She took the eightieth birthday picture off the wall of the old house and set it up on an easel at the cross aisle of the church. Next to the poster, Aunt Tut placed a collage of photographs of PawPaw through the years. High in the center, a solemn little boy in short pants clutched a thick pencil on the first day of school. Below, a very young man stood tall and proud in his uniform for the Great War. Then he and Mama B on their wedding day, smiling behind a tiered white cake with a miniature bride and groom on top. Another photograph showed a young farmer in overalls standing next to his first John Deere. On a third poster, Mom pinned up an array of color photographs of PawPaw with his grandchildren.

The funeral director said he had done what he could with PawPaw's body, but he had a strong recommendation. Close the casket. Uncle Ti and Mom jumped at that. Bub wouldn't have been able to stand the sight. The American Legion supplied a flag to cover the top of the casket. Good. PawPaw was proud to have served his country.

I didn't think there was anyone left around the lake who hadn't already come by the house to pay their respects, but all evening before the service, the line of mourners for the wake stretched the full length of the aisle. More people waited on the steps outside. Aunt Nell had to go into town for a second sympathy book to record the names of the visitors.

The pews of the church filled up for the rosary at seven. Sophie-Claire, my brother Emile's little girl, pulled on her grandmother's skirt and raised her sparkling black eyes. "People, people, lots of people G'Mimi." she said. "I can count to some pretty big numbers, but not this big."

We greeted the entire faculty of Our Lady of the Sea Elementary School where Uncle Etienne's wife Berthe had been teaching third grade for twenty-some years. My dad's firefighters came in uniform, as did the sheriff's deputies who worked with Bub. A tall black deputy stood at attention at the head of the casket. Mom's catechism class arrived together, right behind three nurses who worked with Uncle J. Allen's wife Mathilde at Iberia General Hospital. On and On. Worn down from hours on their feet, the brothers and sisters took turns standing in the line. My Dad brought in a chair for Uncle Bub. All of the family members said the same words over and over. "Thank you for coming." "Yes, I remember."

I remembered PawPaw's smiling face at the head of Mama B's Thanksgiving table. I remembered his steady hand on mine, guiding my fishing rod over the lake. And I remembered my last sight of him—a misshapen bundle being lifted from the water of the Delcambre canal. Anger again surged through my chest. Sweet PawPaw!

Early Saturday morning the line formed again, from the back of the church, past the cross aisle, and up to where the family stood before the altar. Why did so many people come for one old man? Because they knew the family, of course, and because the community had lost a beloved member. But for another reason. Everyone knew they could have been lying there instead of PawPaw. Anyone could have been the totally unsuspecting victim who had an accidental and tragic encounter with a crazy man.

The pews filled for the Requiem Mass. An altar boy came out and lit the candles, then signaled to the funeral attendants to begin the procession. The organ sounded a mournful hymn, and the family lined up to follow PawPaw on his last trip to the altar. Two black-suited men brought the flag-draped casket back to where we had assembled at the foot of the aisle, rotated the gurney, and pointed the flag toward the cross.

Father Martin intoned. "I am the Resurrection and the Life. Whosoever believeth in me shall not die." Six dark suits, six lapels with white carnations, flanked the casket: PawPaw's three oldest sons, Ti Pierre, J. Allen and Etienne on one side, and the husbands of three of the daughters, my Dad Emile, Tut's husband Burt, and Mazie's husband Al, on the other. Dora's husband and the women walked behind with their children. Every female member of the family over the age of fifteen wore black.

And then came the two who didn't keep in step. Bub bumped along on his crutches. Behind him, the frail form of an ancient nun shuffled slowly.

Many years ago, Sister Agnes, PawPaw's sister and my great-aunt, returned from a convent in the Philippines where she had spent forty-five years teaching in an orphanage and mission school. She moved into a home for retired nuns in uptown New Orleans. Today, for her brother's final Mass, an old-fashioned white wimple framed her wizened face. She folded her hands over her heart, on the front of the long black habit the Sisters of Mount Carmel now rarely wore. Her frail form tilted to the supporting frame of a much younger woman clad in the dress of the Sisters of today—pastel, mid-calf polyester skirt, high-neck blouse, large cross on her chest.

The rest of the family followed. As they passed the cross aisle, the poster-sized photograph on the easel drew every gaze. Bright blue eyes sparkled in the smiling face of PawPaw, at the center of his family, celebrating his eightieth birthday.

FAMILY MEETING

"Now don't feel like you're doing something weird, Mom. You know, we're actually reviving an old legal tradition. The Louisiana Civil Code once said you had to have a family meeting whenever there was something important to decide."

I snapped open a borrowed folding chair and handed it to my mom, who set it out with a couple of dozen others in the central hall of PawPaw's house. The two of us, just the two of us, were getting ready for a crowd. We had gathered here during the search for PawPaw, and again after the funeral. The DA had asked for this meeting of the family. Mom let out a disgusted snort, so I kept talking.

"All through the 1800s, the Clerks of the Court would order a family to get together to talk about who should raise orphaned children, plant the crops, and such. Makes a lot of sense to me. Some decisions are so important everyone should have a say."

"A say-so maybe, but this family will never *agree* on anything. Anyway, my dear, we have nothing to decide. Getting us together is going to be another wake. This house brings it all back." She snapped open another chair.

"You're probably right, but we'll be getting information the DA thinks we should have."

Even with a scowl on her face, Mom looked a lot better than she had a month ago, and my dad said she was sleeping OK. But the old house had sunk into melancholy. The venetian blinds sat askew, causing irregular ribbons of sunlight to stripe the wide pine boards of the floor. Mom pulled on the cords trying to straighten the slats.

"Fixing the blinds won't help, Mom. Let's raise some windows and get fresh air in here. The problem is the musty smell."

I tugged at a window, and the sash broke free with a thunderclap, rattling the old glass. Mom jerked her head back as if I'd struck her on the chin. Her nerves had a way to go. Fresh fall breeze chased dust bunnies across the floor. Mom took a deep breath, and I could see her shoulders relax.

"You're right, dear. The air feels good."

The past few years PawPaw hadn't kept up the place, and being shut up tight since the funeral didn't help, but with a lot of work and money, the house could once again be a wonderful home. Not grand like Jefferson House next door, of course. The Victorian mansion was gorgeous.

I glanced around the wide hallway. "I love this old place."

My thoughts drifted. Wouldn't it be great to restore this house? I'd love to see what could be done with the heavy walnut pocket doors separating the side rooms from the hall. Someone could redo the floor and re-attach the ceiling medallions. And the yard! I'd start by trimming the *Magnolia grandiflora* and *Grancy Greybeards* that twin-towered the front yard, and then I'd clear out the sad remains of the haphazard plantings to let the sweet-olive trees waft fragrance across the porches. In the backyard, except for the Satsuma, the fig tree, and the three blueberry bushes that earned their keep with fruit every spring, I'd get rid of everything and open up a view straight down to the lake.

Get a grip, girl. How could you even think of such things when you don't even have a job? The whole house needed to be scraped and painted. The roof probably leaked, the porches needed to be rebuilt, and who knew what else was about to fall apart? Fixing up just the outside would cost more than a year's law school tuition. In this family, only Dora, who lived a thousand miles away, had the means to undertake a restoration. The old house would have to be sold.

When I turned around, Mom had raised her eyebrows in my direction, one hand on her hip. "Honey, no one would ever know you're almost through law school. Don't you think it's about time you dressed a little more professionally? You could run next door and..."

Mom smiled as she scolded; she wasn't really mad. I pushed my bangs behind my right ear, but they dropped back into my face again. What a stupid hairdo—the tousled look. I needed to find a style I didn't have to fool with all the time.

Mom continued her fuss about having a family meeting. "Mr. Strait—of course he's still Jerry to me—is the one who asked me to put this day together, but he didn't see fit to tell me why. I guess we're going to hear how the investigation is going. There's talk around town the cops have a suspect."

Actually I knew that and more, but I wasn't telling Mom. I'd met one of Mr. Strait's assistants, Tom Barnett, at a football party, and I'd seen him a couple of times since. In fact, whenever my phone rang, my eyes shot to caller ID in the hope I'd see his name on the screen. The central hall of the old house had been the command post for the search—which gave me an idea. "Maybe memories of PawPaw floating around will help keep everyone harmonious."

Mom let out another snort. "That's enough chairs for now, Mandy. We have more in the closet if we get a crowd, and maybe *then* someone will give us a hand. I hope this meeting is over before time for lunch." Mom was into resentment today.

"I'll make sure there's something to eat if we're still going strong by noon."

Mom knew I meant a tray of sandwiches from Subway at the Exxon station on the way to town. My generation wouldn't spend time preparing what we could easily acquire.

Mom had good reason to worry about gathering the family. Would they even come? A month ago everyone was of one mind in sorrow, but as the sharpness of PawPaw's brutal death faded to dull pain, and the sheriff hadn't arrested anyone, old irritations began to scrape against one another. Frustrated and impatient, my aunts and uncles looked around for someone to blame. Uncle Ti had his designated villain. He would leap at any opportunity to complain about the sheriff. I hoped he'd bring Nell to the meeting. He was a lot easier to tolerate with his wife around. Uncle Bub would also come. He'd taken the loss of PawPaw harder than anyone. He didn't live alone in his cabin in our backyard anymore but had moved into our house. He slept in my older brother Emile's old room. Uncle Etienne, who lived in town, told Mom he'd be here.

"Do you think Uncle 'Tienne will have anything to say today?" I asked.

"I *hope* we find out what he has on his mind. Maybe he'll speak up and not sit there like Charlie McCarthy."

"Charlie McCarthy?"

"Before your time, honey." Mom almost smiled. "Sunday night radio. Charlie McCarthy was a puppet on the lap of a ventriloquist named Edgar Bergen."

I had a mental picture of 'Tienne perched on Berthe's rotundity!

Mom didn't know if we'd see Uncle J. Allen. Farmers always have some pressing task as an excuse for whatever family event they'd prefer to skip. Aunt Mazie and Aunt Tut would come, but not Aunt Dora. She'd flown in from Atlanta for the funeral, arriving the day before and leaving the day after.

Mom called the convent in New Orleans to ask about PawPaw's only living sibling, Mom's godmother, Sister Agnes. Before she took vows, Sister Agnes was the first Mimi. Mother Superior said a three-hour car trip would be a risk. Not a surprise. When the old nun walked up the aisle at PawPaw's Mass, I thought she'd blow over if anyone so much as sneezed.

Mom didn't extend a special invitation to any of the grandchildren, or even ask for them to be told about the meeting, but a few would show up anyway. No one in this family waited for an invitation to a gathering. Mom had given my brothers and me our orders. Come if you want, but be seen and not heard. I'd tried to make a few suggestions about how the family meeting should go, but she told me to forget *Robert's Rules*. She admitted set procedures help people get through sticky situations, but said since the DA wanted this gathering, he'd have to figure out how to make it work.

At a quarter to ten, Aunt Mazie and her husband Al arrived —fifteen minutes early. Mazie wore a flower-printed mid-calf dress, stockings rolled below her knees, dress shoes. Clearly she had no intention of helping out.

"Oh, Mimi. I just didn't know what it would be like to come back to the house again. No, I didn't know what it would be like today."

"Why does Mazie always say everything twice?" I muttered for Mom's ears only.

"And always the obvious," she whispered back.

You might think Mom would feel motherly and forgiving towards her baby sister, but many times Mom had told me how spoiled Mazie had been as a child, and how her husband Al spoiled her now. One child was quite enough for Mazie, and Al had to do whatever was needed to raise their little girl. Mazie spent most of the day in a lounge chair watching her "stories" on TV. Today she had sticking-up rooster-hair to show she'd logged time there already. Mom scowled in Mazie's direction, then scurried to find a chair more comfortable than the metal ones she had set up for everyone else. Mom spoiled her baby sister once more!

Out front, the doors on the next car to pull up popped open, spilling a half dozen passengers onto the lawn—Aunt Tut and her family. When her children were young, Aunt Tut had a station wagon for car pooling the girls to dancing lessons and the boys to Boy Scout campouts and the ball fields. With two children already married, and four more marriages to go, Tut had just bought a used Chrysler Explorer to taxi around the next generation. Aunt Tut went around to the back hatch and retrieved three plastic covered trays. Mom wouldn't have to worry about lunch after all. Tut always seemed to know what was needed, and she seemed to find the time to go to no end of trouble. Today she had brought sandwiches, drinks, and chips.

Ti Pierre arrived next, his wife Nell with him, thank God. And then Uncle Etienne and Aunt Berthe pulled up. J. Allen came after all. He'd stopped at our house to pick up Bub. We had all the siblings, except Aunt Dora.

And we'd picked up at least a dozen grandchildren as well. They walked into the house quietly enough, but soon greetings bubbled up into chatter. Not even a solemn occasion could keep them from being glad to see each other. We called that 'cousination'.

At ten o'clock, District Attorney Gerald Strait arrived. A tall, suited man walked at his side. Tom.

Mr. Strait moved easily around the room, greeting almost everyone by name. Smooth, he asked about the count of the shrimp in the last catch, the sucrose level in the sugarcane, if the rice fields were ready to be flooded. He knew the predictions for the local football teams and who won the Chevy pickup at Our Lady of the Sea fall festival raffle. Mom had known Gerald Strait since he was a boy. She'd watched with pride as he took the top spot in the power structure of the district—District Attorney. She gave him about fifteen minutes to work the room, then spoke over the hum with the tone of someone calling a meeting to order.

"Quiet, y'all. Let's settle down. Mr. Strait doesn't have all day." Her glance to me said, *You see, Mandy, I really am going to follow some procedure here.* Scraping of chairs on the bare wood floor replaced the buzz of conversation. Women took the front seats, the men drifted to the sides, and the young people clumped together in the back.

"Jerry—Mr. Strait." Mom corrected herself. "Come on up front. I think we're all anxious to hear what you have to say." Mom directed him to a marble-top table at the end of the hall, then she turned and sat down on the front row. Mr. Strait cleared his throat and looked over the crowd. He raised his chin, and his brows dropped just a touch.

"My friends, I would like once again to extend to all of you my deepest sympathy for your loss." For a good three minutes Mr. Strait played the condolence tape. *Yada, yada, yada.* Get to the point, man. Then he moved on to topic number two.

"I know, my good friends, nothing we can do will bring back your beloved PawPaw, but I have important news. The sheriff is wrapping up his investigation." Mr. Strait straightened up to all of his five feet six inches—which reminded me that out in the country they call him *the little man with glasses*. "This morning Judge Bonin signed an arrest warrant for the person the detectives have concluded is responsible for your father's death. His name is Remuald Richard."

He paused, raised his chin. Someone started to clap, and then came a roll of cheers. Half the room rose to their feet, then the remainder joined them. "Yeah, man!" "Way to go!" Mr. Strait's face cracked open in a smile. He leaned back on his heels and let the good feelings roll in. A sputtering of questions bubbled from the crowd. He picked out Aunt Tut to recognize first.

"Is he the same man who, you know, beat up the lady on Captain Cade Road?"

The DA raised his thumb in a congratulatory gesture. "I believe you surmised there might be a connection between two violent crimes in two days, didn't you? Good thinking. Yes, Mrs. Bienvenu. The same one."

"Does he come from these parts?" Al, Aunt Mazie's husband, asked.

"Yes, Mr. Randall. I think he's lived in this district most of his life. We believe he was born in lower St. Martin, moved around a lot, and for a few years worked offshore. He spent his onshore time wherever he could find a bed. We'll be learning a lot more about him."

Mom raised her hand to ask a question. "Jerry, has he been arrested? Is he in jail?"

I knew what she was thinking. Are we safe?

"No, not yet, Mrs. Aguillard." Mr. Strait tossed away the words as if arrest would be a mere formality. Not the case, I knew from Tom. The sheriff had the name of the suspect but the search for his whereabouts had just begun. "He may have fled the State, but the word is out all over the South. It won't be long before we find him. He's just your ordinary criminal type."

Ti Pierre exploded from the side of the room. "Ordinary? Hell, no! He don't sound so ordinary to me. He's some kind of monster."

Mr. Strait smiled. "Of course, Ti Pierre. What I mean is he isn't someone with international connections and a Swiss bank account. He's going to have to find money to live, and his friends around here are the only ones who can supply it. We'll find those friends and they'll talk. Actually, Richard was in our jail on a drug charge not too long ago."

"Shit! That figures. The sheriff had him and let him go." Ti Pierre again. Why on earth did the family allow Uncle Ti to be so obnoxious?

Mr. Strait continued. "The sheriff and I are having a joint press conference at noon today to announce the name of the man we want for these two brutal crimes. We'll be asking anyone with knowledge of his whereabouts to come forward, and we'll let the public know that if anyone gives him safe harbor, they'll be prosecuted themselves. Someone will talk, I promise you."

"Will there be a reward offered?" Aunt Tut asked.

"We've not set that up as yet. If necessary, we will do so."

I'd watched enough TV to know the family would be asked to kick in to the kitty. We'd probably find out about that little detail later on.

Mr. Strait answered a few more questions and then played the political tape. "I want you all to know that the offices of the District Attorney will see to it that justice is done. In a few weeks I will present the case to the Grand Jury. If they return an indictment for first degree murder of your PawPaw, as I expect they will, we will not rest until we have looked at every bit of evidence, until we have prepared the case to the very best of our ability, until we have presented the evidence in the court of law, until we have obtained a conviction. Then we will see to it that the perpetrator of this horrendous crime receives what he deserves."

Mr. Strait passed his eyes around the room. "Of course, we have a long road ahead. We will try the case and then we will endure those long appeals. The trial will be handled by my first assistant here, but of course I will closely supervise everything that takes place. My friends, we will be seeing a lot of each other over the next year."

"The next *year*?" Ti Pierre exploded again. This time he stood up to rant. "You're going to take a year to put an end to the monster?" This time, Mr. Strait ignored Uncle Ti. Good. We'd all had enough of him.

Mr. Strait turned to find his assistant in the crowd. "Mr. Barnett, Tom, would you please come up here and introduce yourself to these good people?"

All eyes turned to the back of the room where Tom was standing—next to me. Mom let out a puff of breath. I'd already told her I'd met the assistant DA who'd be in charge of the case, but she hadn't put two and two together. I watched Tom walk to the front of the group and replace his boss behind the little table. Younger, of course, and taller. Actually drop-dead handsome. I felt hot, and I'm sure my face turned crimson.

Tom had a serious expression, his face pale in comparison to Mr. Strait's. Unlike his boss, Tom didn't take off a couple afternoons a week to go fishing or play golf.

"Some of you may know me already, but let me introduce myself. I'm Thomas Barnett, Tom. For some time I've been handling the serious felonies occurring in this parish." He spoke slowly, with the marked accent of the northeastern part of the state. I remembered what one of my law school classmates said about our torts professor who came from Bastrop—when you heard his accent you had to remind yourself he could read and write.

"We'll be talking together quite a bit over the next few months. Probably y'all don't know all the procedures we have to follow in a case like this, but where murder is involved, we have to start with the Grand Jury. Today, at the press conference, Mr. Strait will announce that once Remuald Richard is arrested, we'll call the Grand Jury back into session and present the evidence the sheriff has assembled. My friends," Tom smiled, "we have very good evidence."

Tom had the full attention of his audience. He looked from

one face to another as if he were already talking to the jury. But he was difficult to understand through the filter of his north Louisiana twang.

"I fully expect the Grand Jurors will bring in an indictment for first degree murder of Pierre Boudreaux, your PawPaw. That's what we have here, first degree murder. For two reasons. First: the killing of a human being when the offender is engaged in committing a felony, and we have evidence Remuald Richard was robbing your PawPaw. Second: the killing of a human being who is over sixty-five years of age. We plan to use both reasons, belt and suspenders, you might say. Then, after the Grand Jury indictment, we'll need a couple months to prepare for trial. After the trial for first degree murder, we'll try Richard for what he did to Mrs. Falgout."

"Wait a minute! Mr. Barnett. I think that's what you said your name was." Uncle Ti stood again. "What if he's confessed? Do we still have to go through all that crap?"

Mr. Strait started to move forward to come to his assistant's rescue. Tom opened a downturned palm to smooth an imaginary ripple in the air, his raised eyebrows asking for the OK to continue. Mr. Strait backed off.

"Mr. Boudreaux, there are different confessions. Some are more like incriminating statements, and even one signed, sealed and delivered, should we be fortunate enough to get it, is not enough evidence by itself. When the crime charged is a capital murder..." Tom trailed off. Oops! This was not the time to bring up the death penalty.

Tom glanced at his boss with a look that said, *maybe I should have let you handle the family after all.* But he couldn't stop; he was in the dance.

"Mr. Boudreaux, over the next few months we'll be seeing each other a lot. We'll talk about the law, the penalty, and the long, long process we'll be in. I'll be trying to move as fast as possible, but we'll all need a good portion of patience."

I looked over at Uncle Ti's scowling face. He wasn't buying the story, and he didn't do Tom the courtesy of standing up to deliver his next shot.

"What a bunch of crap. If you get the evidence the dude did it, if he admits he did it, that's murder in cold blood. He should be taken out to the Delcambre Canal, stabbed, stuffed in his car, and sent into the water to drown. Just what he did to PawPaw."

Nell touched her husband's arm. "Easy, Ti."

Tom kept his cool. "I understand your feelings, sir, but for right now we have to begin with the Grand Jury. That's the law. We need to ask them for an indictment for First Degree Murder. Then we need time to prepare for trial. I assure you we'll all go through this together, as quickly as legally possible."

Tom had looked his challenger right in the eye. With his quiet, deliberate manner, he had calmed the storm. Good job, Tom. I hoped my face didn't flush again.

Uncle J. Allen was thinking a step ahead of his older brother. He'd picked up that the penalty for first degree murder would be an issue.

"First degree murder means he gets the death penalty, right? He dies for this?"

Perhaps only I noticed Tom's brief hesitation. "Sir, one of the penalties for first degree murder is indeed death. That decision—death or life in prison without parole—will be made by the jury, but the possibility of a death sentence is the reason why every step in this process must be taken with great care. Capital verdicts get a lot of attention in the State courts and then, when the State proceedings are done, in the federal courts as well. Year after year, defense lawyers, judges, and the prisoners themselves, go back and look at how the original trial took place. We have to do everything right at every step along the way."

Ti again. "OK, Barnett. If we have to have some half-assed trial, we do it. Then, what *will* he get, the gas chamber?"

"At this time, in the State of Louisiana, if the jury decides on the death penalty, the sentence is carried out with lethal injection."

"Ah, yes. The needle. Good." Ti stuck his thumb between his first and middle finger.

Aunt Tut had the next question. "How about the lady he did such awful things to, Mr. Barnett? How's she doing?"

Tom looked relieved to move to another topic. "Lydia Falgout. She's still in very bad shape, but she's improving every day and might be well enough to tell the Grand Jury what he did. She'll definitely be at the trial. I hope y'all get to meet her soon. She is one brave lady."

Mr. Strait came forward to put an end to the meeting. The ingratiating smile of the seasoned politician reappeared.

"My friends, you have as many questions as those reporters who will be waiting for me at noon." He looked at his watch. "Just an hour from now." He paused. "One more thing. You will not read a lot about this case in the newspapers. We have to be very careful. If we have too much publicity, we give ourselves a problem finding jurors who haven't already made up their minds. We don't want to have to move the trial somewhere else. We want a good group of citizens of *this* parish to be our jury. Justice will be done, my friends, but for now, I'm back to the office to prepare to meet the press."

The sheriff would probably put on some TV makeup and spray his hair. Not Mr. Strait; he'd go before the cameras as is. But they both kept an eye on politics. I remember the DA I'd worked for in Baton Rouge always timed his press conferences for noon so his announcements could make the afternoon papers and be featured on the evening news. I hoped my family had given Mr. Strait credit. They wouldn't be getting their information about the arrest warrant at the same time as the rest of the world.

The DA, Tom at his side, passed out a few more pleasantries as the pair made their way to the door. Once there, Tom turned his head and found my eye. Mom took it all in. I guess a sixth sense comes with the role. Custom around here has the mothers of girls thinking about weddings before their daughters are eighteen. I was twenty-six and had no one Mom called a prospect. She made regular remarks about grandchildren.

As the two suited men walked to the road, Mr. Strait's head bobbing in time to his moving lips, the public smile fell from his face. No doubt he was running through the plan for his meeting with the press, putting in motion the instincts that enabled him to balance the political forces that kept him in power and the analytical brain that allowed him to mine the law for prosecution strategies. Tom had clued me in about the political games of this press conference. The first order of business for the DA would be to get control of the sheriff's mouth. If Mr. Strait let Sheriff Landry face the public alone, the big fella, not the DA, would get the evening headline. To uncover Richard's hiding place, they needed the help of ordinary people, but too many details about the crime might jeopardize the chances of finding impartial jurors.

His expression stern, chin tucked, Mr. Strait headed straight for the passenger side of his SUV. He flipped his hand to Tom to tell him to take the wheel.

What would Mr. Strait say when the press wanted to know if he planned to ask for the death penalty? He'd take on a grave expression, lower his tone, and give the answer of any experienced DA. "I plan to prosecute this case to the fullest extent of the law." He'd leave the details for Tom to deal with down the road.

Watching the two men, and imagining their conversation, I thought about the process that lay ahead. As a member of the family, I would have an insider's view of the prosecution. And I'd get to spend time with a really exciting guy!

Aunt Tut invited everyone to come to the dining room for something to eat. My aunts and uncles were subdued, but the younger generation soon switched to talk about someone who got a bright red Camaro when he turned sixteen, and about the prospects for the local high school in the football playoffs. New Iberia Senior High had a good shot to win the championship. For the younger generation, the sandwiches and chips were no doubt breakfast. Not for me. Sometime in the past year I crossed over the line to be adult about what I put in my mouth.

Before long, the family went their separate ways, leaving Mom and me to pick up the remains of the meeting. Mom looked exhausted.

"Go sit down. I'll finish up here," I suggested.

"I can hold on for a bit more. I'm so relieved this business is finally all over."

I couldn't allow her to be deluded about what lay ahead. "Mom, it's far from over."

She dismissed my concern. "Sure, honey. I understand it's going to take time. But we know who did that to PawPaw. Even when he's tucked away in jail where he can't hurt our family ever again. Now it's just a matter of going through the motions."

"It'll take more than time, Mom. Deciding on the death penalty takes a toll on everyone."

Mom looked puzzled. "Whether he gets the death penalty or not is out of our hands. The jury decides life in prison or death, at least that's what the DA told us."

"Technically, you're right, Mom. If the DA asks for the death penalty, the jury decides whether or not to impose it. But he isn't required to ask for death."

No need to get into the details today. Mom would soon learn almost every DA is willing to cut a deal for a defendant to plead guilty in return for a sentence of life in prison if—and that's the big if—the victim is willing. We had a family of victims. *My* family, and I had at least one uncle who sounded as if he'd insist on going for the ultimate. I wasn't too sure about the rest of them —or myself for that matter.

I folded up the last chair and gave Mom a hug goodbye. When I turned to walk to the door, Mom put her hand on my arm.

"By the way, Mandy, you seem to know that assistant DA, Tom Barnett. I think I saw something going on there. He looks very nice."

"I've met him, Mom. That's all. He called last week and said he'd be handling the prosecution. Nothing to get excited about."

"Really? That call was enough for you to get out of those ratty student jeans!"

"Mom!"

I had taken a little more time with my appearance, but I didn't go into that. Nor did I tell Mom Tom had joined me last Sunday afternoon in PawPaw's back yard. I had wanted to keep Taddy company when he went fishing there for the first time since PawPaw's death. Not having PawPaw was bad enough for the boy, but when he walked down to the water to cast his line, he darn near collapsed. There lay the body of his friend the Great Egret, dark spatters spotting the rock the bird lay on, blood oozing from his belly into the lake. The snow-white neck had been blown apart by buckshot. Three turkey vultures circled overhead, red wattles pointing downward toward their dinner.

While I was consoling Taddy, Tom went up to the shed for a shovel. He came back to the shore and began to dig a hole in the side yard close to my old favorite spot. Silently, Tom buried the bird. That act alone won a piece of my heart.

That night I fell asleep with Tom's face behind my closed eyelids. And another visual rolled into my brain. When Tom had gone back to PawPaw's shed to find a shovel, I had seen a white pickup truck parked in the shell turnaround across the lake. Why was someone out there again? Were we being watched from across the lake?

Or was I just having a flashback of the last afternoon I'd seen PawPaw alive—the Sunday afternoon when the pelicans came in before the storm? I dozed off before I answered my question.

ARRAIGNMENT DAY

Mom sent out her own All Points Bulletin. She commanded my aunts, my uncles, and me to be present for the arraignment of Remuald Richard. I protested.

"This is ridiculous. Nothing important happens at an arraignment."

"He'll be there, won't he? Everyone in the family needs to get a look at him."

I tried my best to make Mom understand Remmy Richard wouldn't even speak. His attorneys would enter a plea for him, and we already knew they'd pronounce him *Not Guilty*. The court officials would just use the occasion to strut their stuff for the voters.

"Empty procedure, Mom. The judge will set a trial date, but even that's fiction. The District Attorney told us first degree murder goes on a special calendar and will be reset for a date at least six months down the road. There's absolutely no point making Dora fly in from Atlanta."

Or making me miss a class.

"We need to be there to show our strength, and Mr. Strait wants a short meeting with the family at nine, an hour before the arraignment."

Ah! That cast the situation in a different light. Mr. Strait would no doubt have his first assistant at his side. Tom.

I tucked my car into an empty space across Iberia Street, behind Migues Grocery. Cooking fumes assailed me as I opened the door. Who should I see getting out of his truck but George Miller, a high school buddy of my older brother. I'd heard he worked for the Clerk of Court.

"Hey George!" I called out. "Is it OK to park here? Everything's full at the courthouse."

"Sure. I park here often, but then I usually eat Sammy Migues' plate lunch. You may want to try one. He fixes extra on criminal days."

"I'm here for just one arraignment. I hope to be well on my way back to class by lunchtime."

George and I walked across Iberia Street toward the front steps of the courthouse.

"Pretty neat building, isn't it," I observed.

"Yup. An art deco treasure, built at the end of the thirties. Renovations and extensive additions in the 1980s changed the wings and back of the building, but thank goodness they kept the clean, symmetrical white facade. It's too bad the old courthouse on the bayou wasn't saved for something."

I paused to admire the statue commanding the top landing like the prow of a ship. Twice human size, one foot forward, palms upturned, reminiscent of the sculpture of the ancient Greeks. "I really like our Lady Justice," I said.

"We've got the sculptor's explanation in the clerk's office. He says she isn't the usual trite representation—robed, blindfolded, holding mechanical scales. Our lady announces that from this industrial, technological building comes justice that is clear-eyed, humane, compassionate and strong."

Hm-m-m. Most of the time, anyway.

We mounted the fifteen steps leading up to the brushed stainless double doors. Stylized pelican-beak profiles pointed at us from the tall windows above and on either side of the doors. Inside, George turned left to the office of the Clerk of Court. "See you at ten. I'll be on duty as Minute Clerk in the big courtroom."

I entered the elevator and signaled the second floor, under a brass plaque placed there in memory of the long time operator. *The Good Lord pushed the button and Charlie Baudoin had to go.* Because he was a beloved character, he kept his job for years after automation had made him irrelevant.

Our family meeting began on schedule. A puff of breath left my mouth when Tom stood before us. I planted both feet flat on the floor so my legs wouldn't wiggle.

"As you'll know, following a very important tip from a citizen, our detectives located Remuald Richard in Birmingham, Alabama, and arrested him for the murder of Pierre Boudreaux, your PawPaw. The Grand Jury met, we presented our evidence, and they returned an indictment for first degree murder. Today Richard is set to be arraigned—formally charged—with that crime and for the attempted murder of Mrs. Falgout. We fully expect to convict Remuald Richard of capital murder and of the other charge as well."

Tom sounded great.

"As we've told you, the process of obtaining a capital crime conviction is reviewed by the upper courts again and again. Volumes of cases parse the fine points of every death penalty decision—both state and federal cases since we're dealing with constitutional protections. We can't afford to take any shortcuts. We have to do everything right."

"Bullshit. Bullshit! That's what I think of what you call 'process.'" Uncle Ti again. He sat in the front row, on the center aisle, the best vantage point from which to rant.

Tom gave Uncle Ti a broad smile. "Mr. Boudreaux, I do believe I agree with you, but we live in America, and I don't think there's any one of us who would want to live anywhere else. The 'process' is the law of our country."

"The word on the street is the dirt bag confessed. Can't anything be done to just get this over and done with?"

Would Tom go there, I wondered? Yes. He put a toe in treacherous water.

"Actually there is, Mr. Boudreaux. If we weren't asking for the death penalty, the process would be much simpler."

Uncle Ti had nothing to say about that alternative. Tom gave him a steady look and moved on.

Once again, Tom's answers to the questions from the family were awesome. I thought so anyway. When he was done, he thanked everyone for coming. He walked down the center aisle toward the rear door, pausing as he passed my seat.

"How about lunch today, Mandy? Want to come by the office after the arraignment?"

I nodded my acceptance but couldn't speak.

A half hour later the bailiff formally opened court in the large courtroom. Forty members of our family were in place on the benches on the right side. In front of the family, within the bar— the railing separating the public from the officers of the court— District Attorney Gerald Strait sat at the prosecution counsel table with two assistants: Tom, of course, and Richie Castille. All three wore dark grey pinstripe suits. The prosecution had claimed the counsel table closest to the box where, at trial time, the jurors who would decide the case would be sitting. Inside the bar on the left, the pair of attorneys appointed to defend Remuald Richard occupied the other counsel table. The Chief Public Defender for Iberia Parish, Sarah Bernard, very tall, very blond, sleekly thin, sat in the center. For this public appearance Sarah had chosen a clinging, sharkskin, cream-colored pantsuit. Tom told me the lawyers referred to her as *The Afghan Hound*. If so, why not dress the part? Next to her, Reginald Denny, co-counsel sent by the State Public Defender Board to assist in capital defense—a dapper young African American with a full afro, a polka dot bowtie, and an unvented, iridescent grey silk jacket—sat at her side. A third chair, at the end of their table, awaited the defendant. The benches directly behind the counsel table, the places customarily reserved for supporters of the defendant, were empty. Remuald Richard had neither family nor friends.

The Clerk of Court himself showed up today, stationed directly in front of the judge's bench. He came to read the indictments returned by the Grand Jury: First Degree Murder of Pierre Boudreaux and Attempted Second Degree Murder of Lydia Falgout. As an elected official, he used the occasion to shine his record-keeping job with a patina of judicial importance. He had George at his side to take the court minutes.

Of course the Grand Jury returned indictments. Only the District Attorney puts on evidence; there's no defense presence. Although no one knew any details about the testimony the jurors heard—the proceedings were closed—the general public skipped right over any problems the prosecution might have in proving guilt. Even my Mom thought Richard's conviction was assured. The sheriff's deputies had good evidence tying Richard to the crimes, and he had admitted his involvement. The only question? Would he or would he not get the death penalty?

For the occasion, Sheriff Septimus Landry had stuffed himself into his dress uniform. With the two lead detectives on the case, Buddy Aymond and Deuce Washington, he leaned against the wall at our right, overlooking our benches. His upturned chin invited the Boudreaux family—voters every one— to feel protected and served by his sheltering presence. In the general audience, I spotted representatives of the media sprinkled among courthouse groupies and the merely curious. Eager young men and women with notebooks in hand, loose shirts concealing tape recorders they had strapped to their chests.

Judge Sosthenes Oliver Bonin, who enjoyed initialing paperwork with the block letters S.O.B., emerged from a doorway behind the bench. An elderly bailiff jumped to his feet and bellowed into the room. "Oyez, oyez, oyez. All rise." The judge mounted five steps to the dais and remained standing while the bailiff repeated his call to order.

Judge Bonin settled his ample width into the high-backed armchair. Today a curtain covered the WPA-funded Conrad Albrizio fresco behind the bench. Damn. I wouldn't get to see this famous example of the Diego Rivera period of art Tom had told me about. The subject? A central figure represented mankind achieving freedom by overcoming the forces of avarice and malevolent power. By some unfortunate coincidence, the flushed red face of the bald figure depicting a corrupt official sweeping coins into his clutches, avarice himself, bore an extraordinary resemblance to Judge Bonin. By order of the court, the bailiffs closed the curtain whenever Judge Bonin presided. I resolved to ask George to show me the fresco on another day.

A side door next to the defense table opened. Two deputies prodded forward a pale white man clad in Day-Glo orange and shackled in leg-irons and handcuffs. Remuald Richard. In black flip-flop shower shoes, he shuffled across the tile floor to stand before the judge's bench. Sarah Bernard and Terry Moore moved forward to flank their client.

"Not Guilty, your Honor," Sarah responded to the reading of the indictment for the charge of First Degree Murder of Pierre Boudreaux. She made this response with an edge of defiance. Did she really believe Richard was innocent? She had vehemently stated the same to the reporter for *The Daily Iberian* and vowed she would prove her case at trial. Sarah repeated the same response after the reading of the second indictment, the charge of Attempted Second Degree Murder of Lydia Falgout.

At Provost's Sports Bar downtown on Main Street you could lay a bet on which fly would jump off the table first, but you couldn't have gotten hundred to one odds of Remuald Richard taking a walk for these crimes.

Minute Clerk George read out a list of dates for discovery deadlines, motion hearings, and plea days stretching forward three months to a trial date in March. The judge rapped his gavel on the surface of the bench, swiveled his neck, and squonked like a foraging goose. "So ordered." The deputies who had escorted Richard into the courtroom stepped forward, nodded respectfully to the judge, and led the prisoner away.

"Court is in recess. Arraignments will resume in twenty minutes." Judge Bonin strode out the way he had come in.

For this we had marshaled the standing army. The whole procedure took no longer than five minutes. My raised eyebrows said *I told you so* to my mom.

Mom refused to adopt my ill humor. "Dora is staying at J. Allen and Mathilde's, of course. I'll be glad to get a chance to visit with her. Come join us, Hon."

"Not right now, Mom. I have somewhere I need to be for lunch, but I'll come on over for a visit this afternoon."

Mom's smile and raised eyebrows told me she knew where I was going first, or at least who I'd be with. Her eyes followed me as I took a left turn out of the courtroom, away from the elevator, and walked down the hall to the office of the assistant district attorneys.

If the early morning rain shower had continued, Tom and I would have gone to *Lagniappe*, a cool little restaurant on Main Street. I loved the place. The courtly proprietor greeted everyone by name and pointed out any additions he had made to the collection of his paintings on the walls—mostly caricatures of his customers—and frequently sat down for a visit. His wife stayed in the back. But with clear skies now, Tom had called ahead to order a couple of po-boys from Bon Creole. We picked them up, headed for City Park, and found an empty picnic table at the edge of Devil's Pond.

"You did well this morning, Tom. I saw smiles and satisfied looks on the faces of my family. I believe they're getting used to you."

"And how about you? Are you getting used to me too?" Tom teased.

"I guess you could say that."

"Not sure I could. You look a bit on edge today."

"OK. I guess you can tell I'm uptight at those family meetings, and maybe the arraignment made me nervous. I'm feeling better already."

"Sometimes I think we design our court proceedings to keep the public intimidated so the judge and the lawyers can have the upper hand. But soon you'll be one of us, Mandy. People will be nervous in front of you!"

I wasn't going to tell Tom he was the cause of my jitters. Twenty minutes watching the ducks glide silently along the surface of the pond, listening to the mocking birds calling from the treetops, the fall breeze on my face, I felt better. Tom is easy to talk with—and also easy to be around without talking. When we finished our sandwiches, Tom picked up our boxes and stood.

"I'd love to take the afternoon off and spend it with you, but I have to get back to an appointment."

* * *

Mom and I sat on a green painted bench on the back porch of the old Darby house. Aunt Dora and Uncle J. Allen's wife Mathilde rocked slowly in a cypress swing. We chatted at first, catching up on each others' lives. We could barely see the bayou through the trees—a shimmering stream of dark-roast coffee undulating a half a football field below the house. Mesmerized by a soft breeze and the rhythmic creak of a rope suspended from hooks in the porch ceiling, we fell silent.

The Bayou Teche in south Louisiana casts a spell, an inspiration for poets and a perfectly legal narcotic for the enchantment of those lucky enough to spend time on her shores. Over one hundred years ago, when Longfellow paid a visit to the Louisiana home of his Harvard roommate, he probably passed time on a porch like this one. Three sides opened to the southern breeze. Beneath branches dipping from two-hundred-year-old live oaks, the sun shed light but little heat inside the railings. We wore light jackets but were far from cold.

Mom had told me that years ago, when best friends Dora Boudreaux and Mathilde Darby were in high school at Mt. Carmel Convent, a casual acquaintance could barely tell them apart. They rolled their pleated brown skirts exactly the same way and went everywhere as a pair. On this day, both pairs of dark Cajun eyes sparkled, but now Dora looked ten years younger than Aunt 'Tilde. An affluent suburban life is kinder on a woman than Louisiana tropical sun and a rice and gravy diet. Aunt 'Tilde's end of the porch swing hung six inches lower than Aunt Dora's.

Aunt Dora tipped up her chin and wrinkled her nose.

"Ah! The smell of the sweet olive. My home in Georgia is beautiful. We have the same azaleas in the spring and the same crepe myrtles blooming all summer long, but there's nothing like the scent of sweet olive blossoms. To me, they are Louisiana. I'll always come back here." Aunt Dora turned to my Mom. "How are things at PawPaw's house, Mimi?"

"Just fine so far. Locked up tight. I check every day, but soon we're going to have to come to a decision about what to do with the old place. We can't just leave the house empty."

Down on the bayou bank, my Uncle J. Allen, tall, grey-headed, in khaki work clothes, bent over a thick, six foot long cypress log. His muscled arm reached out to the shore to grab a heavy chain and hook it into a metal eye screwed into the cut end of the log. He straightened up, surveyed his work, and scratched his chin.

On the porch swing, Aunt Mathilde spoke softly to her rocking partner.

"J. Allen's been working at tying up that log for a couple of evenings now. He wants to watch the snapping turtles toast themselves in the afternoon sun and then, when a boat comes by, flop off into the water. Plop, plop, plop! Why does he want to watch that? Beats me."

Mathilde Darby grew up in this house. At eighteen, she married my Uncle J. Allen, her best friend Dora's older brother. When her parents passed away and the other Darby children, all older, had made their nests elsewhere, she and Uncle J. Allen bought out the Darby siblings and moved back into her old home. That was twenty years ago. Through the years, whenever Aunt Dora came back to Louisiana to visit, Mathilde and J. Allen insisted she stay with them.

Aunt Dora met her husband in college. I don't think he'd ever felt comfortable with our family. Dora said he confessed to her he could breathe a bit better at 'Tilde's than under everyone's eyes in PawPaw's house, but it was only a matter of degree. He'd rather she made these Louisiana trips by herself and leave him behind in Atlanta. A couple of Christmases ago I overheard PawPaw say to Dora, "Nice fella', your husband, but he doesn't eat very much and he doesn't have enough vowels in his name. What kind of a handle is Wyznyck anyway?"

"It's Polish," Dora had answered, laughing. "You know PawPaw, some people think Boudreaux is a funny name."

"My brother is pretty quiet these days, 'Tilde. Is he OK?" Aunt Dora asked her sister-in-law.

"Each person handles grief differently, I've learned over the years. J. Allen prefers to keep his feelings to himself, but even from here I can see a sag in his shoulders. The other day, when he laughed at those flopping turtles, I thought the log project might help put a bit of joy back into his life."

"Has he been fishing in the Basin?" Aunt Dora asked. "As I remember, that's what he liked to do when he could."

"Not one time since..." Her voice dropped off. "Today he left the boys in charge of planting cane, but grinding will begin soon. From then until the end of January he'll be really busy, loading cane all day, dog-tired at night. Work helps but doesn't cure the blues. He tells me he still feels his father's presence on every row of cane."

J. Allen and his father had worked the farm together for over twenty years. When PawPaw couldn't climb into the tractor anymore, he still kept a close eye on operations. Mom told me Uncle J. Allen used to fuss about the constant supervision from his father. Now, the lack of it left a hole.

Down on the bayou, a lone blue heron silently skimmed into view. He thrust his feet forward to break his flight and plopped awkwardly onto a sandbar near the far bank. The neck of the bird collapsed into a crook and his head listed left. Our eyes were drawn to the movement of the bird, but J. Allen, no more than twenty feet away, didn't seem to notice. He bent over a grove of cypress knees standing at attention like miniature soldiers awaiting review. From the opposite bayou bank, the blue heron watched the water with one beady black eye.

My mom interrupted our fixation on the bird. "Dora, what did you think of the guy this morning?" An abrupt change of topic, but Dora knew her sister was asking about Remuald Richard.

"Looked like just any guy."

Aunt Mathilde broke in. "He's been in jail for over a month now, so I guess he's cleaned up. And sobered up, they say. Now he just seems regular. If I'd been behind him in the line at the grocery store, I probably would've told him to have a good day—if he weren't wearing an orange jumpsuit and handcuffs, of course. Mr. Barnett says he'll look even better at the trial when they have him dressed up in street clothes. He may wear a suit and tie! You know, that's just not fair. I think the jury should see him the way PawPaw did, dirty and all doped up. Maybe even holding a kitchen knife. That would be fair."

"I feel really weird about him," Aunt Dora said softly. "He looks like us, grew up right around here, and yet he could do what he did to PawPaw. You never know about people. We once had lynchings right here in Iberia Parish, and in Georgia too, of course. Then there was the Holocaust..."

Was I picking up a hint Dora had what PawPaw would have called "northern liberal ideas?"

Mathilde shook her head angrily. "That woman, his lawyer. How can she do what she does, defend people like that? She mustn't have any principles."

Mom beat me to a response, and smiled at me when she did so. "Tom Barnett made a point of explaining that, 'Tilde. Remember?"

Aunt 'Tilde did a mocking imitation of Tom's speech, complete with the extra syllables of his northeast Louisiana accent. "The defense lawyer's job is to be certain the District Attorney proves his case. Only if both sides present *all* the evidence and their *best* arguments for their positions can we be sure the result is just,' he said."

Mom answered. "Now, 'Tilde. Would you want a system where the government decides in secret who should be punished? Sounds corny, but the work of the defense lawyer preserves civil liberties for us all."

I raised a thumb in approval. Good job, Mom. I couldn't have said it better. 'Tilde was still fuming, blowing out little puffs of air. Aunt Dora changed the subject to try to repair the mood between the sisters.

"Ah, Mimi. I think you've taken a liking to Assistant District Attorney Tom Barnett? That's a good thing since he seems to be sparking after Mandy."

Oh, my. Here come the aunts to comment about my love life. Mom, please get them off the subject.

"What a family! You flew into town last night, Dora, and you already know the gossip."

Aunt Mathilde stayed on the subject of Tom. "I like the young man well enough as a boyfriend for you, Mandy, but prosecuting this case is another matter. He talks funny and he's so skinny he mustn't like our food. I'd be happier if the DA himself took charge. He can really make you feel comfortable. I bet juries eat out of his hand."

Aunt Dora gave her childhood pal an affectionate pat. "One glance at Tom Barnett and I knew he was a runner. My husband has the same look—a neck that's all Adam's apple. People are forever telling me I should cook more. I agree the twang is hard to get used to. I had the same problem when I first heard the voices of the people in Georgia. The extra syllables make people sound like snobs."

Mom added her comment, which I appreciated. "Girls, I like Mr. Barnett because he explained things."

With dusk, the mosquitoes descended. We watched J. Allen slap his neck a few times, straighten up from his project, and climb up the lawn to join us behind the screens of the porch. He pulled over a chair and settled down next to the swing.

"Jay, we've been talking about the arraignment this morning." Dora said.

"Huh," J. Allen grunted.

"What did you think of it?"

"It was OK by me."

"Really? Do you think we're in good hands?"

Uncle J. Allen set his lips together. He'd worked in the fields since he was in high school; years of sun had darkened his face to a permanent tan. When he concentrated on something, his skin looked even darker, almost pecan-shell brown.

"It bothered me to see the District Attorneys so buddy-buddy with the defense lawyers. Shaking hands, laughing, chatting it up."

I answered this one. "That's just the way lawyers are, Uncle Jay. We have to stay on friendly terms so we can work together. Civility is just part of the profession."

At least civility is alive and well in most courtrooms. Legislatures could learn a bit about cooperation and collaboration from lawyers.

"Barnett's OK, I guess. When we first met him he told us what to expect."

"True," said Aunt Dora. "And he told us what's going to happen in the future. A long haul. We'll be dealing with this case for years to come."

Aunt Dora lowered one foot onto the deck to stop the movement of the swing. Clearly, she'd given some thought to what she said next.

"As Mr. Barnett told us, when capital punishment is on the table, a trial takes four times as long as a regular murder trial. And after the trial is over, if the jury brings in death, there can be a half dozen post-conviction hearings. At each hearing the family has to be involved, testifying and reliving the whole thing. A capital process, trial to execution or release, now seems to take forever. We'll be living with a nightmare for years to come, unless —"

Uncle Jay interrupted. "We can't do a thing about it. The jury makes the decision."

Dora looked solemn. "Jay, we could possibly do something. I think Mr. Barnett hinted that sometimes they take the death penalty off the table. Explain that to us, Mandy."

Much as I hated to get in the middle of this, I couldn't resist showing off a little of the knowledge I learned in my internship with the DA in Baton Rouge.

"Sometimes, when the victim and the defendant are willing, the ADA doesn't ask for the death penalty. It may be possible to get Richard to admit everything and agree to a sentence of life in prison rather than going to trial and risking a verdict for death. If he did that, there would be no trial. Our ordeal would be over. Richard would go straight to Angola and stay there for the rest of his life. But the District Attorney usually doesn't even talk about backing off from the death penalty unless the family of the victim agrees."

J. Allen snorted a response. "Well, I don't think we're going to do that."

I continued my explanation. "Also, his lawyer would have to agree. Right now Ms. Bernard is saying her client didn't do it."

Aunt Dora pinched her brows. "Does she really believe that, Mandy? Or is that just part of the way this game is played?"

"I don't know what she really believes. I do know the detectives and the DA are totally convinced Richard is guilty of both crimes."

Dora's expression softened. "Good. At least we don't have to worry about a wrongful conviction, although I have heard that happens some time."

I could see Uncle J. Allen carefully picking the right words to express his thoughts.

"When I think about that guy, on a beautiful day like this, out in the fields on the farm at Angola, enjoying the days the way we're enjoying today, his grandchildren coming to visit with him, I'm furious. After what he did to PawPaw."

Uncle J. Allen put his hands over his eyes before he could continue. He swallowed hard.

We sat in silence. Darkness crept in. Then, as if directed by an invisible baton, the evening concert of chirps and chatters began. The cicadas struck up the band.

Mathilde began to fidget, stood up and broke the silence. "I've got to see about my dinner."

J. Allen had one last word. "Death is even too good for that guy."

If Tom been had been hinting around about getting the family to back off from the death penalty, he hadn't scored with J. Allen or 'Tilde. Maybe Dora would be interested. My aunts and uncles had the say, not in-laws or grandchildren like me, but if anyone asked, I didn't think I'd be interested either. If the evidence proved a crime, the prosecution should swing for the outfield fence.

BASKETBALL

Tom and I had been seeing each other casually for over two months. Brother Andry, the genial proprietor at *Lagniappe*, now greeted us by name. We danced to *Beausoleil* at the Gumbo Cookoff, but mostly we tried to meet in Lafayette for dinner and a movie to keep the office chatter to a minimum. Tom came to Baton Rouge to tail-gate for homecoming. I caught myself talking about him without realizing I was doing so. The lift in Mom's eyebrows told me she noticed.

One night at dinner in mid-November, Tom seemed unusually quiet. I asked him what he had on his mind. Just work, he said. He'd spent the day starting to dig into preparation for the trial of Remmy Richard. The set of his jaw told me he hadn't left his work behind.

"You have an interesting family, Mandy, and there sure are plenty of 'em. I gasped when I saw that picture of your grandfather's eightieth birthday hanging in the hall of the old house. No wonder we have a crowd every time the case comes to court. I envy you. Y'all have so much fun with each other."

"Fun?" I chuckled. "Some, yes. But it's not all fun. We fuss, complain about each other, and we've been known to let the sparks fly like a bunch of Italians. Right now Uncle Ti is on the outs with his brother Etienne over a tractor 'Tienne borrowed and ran without enough oil. Aunt Mazie keeps offering her sister Tut unsolicited advice about Burt, Jr. Mazie thinks she's giving Tut news about her son's drug use when, in fact, Aunt Tut has been coping with that problem for over two years. Advice about someone's children is always a bad idea. *As the World Turns,* Boudreaux style."

Tom wasn't picking up my light mood.

"I've spent some time watching y'all interact, Mandy, and it seems the family lets Ti Pierre speak out. Is he the one who makes the decisions?"

"Hell, no. He's an embarrassment, to tell the truth. The sibs blow him off. Mom steps in when it matters. You'll notice she's the one organizing those family meetings."

"So your Mom is the real decision maker?"

"In some ways, she is. But she doesn't tell anyone what to do."

"What about your Uncle Etienne. He doesn't have a lot to say."

"You got that right. But when he talks, everyone listens."

"So, you're saying if I need an answer about something, I'll have to deal with each family member individually?"

Where was Tom going with this grilling to ferret out the family pack leader? Was he skirting around something?

"Sorry about that, Tom. The short answer is yes. We're a pretty independent lot."

"Actually, one-on-one is better." Tom sat back in his chair, still all business. "The first date set for Richard's trial is only a couple months away, although I'm pretty sure the fixing will be bumped a month or two." The little furrow between his eyebrows deepened. "I can just hear Ti Pierre giving me the business over that."

"Yup, he'll scream."

"The evidence is looking very good, but although everyone complains about how long it takes for the wheels of justice to grind, a cooling off period is probably a good idea. Emotion shouldn't be the driving force in the courtroom."

I still didn't know where he was going. So I asked. "What

answers are you looking for anyway?"

"Right now I'm thinking about who I might want to put on the stand to testify at the trial."

"Wait a minute. The family will have to testify? What do *we* know about what happened?"

"A jury needs to care about the victim's family. I'd like to have your mother and your Uncle Bub, if he can do it, take the stand to tell the jurors what they did when they realized your PawPaw was missing. Their account lets me get some sympathetic trial testimony in the back door. And in the penalty phase, if we have to go there, I don't yet know who I might want on the stand to speak about the family's loss."

"I think this will be a surprise to the family, and not a welcome one. We're all riding along thinking we're mere spectators of the whole process. Remember you told them the jury makes the decision?"

Tom rubbed one hand over his face. "Yeah, I remember. All too well. That was my first day on this case. Faced with that room full of your family, I just wanted to say something and get the meeting over with. Maybe I made a mistake there."

"Or maybe that was a good way to start. They don't know you. You had to convince them they had a prosecutor who would try his damnedest to get Richard the punishment he deserves."

"Right. I didn't want them to think I didn't have my heart in my work. My hope is that as they get to know me better they'll have confidence in my decisions, whatever they may be."

This conversation was making me uneasy.

"What decisions? Like who you want to put on the stand?"

"Yeah. But there are other things they need to understand about the case."

"Like what?" I asked.

Tom took a deep breath. "Like juries can be crazy. You can never be certain what a jury will decide. I lost my first case and learned a valuable lesson."

I prodded Tom to tell me more.

"Right after Hurricane Rita—you remember Katrina's caboose—we had a lot of Mexican workers here, mostly undocumented, doing clean-up. One night one of them took a knife to his wife at a party at the Iberia Inn. The defense was willing to have him plead guilty and go away for a short time, maybe enough time for his wife to find a new life away from his abuse, and be deported. Knowing he'd be back over the border in a matter of weeks, I wouldn't go along. I tried him for attempted murder. The jury listened to lots of witnesses who could barely speak English. They muddied everything up. The verdict? Not Guilty. Talking to the jurors later, I learned they just didn't give a damn about what a bunch of illegals did in their spare time. I care about my victims, consider them my clients., and am committed to serve them to the best of my ability. That time I didn't. I've often wondered if the woman went back to her husband. If so, she's probably no longer alive. Lesson learned—a bird in the hand."

I thought I understood what Tom was talking about. I learned in the DA's office in Baton Rouge that getting convictions is harder than it looks. Jurors watch CSI and expect scientific proof. Without that, you need really powerful witnesses.

Tom continued. "A death penalty trial is an incredible ordeal. Only one person has been executed in Louisiana in the past ten years and that only happened because the poor wretch said he was tired of living and asked to die. His lawyers honored his wishes and took a dive. But if a defendant puts up any fight at all, the post-conviction process goes on forever. And you know, it isn't only an ordeal for the lawyers. The family has to relive the experience at the trial, and then go through the years of post-conviction hearings, again and again. No closure. Once emotions simmer down a bit, families are often open to thinking about ending the process."

"Wait a minute. Are you going to ask the family to agree to accept some plea?"

"Definitely not yet, if ever. Now, I just want them to understand what we're up against."

"I can't see them backing down, especially if you need every one of them to agree. Actually, I can't conceive of everyone in the family having the same opinion about anything. You bring all that up now, and they're just going to think you're a wimp."

Me included.

"Exactly. And that's why I haven't yet mentioned plea agreement. No hurry, but in preparation for the possibility, and just because I want to serve the family, I want to know each one better. And they need to know me."

"All sixty four?"

Now Tom's mood lightened.

"Hell, no. Just the eight children. That's all I can handle."

"Even Uncle Ti Pierre? That should be fun."

"Yes, even Ti Pierre. He needs to see what's ahead and maybe get some understanding that the world isn't black and white."

I found a corner in my mind to remember this conversation, and told myself to listen more carefully to the family talk. Except for one casual reference from Dora, I don't think anyone had even considered anything but a capital prosecution. All I heard was 'go get 'em.'

Actually, that's where I was as well.

* * *

A month later, mid-December, Tom called from work on a Thursday afternoon.

"I think I can make it to your place by 6:45, Mandy. I'll check in again when I'm close."

Tom and I had realized we both liked college basketball. He'd once mentioned coming over to Baton Rouge for the first game of the season, but the conversation had been casual. I didn't know if we had a firm date. Apparently Tom didn't talk just to hear himself. I didn't either, and that may be good or bad. Some people have unflattering names for my list making and careful calendaring of tasks.

The basketball game promised to be a good one, a reprise of last year's SEC conference final that Arkansas had won with a last second free throw.

Tom made it across the Basin fifteen minutes early. He gave me a friendly kiss on the cheek, but even that gave me a warm flush.

We walked through the campus gates, across the parking lots, and up the ramp at the Pete Maravich Assembly Center—Pete's Palace. The facility once deserved the royal designation but now looked more like a commoner's dwelling. Other SEC teams had magnificent new basketball arenas, but I loved the intimacy of the old place—and the fact that tickets for students were virtually free. All through school I'd found the games a great way to escape.

A barrage of three point shots sent Arkansas out to an early lead. We scored, but never a three-pointer. Time and again, our nimble point guard sneaked back door, took the ball underneath the basket, and then either laid it up or kicked it out to the off-guard who had shaken his man with a flurry of deft passes. Tom kept punching his fist into the palm of his other hand as we traded two points for their three and stayed behind, but I wasn't worried.

"Easy, Tom. Look how our guys dominate in the paint."

Sure enough, the Arkansas long range shots stopped connecting, and we caught up. The score seesawed back and forth until half-time.

To the deafening sound of the PA system, the tiger mascot plummeted down from the overhead scoreboard, the Golden Girls gyrated in their black tights and sequined tops, and Pete's Palace rocked. Tom took my hand.

"Let's take a walk. I need to cut the tension."

His touch had the opposite effect on me.

The lead changed twelve times during the second half of the game. Tom and I cheered and yelled as loud as anyone—except those red-clad Arkansas fans in snout masks shouting 'Soo-ee.' One team went ahead two points, then the other. With two minutes to go in the game and the score tied at 63-63, LSU took a timeout.

I stood up and rolled my shoulders to work the knots out of my neck. "I need a timeout too," I told Tom.

The last two minutes of any basketball game can last fifteen. Intentional fouls, timeouts to ice a newbie on the line for a free throw, at least one good argument over a call. This evening our coach picked up a technical for which we paid dearly in a couple of free throws and loss of possession. I could see the headline in the sports section tomorrow. *Coach Thomas's Temper Tanks Team.* Got to have that alliteration.

At minus twenty seconds, with Arkansas one point ahead, the ball in the hands of red and white, not purple and gold, all seemed lost. Tom and I both sat back preparing to accept disappointment. Then our point guard stole the ball. We sprang to our feet and held our breath. Coach Thomas entwined the fingers of both hands on top of his bald head, a sign he had offered up the outcome to a higher power.

"All the way in for a two pointer!" Tom screamed, along with half the fans in the arena, hoping the point guard wouldn't panic and attempt a three pointer from too far out—and miss.

With the time clock showing one second to go, the point guard got off a shot. The ball rolled and rolled around the rim, and dropped through the hoop.

Our customary reserve towards each other vanished in the emotional release of the unexpected victory. Tom threw his arms around my shoulders. We danced up and down with the rest of the LSU crowd. Suddenly, we were still. Tom held me for a moment, then pulled his right hand back and tipped up my chin to kiss me gently on the lips. When we straightened up, I sensed a definite change in the air between us.

Later, sitting in the Pastime with mugs of cold beer before us on the table, we were strangely quiet.

"Shrimp po-boy?" Tom asked me.

"Oh, no! Not this time of year, Tom. Oyster. The seasons for basketball and oysters are the same, you know. The perfect combination."

Tom got up and went to the counter to place our order. When he came back to the table I returned to the topic we had both put on hold. My family.

"Have you decided to talk to my aunts and uncles one at a time, Tom?"

"Yes. In front of the others, no one wants to be labeled as

someone letting the victim down. But singly, maybe I can get somewhere."

A speck of doubt about Tom's principles pricked my brain. I pushed away my beer mug. Where was it he wanted to go?

"So why are you giving me the side eye?" Tom asked.

"Am I hearing the interrogation technique of getting two witnesses separated and telling each that the other has spilled everything? You do things like that?"

"No, no." Tom smiled; a deep dimple dented his chin. "I just want each one to talk to me without the influence of someone else in the room. There's no hurry about this. As the process goes on, I look for opportunities to gain their confidence. If they know me, they'll feel more comfortable keeping me up to date. I'm not only looking for answers. I need to get to know each family member and figure out what makes him tick."

OK. I accepted that—probably because I wanted to.

"Tell me about your Uncle Bub, Mandy. How's he doing? He's the one who seems to be having the most trouble handling the loss."

Tom showed sensitivity and obvious concern for the most fragile member of the family. I liked that.

"He's not doing well, Tom. Bub and his father were inseparable, you know, especially since Mama B died. Our lives are pretty much the way they were before, but not Bub's. His whole world changed. PawPaw kept him going. Most days now he just sits and watches TV."

Should I be telling personal stuff to someone who isn't family? The District Attorney represents the State, but he represents the victims as well. That made Tom our lawyer. I should be free to tell our lawyer everything, right?

I wanted to.

"Bub moved in with Mom and Dad the first night PawPaw went missing. Over two months and he hasn't once spent the night in the barbecue house. He sleeps in our house, in my brother Emile's old room. And he doesn't go to his work at the sheriff's office but maybe once or twice a week. I notice that if he doesn't go in, they don't even call. This is not good for him. When he sits still for a few hours, his stiffness gets worse. At this rate he'll be back in the wheelchair before we know it. I'm glad PawPaw can't see him like this."

Tom waited for me to speak again. Something else I liked about Tom, he knew when to say nothing.

"Mom tells me Bub has been waking up in the middle of the night. I don't hear him, but she does. Bub tells her he sees PawPaw standing by his bed, just standing there, in a grey fog, and the vision terrifies him. After a few seconds, Bub realizes he's dreaming and begins to shake, trying to wake himself up. He can't. Mom sometimes finds him gasping for breath and whimpering like a puppy until he drifts off again."

Tom reached out and took my hand. "Mandy, you know we have counseling for victims. I could arrange..."

"Now I'll give you an example of our crazy family dynamics. Mom wants to have Bub see someone, but Uncle Ti says we don't need any shrinks messing in our private business. Then Uncle 'Tienne agrees. 'Tienne says he had to go to a psychiatrist after he returned from Vietnam, and the guy was a jerk. All in all, Mom is losing a lot of sleep right now. No, Tom. We're not a perfect family."

"But you care a lot about each other. My brother has two boys, and I only see 'em a couple of times a year. I really don't know them at all."

"Tell me about your family, Tom. Do they still live up there on the cotton farm in Shangaloo?"

"No, we have almost no one left. My parents sold the farm when I was in college and moved into a retirement complex in town. Too bad. Now they say there's oil and gas under the whole damn place. But Mom and Dad don't dwell on what might have been. They seem happy enough to do little more than play bridge and take a weekly minivan trip to the mall. I have only the one brother, and he moved to Memphis. So you see, I don't have much to go home to. I go up maybe once a month, and frankly, it's a chore."

Our number came up on the board, and Tom went after our sandwiches. We were quiet for awhile, sinking our teeth into the crusty bread, fat oysters coated with the fabulous Pastime batter and just a squirt of spicy mayonnaise.

"You know, Tom, each one of the family brings his own back-story to the issue of the death penalty. Their experiences are probably a better predictor of their ultimate position than the statements they'll make right now."

"Very perceptive, my dear. There's good evidence to that effect, and that's exactly the reason I want to get to know your family. I'd like to learn those back stories. What about you, Mandy? Are you in favor of the death penalty?"

It took me a moment to answer.

"I never thought so before, Tom. But now, when the victim is my own family? I have a different perspective. I know the arguments backwards and forwards, but it all looks different when it's your loved one who was murdered. No one really knows how they'd feel in a vacuum. If there were some alternative..."

"I know. I get angry when I think about a murderer continuing to live when someone's loved one is gone."

"What about you, Tom? Are you for it?"

"I can't say one way or the other. I took an oath to follow the law, and the law provides for the death penalty for the worst of the worst. That's OK with me. We've got some bad characters out there. But I'm fast coming to the point where I think the burden on the State to get from here to there is overwhelming. As for Remuald Richard, I'm convinced he's a very bad guy. But, oh the agony of taking him to the end of the road! It's my job, but it's a tough one." Tom paused. "Do you know the defense lawyer, Sarah Bernard?"

My mouth full, I shook my head no.

"She's damn good, and drop dead gorgeous as well. Juries love her."

I swallowed, wiped mayonnaise off my fingers, and took a sip of beer before I answered.

"Watch out there, Tom. I hear she just got out of a marriage. You wouldn't want to be involved with someone who's ten years older than you are, would you?"

Tom covered my tease. "No, but maybe," Tom counted on his

fingers, "seven years younger would be nice." His blue eyes twinkled, and he gave me that great smile. "Seriously, it's important to have a good lawyer as an opponent for a first degree prosecution. When I don't, I have to check everything the defense does in order to prevent reversible error. Have you followed *Rompilla*? I think the US Supremes are gonna reverse another death penalty and send the case back down to the trial court, ten years post-trial, on the grounds of incompetent counsel. Now there's a real nightmare, attempting to retry a case after that period of time. Half the evidence comes in as a dry record, testimony of long-gone witnesses read to the jury by some law clerk."

"I'm serious too. From what I see, our family will have two very good lawyers at work. I'm feeling damn lucky to be able to watch it all up close."

Tom sat up a little straighter. He must have given some consideration to his next question as he emphasized each word. "That lets me introduce another thought. Would you be interested in doing more than watch? I've been thinking about asking you if you would like me to approach Mr. Strait about taking you on."

"Taking me on? As what? I'm not yet a lawyer."

"As an intern/researcher for this prosecution."

Wow. I couldn't give Tom a quick answer. I needed time to think. The prospect of working on a real case after three years of nothing but books, and the thrill of a major trial, made my heart thump. But a lot of baggage came with the offer. A case involving my own family? And what about working with Tom? I couldn't ignore how I was feeling about this guy. Heart and mind at work at the same time? Usually a really bad idea, especially when some members of the family were sure to find fault with the way the prosecutor handled the trial. I'd be in the middle. But maybe another look at a prosecution in action would help me decide if I wanted a career in criminal law. I'd been canceling those appointments at the placement office and didn't really know why. Perhaps the right option hadn't yet been put on the table.

Tom watched me struggle.

"That's OK, Mandy. Think about it. In the meanwhile, I do have a couple of evidence questions I need help on. Maybe you could do some research for me. With the law library right here you could—"

I jumped at the chance to keep the offer open. "Yes. I'd be very happy to do some research for you, Tom. At least until after the first of the year when I have to cram for the Bar."

More than happy, to tell the truth. I wanted these meetings to continue.

"The obvious first issue I need to have researched concerns *other crimes evidence*—how we tell the story of the investigation into your grandfather's murder without mentioning the attack on Lydia Falgout. Could you research and write a memo on that subject?"

"You'll have to give me more of the facts."

"Of course. I'll let you see the reports of the detectives and their conclusions. Basically, the case against Richard is circumstantial, but persuasive."

On one level, Tom recounted what the detectives had gathered so far. I asked questions. Beneath the surface, the emotional exchange between us led to a different kind of connection.

I looked at the shock of blond hair falling on the left side of Tom's forehead, the cleft in his chin. I let my left hand inch forward on the top of the table. Tom's right hand moved forward toward mine. I thought about the tabletop game we played as kids, the Ouija Board. What were the spirits telling me now?

Our fingertips touched.

"Maybe you could even be my second chair at the trial, Mandy."

I had kept enough sense to recognize that as a bad idea. I'd research, and maybe I'd intern in the office for a while, but I would not sit at the prosecution table.

"Oh, my no, Tom. You've mentioned Richie Castille. He's the one. He has the experience of a zillion drug trials under his belt."

We were holding hands across the table now.

"You're right, Mandy. Richie wants a break from drug duty. A capital case might even get him to lose the Paul Bunyan-sized chip he's had on his shoulder ever since Mr. Strait gave me the job as first assistant. Richie thought he'd done enough time-in-grade to deserve the promotion."

Tom picked up my hand and brought it to his lips. His eyes locked into mine.

"Mandy, would you like to think some more about all these problems over at your place?"

"Yes."

Tom put my hand down on the table, stood up and walked to the counter to pay the bill. We went back to my apartment and made love. He was tender and skilled. All my reserve vanished. I responded to Tom with abandon. When Tom joined me in a final moment I was not on this earth.

Tom didn't go back to New Iberia until the following morning.

PART II

NEW JOB

Tom had made the deal with Mr. Strait for me to clerk in the DA's office until the Bar Exam results came in. Summoned to report for initial instructions, I rang the door buzzer at eight sharp. The lock clicked. I pushed. The door didn't budge. Shit. Maybe I should pull. Yup. Not a smooth beginning.

A giant copy machine and four unoccupied work stations cluttered with papers lined the perimeter of the reception area. In the center of the room, a middle-aged woman with coal black hair and crimson lips sat straight as a schoolmarm at a U-shaped station.

"Mandy Aguillard?" she asked.

"Yes, ma'am."

"Mr. Strait is expecting you." She pointed to her left. "The door's open."

Mr. Strait raised his chin and, with a twitch of his head, indicated the chair I should take. A number of files lay open on his desk; Post-it Notes decorated the remaining surface. He and his receptionist had probably been at work for some time.

"Good morning, Miss Aguillard—Mandy, now that you're one of us." Just a suggestion of a smile. Not exactly a rousing welcome.

With his left hand on a stack of papers speckled with numbers, his right hand holding a pen poised mid-air over a yellow legal pad, Mr. Strait launched directly into an overview of the work in the prosecutor's office. No social preliminaries.

"I have two requirements of every person who works in the offices of the District Attorney. The first is professionalism. Whether my attorneys are supervising pretrial diversion, screening misdemeanors and felonies, trying a capital case, advising public bodies, whatever they do, they are expected to apply high ethical and professional standards to their work. The staff—investigators, secretaries, bookkeepers, clerks—are expected to exercise the highest principles appropriate to *their* professions. And everyone is expected to respect the independence of all the other attorneys and staff as they do their jobs. Do you understand?"

His words tapped out like fingers on a keyboard, and with no more expression.

"Yes, sir."

"In the three offices of the district you will find dozens of men and women hard at work making decisions that impact people's lives. Some decisions are very difficult, such as whom to prosecute, what charge to bring, what is competent evidence. There are often competing considerations at work. My assistants and staff may seek guidance from me or from my first assistant at any time, of course, but usually I decline to express an opinion. Use your best judgment, I say, and be sure at the end of the day you can look at yourself in the mirror and be proud of your work. Do you understand?"

Translation: Everyone around here is on his own. Don't bother to annoy me with questions because I probably won't answer them.

"Yes, sir."

"Second, in addition to professionalism, I require confidentiality, and this requirement also applies up and down the line: attorneys, a clerk such as yourself, administrative assistants, investigators, secretaries, even the clean-up folks who empty the waste baskets after dark. Everyone.

"You will no doubt see and hear matters that are important, petty, funny, sad, even tragic. What you see and hear in these offices stays here. No exceptions. You will do your job—in your case, assignments from Tom to assist him in preparing the cases against Remuald Richard—to the best of your ability. You will do no one else's job. If another person asks you to do something, check with Tom. Understand?"

"Yes, sir."

"That's it. Professionalism and confidentiality are my only non-negotiables. Breaches of these two requirements are capital offenses."

No smile. He might really mean it.

"Yes, sir." I said again—and felt like an idiot making the same response four times.

Done with business, and without taking his left hand off the pile of papers, he lowered his right hand to the yellow pad and leaned his chair back three inches—no more. His face relaxed a tad, and perhaps, with imagination, I could detect a trace of warmth in his tone of voice.

"I have read your memo on *other crimes evidence*, Mandy. You are quite perceptive about the tightrope Tom must walk to persuade the jury of the integrity of the investigation into the death of your grandfather without them hearing a single word connecting his death to the assault on Mrs. Falgout. Tricky problem. They must convict, if they do so, only on evidence Richard committed the crime at issue and not for any other reason. Unfortunately, two key pieces of evidence we need for Boudreaux were picked up in the Falgout investigation: a wallet found in Richard's car and incriminating statements made to the deputies. Quite naturally the jurors will ask themselves—because of course they cannot ask the attorneys—why the detectives were collecting evidence about Remuald Richard in Birmingham, Alabama."

"Yes, sir." I said it again!

Mr. Strait appeared to have command of our case. Although he had a reputation for detail, he couldn't know every file in the office. Probably only the capital cases—and maybe the political ones as well.

Mr. Strait continued. "Indeed, Tom runs the risk of mistrial or ultimate reversal if he so much as hints that Richard did something criminal other than the events for which he is on trial. Your research was thorough and your report persuasive, exploring some wise procedures Tom might employ. He will benefit from your analysis of the problem and your creativity in considering solutions. Good work."

"Thank you, sir."

And thank you, Tom, for passing on my memo. I know I flushed at Mr. Strait's compliment. I had thrown myself into the project and probably spent over a hundred hours over the Christmas break putting it together.

Mr. Strait continued. "We are now at the point in the Richard case when the prosecution must evaluate what the detectives have uncovered. All circumstantial. No scientific evidence and we have no eyewitnesses. The analytical abilities I see in your memo will be beneficial."

Mr. Strait's speech had the precision of legal document. Gone was the smooth and amiable politician who charmed the crowd at our family meeting. I wanted to thank him for offering me the position, but before I could get the words out of my mouth, a red phone on the back table buzzed. Mr. Strait turned his chair to the right to reach the instrument, showing me the left side of his head. Without a word, he lifted his left hand in a dismissing wave. I stood up and backed out of the room as if I were leaving a royal presence—and stumbled trying to straighten out my feet.

Back in the reception area, the same secretary, who introduced herself as Bonnie, jumped up to steady my step. A smile conveyed her amusement and also her empathy.

"Mr. Strait can be a bit intimidating, my dear. He has a lot on his mind this morning. He's giving a statement to *The Daily Iberian* in about an hour. After that, he'll be filmed for the evening news on Channel Three. Big scandal in the Housing Authority. Missing funds. You'll read all about it in the afternoon paper. The job of the District Attorney involves a lot more than prosecution, you know."

And I should be damn grateful to get one little sliver of her boss' time, she implied. I took a deep breath. I'd be OK in a minute. Her kindness would help me get there. A whimsical pink butterfly decorated her oversized glasses. Nice.

Bonnie invited me to follow her through a door at the rear of the reception area, into the library, and then to a small room off to the left. A battered wooden desk, a plastic covered chair—original color no longer discernible—and a three-shelf bookcase filled up the room no larger than a broom closet. Only two books sat in the bookcase—last year's paperback *Louisiana Criminal Code* and a two-year-old *Code of Evidence*. No window, and if I wanted to close the door, I'd have to climb on the desk to accommodate the door's path.

"Not grand, my dear, but it's all yours!"

Not really. From my cubbyhole I'd be able to overhear everything taking place in the combination library and conference room next door, and anyone there would know what I was doing as well. Obviously, a clerk didn't merit private quarters. I wouldn't need to worry about the place being bugged. Ears would do the job of surveillance just fine. No wonder confidentiality was number two on Mr. Strait's short list of requirements to work in this place.

I sank into the chair and grasped the arms to still the tremble in my hands.

Bonnie returned five minutes later, pushing a cart of goodies that included a late model Dell computer, a flat screen monitor, and a snake's nest of cables. With the expert movements of a veteran of a geek squad, she inserted a few plugs, pressed a few buttons, and the distinctive Microsoft melody played. I was in business. In addition to Microsoft Office for word processing and calculations, I'd been given two special programs: *Crimes*, a database of the district's criminal records; *Westlaw* for nationwide legal research. Things were looking up. I could feel my shoulders relax as I logged onto familiar sites.

What did Mr. Strait mean when he said we were to evaluate the evidence? Was he saying the evidence might be insufficient for a conviction? I didn't want to think about that.

I sensed a presence and glanced up to see Tom occupying the doorway. All of it. He's very tall. The back of my neck tingled with excitement.

"You look good there." Tom leaned against the door frame and smiled. No kisses in the office must be another rule. "Sorry about your accommodations. The DA's office has spread like kudzu throughout this building, but we still don't have enough space for all our functions."

I think I told him everything was fine.

"So, did you get the two-part lecture on professionalism and confidentiality? 'At the end of the day, Ms. Aguillard, be sure you can look in the mirror and be proud of what you see.'" Tom mimicked his boss's voice, precise diction, and cadence. So, Tom could lose the north Louisiana twang if he wanted to.

"He called me Mandy."

"Well, that's a good sign."

"So, Mr. Strait's introductory remarks are always the same?"

"Yup. You haven't met everyone around here yet but you will. ADA Richie Castille can repeat the entire speech word for word, complete with the stern face, bobbing head, and no pause to take a breath. In addition to some less admirable proclivities, Richie's a bit of a stand-up comic. He entertains us at every Christmas party. Maybe next time he'll turn his monologue into a skit so you can play the part of a terrified new hire."

"Please, no! Gimme a break."

"One of his best personifications is of the courthouse ghost. Woo-ooo!"

"Courthouse ghost? This place is haunted?"

"So-say. When this courthouse was built—1940, I believe—the next big event after the ribbon cutting was the hanging of Honoré Migues, the first white man in the parish anyone knew to get the noose. Richie loves the story. Old timers tell us they strung him up over a trap door, and then let it drop to accomplish the deed. Richie can do a pretty fair twitchy dance of death. Another so-say, the ghost of Honoré is still around. If you work too late, you'll hear him walk."

"Sounds like a convenient urban legend to use to keep from

having to work late."

"Right you are, and Richie's been known to use the excuse, but if I did nothing but drug cases, I'd be looking for closing time. I guess you met Bonnie, Strait's top sergeant. She's devoted to her boss, maybe even more than that, not that Mr. Strait would even notice her feelings. She smoothes a lot of rumpled feathers."

"I gather she handles the computers. Invaluable. Mr. Strait gave me a nice compliment on the memo I wrote for you on *other crimes evidence*, and I thank you for that. He's pretty scary."

We moved into the library. Tom set a red accordion file labeled *State v. Remuald Richard* on the conference table and explained he was overdue turning our case material over to the defense. He'd given Sarah the affidavits for the arrest warrants, some initial statements from a witness who identified Richard at one of the bunkhouses at the docks, the tape of the tipster who sent the detectives to the Birmingham hospital, and a couple of crime lab reports, but we'd gotten in a lot more since then.

"We'll need to copy the rest to be ready for Sarah's visit tomorrow."

I jumped up and reached for the file, assuming his words were an instruction to me to start on the copying task. Tom laughed and touched my arm.

"Easy there. For now you can just familiarize yourself with the material."

I had a lot to learn about being Tom's assistant. Like not to shiver at his touch.

Tom continued. "The trooper who found Mrs. Falgout is coming in at one this afternoon, and after that the detectives will bring us their investigative file. We're responsible for their material as well as ours. We need to go over everything they have and put a package together for Sarah. You can help me with that."

I'd show Tom I could look at all this like a lawyer.

"We only need to turn over the evidence that's exculpatory, right?"

"Technically. But exculpatory is not only what now looks as if it might diminish the defendant's fault. We have to predict what some appeal court down the line might one day consider could have led to a possible defense. It's impossible to make the call. We just give the defense everything we have, including the investigators' files."

Tom took a big stretchable fastener off the red file and patted the chair for me to sit down. I had some questions.

"May I ask you about the defense? Sarah Bernard is putting out to the newspaper that her client is really not guilty. She told the paper he was around for what happened to Mrs. Falgout but didn't beat her up, and he was nowhere around for PawPaw. What about that?"

"Bullshit. Defense lawyers always sing the same tune at the beginning. 'I will prove at trial my client is not guilty of the offense with which he has been charged.' Then a few months later they stand next to the guy while he owns up to everything and pleads guilty. Sarah's just waiting to see what we'll offer. Standard operating procedure. Like every defense lawyer, Sarah's all about the deal."

There he goes mentioning deal again. Is Tom considering taking the death penalty off the table? I don't think I showed my concern, or perhaps Tom just didn't notice. He kept talking.

"I have to go to St. Martin Parish this morning to cover a couple of tricky motions. My regular duties don't stop, you know. I'll be back this afternoon. How about you study up on our file between now and then. That'll give you some background."

He touched my hand and left, answering one question in my mind. I wouldn't get an invitation for lunch. Fine. I wanted him to leave. I'd be able to turn my attention to what I'd spent three years learning to do and let my heart rate slow to normal.

* * *

No time to go anywhere to find something to eat, but I needed something. I had no idea how long workdays were in the office. I picked up one of those triangular, cellophane-wrapped sandwiches from Jacques, the blind man who ran the snack stand in the basement. When I came back upstairs and entered the reception area, a handsome, just-past-middle-aged man dressed in the distinctive bright blue uniform of the State troopers sat on the visitors' bench. He held his Smokey the Bear hat in his left hand and displayed a colorful collection of badges and pins on his upper chest. State Trooper Ron David. I stood on one foot and then the other. Was it my place to invite him back to the library? Just before my awkwardness caused me to say something idiotic, Tom appeared and took charge. We settled down at the table in the library.

"You've met Mandy Aguillard?" Tom asked.

The trooper dipped his head. "Howdy, ma'am."

Yup, that's really what he said. I guess talking western went with the hat.

Tom got the trooper's OK to tape the conversation. I knew how to operate a tape recorder so I snapped in a cassette. Tom reached across and punched the start button.

"So tell us, Ron. From the beginning."

"Sure thing. I finished my shift doing traffic on Highway 90 and called in my last report of the day. I shoved a stick of gum in my mouth to stave off the craving for those damn cigarettes I gave up for the umpteenth time, and headed home. I turned off at the Coteau exit. The radio was cracklin' on my dashboard, dispatch reporting a house fire close by. I took a little detour to see if the firemen needed a hand."

"I suppose a good trooper is never off duty."

"Right you are. Three fire engines had pulled up into the yard of a house on Captain Cade Road—two old fire-engine-red rigs and a shiny new yellow pumper."

"The *infamous* yellow pumper, I suppose." Tom turned to me. "You'll enjoy this story. When the Coteau Volunteer Fire Department got a federal grant and bought a new rig, they threw a celebration. All the firemen in the parish congregated at the station for red beans and rice, with plenty of beer for those not on duty. Maybe you heard about that?"

My Dad actually cooked the red beans, but I didn't come clean. Best to let someone recount a story he's itching to tell, and I was pleased Tom had included me in this exchange.

I shook my head. "No. Tell me."

"Well, caution lost out to the effects of the brew. The firemen mounted the pumper for a celebratory spin 'round the town in the new rig. Following the victory lap, the captain drove the pumper back to the firehouse, its new home. That's an accurate statement. The captain drove the pumper *to* the firehouse, but not inside. When the lift on top hit the lintel over the door, the captain pulled up short. He backed the pumper into a side yard, and went hat in hand to the fourth floor of the courthouse to appeal to the parish government for money to raise the station house roof. The council had to come through. They couldn't have that expensive piece of equipment left out in the elements."

The trooper slapped his hand on his thigh in appreciation of Tom's story. Actually, I wouldn't have been surprised to learn he'd also heard it before. The trooper resumed his report.

"A thick canvas hose stretched from the pumper, across a dry brown field, to a frame house set back a couple hundred feet from the road. Correction. I couldn't really see a house. All I saw was a great cloud of smoke and flashes of flame, but I soon learned a building was burning down in there. If y'all recall, last summer we had a drought. No rain for over a month. It's hard to imagine, but we were looking forward to the hurricane to bring us some rain."

Tom nodded. I remembered also. My uncles were worried about the cane crop.

"Anyway, every twenty-five feet or so, a fireman in high boots and bunker gear held the hose off the ground. Water arced into the air and dropped into smoke so thick you couldn't see the nozzle. When the wind swirled the smoke, the fireman took a step away from the blaze and bent double in a choking cough. I shouted out to ask if I could give 'em any help."

Up to this point the trooper had told the story smoothly, without a prompt. Now he pulled a little note pad out of his shirt packet and flipped a few pages.

"'We've got it under control,' the fireman shouted back. I asked if there was anyone in the house. 'Sure hope not,' he answered. 'No one could survive in this inferno'".

A frequent first responder, the trooper must have been called upon often to give testimony in court. In preparation, he had made a practice of taking down direct quotes.

"I turned to walk to my unit, thinking that as usual 'under control' meant the firemen had saved the ground the house was built on." Trooper David smiled, appreciating his own joke. He would not only be a smooth witness, he'd charm the jury— especially in his Louisiana State Trooper blues. Tom's relaxed expression told me he agreed.

"Then I saw something odd. When I was almost back to the road, next to what was left of an old fence marking off the boundary between the front field and the neighboring farm, I saw a white stick waving out of the top of a pile of brush. The stick jerked, fell back down, poked up again, and dropped once more. Something's wrong. I walked toward the pile. Damn! The stick looked like a human arm. Arm? I know I cried out loud. 'Ho-lee shit!'

"I was running now. The white stick rose, fell down, and lay still. I dropped to my knees. As fast as I could, I picked off sticks and leaves with my bare hands, trying to clear away debris. I heard a whimper no louder than a hungry kitten."

Trooper David's bright eyes flashed.

"The leaves were damp and sticky. Blood. I picked at the trash with my fingers and a face appeared." The trooper instinctively rubbed his fingertips on his pant leg.

I had already read the trooper's initial statement, but the story straight from his mouth made my throat tighten. My face must have betrayed me. Tom touched my hand.

The trooper continued. "I yelled to the guys to call 911. Two firemen came running, tore off their big gloves, and dropped to their knees. We worked fast, but carefully, and uncovered the upper torso of a woman. The face, really just a lump, moaned again. Through blood and dirt, one terrified eye stared up at us. The other eye dangled out of its socket."

I swallowed hard.

"I leaned close to where the woman's lips should have been. I couldn't make out most of her mumbles, but I did hear a few words." The trooper looked at his notebook and read, "'Don't let him get me again. Please! Oh God! Please don't let Remmy get to me again.'"

Tom and I were totally into the scene. Tom recovered first.

"Good stuff, Ron. Damn shame I can't start this trial with you on the stand. The jury would give me a unanimous verdict of guilty in no time."

I forgot law clerks should be seen and not heard. "No way you can introduce that evidence in the trial for the death of my grandfather, Tom. What happened to Mrs. Falgout is a clear example of evidence of *another crime*."

Tom could have put me down for stating the obvious, but he didn't. "Right. Not in the guilt/innocence part of our trial, Mandy, but I can go full speed ahead in the penalty phase. If that evidence doesn't show Richard's *character and propensities*, admissible evidence for penalty, I don't know what does."

Tom was right-on. The trooper clearly heard Mrs. Falgout nail Remmy as a monster. If we got a verdict of guilty in the guilt/innocence phase, hearing from the lady with one eye would lock up the capital penalty.

Trooper David said the EMTs arrived and took over the scene. Deputies and detectives came later.

Tom had a question for the trooper. "I guess you know we found the defendant in a Birmingham hospital with a nasty tear on his arm. He said something about cutting himself on a fence. Did you examine the fence near where you found Mrs. Falgout?"

"I didn't *examine* the fence, but I do remember it. Barbed wire, partly falling over, rusty."

No chance for DNA. The hurricane rains would have washed all that away.

Tom turned off the tape recorder. Trooper David held out his little notebook, which Tom waved in my direction and placed in the file. "Something else for your review."

I must have been smiling like a ninny. I was so damn excited to be there.

I wondered what Tom thought about having me at his side.

DETECTIVE AYMOND REPORTS

Detective Buddy Aymond showed up an hour late and alone. Thick-set, probably pushing sixty, his face pillows of rosy flesh, ears as bumpy as an old boxer's. I always thought a detective wore a suit and carried a briefcase but maybe only in big cities and on TV. Detective Aymond wore khakis and carried a red accordion file like ours. He paused at the door. When he looked in my direction a deep crease cut between his brows.

"You're one of the Boudreaux family."

"Yes. I'm Mimi Aguillard's daughter, Mandy."

"And you're here for this meeting?"

"As of today, I work here. I'm very happy to meet you." I'd be gracious even if he wasn't.

All this amused Tom. "It's OK. She's had the standard instruction from Mr. Strait."

The set of his mouth told me Detective Aymond still had reservations. "Have any coffee around here?" he asked, adjusting the holster on his hip.

A frown flicked across Tom's face. "Too late in the day, Buddy. Solid acid by now. We need to get going. Is your podnuh Deuce behind you?"

"No. The boss called him to another duty. You'll just have to make do with me."

Tom reached for the phone. "And what piss-ant excuse did the sheriff give for sending Deuce away? This case is top priority. I'm callin' him."

"Ease off, Tom. I can cover. The narcs in Lafayette needed reinforcements for a big operation. The boss sent everyone in our unit—and Deuce—over there. Remember Deuce used to be a narc before he came to me."

Tom pinched his lips together. "Big operation? How many times have I heard 'em say they're about to nab the biggest drug dealer in Iberia Parish—only to find out later they're puttin' on another one of those chicken-shit reverse stings?"

Tom picked up the language of the detectives when in their company—fortunately not the full repertoire of expletives.

"Easy, Tom. The Feds are all over this one. Something about cocaine coming in from Mexico under pallets of lettuce. Not money, the leafy kind. Operation Rough Romaine, they're callin' it. Deuce is a key player 'cause he recruited the inside snitch."

Tom's face relaxed; he accepted the situation.

"Are you happy with Deuce as a partner, Buddy? The word is you're doing a fine job bringing along the rookie detective."

Buddy put up his thumb in a sign of approval. "He's damn good. I don't mind telling you I was pissed when the boss assigned him to me. Four years until my retirement, I thought the sheriff was pushing me out the door and piling on by making me train my replacement. A nig—;" Detective Aymond cut an eye in my direction. "A black man to boot. But a couple weeks with Deuce as my partner and I was OK with him. He's got my back."

Tom had told me the story. The pair answered a call to assist patrol with a domestic disturbance in a four-block grove of house trailers on Shotgun Alley. A crowd gathered and the scene turned ugly. Deuce stepped in front of his older, white partner, figured out who was instigating the trouble, and whipped the punk's shootin' arm behind his back. Then Deuce talked the all-black crowd quiet. The code of the cops: nothing ranks higher than fast action and loyalty at a time of trouble.

"You know he's got the genes for this work. His father,

Thomas Washington Sr., was the first black State cop in Troop I. He was good. Died way too young," Tom said.

Tom indicated where the detective should sit and got permission to run a tape. Detective Aymond reached into his file and extracted a folder labeled FALGOUT in black ink and BOUDREAUX in blue. He unclipped papers attached to the inside front cover and handed them to Tom, who set them on my side of the table. Statements. The detective unclipped another stack of papers from inside the back cover. More statements. I guessed all these would be part of my copying task. He pulled out the one remaining item—a notebook. Tom signaled me to turn on the tape recorder. Ah-ha. A promotion.

"So Buddy, let's start with your call to go to the fire at the Falgout's house on Captain Cade Road. That's the beginning of the investigation into the Pierre Boudreaux murder, right?"

The detective nodded. "Right. Boudreaux starts with Falgout. As you see, we've got them in the same file."

"So what time did you and Deuce get there?"

Buddy thumbed through the notebook to find the page he wanted. "September 1, 2006, 1600 hrs. We got there at 4:00 p.m."

"Wait. Are you reading directly from that notebook?" Tom asked.

"Yup. Deuce kept a detailed record, even drew us some pictures."

Tom turned to me. "A job for you, Mandy. We'll have to go over every word and every drawing in that notebook. Any discrepancy between the contemporaneous notes, the sworn statements, and testimony on the stand at trial is an opportunity for Sarah to go to town on cross. I can hear her now. 'You mean you wrote down one thing at the time and now you say something else? Were you lying then or are you lying now? Which is it, detective?'"

Buddy knew a few more verses to the song.

"Sarah's a piece of work, that one. When she's got no legitimate defense, she puts the cops on trial. 'You mean to tell me you talked to twenty-five people before you found one who knew anything about these events?' You bet we did! That's how fuckin' hard we work to get information. But Tom," the detective raised his eyebrows, "the notebook a problem? Any time you want me to lose it, or maybe a page or two, just give me the word."

"We'll see about that down the road. Mandy'll look for any inconsistencies."

Whoa! Red flag. Did Tom just sign me on to be party to compromising evidence? He picked up the alarm on my face.

"Easy, Mandy. If we find discrepancies, we work on an explanation to have ready for the trial. I've seen Deuce's work before. His meticulous detail will make our case better."

Detective Aymond narrowed his eyes.

"You know, Tom, when we prep Richie we don't turn over everything some fuckin' defense lawyer might use to mow us down."

"Drug cases are a whole different ball game, Buddy. No matter how serious the charge might be, Richie's not lookin' at the endless post-conviction process we have for capital convictions. He can count on no more than three years of post-trial scrutiny."

I already knew capital cases were damn near eternal. In Baton Rouge I'd done research on convictions over fifteen years old. Who could predict what an appeal court judge—probably just trying to dodge signing an execution order by sending the case back down for another hearing—might think should have been done differently? The U.S Supremes were constantly moving the bar.

Detective Aymond smiled. "At least for this trial, we get Sarah Bernard doing the grilling. Some eye candy to go with the abuse she dishes out. Flashy broad, that one."

I felt better about Tom, but I'd keep an eye on Detective Aymond, especially when those eyes narrowed into a leer. His comments about Sarah Bernard made me feel like a dull little mouse.

Tom prodded. "You say you arrived at the Falgout house at 4 p.m. Then what?"

"Yeah. That afternoon I was nodding over computer printouts stacked up on my desk in the basement of the courthouse when the sheriff's voice came over the intercom. The voice of the man himself, not Elnora from the switchboard, so I knew there was something big going on. I was damn glad to put aside that white-collar crap I'd been working on. I hate paper cases. At the end, there's always some deal to get restitution, and the crook doesn't spend a day in jail. Now violent crime? That's good duty. Find the guy who did it, and your boss and mine marshal all forces to put him behind bars for *very* long time."

Buddy kept turning one page back to tell what had taken place previously. Tom's scowl told me the pattern got on his last nerve. Did Buddy do that on purpose? His smile said yes.

"Meanwhile, back on the ranch. Let's get to the Falgouts."

"Right. The sheriff ordered me to go to the scene of the fire on Captain Cade Road, ASAP. Said they'd taken a vic to Lafayette General Hospital. She wasn't burned in the fire, but beaten up within an inch of her life. Fucked over pretty good, really. Looked like aggravated battery at a minimum, the sheriff said. Maybe attempted murder or even first degree murder if the lady didn't make it." Buddy slapped his pudgy hand on the tabletop. "And then this! 'Buddy, you'll need to take statements from the trooper, the victim, any bystanders.' Can you imagine he said that? As if I didn't know what to do after thirty-five years on the force. I've been at this job with two sheriff's before that guy, since he was in short pants."

"And then?" Tom prodded again.

"OK. OK. By the time Deuce and I got out there most of the rubberneckers had gone. The trooper, a couple firemen and the patrol deputies hung around. We took a statement from the trooper—I think you have that one—and a couple from firemen. One of the firemen thought the victim had called her assailant Hemmy not Remmy, but both agreed about what she said. 'Don't let them do it to me again.'"

I wondered if Tom caught what I caught. Don't let *them* do it to me again. The trooper had told us Mrs. Falgout said *him*, singular. Sarah was putting out to the press that Richard was present but someone else did the deed. Was a fireman going to make her version credible? I reached for a legal pad and wrote down the detective's words. I'd give Tom my thoughts later.

Buddy continued his narrative. "One of the firemen—" He thumbed through a couple of pages of Deuce's notebook to find the place he wanted. "One of the firemen put it this way. 'The left side of her face kinda wasn't there, and the right side looked like a purple sponge smeared with egg yolk. Her left eyeball, bloody white jelly, dangled an inch out of the socket. Bigger than a marble, smaller than a ping pong ball. She was quivering all over.' The fireman closed his eyes and shuddered. 'I've been a fireman for thirty years so I've seen a burned body or two. It's worse when they're *living* mush,' he said. 'They shake like Jell-O.'"

"Deuce took down the fireman's actual words?" Tom asked.

"You bet. He can use them on the stand, right?"

"We'll find a way. Keep going," Tom instructed. I checked the tape recorder.

Buddy said the trooper thought the lady was a goner, but the EMTs who put her in the ambulance found a pulse. Barely. Her house was no more than a pile of smoldering ash.

Buddy flipped a few more pages of the notebook. "The patrol deputies had talked to bystanders to pick up background. The house belonged to a couple named Falgout, Jim and Lydia. They had no kids but kept two dogs in a pen at the back of the house. 'Burnt to a crisp, detective,' one deputy said to me. 'Don't go out there unless you got an iron gut.' I took a look at his snake-belly-grey face and knew he didn't. Sure enough. At the sight of the crisp animals he'd torn off his mask and made a quick trip behind the bushes to puke."

I could never do the job these guys do. I wanted to get the necessary horrible stuff written in words on a clean piece of paper.

Buddy turned to a drawing in Deuce's notebook. Deuce had estimated the area as a four-acre tract, five arpents as they say in the country. He sketched in the remains of the house about two thirds back from Captain Cade Road and drew in the side driveway and the wire fence on the left boundary next to the ditch where the trooper found Mrs. Falgout. Two narrow lines marked ruts leading from the shell driveway to the ditch. He gave the distance between the house and the ditch as thirty yards, plus or minus.

"Any other witnesses have anything for you?" Tom asked. "I'm particularly interested in what was said about this guy Remmy."

"Yeah. A grey-haired dude, pressed checked shirt and dress pants, walked toward us from the rear pasture. He identified himself as Frank Delasbour, the one who called in the fire. He'd been on hand when the trooper found the woman, but had to leave to get control of himself. Said it was fuckin' awful. I asked if he knew where Jim Falgout might be. Probably offshore, Delasbour said. Falgout worked seven and seven for Diamond Services and had been at the house last week. But now everyone was coming in from the Gulf because of the storm."

Buddy picked up one of the statements he'd taken out of his folder.

"Here it is. Delasbour said the last time he actually talked with Remmy was months before. Remmy had come by to pick up the mail Lydia had left for him in a box on the front porch. Delasbour remembered telling his wife Remmy wasn't looking too good. Thought maybe he'd been sick."

"Did he have a last name for Remmy?" Tom asked.

"Nope, that was our problem. Said he'd never heard it, and of course the name was exactly what we needed to get going on the investigation."

"How about a description?"

"Delasbour said 'ordinary.' When I pressed for age, height, hair color, weight, any distinguishing marks, Delasbour came up with this: late thirties, maybe five foot nine, hundred and fifty to a hundred and sixty pounds, thin hair."

The folds of Buddy's bulldog face shifted to accommodate a smile. "I remember a side play here. My partner interrupted to ask if Remmy was a white man. Yes. Delasbour didn't say 'of course', but implied so, and then flushed beet red. We do assume white is the norm."

Buddy wasn't the bigot I first thought. Maybe time with his new partner had brought him along, but he still had the language he grew up with.

Detective Aymond said they left the patrol deputies on duty at the site, instructing them to get the names of anyone who came by, and ask every one if any version of the name Remmy rang a bell. No one was to get anywhere near what used to be the house or the pile of trash where they'd found Mrs. Falgout. Buddy said he called in to the station.

"You know what? They didn't give a fuck. They were all into prep for Hurricane Hannah. So we headed out to Lafayette to find Mrs. Falgout on our own. We needed a last name for the perp and knew Mrs. Falgout would have it."

Tom complimented Buddy, but spun his fingers again in a signal to keep the story moving along.

"The nurse at the window of the emergency room at Lafayette General set up a stone wall. There was absolutely no possibility we could see the patient, she said. A half dozen doctors were back there evaluating her injuries. She invited us to leave our names and someone would call when Mrs. Falgout could have visitors. I got the impression that would never happen. The nurse didn't care one bit about locating the guy who turned her patient to mush."

I checked the tape and saw the end coming up soon. I signaled Tom to hold up a minute. He gave me a nod, waited until I was done, and spun his fingers again for the detective to continue.

I was loving this.

Deuce had called the Lafayette sheriff's office to ask for a courtesy intervention with the hospital bureaucracy. They tried, but the hospital administrator gave the locals the same treatment. The patient was critical. Her condition overrode all other considerations. Mrs. Falgout could not be questioned.

Buddy said he went to the soft drink machine, got them each a coke, and sat down to think. He came up with a plan. He went to the window and told the nurse that if he had use of a phone, he could help locate the patient's husband. That got her attention. Finding next of kin probably headed up her to-do list. Open sesame. Buddy found a number for Diamond Services in Lafayette. They said offshore operations came out of the Morgan

City dock. A voice at that location said they'd just given the order to secure and shut down the rigs in the eastern Gulf and had dispatched choppers to evacuate all personnel from the platforms. Everyone would be on shore by noon the following day. No, they couldn't possibly single out one person for special transport. Buddy told them the man's wife was critical; noon tomorrow might be too late. They said they'd try to get Falgout a spot on board the next chopper.

"On to plan B," Buddy continued. "The tag on the nurse's uniform read Mrs. Dartez. I turned on the charm."

Now that was hard for me to imagine.

"'Mrs. Dartez. Ma'am,' I said. Could you get the doctor's permission for us to ask one question, just one?' Negative. 'Could a doctor ask the question for us? It's really urgent, ma'am. We need the name of the guy who did this and she knows it.' The nurse went through a curtained area and came right back out. 'Not possible,' she said. 'The patient isn't communicating at all.' I gave the nurse my card. She said she'd be off tomorrow, but she'd leave it on the station. I was pretty sure that'd be where the card would stay until the end of time."

Tom tapped his pen on the tabletop. Aymond smiled.

"I figured we were at a dead end, but I hadn't counted on our secret weapon—my partner Deuce. While I was at one end of the nurses' station charming Mrs. Dartez and working the phone, Deuce was at the other end inching closer and closer to the curtains separating us from the patients. He overheard someone say Mrs. Falgout had been stabilized and would be sent by AirVac to Ben Taub Hospital in Houston. They had a particular kind of specialist in ocular reconstruction. The dozens of broken bones and internal injuries were apparently now a lower priority than the destruction to her face. We came on in to the station. Well, there was nobody there except a grass-green rookie and Murphy, the sheriff's schnauzer. Do you know Murphy? Wears a badge on his collar, you know. A great dog—"

"I know him, Buddy. Keep going."

Buddy now gave us the weather report. Tropical Storm Hannah had crossed the tip of Cuba and entered the lower Gulf, the path to shore unknown. A named storm in the Gulf required a whole protocol of preparations along the coast. The Sheriff and Big Theriot had gone out to Lake Peigneur; everyone else was across the street at a briefing by Homeland Security. Buddy and Deuce decided to create their own orders. They made a plan to meet the next day at 6 a.m. and drive to Houston to find Lydia Falgout. Deuce went home to his wife and kids and his own hurricane preparations. Buddy stopped at the Mirror Room for a few beers.

Tom frowned. "Buddy, you know you're—I know. None of my business." Tom stood up. "Let's take a break. I'll go ask Bonnie to make a new pot of coffee. We got to get to the part where you pick up the last name of our suspect. Sometime in the near future, I hope."

We should have given Detective Aymond coffee to start with. Fueled by caffeine, he stepped up the pace of his report.

"Do you know Ben Taub? The Texas version of Big Charity in New Orleans, but even bigger? The whole place is a fuckin' Intensive Care Unit. Jim Falgout got there before us, but it took a while to pick him out of the crowd of misery in the waiting room. Oh yes, Falgout knew his friend Remmy's last name all right. Richard. Bingo! I called back home and found someone at the jail who could get started running the records. Remuald Richard, aka Remmy. Would you believe it? He'd been our guest about five years ago."

Tom interrupted. "I'm looking at the paperwork on Lydia Falgout. I see a report but no signed statement. Did you get to talk to her?"

"They let us in to see her, but we didn't really *see* her. If they hadn't put a sign on the foot of the bed I wouldn't have known there was a person inside that mummy. No way she could sign her name to an affidavit. Her left leg and left arm, covered in plaster, hung from a contraption over the bed. The one eye not under bandage opened no wider than a pencil. A raspy voice creaked out of the mouth hole. 'Pleased to meet you, guys. Sorry I can't get you a cup of coffee.' Can you imagine?"

Unfortunately, I could.

"I asked her how she was doin'. 'So how you think? Fuckin' wonderful!' She made a sound that could have been a laugh. The docs said she was going to lose an eye but they'd build her face back up to look like it did before. 'You'd think they could at least make me pretty.' Then just wheezing. Damn courageous broad."

They had the name, so Deuce, the softie, wanted to leave the poor woman alone, but Buddy knew the importance of first reports. He asked Mrs. Falgout to tell them more. She managed to get out that Remmy ran over her with his truck and beat the shit out of her with a tire iron. At that, Deuce made Buddy stop, and they told Mrs. Falgout they'd be back for details when she was feeling better.

"Now, looking through the file, I see we never did get a signed statement. I'll talk to Deuce about follow-up," Buddy said.

"Do that. Top priority."

"That it for now?"

"Not quite."

Tom foraged around in the stack of statements and pulled out one signed by Skipper Domingue, the manager at a bunkhouse down near Intracoastal City called *The Southern Wave*.

"Speaking of statements, tell me about seeing this guy."

The detective started to get up, but Tom put a hand on his arm.

"You've got to move on, Buddy. Past history, water under the bridge. *The Southern Wave* bunkhouse didn't even exist back when you worked down there. Vermilion Parish tells me no one's ever had trouble with *The Wave*. Skipper Domingue's testimony is critically important to our case. We need his recollection to *stay* recollected. I want you to keep him warm, touch base with him every few weeks. Just mention what he says he saw so the story doesn't fade."

A frown cut deeper creases in Buddy's face." You made me go over there and we got you the damn statement. Talk to Deuce if you want to know more."

I understood what Tom was saying about the critical nature of Skipper Domingue's testimony, but not why Detective Aymond had a problem. I needed to be brought up to speed.

Bonnie came to the library door. "Sorry to interrupt, gentlemen. Detective Washington is on the line and he says it's urgent."

Buddy lunged for the phone, clearly anxious to change the topic. He listened, then responded. "Copy that."

"I got to go meet my partner, guys," he said. "Looks like they may have to scrub the drug operation in Lafayette, and Deuce needs a hand shutting it down. The Remmy Richard report is continued to another day."

He wanted out of there.

"Tomorrow. Tomorrow morning. Come at 9 a.m." Tom said. "We've got to go over your trip to Birmingham. We'll be waiting for you."

I had a question. "Could we keep Detective Washington's notebook? I want to read it with care."

Tom looked questioningly at the detective, who nodded. I guess he'd decided I could be trusted. Buddy moved quickly out the door.

The pages of my Bar Exam notes on eyewitness testimony flipped through my head. A woman who had every reason to expect imminent death had made a clear identification of her assailant, and he was someone she knew well. Three people, the trooper and two firefighters, overheard. Good stuff. But was that her *assailant*, singular, or one of her *assailants*, plural? Was there anything to Sarah's contention that Remmy Richard was at the Falgout house but didn't hurt her? Mrs. Falgout's testimony would be critically important to sorting all that out. And all of the above had to do with the search for the man who beat up Mrs. Falgout. Not my main interest, or even what was now on our plate. Trial for PawPaw's murder would come first.

"Buddy didn't seem a bit happy you assigned him to keep in touch with Skipper Domingue. What was that all about?" I asked Tom.

"He's not happy to have anything to do with the bunkhouses. All part of the history around here, even before my time, but it's not important now. I'll make sure Deuce follows up."

"Seemed very important to Detective Aymond."

Tom stopped packing up the file and sat down again. "I guess you should know. About ten years ago Vermilion Parish asked for help cleaning up what was going on at the bunkhouses down the road from Delcambre. Prostitution, mainly. The sheriff lent them Buddy to go undercover. He worked over there for a couple months and did a great job getting evidence on a couple of the managers and on the absentee owners. Charged and convicted. From then on, all Vermilion had to do to keep everything clean was make periodic unannounced checks. But Buddy's wife ended up leaving him over it, taking his children with her to California. Buddy went through a pretty bad patch after that. In fact, he's had several bad patches between then and now. Depression, alcohol."

"She left him just for doing his job?"

"He did kind of go overboard. He became obsessed trying to save a fourteen-year old girl caught up in the trade. Instead of letting her go to delinquency court and ending up with a record, he arranged to have her taken into the State welfare system. The girl ran away from her foster home, from a group home, and then just disappeared. You know our kids in care are prime targets for traffickers. For the next six months Buddy spent every off-duty hour trying to find her—and never did. He felt guilty. His wife didn't understand his obsession."

"She shouldn't have married a cop."

Tom dipped his head and fussed with his papers. He wanted to close out the topic. "We'll talk more another day."

I stood up and reached for the detective's notebook. Tom put his hand on my arm.

"You can't take that home for bedtime reading. Originals live in our locked evidence closet under Bonnie's watchful eye. And we need to get out of this building before the ghost of Honoré walks. Anyway, we might find something better to do with our evening."

Tom circled a strong arm around my shoulders.

"I'll take the offer," I said.

DEUCE'S NOTEBOOK

The next morning I made a quick detour home to change into a different outfit and took care to arrive at the office fifteen minutes after Tom. Better to risk a comment about being late for work than give the pool of secretaries a juicier topic for their wagging tongues. Tom had warned me they could multi-task, engaging in gossip as they mechanically posted into the *Crimes* database the stacks of traffic tickets and misdemeanor citations arriving every morning. The requirement for confidentiality apparently applied only to the subject matter of their work, not anyone's personal life.

Bonnie, the early bird, had messages waiting for me. The detectives wouldn't be able to make it in this morning to continue Buddy's briefing, and Tom had postponed our afternoon appointment with Sarah. Good. I'd have all day to study how the investigation had unfolded. To this point, I had researched several evidence problems—most notably how Tom could explain the detectives' presence in Birmingham, Alabama, without mentioning what happened to Mrs. Falgout. Admittedly, they had the benefit of my research into past cases, but in fifteen minutes of collaboration, the pair came up with Plan A and Plan B.

Plan A: Have the deputy sheriff in Alabama testify he'd had a call from a hospital about a man mumbling something about knocking off an old man. He'd followed up, talked to the EMTs, and interviewed patrons of the bar where the man had collapsed. If Sarah, on cross-examination, asked why he thought the man "knocked off" might be PawPaw, she'd be opening the door for Hamilton to walk through. She, not the prosecution, would be eliciting evidence of *another crime* her client might have committed. Plan B: If Sarah tried a pre-emptive strike at her pre-trial Motion to Suppress by trying to have Judge Bonin exclude any mention of what happened in Alabama as a reference to *another crime*, Tom would put Deuce on the stand to say the Iberia Parish Sheriff's Office had received an anonymous call telling them to check on a man in a hospital in Birmingham. Plan B had the extra advantage of being true—but incomplete. So Richie and Tom had come up with two strategies in fifteen minutes for what I'm sure cost me hours of sleep!

I retrieved the red file from Bonnie's secure closet, pulled out Deuce's notebook, and settled in for serious reading. I needed to review the investigation to understand just what the detectives had told the DA for him to bless a warrant of arrest for a capital crime. Mr. Strait had been clear; we had no eyewitness testimony, DNA, ballistics or any other scientific evidence. I needed to know what Tom believed was circumstantial evidence strong enough to *exclude any reasonable hypothesis of innocence*, as the law requires.

I had a bit of trouble getting started. I kept closing my eyes, the better to picture Tom's face and remember the warmth of his bare chest against me. Get on with the job, girl.

After entries about the trip to see Mrs. Falgout at Ben Taub Hospital in Houston, diagonal lines crossed the next three pages of Deuce's notebook, with one notation—Hurricane Prep. Except for the deputies assigned to PawPaw's house for the search, the storm had consumed the attention of the entire department. The Falgout investigation picked up again on Saturday.

The APB—All Points Bulletin—for Remuald Richard had triggered a flurry of calls from amateurs who saw suspicious characters under every bush. The detectives ran them all down. Sarah was going to have a field day at trial ridiculing the activity. As I leafed through the twenty pages documenting mostly dead ends, several entries caught my attention.

First, a probation mug shot of Remuald Richard taken five years ago after he'd served time in the parish jail for possession with intent to distribute cocaine. He looked a good fifteen years younger than he had at his arraignment for the murder of PawPaw. He'd given his address to the probation officers as c/o Jim Falgout, Captain Cade Road. I put a post-it note on that entry. I remembered Professor Joseph demonstrating the unreliability of eyewitness testimony, but accuracy improved substantially if the identifier previously knew the person identified. Lydia Falgout knew Remmy well. Her ID would have cred.

But, damnit, I had to remember Lydia Falgout couldn't be spoken about in the guilt phase of PawPaw's trial.

I picked up another interesting entry in Deuce's notebook. Before the body of PawPaw had been pulled up from the Delcambre Canal, a sugarcane worker reporting for work across Lake Road from PawPaw's house told his boss, my Uncle J. Allen, that he'd seen someone who met the description of Mrs. Falgout's assailant driving a truck out of the driveway of Jefferson House. A white truck. Initially, J. Allen didn't find the report worth calling in. For all he knew, the Alexandria's caretaker, like half the people around, drove a white truck. But when J. Allen went to the grocery store in Coteau to pick up something for lunch, he stood next to an unfamiliar man who met the same description. At the sight of Uncle J, the man had tucked his chin, snatched his po-boy off the counter, and double-timed out the door. To a white truck. According to Deuce's entry, dispatch relayed Uncle J's message to the detectives, and Buddy and Deuce drove out to the mansion to check out the report. Patrol was already on the scene, as was neighbor Mimi Aguillard.

My mom? I didn't recall her telling me about that. I must have been back at school. Or perhaps Jefferson House was way down Mom's list of concerns while PawPaw was missing.

The deputies had found the house itself secure, but the lock on an outdoor shed had been broken. Inside the shed, the detectives found signs of occupancy: a pile of blankets, an empty tuna fish can, some burned-down candles.

Detective Aymond called Jack Alexandria, the owner of Jefferson House, at his home in Nashville, Tennessee. They determined nothing was missing. Deuce noted their conclusion —probably a homeless man had found shelter from the storm. When the weather cleared, he'd moved on. Alexandria said he'd call a locksmith and a carpenter to make repairs.

Deuce recorded what he thought an interesting remark Jack Alexandria had made. *No one is supposed to be at the house, but I have a nephew who's caused my sister no end of trouble. He just finished a stint in rehab and disappeared. He could've drifted down there.* Alexandria provided a sketchy description of the nephew. Name: Mickey Brown. Stats: thirty years old, five foot ten, light eyes, about one hundred sixty pounds when Alexandria last saw him a year ago. Probably weighed more now, if he was off drugs. Alexandria told Detective Aymond he didn't know if the nephew drove a truck. The boy had a history of wrecking whatever vehicle his mother gave him. But eating tuna fish out of a can? Probably not his nephew, Alexandria had said. Mickey had expensive tastes. Remuald Richard wouldn't have expensive tastes. Maybe *he* had holed up in that shed. If I had that thought, I bet the detectives did too.

Once again, not admissible in PawPaw's case, but increased the detectives', and Tom's, confidence they had the right man.

I could just imagine the cross-examination if Buddy or Deuce testified about this part of the investigation. *Now tell me, detective, just how did you follow up on the discovery of the break-in? You didn't follow up? You didn't call in forensics? You didn't even dust for prints? You just assumed a homeless man had been sleeping there?* Alas, country investigations never measure up to the expectations the public has developed from watching TV crime drama.

This job had me so damn excited—Tom and I working together for the good guys. I probably lost a few minutes as my mind again slipped into thoughts about Tom.

A post-it note already marked the next page in Deuce's notebook: a significant development in the investigation. The break they'd been hoping for.

Two weeks after the beating of Mrs. Falgout, an anonymous call came in to Elnora on the sheriff's switchboard. *You guys looking for Remmy Richard? Try the County Hospital in Birmingham.* The call ended.

Buddy and Deuce made contact with a Deputy Mark Hamilton in the sheriff's office of Jefferson County. Birmingham had no county hospital, but there were several large medical facilities in the city. The deputy conferenced Buddy with each one. They hit pay dirt at the University of Alabama Medical Center.

The emergency room of UAMC had admitted a delirious white man in his mid-thirties who had collapsed in a local bar. He had a badly infected laceration of his left arm, was sniffing like a bloodhound, and couldn't get enough water or beer to quench his thirst. Signs of drug use. He carried no ID, but the ER found a receipt from a gas station in Baton Rouge in his pocket. Deputy Hamilton located the patient's truck outside the bar and traced the Louisiana license plate. Remuald Richard.

Deuce noted Buddy's instruction to Deputy Hamilton. *Freeze the guy. Document everything he says whether you can make any sense of it or not. Impound and seal his vehicle.*

Apparently, Deputy Hamilton did as instructed. In fever delirium, the patient mumbled: *lady had some bread; needed a fix; truck got stuck in a ditch; tore up my arm on a rusty old fence. Yeah, knocked off an old guy, too.* Deputy Mark Hamilton had searched Richard's car and found a well-worn wallet on the floorboard. Empty. He sealed it in an evidence bag. A marginal note referred the reader to a later page in the notebook where the detectives reported taking the wallet back to New Iberia and showing it to my Uncle Bub for identification. Bub said it looked like PawPaw's.

Hallelujah! We had one item of physical evidence for our case —PawPaw's wallet. 'Looked like,' anyway.

Buddy and Deuce drove to the Birmingham hospital the next day. The patient admitted he was Remuald Richard and blurted out *two dead on my watch*. Buddy read him his rights and placed him under arrest for the attempted murder of Lydia Falgout. Richard refused to say anything more. Three days later, the hospital released Richard into the custody of the detectives.

I checked the stack of witness statements the detectives had taken but couldn't find one from Deputy Hamilton. Tom needed to get the detectives on that right away, before Hamilton forgot the whole scene.

Then I ran into another critical piece of information. After bringing Remuald Richard back from Alabama, the detectives visited the docks. Only then? Hadn't Uncle Ti told them they should do that earlier, when PawPaw first went missing? I found a margin entry directing the reader's attention to the initial report by Detective Ted D'Aquin, the detective on loan from St. Martin Parish when Buddy and Deuce were over in Alabama. I found D'Aquin's report attached to the inside cover. His trip to the docks had yielded nothing.

Now Deuce's notebook recorded the detectives' revisit to the area. Armed with a name and the mug shot from Richard's prior incarceration, they worked through every corner of Delcambre and then on down the road to Intracoastal City. They scored a hit at *The Southern Wave*. The manager there, who gave his name as Skipper Domingue, said he recognized the man in the mug shot. He looked like a guy who'd been around the bunkhouse at the critical time.

Ah, ha! This was the visit Tom talked to Detective Aymond about, the visit Aymond had been reluctant to make and didn't want to repeat.

At *The Southern Wave*, Deuce had another opportunity to use his artistic talent. A careful drawing of the ground floor living area of the bunkhouse—sleeping took place upstairs—spread across two pages. A kitchen held down the mid-section of the long side of the large open room. Five picnic-type tables, benches on either side, occupied one end. Fifty feet away, on the other end of the room, two sofas and a couple of metal chairs sat in front of a TV. One of the picnic tables had been marked with an X, as had one of the chairs on the opposite end of the room. Deuce had written the name Skipper Domingue next to the chair. I searched in the file for an account to see what this witness might have had to say, and this time I found a signed statement in what seemed to be Domingue's own words.

> *September 1. Two men sat at a table at one end of the room. I didn't know their names but I'd seen them around before. Big argument... seemed to be about getting money for drugs. They talked about a score the day before. One guy tried to persuade the other one to take his truck out to get more bread. He refused. At one point the second guy said he didn't expect the first one to off the old guy. They kept jawing at each other until finally the second guy got up and said OK, we'll use my truck. The first guy looked like the mug shot of Remuald Richard.*

Now the detectives had a second reference to the death of an old man, and Skipper Domingue ID'ed Richard as the one who *offed the old guy*. Bingo.

I went back looking for the initial description of the two speakers. Not much detail. In fact, the descriptions of the two men were virtually interchangeable. Thirties to forties, not heavy, light hair, white shrimper's boots. One wore jeans; the other khakis. One had a darker complexion than the other, but Domingue wasn't sure which was which. Maybe someone could hear a conversation across that big room, but could he identify the speaker from such a distance? How sure was Domingue? Pretty shaky evidence.

Now I had a good fix on the two key witnesses Tom had for PawPaw's case—Deputy Mark Hamilton and bunkhouse manager Skipper Domingue. The detectives made a full report of their investigation to their boss and DA Strait. Both gave them a green light—Deuce's word was *instruction*—to prepare another warrant for Richard's arrest, this time for the first degree murder of Pierre

Boudreaux—my PawPaw. They served the warrant on Richard in the parish jail.

I turned the next page and read Deuce's notes about checking the coroner's report. I kept going but found no more direct, circumstantial or any other kind of evidence linking Remuald Richard to the murder of PawPaw. Damn.

So that was to be the evidence the detectives had to give us. Without saying anything about the crime against Mrs. Falgout, Tom would have to ask the jury to convict Remuald Richard of first degree murder, death penalty recommended, based on Richard's own feverish mumblings about *knocking off an old guy*, an incriminating statement about *two dead on his watch*, an overheard conversation at a bunkhouse down by Intracoastal City, and an empty wallet that *looked like* my grandfather's found in Remmy's car. My God. I felt slightly sick.

No wonder Tom had thoughts of a deal for a plea of guilty in return for a sentence of life without parole. My family would gag, but maybe they'd go for life in prison rather than have Remmy walk. And maybe Sarah wouldn't want to take the risk of going to trial. She had to face the fact that if Tom did get a conviction, and he put Mrs. Falgout on the stand in the penalty phase, she'd be dynamite. One look at her face and every juror would be totally convinced someone who could do that would be capable of anything.

ETIENNE'S STORY

"Uncle 'Tienne had an appointment to talk to Tom. Did 'Tienne tell you how that went?" Mom and I were having an after-dinner visit on the back porch.

Mom smiled. "Honey, I think you've the best window into that conversation. From the outside looking in, I'd say you're enjoying your job at the DA's office."

"It's a great experience. But no, I don't have a special window. I'm just doing my work and trying not to get caught in the middle. Tom tells me he talked to 'Tienne, but they didn't really get to the meat of anything. I let it go at that."

"Sounds like how it would go, Etienne not saying much. But tell me, what's Tom trying to accomplish by talking to the family members one at a time?"

I punted. "Oh, I think Tom just wants to decide who to put on the stand to tell the jury about the loss the family suffered."

"Well, we know who'll demand to be the one!"

"Right. Uncle Ti. But I can almost guarantee Tom won't do that. Ti doesn't exactly have jury appeal. Maybe Bub. Do you think Bub could do it?"

"It'd be hard for him, but he'd walk on hot coals if he thought he could help his PawPaw."

I decided to come clean. "And while Tom is talking to y'all, Mom, getting to know you, as he puts it, I think he's feeling you out about the possibility of the family agreeing to let him ask the defense if Richard would take a plea to life in prison. You know, admission of guilt, no trial. All over in just a short time."

"Family agreeing to waive the death penalty? Everyone? No way. Ti Pierre would never go for that."

"If Ti were the only one in opposition, it wouldn't be the first time you disagreed with him. What do you think about the others?"

Mom tilted her head before answering. "J. Allen might go either way. And 'Tienne? I don't know. He's the brother who doesn't talk."

"By everyone, Mom, Tom means the sisters also." The old patriarchal society dies hard with Mom's generation.

Mom continued. "Dora would back off the death penalty, I'm pretty sure of that. She spoke out pretty clearly against capital punishment when we were over at 'Tilde's after the arraignment. She can't get over the reports of guys who turn out to have been wrongly convicted, even though there isn't a chance of that here. Me and Tut? We'd have to talk. And, of course, there's no point in us even looking for Mazie's opinion because we couldn't find it. A babbling goose running all around the barnyard, that's what she is."

"Mom! You should be ashamed."

"And I am."

"Back to Uncle 'Tienne, Mom? Would he consider the plea? 'Tienne's opinion carries a lot of weight."

Mom raised her eyebrows a good quarter inch. "I'm inclined to think that how 'Tienne has learned to live with his Vietnam experience will determine his position. Could go either way."

"What was his experience in Vietnam, Mom? He never talks about it."

Mom sat quietly for a few moments. "I doubt he's even told Berthe what he went through over there. That's not good. A wife should know everything, but it isn't my business to tell her. That's between 'Tienne and Berthe. PawPaw talked some. Now that

PawPaw's gone, I guess I should tell you."

"Please, Mom." I sat back on the sofa and Mom did the same, but in a moment she jumped back up.

"Wait, I wrote down something about this. It's in the bottom of my desk."

She left the room and came back with an envelope, which she opened. She glanced through five yellowed pages that had been folded inside, but then set them on her lap and just talked.

"The year was 1968. I was just a girl then, so what I tell you is mostly from these papers and a couple of conversations I had with PawPaw later on. It's a story, all right."

I urged Mom to tell me.

"PawPaw said that when 'Tienne stepped off the bus in Lafayette, Mama B called out 'Holy Mary, Mother of God.' After two tours of duty in Vietnam, 'Tienne had spent a week in California telling the Army psychiatrist what he wanted to hear in order to get released from the service. He'd gotten a real haircut and found some clothes he could hang on his pared-down frame. The sight of his parents, his brothers and sisters, and Ti Pierre's new baby boy, put a smile on his lips but not in his eyes. No one could do anything about those hollowed-out eyes." 'Tienne moved into his old room. Two brothers, J. Allen and Bub, and we three younger girls, were still home then. 'Tienne never was a big talker but now, hardly a word. Some mornings Mama B found his bedcovers undisturbed. We kids didn't notice, of course. You know adolescents. They think they're the center of the universe."

That made me smile. Always has been true, apparently.

"When Mom's brother Nonc, who was 'Tienne's uncle and *parrain*, asked the men and boys in the family to join him at his duck camp at Pecan Island for opening day of the season, Etienne said no thanks. But Nonc kept asking, begging really. J. Allen had just gotten his first shotgun. The favorite cousin, Nonc's oldest, would be there and really wanted to spend time with his hero. Etienne still said no. Then PawPaw played his trump card. He told 'Tienne he'd take a couple of days off from the field so he could join them. Ti Pierre worked for PawPaw then and said he'd pull the extra time."

Mom's hands were clenched together. Just telling this story caused her pain.

"Apparently they followed the same routine they do today— leaving after supper Friday so they could get a good night's sleep at the camp, then up early to be in the marsh before light. They shot birds, mostly mergansers PawPaw said, and had their limit before noon. Shooting over, PawPaw said he saw 'Tienne's shotgun on the floor of the blind, unused. He asked 'Tienne why he hadn't taken a shot. Tienne said he just didn't feel like holding a gun. He never wanted to hold a gun again.

"Planning for another hunt the next day, I'm sure they napped, cleaned the ducks, and started a gumbo. PawPaw said after supper he made a point of getting 'Tienne alone on the porch. They propped their feet up on the railing, and PawPaw worked the conversation around to asking 'Tienne what he was thinking about out there in the marsh. 'Tienne told PawPaw he wouldn't want to know. But PawPaw persisted.

"PawPaw said he told 'Tienne some people were saying it wasn't going too good over there in Vietnam, but he wanted 'Tienne to know he was proud of his soldier. The President said the country was in danger from those communists. No matter how the war turned out, 'Tienne had done his duty for the free world. Sounds corny, but PawPaw believed it. He said if people hadn't done that before, we'd be talkin' German right now, if we'd lived long enough to talk at all. Sometimes you just have to do things you never thought you'd do. For your country and for your family."

I nodded my head but didn't speak. I didn't want to interrupt Mom's concentration on her memory.

"PawPaw said 'Tienne didn't respond for a good ten minutes. He'd just about decided that was going to be it for their conversation when Etienne opened up. Mandy, I came home that night and wrote down 'Tienne's story as best I could. I was afraid I wouldn't remember it, and I felt I'd heard something important."

Now Mom picked up the papers she'd taken from her envelope, and read.

Etienne's Story

When we first got over there I led patrols. We did that for six months or more, I can't quite remember how long. We'd take the chopper out at dusk. The mission was to search and destroy, to hunt and kill North Vietnamese, and to wipe out anything the Cong might find useful. Sometimes we'd find a village empty, so we'd shoot every goat and chicken, call in the artillery to torch the place, and pull out. Sometimes there were people. We made some tough calls about what to do with them. Then the chopper would come to pick us up, take us home, and we'd sleep in, only to go out again the following night. Sometimes we had to stay out there a couple nights.

One time, before the chopper came to pick us up, we caught fire from a hill about five hundred yards yonder. I waved off the ride home so air support could hit the hill and take out the rest of the VC. Then it was too dark for the chopper to find us.

During the night the rains came, slow and steady. We pulled out our ponchos and waited. We'd wandered off course. I really didn't know where we were. I'd lost the rest of the platoon. Doggie caught a bullet in his left thigh. He didn't let on right away. I didn't know why he didn't tell us, but I figured it out later. He now had his pass to get out of this hellhole. We huddled like possums in a ditch, our boots sunk into six inches of mud.

In the morning I raised my head, parting the reeds with my left hand, M-16 at the ready in my right. I thought maybe VC would think I was a turtle. The sheen of the rice paddy stretched as far as I could see. I checked the other bank. Same empty view. Silence, dead silence. No sound but our own breathing, the whir of bugs, the croaking of frogs, and the weak swish of a breeze in the reeds rising on each bank. And the smell—the sweet smell of decaying vegetation.

'Movin' on. Pass the word.' I sucked my boots out of the muck. 'Strap down that grenade Corporal, I whispered to Jefferson. 'Sounds like a fuckin' cowbell.' There were eight of us walking, and one wounded. Doggie lay on a litter between the third and fourth men. He wouldn't be out on patrol again. For that duty you need two good legs. Some genius in the Pentagon sent me here thinking *that I'd seen a rice field before and wouldn't rot easy. He was right. I may be a wiry little Cajun but I'm tough. Even then I figured I'd survive, but I wasn't so sure about my men. I could feel their fear.*

We made it in.

I did maybe forty patrols like that and was looking at as many more before the time would come for the end of my tour. Some nights we couldn't call support to wipe out the VC. We had to do it ourselves, face to face. Same story every patrol, only some nights more men caught the bullets. We went down to six men. Mac took a knife between the shoulder blades and Romano—he got crazy. That happened after a real bad night. We'd walked onto another patrol that had caught it head on. A dozen bodies lay in a bloody heap, some dead but others gasping, writhing, moaning. Our guys. A medical chopper was landing nearby to clean up. After that patrol, Jefferson didn't bother to hide how he coped with the horrors. He'd roll a joint, light up, and pass it around.

And then it got worse. Headquarters moved inland. The Captain said that was a sign of our improved position, but no one believed his crap. Winter set in. The night rains turned cold and the day rains steamed up off the muck. And there was always an endless stream of new VC, and another assignment to 'find and destroy.'

One night the tarp slipped off my face, and I felt a rat scurry across my cheek. I wanted to scream, but a greater fear triumphed. Who would hear me? Not friends because there were none out there. I lay still and waited for the rats to move on.

Always keep your feet dry, the Captain had said. Now how the hell could we do that? Back in headquarters we toasted our boots over the sterno, but the next night sloshed through six inches of mud in another downpour. Fungus crept into our boots and socks. Not a surprise that our feet turned white and spongy.

We could see mountains in the west and sometimes at night felt a breeze from that direction. We dreamed we were there, lying next to a clear stream.

When Joe Bob stepped on a mine and blew off his left foot, the Captain put the remnant of my men together with another pared-down squad to make an almost respectable-sized platoon. Like us, the new guys had long dirty hair, scraggly beards, and hollowed eyes that said there's nothing you can show me that I haven't seen before. They'd been over here for months so I didn't have to tell them the obvious, like clean your weapon and never forget to fill your canteen.

One winter afternoon the orders changed. The chopper took us farther inland and some to the north, to a tunnel complex at the foot of the mountains. Now we carried explosives along with everything else, and we had a guide, a 'friendly' they called Joe. He'd been fitted out with a flak jacket and boots, but was still almost small enough to fit in one of our packs. Joe spoke maybe a dozen words of English. He made hand signals and squeaked out through thin, grinning lips.

We did our job on three of the four tunnels we were assigned. Three guys went down the tunnels first. Joe and the rest of us waited and made our minds think about what might be worth waiting for —home, women, real food, the end of this shit. The three came out, their faces wearing mud and as close as any of us ever got to a smile. We strung wires, detonated the charges, and then we moved on. We were just ready to blow the last tunnel when we spotted a file of natives moving silently on the trail we had just come in on. Their guns weren't US issue. VC. My patrol sank down into the dense brush and let them go on by. If we'd been only fifteen minutes later... No one wanted to think about that.

Now what? I radioed to the base with our coordinates but got no response. I couldn't rouse HQ. Were they wiped out? After an hour of dead air I knew we were on our own, and I knew why the Captain sent us out with a friendly for a guide. We were going to need more than a map and compass to find our way back to HQ. And back to who knew what.

The first day of the return felt like an exercise at Camp LeJeune —tough but we'd done it all before. We organized into squads. The squads went out in turns with Joe. When they came back with an all-clear, the rest of us followed. That night we dug in and slept. One squad kept watch. I figured we were four days out, and that we had three days' rations of food and water. With care and no bad news, we could make it.

The second day was the same. On the morning of the third day two things went wrong. The brush at the foot of the mountains gave way to those goddamned paddies. No cover. And it began to rain. We could move in the daytime, following the same routine, but at night had to bed down in a ditch. And we couldn't find a dry hole. Two ponchos could work to make the best of a bad bed—one poncho on the mud, the other as a tent to keep off the rain.

I woke up the fourth morning and realized I'd been asleep too long. Two hours ago I should have heard one duty squad replace the one before. When I checked, both squads were missing, vanished without a trace. Six men gone. Jefferson was one of them. And then I saw three natives moving single file up the trail, carrying rifles pointed at the ground, again not US issue. I ordered my men to 'freeze.' A dozen VC passed back and forth until late afternoon, keeping us pinned down like snakes in two feet of mud.

When we hadn't seen anyone for over an hour, Digger opened a can of sterno to heat up an MRE. A sappy grin broke up Joe's wizened, sun-browned little face and he scampered up the bank. He found a stiff piece of reed, speared a toad, and held the wiggling little critter out over the flame. OK if I cook it? his eyes asked. When the toad stopped sizzling, Joe popped it in his mouth. Digger retched. He jumped out of the ditch and puked into the reeds.

That night Joe disappeared.

The next day we came upon our lost men. Cut to bits. I gave the order to leave them, and wept.

That night we cooked and ate six toads. It was toads or leeches, and Joe had survived eating a toad.

Once we had been an almost respectable platoon of four patrols. Now we were down to six men. I tried the radio one more time, but again no one answered, so I pitched the device. So what if VC found it? Obviously, they already knew we were out here. I was weak and could do with one less thing to carry.

Four days later we made it back into camp. There it was, just the way we left it. The Captain gave us a day off. Get a good sleep, he said, because there's another patrol for day after tomorrow.

A couple months later I made Captain. I didn't have to go out on search and destroy any more. I stayed in the pagoda and gave the orders to send out the others. I remember a guy named Belker from Detroit, a broad black face with yellow eyeballs. I remember Possum from Alabama. But I've forgotten most of the other names. Mostly I remember the look in their eyes when I gave them the speech. I had several versions: Patriotism—You're making America safe for your children and grandchildren; Shame—go on out there or you're off to the court marshal; Pride—you're a Marine, you fucker.

I sat there safe under a tin roof and sent them out, one after another—to die.

When Mom finished reading Uncle 'Tienne's story we were both choking back tears. "It's a wonder Uncle 'Tienne talks at all, Mom, if that's what he has to say. I'm so glad you wrote that down. Some day..."

"Yes, some day. This envelope will be in my desk, with your name on it. And your Dad knows where it is. Maybe you'll give it to 'Tienne's children. I don't know. You'll have to figure that out when I'm gone."

Mom continued. "There's one more thing that may matter now, Mandy. I remember PawPaw saying he told 'Tienne that if anyone did anything to Mama or to one of the kids, he wouldn't rest until he'd done it back to them. I wonder if 'Tienne remembers those words."

"Good question, Mom, and 'Tienne isn't talking."

Would the clearly traumatic experience of sending men out to die turn 'Tienne against another deliberate killing? Maybe his opinion would depend on what thought had the dominant spot in his brain on a given day. Is that the way it is for jurors as well? Changing with the wind? Maybe. Some days I felt one way, some days the other. Tom was telling me he had to represent the best interests of the victims, my family, and that was why he needed to talk to each one of PawPaw's children. Would what they said one day be what they thought tomorrow?

Being a prosecutor was turning out to be much harder than it looked from the outside.

TWO DINNERS

"Mandy, we really need to have Tom for dinner. We've only exchanged pleasantries when he comes to pick you up, and your Dad hasn't even been around for that."

Mom had ignored my absences at night, but clearly she'd figured out what was going on.

"Sure. When would be good? Maybe Sunday?"

"Perfect. I'll call him."

"No-o-o, Mom. Let me do it. He'd be freaked out by a dinner invitation coming straight from my mom." Tom wasn't totally at home with the mores of south Louisiana.

"Sunday? Does that mean I have to go to church with y'all?" Tom asked when I conveyed the invitation.

I told him not to worry. Mom's easy. Her invitation covered only lunch. We all went to different churches, on different days, at different times, and some in the family didn't go at all. My grandmother Mama B used to check the religious observances of her children, and she tried to carry her governance over to the grandchildren as well, but she gave up. My aunts were regular churchgoers, but my uncles may have made it to Mass on Easter and Christmas. *Chreasters*, Mom had been known to call them.

"Dinner will be around two. Dad will probably barbeque.

Very casual. Mom may invite Aunt Tut or someone else who wouldn't give you a hard time, but this will *not* be another family meeting. Ti Pierre won't be there, and I promise you the subject of religion will not come up."

The lunch went well. Tom seemed comfortable with the group, which turned out to be Mom, Dad, Taddy, Aunt Tut, and three of her children. We ate at a picnic table on the screened back porch. Tom scored by asking Dad about one of his favorite subjects—the day Lake Peigneur disappeared.

"I've heard about the lake draining into the salt mine, but now I'm realizing that must've been a traumatic experience for those of you who were living so close. You were here then, right?"

My father, usually withdrawn in the company of more than two people, sat up straighter. "We sure were."

"What was that like? Could you tell me?"

He could and he would. We say everyone in south Louisiana "dines out" on hurricane tales, but those who live by the lake have an additional disaster to recount. They take every opportunity to tell what happened on November 20, 1980.

Taddy and Tut's children were rolling their eyes. They'd heard my dad's account too many times before.

"First a question, sir." Tom asked. "The name Lake Peigneur. Where does it come from? I would've thought you'd call the area Pirates' Hideout or some other reference to Jean Lafitte. He's supposed to have wintered around here and buried part of his treasure on the shores, right?"

"Right. Treasure hunting frenzy comes in waves every few years, but other than the discovery of salt, a valuable commodity at the time of the War Between the States, the only treasure people have found is bones and crockery. Maybe a few coins, but not old ones. My brother-in-law, Ti Pierre, is forever trying to get up a party to take the Boudreaux map out there for a dig. If you're interested..."

I gave Tom a wink. I knew he wouldn't want more time listening to complaints from my uncle Ti.

Dad told Tom the French-speaking Acadians who settled the area in the 18th century gave the lake its name. They thought the kidney shape resembled the fine-tooth combs, or *peigneurs*, the early settlers used to card the wool from sheep.

Dad continued his tale about the catastrophe. "The lake's not the same shape anymore, you know. That day changed everything. We're sittin' on top of two underground domes of salt they tell me are as tall as those twin towers in New York City used to be before 9/11. Above ground, all we could see back then was the rickety-looking six-story structure of the mining operation and a seventy-five foot oil derrick in the water near the western shore. But down below, in the cavities, fifty-five men were hard at work.

"The Texaco drilling crew on the platform had put down an exploratory well outside the dome of salt—well, mostly outside. They'd made a slight miscalculation. A fourteen-inch drill bit punched into the salt dome and then into the mine. Water began seepin' in. You know, the only way up or down most mine shafts is a bucket takin' up four men at a time. The biggest miracle of the whole tragedy is that nobody drowned. The well-trained crew just calmly lined up for a turn to be taken to the top."

"Must've been frightening to be so close to all that."

"Actually, in the beginning we didn't know enough to be scared. It was hours before we even realized anything was going on."

"What time of day did it all start?" Tom asked, drawing out my dad.

"Before dawn. We woke up to the sound of sirens and a policeman knockin' on the door. He told us there was a problem with the salt mine, evacuation in progress. At first we didn't have to leave; that came later. We just got dressed and went over to PawPaw and Mama B's to tell 'em about it."

"I guess you could look out across the lake from there and see the whole scene."

"Nothin' to see. Looked like usual. Some barges and a couple fishermen in pirogues on the water. Things looked peaceful enough, maybe a little more movement than usual, but not much. Suddenly, the oil derrick just disappeared. Slu-urp! A fifty-foot high structure vanished straight down into water only 15 feet deep."

"Wow!"

"Then we saw current, the water in a whirlpool on the far side of the lake. One after another, eleven barges disappeared. Then the water level began to drop. A fisherman's pirogue sat high and dry—well, not really dry, marooned in sticky mud. Astounding, really. One fisherman, Aristide Romero, we called him Teedy, had his fifteen minutes of fame. Someone on shore caught the scene on a camcorder, Teedy climbing out of his pirogue onto the yucky lake bottom, one hand on his straw hat, 'deer in the headlights' look on his face. He was interviewed later and the clip played on the national news for three whole days. Wait." Dad turned to my Mom. "Mimi, you do the Cajun accent better than I do."

"No, Emile, you got it goin' now," my mom said, loving that my Dad had another chance to tell the story.

"OK. Wide-eyed, open face, Teedy said to the Channel 10 reporter, 'I taut it gonna be da en' of the whirl.'"

Tom loved it, too. "But then the water came back?"

"And how! With a vengeance. First there was just a trickle. Once we learned that all the miners were safe, we were calm about the whole thing, stunned but not panicked at all. We had no idea people on shore would have any problem. That changed. Water in the Delcambre Canal, which usually flows south to the Gulf, began movin' in the opposite direction, pourin' saltwater into the lake. I've seen pictures of the huge waterfall it created, but by then we weren't hangin' around to see for ourselves. The sirens had started up again. Another policeman came to the door, and we took his advice to move across the road to the farm. We missed seein' one of the famous sights, the eleven barges that had gone down the hole poppin' back up to the surface—pop, pop, pop—and we didn't see the last shot of Teedy climbin' back into the pirogue, then just sittin' there in his straw hat, dazed, waitin' for lift-off. When there was enough water in the lake, he bowed his back and paddled like hell for the shore."

My Dad gave us a demonstration.

"But then came the real catastrophe, the onshore destruction that followed. Our area was OK, but down farther, not so fine. The water rushin' in scoured out the bank. Three-hundred-year-old oak trees, a garden of fancy plants collected from all over the world, a bunch of houses, all toppled over and disappeared into the maelstrom, as they called it. Three days later, when everythin' had settled down, sixty-five acres of land had washed away. Parts of the gardens and plant nursery have been restored, but the entire shape of the lake is changed. The water that was six feet deep before the catastrophe is now way over a hundred. You can still see the brick chimney of one of the houses sticking whop-a-jawed out of the water, kind of pointin' to where the vortex had taken place."

Dad's face cracked open in a smile. "Better fishin' now, though. We got saltwater fish to catch."

My mom added her latest concern. "I heard the other day there's some kind of bubbling or foaming going on out there now."

"And no explanation of what it is," Dad said. "That's the problem. When you deal with the forces of Mother Nature, you just can't be sure of anything."

Tom asked what happened to the salt mining business and the oil drilling.

"No more and never will be, if I can help it," my dad said. "The salt mine never reopened, but that doesn't mean people aren't always tryin' to use the underground cavities to store stuff. Natural gas, I hear. Texaco shut down its operation and didn't drill again, but oil and gas companies are forever schemin'. Oil is found next to all the salt domes around here, you know. We're snake-bit. We stay busy fightin' every attempt to use the area in any commercial or government scheme whatsoever. Even though people keep tellin' us this or that can be done safely, we don't want to take the chance. I'm against anyone who wants to do anythin'. I think that chimney on the sunken house is pointing a scoldin' finger toward the site of the whirlpool and sayin', 'World, keep your cotton-pickin' hands off our lake.'"

I was glad Tom got to hear what makes my family so paranoid about 'development.'

After lunch, Aunt Tut and I helped Mom clean up the kitchen. Tut's boys and Taddy went out into the yard to throw a football back and forth. Tom joined them, and I watched him carefully place the ball in Taddy's hands, fingers on the lacings. Hmmm. I liked that.

When the others left, Mom, Dad, Tom and I settled back down on the porch. Tom took a chair where he could look out over the lake.

"You have a lovely spot here, Mr. Aguillard. The lakefront is so peaceful."

"Yes, we're here thanks to my wife's family. PawPaw arranged for us to have this strip right next to his house."

"And the big house up there to the right? Jefferson House, you call it?"

"That's the real prize. Joseph Jefferson, the famous actor who played the part of Rip Van Winkle in a traveling theater company, fell in love with the spot when he was on tour in New Orleans. He bought what was then known as Orange Plantation and built that mansion on the butte, or dome, overlookin' the lake. Jack Alexander owns it now. As you know, the Alexander family lives in Nashville and only spends summers, huntin' season, and some holidays down here."

"If that place were mine, I'd be here every day of the year, and I think I'd never go to work. I'd spend all my time on one of the porches looking out on the water."

Soon the conversation got around to PawPaw's empty house —what the family was going to do with it—and then to Mama B. Mom wanted to tell Tom about my grandmother's last days. I tried every way I could to steer the conversation to a more cheerful subject, but Mom wouldn't let go.

"No, Mandy," she insisted. "Tom should know one of the reasons we're all so angry about what happened to PawPaw."

I resigned myself to wait out her story and apologize to Tom later. She told him Mama B was sick for many years, but she and PawPaw mostly handled everything by themselves. Surgeries, chemo, radiation—the works. Through it all, Mama B was sure she'd get well. The next therapy was going to do it, she'd say. She went to daily Mass, walked every day no matter what, and always wanted to talk about anything other than her health. We thought her optimism and fight kept her going, and, for sure, eased the burden on everyone else.

One morning, when she put her legs over the edge of the bed and tried to stand up, she fell back down. She couldn't hold her own weight. PawPaw carried her to his truck and drove her to the emergency room in town. The hospital took a bone scan. PawPaw said the picture of her skeleton was lit up like a Christmas tree. They only kept her at the hospital for a couple days. PawPaw put her bed in the hall, next to his recliner.

I couldn't take any more. "Mom, Tom doesn't need to hear all this."

"Yes, he does need to hear it, Mandy. He's asking questions about the family, and this is where we're all coming from."

She went on, telling him PawPaw stayed right by Mama B's side, holding her hand day and night. The rest of the family came and went, did what needed to be done, but when the lights went out at night, it was just PawPaw and Mama B.

"Funny how peaceful—and how beautiful—those days were for us," she said. "Mama B didn't seem to be in pain. We didn't understand how that could be until the doctors explained. Sometimes bone cancer hitting the spine kills the nerves first. God's mercy, he said. Every child, every grandchild, visited. Some of the little ones didn't know what to say to her so we told them to write her a note. They scribbled, 'We love you Mama B', and tucked the pieces of paper into her covers."

There was nothing I could do the stop my mom. We were all changed by those six weeks, but did our lawyer need to hear the details? And that's what Tom was to the family—the lawyer. So far, at least.

Mom plowed on. "The immediate family is a special unit, but you have no idea how close everyone is until you see a gathering around a mother's deathbed. Each person goes home with a deeper understanding of family, of life, of death." She looked Tom straight in the eye. "We couldn't be there for PawPaw when his time came, and that makes us angry."

Tom nodded.

She continued. "I know anger eats the container it's in, so we're the ones suffering. We should get over it, but we can't. And as for Christian forgiveness? As long as the pain that guy caused is still at work in our hearts, we're a long way from coming out the other side."

Tom stood up, went to Mom's chair and touched her shoulder.

After goodbyes to Tut's family, Tom took my hand and we walked down to the lake to watch the sunset.

"Today I learned something about picking jurors," Tom said.

"And what was that?"

"For our trial, I'm going to try to find some men and women who've cared for an elderly parent."

I guess that's what a prosecutor thinks about—how to win. Getting prosecution-minded jurors is a critical part of a trial, but I knew my Mom. She treasured the memory of Mama B's death but wouldn't necessarily choose the ultimate penalty for the man who deprived her of the same experience with her dad. Mom was revealing her own spiritual struggle with Christian forgiveness, not thinking about the trial.

And I remembered Dora's conversation on Aunt Mathilde's back porch after the arraignment. She'd beaten herself up about not being there for Mama B, but that didn't determine her attitude toward capital punishment for the murderer of PawPaw. She was against it. Tom had missed the point.

When the mosquitoes started buzzing, we picked up our chairs and walked back up to the porch.

"By the way, Tom. I left you a note after I read Deuce's notebook."

I guess I was just as bad as Tom—obsessed by the trial.

"Deuce's good, isn't he. What did you think?"

For a few seconds I considered telling Tom I was concerned about the scarcity of hard evidence needed for a conviction, but decided to leave that alone. I'd stick with subjects more appropriate for my lowly status as an intern.

"I couldn't find a statement from that deputy in Birmingham

—I think his name was Hamilton—nor a lab report on Remmy Richard's car. And I didn't see a statement signed by Mrs. Falgout."

"The lab report on the car came directly to me. Might be still on my desk. Just another white pickup. A five-year-old Nissan, I believe. Nothing helpful except of course the wallet they sent us. Deuce got Hamilton's statement this week, and I think he's made an appointment to see Mrs. Falgout on Wednesday." Tom put his hand on my arm. "Maybe you'd like to go with him. It would be good experience to go on an investigation."

You bet I'd like to go.

* * *

Mr. Strait had a special invitation to have dinner on Friday at *Lagniappe,* the fun little restaurant on Main Street, but he had a conflict—command performance to make a kick-off speech at a campaign event for the Sheriff of St. Martin Parish. He'd make it to *Lagniappe,* but late. He asked Tom to cover. Not a problem. Tom and I loved the place.

Usually Brother Andry only opened the restaurant for lunch, but tonight was special. His birthday. Not that he didn't consider every day a reason to celebrate. Tonight he planned to wear his bright red apron (which never got near enough to the kitchen to be soiled by a spot of food), graciously accept a few bottles of wine from his regular guests, and share stories with the diners at every one of the twenty tables. Although Tom and I'd be the youngest guests, I was delighted to be included. Brother planned to unveil his latest work of art—a caricature of Mr. Strait.

Brother Andry's wife Evelyn made stocking dolls, which she tucked around the room on the window sills, the piano, and on top of the bar, but the walls were reserved for Brother's art. He had one large painting of the Billeaud Sugar Mill, where my brothers took their cane—if I'd had money to burn I'd have bought it for my Uncle Jay and Aunt 'Tilde—but the real drawing cards were Brother's whimsical caricatures of his own customers —and Evelyn's cooking.

I couldn't wait to see what Brother would do with Mr. Strait.

The evening was great fun. The usual daytime waitresses were at work. Mona, a lady of at least eighty, banged out show tunes on the piano. Some man tried to make a request, but his words literally fell on deaf ears. Mona couldn't hear. She just smiled and kept playing. The food was super. Evelyn did something wonderful with speckled trout. Well into the evening—late for this crowd—the boss hadn't shown up. Tom got antsy.

"I'm going outside to give him a call."

Tom came back relieved. Mr. Strait had just climbed down from the back of a pickup truck where he'd harangued the crowd in Les Doux Subdivision and would be at *Lagniappe* in fifteen minutes.

Finally, he showed, and Brother called Evelyn out from the kitchen. The extra beads of sweat on her brow revealed that her husband's birthday wasn't her celebration, just meant more work. She set down a special banana mango cake in front of her husband, but before Brother led the group in "Happy Birthday" to himself, he unveiled his latest work. He'd captured the boss, for sure. Grey suit, graying hair, intense eyes behind big round glasses, hands snapping in half a yellow number two pencil.

Brother called out for champagne—on Mr. Strait's tab, of course.

Tonight's *lagniappe*—the little something extra in the bowl at the cash register—was a homemade chocolate candy, not in the shape of an Easter bunny but of Lady Justice. Creating that little favor had probably taken all of last Sunday and had put another ribbon of sweat across Evelyn's forehead.

INVESTIGATING WITH DEUCE

Deuce picked me up in a patrol car. The green-leaf air freshener hanging from the rear-view mirror did little to mask the odor of a thousand drunk-runs wafting from the back seat. I could fit on the passenger's side, but only because I'm small. A computer screen hanging from the lowest point on the windshield, angled to the driver, filled up the space between us. A stack of papers on the floor left little space for my feet.

"Does Detective Aymond ride with you often?" I asked, deadpan.

That brought a good chuckle from Deuce. "Naw. When it's the two of us, Buddy drives. I squeeze in over there. Maybe one day we'll get some new vehicles with all the techie stuff built in. Ever seen the inside of a State Police unit? Uptown. They even smell better."

We'd met briefly at the office last week. Deuce seemed very formal then, calling me Miss Aguillard. I'd praised the meticulous work he'd done on his investigation notebook, but he turned aside the compliment. Today he seemed a lot looser. I think he liked to be out in the field. I warmed to his big, open face, and I knew from the bulges under his shirt that wherever we went, no one would get very far trying to give us grief. Deuce turned onto

Captain Cade Road.

"So the Falgouts still live in the same place?" I asked.

"Yeah. DA's Victim's Assistance is renting a FEMA trailer for them until their insurance comes through. You can guess how that will work out—slowly. A fire is the worst disaster a home can have, you know, especially when you aren't around to save a thing. They'll never be able to replace what they lost, and of course a lot of what we treasure is irreplaceable."

We pulled up in front of a weedy patch of land. A mobile home shaped like a silver cigar-case perched twenty feet back from the road. Three piles of fire debris lay stacked at the rear of the tract. Concrete steps led up to a door in the side of the trailer, which shuddered under Deuce's knock. Jim Falgout appeared and showed us to a sofa on the far side. Deuce had to duck his head to avoid a collision with the light fixture dangling from the ceiling.

Lydia Falgout stretched out in a lazy-boy. A plaster cast swathed her left leg; her bandaged left arm crossed her chest. White gauze covered the left side of her face, but below the bandage, her lips opened in a broad smile. Lipstick, even. She held out her right hand. She said she had a dim memory of meeting Deuce and another detective in the hospital in Houston.

"The other guy was Detective Aymond, ma'am. This is Amanda Aguillard from the DA's office," Deuce said.

Hey! I liked the sound of that. Amanda Aguillard from the DA's office.

Deuce took charge of the conversation. "We never got back to you for a complete account of the events of last September. We'd like to go over the details."

She agreed, and let us run a tape. I opened my brief case and looked around for a spot for the device. Mr. Falgout jumped up to clear the end table at Mrs. Falgout's right.

"Let's start at the beginning. Can you remember what time of day this all began?"

"Not exactly. Mid-morning, I'd say."

"You heard a knock at the door, or did someone ring a doorbell?"

"A knock. My doorbell don't work."

"Did your door open in or out?"

"Opened in."

"And you recognized the person at the door?"

"Yeah. In the doorway. I recognized my good friend Remmy Richard. He lived with us when he and Jim came in from offshore. That dick-shit. Sorry, ma'am," she said in my direction. She shrugged her right shoulder. Her right eye—her only eye— didn't quite center.

"He spoke to you? Can you tell me what he said?"

"Not word for word, but he asked if Jim was home. I said he was offshore. He asked if he could do anything for me!" She rolled her eye. "Ha! How you like that? Wasn't that just so sweet of him to be asking. I said I was fine. He asked if I had enough money. Dumb me thought he was going to offer me a loan. I said I'd cashed Jim's paycheck so I had enough to last 'till he came in."

"I start to boil whenever I think about this." Jim Falgout interjected.

"Yeah. Then, whammo! Remmy pulls out a knife. He pushes it at me and says, 'Go get your damn money.' I couldn't believe it."

"Can you show me how he held the knife?" Deuce asked.

Mrs. Falgout made a fist with her thumb on top.

"Right hand?"

"Yeah."

"Kitchen knife? Pocket knife? Switch-blade? What did it look like?"

"Kitchen knife, I'd say. But not a big chef's knife. Medium size."

Deuce scribbled in his notebook. He must've started volume two because his first notebook rested in the security closet in Bonnie's office.

"OK. So you did what he asked?"

"Sure did. I went to the bedroom and picked up a couple hundreds I had in my bureau. I took my time because I was trying to think if I had any alternative. When I came back up front, whack! I got conked on the head and went out cold. I remember coming to and stumbling out of the house. I saw his truck down the driveway. I don't know what possessed me, but I just took off after it until I stumbled and fell down. He spun the truck around and headed right at me. Ran right over me, the fucker." Mrs. Falgout looked in my direction. "Sorry for my language, ma'am, but that's when my leg got crushed to smithereens. Then I think I remember him hitting me with something big. A tire iron maybe."

Deuce went back to get more details. "Before he pulled out the knife, did you notice anything unusual about him?"

"What do you mean unusual? He was just Remmy."

"Was he disheveled? Did he seem drugged up or anything?"

Mrs. Falgout laughed. "Well, Remmy never was Prince Charming. Same old jeans, same stringy hair. On drugs? I wouldn't know. He liked to smoke weed and have a few beers, but I couldn't say if he had anything special that day."

She didn't remember anything after she was run over and beaten. She woke up to feel the trooper picking leaves off her face, asking if she was OK."

"And during all this time, Remmy was alone?"

Mrs. Falgout hesitated, then said, "I didn't see anyone else, if that's what you mean."

Deuce turned to me, inviting my questions. Me? Could I do this right?

"Mrs. Falgout," I began, "Do you have pictures of your house you could show me?"

She shook her head. "Nope. We lost everything we had. Even my dogs—Jake and Lucky."

I could have bitten off the end of my tongue for that thoughtless question. Deuce nodded for me to continue.

"Could you tell us exactly where Remmy Richard was when you first saw him? Was there a porch, or did steps lead directly up to the door?"

"A porch ran all along the front of the house."

"Beyond the porch, could you see the vehicle he came in?"

"Yeah. I recognized his truck. A Toyota, I think. No, he had a Nissan. Well, I really don't know exactly. A beat-up white pick-up, that's for sure."

"Did you see anybody else, either in the truck or in the yard?"

"No. I don't think there was anyone else, but I was kind of looking at the back of the truck. He'd pulled up a way past the steps."

"OK. When you went back to the bedroom, where did he go?" She had a *how would I know when I wasn't there* look on her face. "I mean, was he right there when you came back?"

"I dunno. I never saw nobody. I just got bashed on the head and went down. When I came to, there was nobody around."

"So you didn't actually see him hit you?"

"No, but somebody sure as hell did. I saw stars, I guess you could say."

"How long were you out from that bash on the head? Can you guess?"

She paused and thought for a few seconds. "No. I just woke up on the floor and stood up. I went out the door and saw the truck going down the driveway. I took off after it—screaming bloody murder."

"Back up a minute. Did you notice what happened to the money you got from the back."

She laughed. "Hell, no. Maybe Remmy took it or it got burned up. No idea."

Of course. Not what she would think about at that point.

"So you ran out after the truck. Could you see the person who was driving?"

"Not really. I had blood streaming down my face. I assumed it was Remmy."

"Then I think you said the truck turned around and came back at you."

"Yeah. Sure did. Goddamned Remmy ran right over me. Sorry for my language, ma'am."

"You say Remmy ran over you? Could you see it was Remmy driving the truck?"

"Well, no. Remmy's truck ran over me, I should say."

"Did you see anyone else in the truck?"

"No, but I could barely see at all by then."

"OK. Then what?"

"I think I ran after the truck again, but I'm pretty fuzzy from then on. In and out. I think someone came after me with a tire tool in his hand and I got it again. Next thing I really remember was being under sticks and trash. Someone was talking. I was spitting out leaves and a few teeth. I hurt like hell."

Deuce had leaned back in the sofa, a smile widening his full lips. His round, deep brown eyes sparkled.

"Sorry, Deuce. I kinda got carried away," I said.

"You did good, Mandy." Now he used my first name. I think I just passed a test.

Deuce asked Mrs. Falgout what lay ahead for her. She said more surgeries. The leg was about as good as it was going to get except for rehab, and they'd about finished her arm, but she had a good way to go with the face. Eventually she'd get a glass left eye. Her right eye was cockeyed but they'd straighten it out pretty soon.

"They say my face is going to be just about like it was before. I told them they could at least make me prettier while they were at it."

One gutsy broad.

On the ride home, Deuce was complimentary.

"Have you taken a course in interrogation? Or are you a natural?"

"Thanks, but she didn't see anyone except Remmy, and she can't say one way or the other if there was anyone else. Tom will have a tough job proving a negative."

"Sarah will hammer reasonable doubt, but Tom will be prepared. Not even Sarah's going to get a bit more out of her than you did."

I could picture Mrs. Falgout coming through the back door of the courtroom, dragging her crippled leg all the way up the center aisle, past the jury, taking her seat in the witness box, and looking over at the jurors with half a face. She hardly needed to tell her story. If she said Remmy did that to her, the jury would believe he did. But could she say that?

Deuce returned to the subject of my questions to Mrs. Falgout, at least I guess that's what led him to talk about his future and mine.

"Have you ever thought about going to work for the FBI, Mandy?"

"What do you mean? I'm gonna be a lawyer."

"I know, but that's who the FBI wants to hire these days. I know because I've applied. They said if I had a law degree I could move right in."

"Your father had a fine career in the State Police. I thought you were headed there."

"They want me to put in a few more years with the sheriff first, and I don't know if I want to do that. I'm almost thirty. But back to you, Mandy. Let me plant a seed. Lawyers play games with one another and then put on a play for the jury. Investigative work is straightforward. You start with a crime and follow the evidence. Straight pursuit of the truth. Think about it."

I told him I would, but just to be polite. If I could, I'd be working for the DA. And Tom.

Now I had an opportunity to ask about Detective Aymond's story.

"Deuce, it happened before your time on the force, but Tom told me something about Detective Aymond and the Vermilion Parish bunkhouses."

Deuce jumped as if he'd taken a shot in the back. "What? He told you about Mary Jane?"

"No-o. Who's Mary Jane? He said Buddy did great undercover work that cleaned up the place but was bad for his marriage. Then he clammed up. What's the story?"

Deuce's face opened in a monster grin. "Miss Aguillard, I believe you need to get that bit of information from Tom."

Now I was really curious. Somehow the story went from kudos for Buddy's detective work, to the tragedy of his marriage, to something no one would tell me about. Who the hell was Mary Jane?

We were halfway back to the courthouse when I noticed Deuce's eyes make quick cuts from the rearview mirror to the side ones, back and forth.

"Is someone following us?" I asked.

"I think so."

I turned around to look out the back glass.

"Damn, Deuce. A white pick-up. No plate on the front."

"Yeah. Following way too close. He's an amateur. Hold tight and watch this."

Deuce slammed on the brakes, turned sharply to the right, and dove into a driveway. Hard surface, thank goodness, or we'd have spun out of control. The truck sped on by.

"Did you get a look?" I asked. "I was too busy just trying to hold on."

"License covered in mud. He'll be back in a minute." Deuce had that wide grin again.

"You're having fun! Why is someone following us?"

"Now that's a down side of being a cop. We get followed all the time. There's a whole universe out there listening to police radio, trailing our units, looking for anything exciting. Sometimes I oblige 'em. Don't tell my boys I do this. I won't even let them race their tricycles."

Deuce pulled the unit out of the driveway and backed in again so we could see the road through the windshield. Not two minutes later the white pick-up came sailing back past us.

Probably a man, but that's all I could say. The driver's window was as muddy as the license plate.

"He's gone. Another lesson in investigation, Mandy. Beware of paranoia."

* * *

Three days later, Tom and I completed putting together the first discovery package to deliver to the defense. My fear that Tom might not turn over everything had been unfounded, and I kicked myself for my doubts. True to his word, Tom had me copy Deuce's entire field notebook, tapes of our interviews, and every single statement he and Detective Aymond had taken. The only papers I didn't include in our package were our research notes. Privileged *attorney work product*, as it's known. Bonnie, the tech-savvy one, put almost all the material on a CD, and we were set for a conference with the defense. Sarah Bernard.

Sarah breezed into the DA's office like a star walking the red carpet at the Grammies. She kissed Bonnie on each cheek. Right, left, right. Three times—like a Parisienne. Rumor had it she took vacations over there with a French boyfriend. She moved quickly past the other secretaries, flashing a brilliant smile and a cool wave as she strode back to the library. She set down an alligator briefcase, pulled out the chair at the head of the conference table, and tossed back her thick blond French braid. God, she looked good.

Sarah had started out stunning to begin with. Flawless skin, long legs, stately carriage, clear emerald green eyes, but she also must have spent hours working on herself. Lean toned body, whitened teeth, French manicured nails. She knew how to apply mascara and just a touch of eye shadow, and she smelled good. Her outfit matched, even to the shoes a shade darker than her peach-colored suit.

I wore my usual office uniform of black pants and white shirt, jacket nearby in case I had to go into court. Damn. When Sarah crossed her legs, I swear Tom sucked in his breath to keep from drooling. Sarah struck first.

"Guys, as you have no doubt heard, my client says he was around for the attack on Mrs. Falgout but nowhere on the scene when Pierre Boudreaux took the knife. Didn't know about it beforehand nor until the next day, so he wasn't a principal either."

"Sarah, wake up and smell the coffee. The guy admitted guilt. He said he'd killed two people! The bunkhouse manager heard the same. As for Falgout, pretty hard for your client to give us the usual *another dude did it* when the surviving victim knew and named him."

Sarah uncrossed her long legs and then crossed them again in the other direction, moving slightly away from the table. Tom's eyes dropped to take in her maneuver. I bet she practiced.

"Take another look at that Falgout statement, Tom. Lydia Falgout saw my client come to her house but never saw the guy who hit her on the head and turned her into a pile of shit. Read it. Another *dude* really did do that."

"And tell me who that *other dude* might be? She never saw

anyone else. You have a name for me?"

"You have the burden, Tom. I just have to raise reasonable doubt, and I'm working on that. And I don't put much store in the meeting that took place at *The Southern Wave*. Cross-examination will be fun. The guys who spend onshore time in bunkhouses have no cred. Remember, I represented a bunch of defendants when Buddy helped shut those places down ten years ago. I've got the ammunition to give the jurors a history lesson."

What was that all about? The topic of Buddy and the bunkhouses kept coming up.

"Tell me how you explain away your client's admission that he killed Pierre Boudreaux?"

Sarah rounded her lips like little goldfish. Cute.

"Correction. Richard didn't really admit to *killing* anyone. He thought he was responsible for two deaths. Maybe because he provided the marks for robberies and the *other dude* used his car. My client swears to me he wasn't even on the Boudreaux job. Bottom line? You have no direct evidence and piss-poor circumstantials. I'm pumped for this one, Tom."

I was shaken. I'd already figured out Tom had weak evidence to prove first degree murder. Could the reason he had weak evidence be because the guy wasn't guilty?

Another thought took up space in my head—and scared me. If Remmy didn't do it, PawPaw's murderer was still out there. Were we safe?

Tom didn't show a speck of doubt.

"Remember, Mrs. Falgout recognized Remmy's pickup, the little Nissan, as the one at her house. Did you look at the lab report from Birmingham? Only Remmy's prints in the car."

"That's odd in itself, Tom? I bet all of 'em were fresh. How many prints do you think a good techie could get off your car? Lots, or at least those of the last guy who did the routine service. I'd say someone wiped the car down, and Remmy's prints are recent. After the fire."

"We'll have fun with all this, Sarah. But what's with this righteousness all of a sudden? You've told me before you never even ask your clients if they're guilty because if they are, they'll just lie. Guilt or innocence doesn't affect your work. You give your clients the very best defense you can dream up whether they're guilty or innocent. That's your job."

"I didn't ask Remmy if he did it. I didn't have to. He denied anything to do with Boudreaux from day one. And he insists. You know, Tom, once in a while we get someone who's innocent. We always need to pay attention to the possibility."

Tom blew off the idea. "We've done a lot of cases together. You're all about the deal."

That's what I'd heard about being a criminal defense lawyer. Ninety-nine percent of the clients are guilty of something. You just have to work to get them a good deal.

"Give it a try, Sarah. We might be able to take death off the table if..."

Sarah was adamant. "Never. I'm never going to be able to get this guy to take life."

"OK, Sarah. You do your job and I'll do mine." Tom put away the papers in his hand and reached for our file, volume two. "Here's the rest of the discovery. Richard is a very bad guy who was on a three-day alcohol and cocaine bender that drove him to do anything to get money for another fix. That's my case."

Sarah gave us that dazzling smile. "You have the burden, Tom. If you get a conviction, which I doubt, the jury will never give him death. I'll have strong mitigation for the penalty phase. I've got an expert who can tell us what the deadly combo of alcohol and cocaine does to the brain. Not enough for an intoxication defense on guilt/innocence—unfortunately, if you can stand up or drive a car you don't meet the threshold for that defense—but Richard's life story is going to curl the hair of every juror. Members of his family will tell us all about that. I've got my shit together on this one, Tom. Life's the worst he's likely to get."

Tom leaned back in his chair. "Sarah, I have Mrs. Falgout."

I know I saw Sarah flinch, but she kept her cool. "As they say, I'll see you in court."

Sarah left, our discovery in her alligator briefcase. No messy red accordion files for her.

Concern must have been all over my face. Tom gave me one

of his reassuring smiles.

"Welcome to the opening act of the drama. I know Sarah well. She's playing her cards. Her main goal is to get me away from even asking for the death penalty. And you know, I wouldn't mind doing that if I could get your family on board."

"Are you saying she really thinks her client is guilty of killing PawPaw? That she's just doing a dance for a deal?"

"I'd bet my life on it. Well, not maybe my life, but at least a few back rubs."

Tom patted my hand. A touch condescending. Hm-m.

"Something is bothering me, Tom. Remember the fireman who reported that Mrs. Falgout said, *Don't let them get me again* —plural. When I talked with Mrs. Falgout she didn't ever think there was anyone there except Remmy, and I didn't want to say too much, to put ideas into her head. I think the firemen misheard. We'd better talk to them and get that straight. Maybe what she said was *don't let him get me again. Him* sounds the same as *'em.*"

"Now you *are* thinking like a prosecutor, suggesting to the witness what he *really* heard."

Ouch. Tom changed the subject. "Anything special on for tonight, Mandy?"

"I promised Taddy I'd go to his soccer game at five. You sure can come too."

"I accept. And then dinner?"

"Yes."

The trial didn't leave Tom's thoughts for long. As we walked down to the parking lot he pulled out his cell phone and began to swirl through his contacts.

"We learned something from Sarah today. I'm going to get an investigator to do more digging to find Richard's family. I hear from Buddy the mother is round-the-bend crazy, but maybe Sarah has found someone else. We'd better look ourselves." Then he had another thought. "Sarah has to disclose to us the name of her expert witness on the effect of cocaine and alcohol. If he's that guy from Florida with the wacky institute, I don't think Judge Bonin is any more likely to accept him as an expert than the judges who knocked him out the last couple of times a defense lawyer tried to get him qualified. I'll be asking you to get the scoop on him and to absorb those dense papers he writes. I sure like the decision in the *Daubert* case. Until recently we had all kind of quacks paraded before our gullible juries. Now the judge decides if they're legit."

Did Tom plan to leave the defense with no expert? I thought I remembered hearing that could be a problem. A defendant has to be allowed to make some kind of defense.

* * *

"Tom, who's Mary Jane?"

"Mary Jane who? I don't know any Mary Jane."

"The Mary Jane who has something to do with Buddy Aymond. The mere mention of her name makes Deuce double over with laughter, and I think she's the reason you stopped dead in your tracks when telling me about Buddy's marriage breaking up after he cleaned out the Vermilion Parish bunkhouses."

"Oh, yes. Deuce is right. You do have the curiosity of a detective. But trust me. You don't want to know about Mary Jane."

"Oh, yes I do."

Maybe because we were both totally relaxed, sated with sex, good food, wine, happy with where we were with our case, whatever. Tom broke down and told me.

The first part of the story continued his account of Buddy's fine undercover work at the bunkhouses, and his success in getting a fourteen-year-old girl away from her pimp. But when she vanished, which is not uncommon, Buddy wouldn't give up.

"Half of the girls who run don't survive more than a year. Buddy felt responsible. For six months, he used every nonworking hour on the hunt. His wife misunderstood. He never found the girl, and she's probably dead by now."

I'd read Buddy wrong. He had a heart, after all. I had to remind Tom we hadn't gotten to Mary Jane.

"OK. Buddy continued to help the Vermilion deputies with their surprise monthly checkups at the bunkhouses, and everything seemed to be under control. Then one night..."

"Keep going, Tom."

"You asked for it. Buddy got to wondering about a lamb he kept seeing chained to a fence behind one bunkhouse called—I'll never forget it—*Old MacDonald's Barnyard.* No girls around anymore, of course, so the guys used a sheep. They named her Mary Jane."

"What? What are you saying? A sheep?"

"I told you, you didn't want to know about this."

"My god! That works?"

"Hell, I don't know. But you put guys out on the water for months at a time, then in an all-male bunkhouse when they're on shore, and they'll think of something."

When I recovered my cool, I got to thinking like a prosecutor.

"What charge do you bring for that, Tom? Aggravated Animal Cruelty?"

"Hell no. The DA couldn't let the story go public, be picked up by national news, and make us a laughing stock. He took a plea to some unknown misdemeanor with *parish line probation*— go away and don't come near Vermilion Parish ever again."

SISTER AGNES' JUBILEE

While Mom swept up the rust-colored blanket of fallen cypress needles on the patio, I answered the phone. "Aunt Mazie calling for you, Mom."

Mom scowled. She propped her broom against the railing.

"Doggone it. I bet someone told her we were going to New Orleans to see Aunt Mimi. Probably Tut. She's nicer than I am. Mazie's gonna want to come along."

"That's OK. We have four places in the car. You, Aunt Tut, me and now Aunt Mazie."

"That's OK for you to say. You'll have your hands on the wheel and your eyes on the road—an excuse not to have to listen to her. Tut and I'll be captives for three straight hours each way! I hope to heck she doesn't have some new ailment to tell us about." Mom sighed. "Oh my goodness, listen to me. On my way to see my holy aunt, and I've nothing but ugly thoughts. I might as well take a deep breath and face the inevitable."

Brushing her hands on her jeans, Mom picked up the phone, gave me a wink, and invited her sister to come along for the ride to Aunt Mimi's Golden Jubilee.

The Sisters of Mount Carmel are teaching nuns, and teaching clearly called PawPaw's younger sister Mimi. By the time she was twelve years old, she had become Mama B and PawPaw's best nanny for their brood of eight. Years later, the nieces and nephews never forgot their aunt's devotion. Aunt Mimi became *marraine*—godmother—to five of PawPaw's grandchildren, including me.

Aunt Mimi went to what they called the Normal School to study to be a teacher and then took her vows as Sister Agnes. The order first posted her to an orphanage in the northern Philippines. She returned home five years later, taking a position teaching second grade girls at Mt. Carmel Convent in New Iberia. Religious customs changed, but not Sister Agnes. She always wore a long black robe and white wimple, keeping traditional dress long after her fellow sisters changed to pastel polyester skirts with matching long-sleeved shirts.

Every few years the staff at Mt. Carmel lost nuns and gained lay teachers. When Sister Agnes retired, nuns no longer drilled arithmetic into the heads of little girls in brown plaid skirts quaking before chalk-covered blackboards.

According to the custom for retirement, she went to live at the mother-house in New Orleans. Within a year of the move, her health began to fail. The family wondered if she'd retired because of illness or the other way around. Perhaps she faded because she mourned the loss of the work she loved. We had no one to ask. Aunt Mimi belonged to the order, not to her family.

Mom and I picked Aunt Tut up in town, and the three of us had a good visit during the first part of the drive to New Orleans. We exchanged what we knew of family news and shared a few laughs. When we stopped in Houma to pick up Aunt Mazie, the mood soured.

"So, Tut," Mazie asked her back seat partner, "what's your daughter Eula Mae doing these days? Did she get back into college? Back into college? Or does readmission have to wait until next semester?"

I looked in the rear view mirror and saw Aunt Tut's upper lip stiffen.

"I'm not quite sure, Mazie."

"And how about Burt, Jr. Is Burt, Jr. doing OK?"

"He's just fine."

"I'm sure he is. Yes, I'm sure he is. There are wonderful treatments available today. Wonderful treatments."

One topic Aunt Tut wanted to discuss even less than her daughter Eula Mae's academic difficulties might have been Burt, Jr. getting busted. Then Mazie turned on Mom.

"Have you put on a few pounds, Mimi? Becoming on you, I think. You know, I always say we need a little more weight as the years go by. A little weight as the years go by, I say."

Does this woman eat bitter lemons for breakfast? My turn came next.

"Mandy, am I hearing you're our prosecutor Tom Barnett's latest fling? That man does indeed like to find 'em young, that's what he does. He's a good-looking fella, all right. Good looking. Young women just can't seem to resist his charms, although I don't much like the accent. Quite a north Louisiana drawl, he has."

Her comment stung. I caught my breath to cut off a response. Aunt Mazie kept at me.

"I suppose you'll hear the results of your Bar Exam pretty soon. Pretty soon now. And then I guess you'll stay around here with us at long as the romance lasts. Or maybe until our trial is over. Until the trial, right?"

I gripped the steering wheel and fixed my eyes on the road ahead. I heard Mom exhale. Mom and Aunt Tut were right. Poison. I could be grateful for one aspect of Aunt Mazie's chatter; since she didn't listen to anyone, no responses were necessary. In fact, she let the dig about my private life blow away in the wind. With hardly a pause to take a breath, she moved right on to disparaging comments about 'Tienne's wife and Ti Pierre's grandchild.

My stomach felt like I'd swallowed a bad oyster. Any normal man over thirty had some history. I expected that. I was only twenty-six and had my own. And I really didn't care anything about who Tom had been seeing before I came on the scene. But was I just another fling? Tom and I never talked about where our relationship might go. Did that mean something?

I pushed my questions down, out of sight, resolving to ignore Aunt Mazie's venom.

As I expected, the Golden Jubilee Mass for Sister Agnes warmed our hearts. In order for all the old sisters to attend, Mother Superior moved the service from the little chapel in the retirement home to the church next door. An attendant from the home, also retired, doing her duty as a geriatric nurse, rolled Sister Agnes' wheelchair right up to the altar rail. In praise of her lifetime dedication to children, the homilist preached on Jesus' words, "suffer the little children to come unto me," and "in as much as you have done it to the least of these..." He delivered a message far better than what we hear from our country priests.

Aunt Mazie sat enraptured, her hands folded across her breast, but I heard Aunt Tut whisper to Mom. "This priest is gettin' to me, sis. It isn't Aunt Mimi's funeral." To tell the truth, Sister Agnes looked as if it could be. Her little frame curled into her wheelchair, still and pale as a corpse.

The Mass over, Sister Agnes invited us to join her in her room while she took a rest. We entered a stark cubicle no more than ten feet square. Only a simple crucifix, a framed picture of Pope John Paul, and a statue of the Blessed Virgin—the Sacred Heart version with the droplets of blood on her breast—adorned the white walls. The attendant helped her to bed, pulled up a cover, and brought four straight wooden chairs in from the hall. No need to have seats in each room; few here had much company.

Mom, Aunt Lou, Aunt Mazie and I took our posts at bedside, in vigil over a devoted servant of God resting from a lifetime of prayer and service. She dozed off. The attendant slipped out, on the way assuring us that Sister Agnes would want to visit with us again when she awoke.

We waited. Not even Aunt Mazie dared to break the silence. We were surrounded by a faint scent of candles, and a strange calm prevailed. Mom closed her eyes; she looked as if she wished she could slip in beside her aunt. I pulled a book out of my purse and read to myself, frequently pausing to conjure up the natural world evoked by my new favorite poet, Mary Oliver.

An hour later, Sister Agnes opened her eyes and stretched out her arms to her nieces.

"Thank you for your patience, my dears. You minister well—the ministry of presence." She wanted a complete report on the family, inquiring about the health, occupations, and the happiness of each of PawPaw's children. Recalling the names of all of the grandchildren put her memory to a test. She passed.

"Are there any vocations?" she asked.

"Lay Eucharistic Ministers we have aplenty, but no priests or nuns," Mom replied.

"Without imports from other parts of the Catholic world, I fear for our future. Our schools have all lay teachers now, and I understand that in the country our priests must travel every Sunday to say Mass in several parishes. That cuts down on their availability for pastoral care. I've been blessed by a life of prayer and service and have wanted nothing else, but men and women today are not so inclined. Good people, mind you, but unwilling to take on the sacrifice of total commitment to serve Christ."

"Your life has been a blessing, Sister Agnes. A total blessing. Yes, your life has been a total blessing." Aunt Mazie again.

Aunt Tut put a hand over her eyes. "This time the cock crows thrice!" she muttered.

Sister Agnes changed the subject. "Tell me, my dears, about the man who performed that dreadful act on my brother. I hope you are praying for his soul."

Mom and Aunt Tut started and looked up quickly. Mom's left brow pulled toward her nose. Aunt Tut recovered her composure first. "Aunt—Sister Agnes, did you know that the person responsible for what happened—his name is Remuald Richard—will soon be going to trial? The police tell us there's no doubt about his guilt. He's admitted his responsibility."

"And so he *should* be tried, my dears. His responsibility for the death of my brother should be determined legally by the civil authorities."

Mom had the guts to take the next step. "One of the possible sentences the man could receive for first degree murder—that's the crime he's charged with—is the death penalty. The district attorney has hinted to us that whether he will ask the jury to impose that sentence depends on what the family wants."

"Human life is a gift from God, my dears. Only God decides when this life is over. I hope you're very clear to your district attorney about that. We cannot teach killing is wrong by asking for killing in return."

I expected that to be her opinion.

Mom responded. "Not everyone in the family thinks that way, Aunt Mimi. Ti Pierre, for example, is adamant. He believes PawPaw would want us to avenge his death." Mom's voice quivered, and she forgot to call her aunt 'Sister Agnes.'

"In that case, I will pray for Ti Pierre as well, my dears. And so should you."

And please pray for a few more of us.

Sister Agnes wilted. Her eyes glazed over; her chin dropped. Mom glanced at Aunt Tut, who nodded in agreement with the silent message. We needed to leave the old one to her rest. Mom and Aunt Tut stood up, stepped softly forward, and touched their lips to their aunt's forehead. Aunt Mazie and I followed. The attendant outside the door must have been listening for the scrape of our chairs. She came into the room and adjusted the pillows on the bed.

We'd all been full of joy during the Mass, but now Mom had the courage to speak about our thoughts.

"Where are you on all this, Mazie. Would you be in favor of asking the district attorney to let Remuald Richard plead to life in prison?"

"Me? Oh, me. Oh, my," Aunt Mazie sputtered. "I leave such matters to Ti Pierre. Yes, let the oldest son in the family make the decision for all of us. That kind of decision is not for us. No, No. Not for us to decide. Men decide those things." Her words kept rhythm with the quick tapping of her steps.

I could just about feel the steam coming from Mom's ears. Her words tumbled out. "There's one thing I'm absolutely sure of, my dear sister. We girls have as much right to have an opinion on this subject as anyone. In fact, we have an obligation." Mom turned to me. "Let me drive home, Mandy," she said. "Tut, sit in the front. We have some talking to do."

When Mom gave crisp instructions, I always obeyed. And so did Aunt Tut. Before we left the city, Aunt Mazie had fallen asleep on the other side of the back seat. I thanked God for that mercy.

"How about you, Tut? I'd like to know. Where are you on this?" Mom asked.

"I've been doing some thinking, of course. Aunt Mimi's— Sister Agnes'—words touched me. Human life *is* a gift from God. But there's something else on my mind. Remember before little Jeanne-Claire was born, when my daughter Eugenie was in the maternity hospital in Dallas and I went over to be with her?"

"Sure. I remember. All of us were so happy to get the news Genny was expecting after eight years of marriage, and we got down on our knees in thanksgiving," Mom answered.

"Did I ever tell you about visiting the neonatal unit?" Aunt Tut asked.

"Not that I remember. Tell me."

Aunt Tut took a deep breath. "It's kind of a long story but explains some things. Precious little Jeanne-Claire has a special place in my heart, you know. When my sons had babies I was excited, of course, but nothing prepares you for all the emotions you have when your daughter becomes a mother for the first time. It's all part of that mother/daughter bond. You'll learn about that when Mandy becomes a mother." She turned around in her seat and gave me a smile.

Mom prodded her sister to tell her story. "Go ahead. We've got miles to go."

"As you may remember, everything went well for Genny the first twenty weeks of her pregnancy, but then she threatened to miscarry. When Charlie called, I jumped in the truck and drove over to Dallas. By the time I arrived, the crisis had passed. I'd overreacted. I visited for a day, and drove home. Genny and her husband have busy lives, and I didn't need to be in the way. But at about twenty-five weeks, Genny's problems began again. The doctor put her on bed rest with a fancy monitor on her barely rounded belly. Time and again, in the middle of the night, they tore across town to get to the neonatal emergency room. After the fourth nighttime rush, and the fourth all clear, Charlie agreed with the doctor they couldn't risk the distance. He checked Genny in for the duration, and we prayed she'd be there to term. Each morning the nurses took her for an ultrasound. During the day she rested, read, did crossword puzzles, and waited for the evening when Charlie would come to visit after work. The emergencies continued, and passed. She didn't tell me about most of them."

I was too young to remember, so I was interested in the story. Aunt Tut said she went for a visit and to do her daughter's Christmas shopping. When she walked into Genny's room, she found her perfectly relaxed, glowing like any other expectant mother in her sixth month, only this prospective mother lay flat on her back in a hospital bed. And then Genny admitted that just the night before she'd had a period of contractions. The doctor had feared she wouldn't carry until the morning. When Dr. Melancon, the neonatal specialist, made his rounds, Tut asked him what would happen if the baby came at that point. Genny had hit it off with the doctor right away. He'd grown up in Iberia Parish. The nurses teased Genny about him all the time, said she was the only one who could understand his talk. They couldn't even pronounce his name. Trying to soothe Aunt Tut with information about the facilities the hospital had to offer, Dr. Melancon gave her a pass to go down to the NICU, neonatal intensive care unit. He thought she'd feel a lot better about everything if she saw the care they had available for premature babies.

Tut continued her story. "Charlie said he'd like to go with me. Thank God. We got in the elevator to ride down the twelve floors to NICU and noticed right off the bat the big red label over the button for the basement. NICU-NO VISITORS. We pressed the button anyway. When the door opened, we faced a closed double door again labeled in red. ADMITTANCE BY PASS ONLY. We pushed on through. One of the nurses stood up and came toward us.

"'Hello there,' she said, a warm smile changing her expression to a welcome. 'Dr. Melancon asked me to show you around. My name is Gloria.'"

Aunt Tut said that except for the clear plastic tents over the little baby baskets, the room looked very much like any hospital nursery. Gloria told her these babies would be going home in just a few days. Then they went on to the second room.

"In this room," Aunt Tut said, "a spaghetti of tubes snaked out from under each tented bassinet, some ending on a night stand and some leading straight overhead to a grate in the ceiling. Gloria took pride in the work going on here. She chatted cheerily as we approached each crib, but at the sight of the little bodies lying naked under plastic, I squeezed my son-in-law's arm and swallowed hard. I felt faint. Oblivious to my anxiety, Gloria continued her chatter.

"She said these babies were all in warmer beds. Tubes reached into the overhead heater. Their skin was immature, and they had very little body fat. Most of them were still on ventilators to help their breathing. She pointed out one who had come in six weeks before, weighing just over three pounds. They had started to wean him from some of the equipment, and he'd be moving out to the other room in a few more weeks, maybe sooner. He was able to swallow, so he could handle a feeding tube in his mouth rather than his belly. He was doing beautifully, Gloria said. Doing beautifully? The tiny body lay on his back, buck naked, limbs twitching. I watched him push out his arms and legs. Instinct. No personal trainer had to tell him to do his exercise, to use it or lose it! A wide blue bandage covered his eyes. 'What about his eyes?' I asked Gloria. 'Oh,' my guide chirped in response. 'His eyes are still sensitive to light.'

"Charlie and I followed Gloria down the row of bassinets. She chatted on about how they were monitoring blood pressure, heart rate, breathing, temperature. At several of the cribs a nurse reached her arms into the sides of the tent so she could tend to the little occupant. Covered fingers stroked the quivering chests —the only affectionate contact the little ones could receive. I couldn't help thinking of the racks of books new mothers read about the critical importance of early touching and nurture. What if all a baby receives is an occasional latex-gloved fingertip on his chest? What does that mean for their emotional health? I asked Gloria if they'd be alright, and she told me they might have a few little problems here and there, but the little ones fight like tigers to stay with us. That expression stuck with me, Mimi. They fight like tigers to stay with us."

Aunt Tut said Genny's husband hadn't had much to say, but now he asked how old these babies were when they were born. Gloria told him they were mostly twenty-eight weeks or more. The drugs today made a tremendous difference, she said. President Kennedy's premature baby had hyaline membrane disease from not-yet-developed lungs. Unheard of now. Corticosteroids mature a baby's lungs in as short a time as twenty-four hours.

"Charlie steered me back to the central station. We turned to the third spoke from the hub. We had to put on a gown and mask to enter this room, a nurse at the door helping us into green shrouds. We could only take a few steps inside. Here each bassinet station had not one but three nurses in attendance, and these nurses didn't sit on stools. They bent their backs over their little charges. Gloria said most of these little ones were born at twenty-three, twenty-four weeks, weighing less than two pounds. She said most of them would do quite well. I couldn't believe it.

"They were pitiful. Mimi. My throat closed, and I felt a wave of heat. I mumbled something beneath my mask, and Charlie pulled me to the door. 'Thank you so much Gloria,' he said. 'We'll be going now.' He led me to the cafeteria, found me a coke, and handed me a wet napkin for my throat. Fifteen minutes later we returned to Genny's room with optimism pasted on our faces.

"So why am I thinking about all this now, Mimi? I'm remembering those little ones fighting as hard as they could to stay alive. Shouldn't we have the same fight for life? I also remember another thought I had then. When Genny's baby was born at term, perfect in every way, I remember my vow. Charlie and I held those little fingers and swore to each other that if anyone ever harmed this precious child, we wouldn't rest until that person had paid the just price. Should I do the same for PawPaw? Make sure that his killer pays? Mimi, I'm torn."

Like Uncle Etienne, Aunt Tut was probably another of the siblings whose opinion about the death penalty depended on a back story, and which part of the back story floated to the top of consciousness at the moment of decision. The possibility an innocent person might be put to death haunted Aunt Dora. Sister Agnes opposed the penalty even for the truly guilty. Where was I on the question?

With a catch in her voice, Mom spoke to her sister.

"Tut, I'll confess to you that in the very beginning, when we didn't know who did that to PawPaw, I was vengeful. I was really just scared the person might come after someone else in the family, return to the scene of the crime and all that. But once he went to jail, and we knew he wouldn't get out no matter what the jury decided on the penalty, I just didn't care one way or the other."

Aunt Tut took a good while to respond.

"If you speak out to let the DA make a deal for life, Mimi, I'd stand with you. Sister Agnes persuaded me. I know what Ti Pierre will have to say about that, but I don't care."

"And poor Bub, too. The pursuit of vengeance may be what's keeping him going."

"Perhaps, but maybe keeping him from moving on."

What should I tell Tom about this conversation? I could say there was some sentiment among my aunts and uncles for asking for a plea deal. No. It wasn't fair to put me in the middle.

* * *

We dropped Aunt Tut off in town and drove out to the lake. As soon as we were alone in the car, Mom brought up the subject of Tom.

"Hon, I'm sorry Mazie gave you one of her poison darts this morning—commenting on Tom's past history."

"That's OK, Mom. She's just like that."

"I want to say a couple things, even though you may think I'm butting in."

"Go ahead, Mom."

"I really like Tom, and he's been very kind to all of us at a difficult time. And I admit to going off into thoughts of you staying here, maybe even living right on the lake next door in PawPaw's house. If Tom came into our family, that would be more likely,"

I'd be lying if I said I hadn't had the same thought. Many a night I fantasized about what Tom and I could do with the old place.

"He's given you an amazing professional opportunity, opening the door for you with the DA. I appreciate that. But... Here goes." She took a breath. "I wonder if you're being carried away. More sophisticated man, a prosecutor. Also, to use a very old fashioned term—but one that has meaning—I hope he has serious intentions."

Mom was correct the first time. I didn't want to hear this.

"We're fine, Mom. At this point I don't think either one of us has what you call 'serious intentions.' I'll let you know if and when we do."

But Mom underlined a thought throbbing in my head—when I was rational enough to get beyond the euphoria of our exciting relationship. Tom never did talk about our future. Perhaps Aunt Mazie was onto something. Was I just his latest fling?

We pulled onto the road that skirts our side of the lake. Up ahead, parked in front of our house, was Tom's black truck. My pulse quickened. The prospect of being with him chased away all my musings and misgivings. Right then I just wanted to see his face.

Wait. Tom shouldn't be at the house. When we talked the previous night we'd agreed I'd see him at the office Monday morning. He'd have material for me to look at for the pretrial motions set to be argued the following week. And what was all that commotion I saw farther up the road, toward the long driveway to the Jefferson House? Blue lights flashing. Concentrating on making the left turn into our driveway, Mom probably hadn't seen the lights.

"Look, Mandy. Tom's here," she said. "Maybe he'd like to come on in and have a beer. It's been a long day. OK if I ask him?" She rolled down her window.

Mouth set in a grim line, Tom spoke before I could answer. "Mrs. Aguillard, Taddy had a pretty bad scare this afternoon. He's not hurt. Really, he's fine. He's inside the house with his dad. But I know you'll want to go in and be with him."

"What is it? What happened?"

"They're both fine, really, but he and his cousin Jay stumbled on a body when they were walking along the lakeside, down from the Jefferson House."

"What? What are you saying?"

Tom took Mom's arm and walked with her to the door.

PART III

ANOTHER BODY

Mom caught her foot on the car doorsill, wobbling like a spindly plant in a strong wind.

"What? Taddy *stumbled* on a body? What are you saying?"

Tom reached out and caught her just in time. "They'll tell you inside, Mrs. Aguillard. The boys happened onto a pretty grim sight over at the Jefferson House. Scared them good."

"Oh my God. Oh my God. Poor Taddy."

Mom broke from Tom's grasp and ran up the walk to the front door.

I clutched at Tom's arm. "What do you mean? A body? A dead body? Who is—was—it?"

Tom's circled my shoulder and held tight.

"Nothing to do with any of us, Mandy. Detective Washington knows who he is—was—and says the guy was part of a drug operation in Lafayette. Let's go inside. Taddy had a fright, but you'll feel better when you see him. Strong kid. Then we can go on over to Jefferson House."

Tom and I drove up the long gravel drive from the Lake Road up to the house, parked, and walked around to the shell lane leading down to the dock. I hadn't suggested taking the shorter route by the footpath along the shore. With the light already beginning to fade, I feared we'd end up stumbling back in the dark. No telling what was out there. Or who.

At the dock, a crowd had gathered just outside a sixty square foot patch cordoned off with yellow crime scene tape. Muscular guys in tight black T-shirts, FBI stenciled in huge yellow letters on their backs, outnumbered the local deputies. Bright white coats of the forensics teams dotted the assemblage. Everyone wore gear for a crime scene—booties and gloves.

Detective Aymond spotted us and beckoned us over. Tom and I walked toward the object of everyone's attention. Detective Aymond lifted the tape to let us into the theater of operations where spotlights from the sheriff's jacked-up 4x4s lit the scene like high noon.

"Do we have ID on the vic here?" Tom asked.

"Shit, yes. He is—was—the confidential informant Deuce recruited for the big federal drug operation. You remember when Deuce missed our meeting last week because Lafayette called him to help out?"

"Yeah, I remember. And you stopped me from climbing the sheriff's ass about letting Deuce go."

"Well, the CI failed to show up for work the day he was supposed to meet the shipment of lettuce coming from Texas. You know, the lettuce packed with cocaine. He hasn't been heard from since. Now he turns up like this. Bullet in his brain."

"Then the dead guy really is—was—Deuce's inside informant?" I asked.

"Yup. Name: Glen Mitchell. Age 24. Deuce is wiped out about it. The major operation was ninety percent successful. DEA nabbed the guys working the transfer unit in northern Mexico, and the FBI got the truckers at the Houston company that took the goods across the border. We shut down the wholesale distributors in five locations in Texas and southwest Louisiana. Close to fifty people have federal charges now, but right when we were closing in on the Lafayette distributor, our key inside CI goes AWOL. Big shit storm. We had to scrub the rest of the Lafayette operation. You remember the day. But for once, at least, we got most of the main players."

And had one casualty. I didn't want to look at the spot where everyone clumped together.

Buddy's voice had lowered at least two keys. He relished his role as our guide to the excitement.

"Cause of death?" Tom asked.

"The coroner's still working on that, but so far looks like the guy took a bullet in the center of the forehead—in the front, then out the back, gangland style. Big piece. Maybe .25 Beretta Bobcat. Could be the Juarez cartel or Los Zetas. That's their MO."

"And Taddy and Jay found him," I mumbled. "God!"

My legs felt like spaghetti, and my stomach roiled. I caught sight of Deuce leaning against one of the sheriff's vehicles, shoulders slumped, eyes on the ground. I picked him for my exit plan. I ducked under the tape and walked toward him.

"Deuce, I'm really sorry about this."

"A real fucker." He looked up at me. "Sorry about my language. Really decent young guy, wife and kids. One big mistake put a serious drug distribution charge hanging over his head. He was looking at maybe twenty years, then I came along and talked him into this."

I leaned up against the vehicle, by Deuce's side, hoping my company provided some sympathy. Sister Agnes had taught me that when you don't know how to comfort, just be there. I needed support myself, and sought it from the presence of Deuce. I could see Buddy strutting around the crime scene, chest puffed out, rolling his shoulders. Damn! He was enjoying himself.

"How are the boys doing?" Deuce asked me. "Must have been quite a shock for them."

Deuce had just lost his CI and yet thought to ask about the boys. Buddy Aymond hadn't. I'd softened on Buddy when I heard about his search for the girl from the bunkhouse, but I think I'd called it right to start with. Personal problems or not, he was a jerk.

"The boys are OK, Deuce. Thanks for asking."

"You know, half our drug busts rely on the work of CIs we recruit to work off charges. I hate the practice, really, but this time we weren't going after just one poor schmuck. We had a major distribution operation to shut down. I persuaded Mitchell to go for the deal the feds offered. I told him they'd be monitoring everything. Well, they lost him. Thank God this is the last time I get into this, now that I've moved over to detectives."

Deuce's breath wheezed in and out. I waited.

"That white boy trusted me. Plea of guilty, cooperate in setting up the Lafayette bust, and he'd be in line for a probated sentence with a real possibility the conviction could come off his record. Most important, he could return to his family." Deuce pressed his hand to his forehead. "I led him to his death, and now I've got to go see his wife."

Deuce stood up, turned around, drew in a deep breath, and a shudder rippled through his torso. When I saw him clench his right fist and face the black-and-white he'd been leaning on, I shrank away. Instead of punching the door as I expected, he reached for the handle, pulled open the door, and climbed inside. Before closing the door, he raised his head and looked straight at me.

"Cracking this case just went to the top of my list, whether my boss goes for it or not." His face set, he said one more word. "Thanks."

Seeing a dead body couldn't be nearly as bad as facing the family of the man you set up to die. If Deuce could go do what he had to do, at least I could look at the crime scene. I walked down to the dock and back under the tape to where Detective Aymond stood with one of the FBI agents, close to the body. My throat closed to block out the sweet smell of rotting flesh. I still hadn't really looked. I pictured Taddy on the path, leading his pal Jay. Two carefree kids.

"Detective, is that where the boys found the body? Right by the dock?" I asked, trying to tend to business.

"Yes ma'am," the FBI agent replied for him. Of course he did. Once the FBI takes on a case, the locals get outranked and have to yield. "Not a pretty sight. The coroner says he's been there a couple days. Dogs, rats maybe, got to the face, and who knows what got to the legs hanging in the water."

I dropped my eyes for a quick peek. Half a face, wiggling with critters. A white coated man bent over the body, expressionless, studying the head with no more emotion than a master gardener who'd found a new shoot on a rose bush. I squeezed my eyelids together, closing out the sight. A couple of seconds and I'd seen enough to fuel my nightmares for weeks to come.

I took a few steps to where Tom chatted with a man in camo, gathering information in a cool professional manner. Would I ever be able to do that? I willed myself to stand upright, although I could have made good use of a nearby tree trunk to lean on.

"Was he killed right here or just dumped?" Tom asked.

"Probably killed right here. We haven't picked up any drag marks, but we haven't found the bullet either, and there's some compromise from whatever dined on the body. The forehead entry wound is bloodless, and the exit on the back of the head sent blood pouring down onto the rocks. We need time to look at all the evidence, Mr. Barnett. We'll be in touch."

Agent Taylor came over and handed business cards to Tom and to me. I felt relief when Tom said we needed to go. I'd made it through without puking.

Back at the house, we found my Dad sitting alone in the living room. The TV screen flickered, but he'd muted the sound. His shifting eyes told me he wanted to talk to me one-on-one, without Tom. I took Tom's arm and steered him out to his truck.

"Tomorrow, Tom. I'll meet you at your house and you can get me started preparing the pretrial motions set for next week."

Tom tipped up my chin for a long, sweet kiss. Just what I needed. His strong arms encircled me and I clung to him, absorbing strength, until I felt calm. The hell with Aunt Agnes and her poisonous comments. I loved this guy.

"Come sit here a minute, Mandy." Dad patted a spot next to him on the sofa. "Your mom is upstairs with Taddy, and they're probably both asleep by now."

"Is Taddy OK?"

"He's all right, but that's what I want to talk to you about. Your Mom and I just had a big fight about how to deal with this."

"Fight? You and Mom never have a big fight."

The worst I'd ever seen amounted to no more than a few extra words from Mom and Dad's upper lip stiffened into a tight line.

"I guess you'd say we had a disagreement rather than a fight, but the way we usually handle problems isn't working for this one. We talked and talked, but at the end we still had a difference of opinion about what to do."

"About what? What's the problem?"

Dad shifted his weight on the cushions.

"Let me tell you how this played out. I'd just gotten home this afternoon when Taddy and Jay came tearing back from the lake. Jay was shaking; Taddy just looked dazed. He stammered out that he'd stumbled over a body at the Alexanders' dock. First thing I did was call 911." Dad raised his face to me, coming close to a smile. "I'd never done that before. I'm usually on the other end of that conversation. Then I called Aunt Mathilde to come pick up Jay. The boys didn't want to talk so I just sat here with them and waited. Mom had called home when you dropped off Mazie so I knew you'd be here soon. The boys had calmed down by the time Aunt Mathilde drove up, about the same time as the sheriff's patrol answered the 911. All OK, so far."

"OK. And then?"

"The boys told their story to the sheriffs. They'd run into a body by the dock. Actually, Taddy told the story; Jay just sat there chewing on his fingers. After Aunt Mathilde took Jay home, and the cops had left, and you and Mom weren't back yet, I was here alone with Taddy. That's when he told me more." Dad ran his tongue over his upper teeth. "He said he'd seen a man. A *live* man."

"What? Somebody else was out there? I haven't heard anything about anybody but the dead man. This is really important, Dad."

"That's what I say, Mandy, but Taddy said we couldn't tell anyone. The man had grabbed him by the arm and said if he told anyone he'd end up just like that body."

"Jesus! So you did tell Mom, of course. What did you two disagree about?"

"Mom says we can't let the detectives know. Tell one person and everybody knows, she says, and there's nothing to be gained since Taddy doesn't know anything about what went on over there. He couldn't identify the man because he didn't really see him."

"The detectives would be the FBI. Once the FBI is on a case, they're in charge. I gather you think we should tell them."

"You bet I do. They'll know what to do with the information. Maybe nothing, but we shouldn't handle this on our own. I know Mom's thinking first of Taddy and doesn't want him in danger, but what do we know about dealing with something like this?"

Then Dad surprised me with how cool he'd been.

"Mom wanted me to just leave Taddy alone, but I went back to his room and asked if he'd ever seen the man before. He said no. Could he describe the man? He couldn't. The man grabbed his arm, said what he said, and disappeared. I think Taddy was on the run by then. So Mom's right; Taddy couldn't ID him. But here's what's bothering me. The man may not know that."

That roiling gut I'd felt down at the lake started up again.

"I think just being in contact with the man puts Taddy in danger. The man has no way of knowing if Taddy could finger him. He might think he shouldn't take any chances."

Oh, my God. Dad was right on. Would the man come after Taddy just to keep him quiet? I let my mind think of the consequences of the two possible courses of action. Tell or not tell.

"This is really scary. We don't know what we're dealing with. You know, the FBI thinks the dead man took the hit from a Mexican drug cartel."

Dad dropped his face into his hands. I flipped open my phone. Dad looked up, startled. He thought I was about to call the detectives on my own.

"No, Dad. I'm not calling anyone. Just checking the time. It's almost midnight, and Mom and Taddy are no doubt sleeping by now. Taddy is safe in bed and we're right here. I don't know how much you and I will sleep, but let's try. Tomorrow morning, first thing, we'll take this up again with Mom." I stood up and kissed his forehead. "Goodnight, Dad."

"'Night, Hon." He didn't make any move to go to bed.

I turned off my light but not my mind. Why all this criminal activity in our sleepy neighborhood? First PawPaw, then the shed break-in by the homeless man, now a body. Could all these events be connected? One thing I'd come to believe, most coincidences aren't. Something was going on. What could possibly tie all this together?

I considered calling Tom to talk it through. No. Tom's priority these days was getting ready for the trial. He'd pause long enough to look at another crime scene, but that was about it. This was a problem for our family, and my little brother headed my list of concerns. I dozed off and on. With morning came one clear thought. Dad was right. We were in over our heads. We needed the professionals on the job. I found Dad sitting on the sofa exactly where I had left him the night before.

Mom had a hard time accepting our viewpoint. She paced around the kitchen table while we pleaded our case. Eventually, the argument that Taddy would be safer with the FBI calling the shots won her over. I called the number on Agent Taylor's card.

"Taddy is eight years old? The first forensic interview of a child is critical, but we don't have the luxury of waiting for a specialist to come from Baton Rouge or New Orleans. Detective Washington has been through some forensic interview training, including interviewing children. He can be at your house in a couple of hours."

Deuce and Agent Taylor arrived in less than an hour.

Deuce began very slowly, quietly talking to Taddy about the lake. Agent Taylor stayed in the background. Before long, Taddy told Deuce about fishing with his grandfather, where they kept their poles, the best place to dig for worms, how he cast his line. "We get bream once in a while, but mostly catfish too small to eat. We throw 'em back." After maybe ten minutes, Deuce's conversation—not really questions—led Taddy to describe the route they'd taken along the shore from PawPaw's bulkhead to the Jefferson House dock. At first they splashed in the water. I could picture it; exposed shells made a bed firm enough to walk on almost all the way.

"Does your mom fuss about you getting your shoes wet?"

Deuce gave Taddy a smile to go with the puff question.

"Not Mom. But Jay's mom does."

"So did you walk side by side with Jay? Or one of you in front of the other?"

"I walked ahead."

"What did you two talk about, do you remember?" Deuce asked.

"I don't know. Maybe some about those dinosaur birds—the pelicans that came in before the storm. Not much, really. We hadn't talked for awhile 'cause Jay was behind me."

"Did you stay in the water, or did you go up onto the path?"

"We'd just left the water and were on the path when..."

"When?"

"I bumped into something?"

"Tell me about that."

Taddy's right hand gripped the arm of his chair.

"The body lay across the path, the legs in the water. I almost fell over his head."

"What did you do?"

"Nothin'. I guess I froze."

"And then?"

"I saw a guy standing there, lookin' at me."

"Was the guy ahead of you, toward the dock? Or was he on your right, up the slope toward the house?"

"He was just kind of right there. On the right, toward the house, I guess."

"And I think you told your dad he touched you."

Taddy swallowed. "He grabbed me. Grabbed my arm."

"OK. And he spoke to you?"

"Yeah."

Deuce waited. He wasn't going to put words in Taddy's mouth. After a pause, Taddy squeaked out what the man had said. "'You tell anyone you saw me here and you'll end up like that body.'"

"Is that the only thing he said?" Deuce asked, slowly.

"That's all I heard. I guess I just turned around and started to get out of there. Jay was behind me, and I ran smack into him."

"Did Jay see the man too?"

"No. He was back a ways when the man talked to me. He didn't know why we had to run. I had to make him go."

"Tell me this, do you think the man saw Jay?"

Taddy paused a moment before answering. "No. I don't think he could've. Jay was too far back."

Mom had put a couple bottles of water on the coffee table in front of us. Deuce picked up one and took a long sip.

"Taddy, tell me what the man looked like. Can you describe him?"

"Not really. I heard him more than saw him. He was just kind of in the bushes there."

"White man or black?"

"White, I think."

"Anything noticeable about him? Bearded face? Very tall or short? A hat maybe?"

"I didn't notice anything like that, but I just didn't look at him good."

"Any idea how old?"

"No. Not an old man or anything. I didn't notice nothin' special. When he spoke to me, I just tried to run out o' there and get Jay to get a move on."

"OK, how did he sound? What about his voice? Did he talk like someone from around here?"

Taddy turned to Deuce. A shadow of puzzlement crossed his face. "No. He talked funny."

"What do you mean by 'talked funny?' Did he have a foreign accent?"

"No. He just talked real slow. I guess a kind of a drawl. He didn't talk like we do."

Deuce leaned forward. "Could you imitate how he talked?"

"No-o. I'm no good at that. Just real slow. Kind of like 'baw-dee.' 'You'll end up like that baw-dee.'"

Deuce let it go. "Taddy. You've been a terrific help to us. I thank you very much."

"Can I go now?" Taddy asked.

"You bet."

Taddy stood up. Deuce stood up also and put his arm around Taddy's shoulders. Taddy let himself receive the slight hug, then walked quickly down the hallway to his room. In a second he came back out carrying his jacket, ran onto the porch, out into the yard, the porch door slamming behind him. I figured he was on his way down to the lake.

"Mr. and Mrs. Aguillard, you have a fine kid there. I want to confer with Agent Taylor for a minute, and then tell you what we think we should do next. OK?"

Deuce nodded to Agent Taylor to go with him to the porch. Mom, Dad, and I sat in silence. I was amazed my brother was so cool.

A few minutes later the screen door on the porch slammed again. Taddy reappeared. Odd. For Taddy, a visit to the lakeshore usually lasted until we called him in.

"Everything OK, Taddy?" Mom asked.

"Yes, ma'am." He threw the words over his shoulder. He grabbed the video game controller from the coffee table and scurried back to his room. From that morning on, I don't remember Taddy going down to the lake again for a long time.

Agent Taylor and Deuce came back into the living room. Agent Taylor took the lead.

"Mr. and Mrs. Aguillard, Detective Washington and I have the same impression. Our thoughts are preliminary, you understand, but the nature of our business requires us to make a decision about what to do even though we don't know all we'd like to."

Dad drew his lips into a stiff line. Mom's face creased with worry.

"I guess you're aware that the victim—the body—was a confidential informant working for us in a major narcotics investigation. All indications are that a professional hit man killed him. From what we know now, the man Taddy saw last night by the body was *not* a professional. A professional hit man wouldn't stick around after doing something like that, and he wouldn't speak in an unprofessional way, probably wouldn't speak at all. Who he was, why he was there, we don't know, but we both think his so-called 'threat' to Taddy was more of a smart-aleck comment than a warning of consequences."

"Are you saying Taddy isn't in any danger from any of this?" Mom asked. She wanted an answer to the big question—was Taddy safe?

"That's our view right now. The professional killer is probably long gone. He had an assignment, finished it, and left. We don't know why the other man, the one who spoke to Taddy, was there, but what he said sounds more like he was trying to scare a young boy. An idle threat."

Mom closed her eyes and mumbled, "Thank you, Jesus."

Dad's shoulders dropped as worry drained from his body. He sat back on the sofa.

"Yes, Mr. and Mrs. Aguillard, that's our opinion, but I assure you we aren't going to take any chances. We'll be keeping a close check on the boys to make sure they stay safe."

Deuce added, "I strongly advise you not to talk to anyone about this."

Thank God he said that. We sure didn't need second-guessing from all the family.

Deuce took over with some questions for Dad.

"The people who own the Jefferson House are from Tennessee, right Mr. Aguillard?"

"Yes. The Alexanders."

"You know them, pretty well, I suppose?"

"Not well. PawPaw knew them best. In the summer they often have guests who have children. Then Taddy has kids to hang with. We hear the house is for sale now. In any case, we don't expect them down here until Easter."

I wondered if I should mention on the Sunday afternoon, before PawPaw went missing, Taddy thought he saw someone on the dock. Before I decided whether to do so or not, the conversation had moved on.

"Do the Alexanders have Tennessee accents?" the detective asked.

"Sure do. I know that much. Do you think—?"

"We don't know anything yet, but we'll be investigating. As I say, you don't need to restrict Taddy too much. We'll have patrol around when he goes to school and comes home, visits his friends, and of course you need to let us know if you have any questions or see anything that troubles you."

Agent Taylor put another one of his business cards on the table. "Any time, Mr. Aguillard. Day or night."

I read the card. *Special Agent Robert Taylor, J.D.*

"J.D.? You're a lawyer, Agent Taylor?" I asked him.

"Yes, ma'am. That's who the FBI hires these days." He looked at me and smiled. "I hear you're job hunting. You might want to consider the service."

Now that was interesting. I'd picked up that Agent Taylor and Deuce seemed to know each other from before all this. Maybe he was the one Deuce spoke to about going to work for the FBI.

Agent Taylor thanked Mom and Dad for letting him talk to Taddy, and he congratulated them on how perceptive their son had been. I was proud of my little brother.

I called Tom and told him what happened. Tom said the right thing—he was glad for the good news about Taddy's safety—but he quickly turned to the upcoming motions, asking me about my research into the background of Sarah's experts. My thoughts stayed fixed on Taddy. The prosecution of PawPaw's murderer had dropped down my list.

Tom didn't mention the time ticking down for me to hear the Bar Exam results, which was also beginning to haunt my dreams.

DEFENSE EXPERTS

At the last minute, Sarah slipped in a motion to continue the trial. I knew Judge Bonin would hear her motion first, and he would not be happy.

I felt more comfortable now coming into the courtroom. Was it only a month ago I had to pause to gather courage to push the metal door? The courtroom was becoming a workplace, and I did enjoy the intellectual sparring of a good criminal motion day. At least as long as I wasn't yet a contestant! The curtain had been drawn over the Albrizio fresco painting that bore such an extraordinary resemblance to Judge Bonin.

"Your motion to continue the trial, Ms. Bernard."

Sarah stood. "Your honor, I regret having to come before you with this motion, but I feel I have no choice. My professional obligation is to give my client, Remuald Richard, a good defense. The trial is now just a few weeks away, and I need the testimony of his family for the penalty phase. I've been totally stymied trying to find any of them."

Next to me, Tom smiled, relishing his adversary sloshing into deep shit. Our investigator hadn't come up with any information about Remmy's family, and apparently neither had Sarah.

Judge Bonin, Judge Sosthenes Oliver Bonin, aka SOB,

scowled. Judges are always protective of their schedules, but they're most protective about a capital trial fixing. With good reason. Judge Bonin had ordered 350 people to disrupt their lives for jury duty, and he'd cleared three weeks on his complex, general jurisdiction trial docket. Tom wouldn't need to argue. Judge Bonin would oppose this motion all by himself—with relish.

"Ms. Bernard." Judge Bonin raised his shoulders, dropped them again, and straightened his back. He leaned forward over the bench, arching his eyebrows. At least ten seconds ticked by. "Ms. Bernard," he repeated, "you have been the attorney for Mr. Richard for over six months. Are you telling me you have not yet gotten around to talking to your client's family?"

"Your honor, I have talked with my client's mother on several occasions." A quick glance to our table. "I'm not revealing anything to the prosecution when I say she probably will be unable to testify at trial. She is in very poor health."

Tom leaned a few inches closer to me. "Poor health? Every cell in her brain is pickled past function. Remind me to tell you about when the detectives went a-callin' on Mommy Dearest."

"And other members of his family, Ms. Bernard?"

"He has a sister, your honor. Beverly Dubois. My investigator learned of Ms. Dubois only recently, and so far she's been reluctant to talk with us. My client and his sister are estranged. But if I had more time—"

"Does the sister live within the State of Louisiana, Ms. Bernard?"

"Yes, sir. She actually lives in this judicial district, in St. Martin Parish."

Judge Bonin put his hand over the little microphone on the bench and looked down to the minute clerk. George, demonstrating his Marine Corps past, snapped to attention and wiped all expression from his face. He handed the judge a thick file, the most recent of the four-volume court record, open to a page near the end.

The judge lowered his reading glasses. "I am looking at the subpoenas you have requested for the trial, Ms. Bernard, and I do not see one for a Beverly Dubois."

"No, sir. I haven't yet asked for a subpoena."

"No? A simple request from you will command her attendance at court."

"Your honor, I would like to prepare her for the appearance of a uniform at her door."

"Oh, I see. How very considerate of you." The judge took a deep breath and glared down at Sarah. "You cannot be serious, counselor. You are asking the court to upset the work of many months so that a possible witness will not be perturbed by a visitor?"

"That's not all, sir. I need time to talk with Mrs. Dubois, to go over her testimony."

Judge Bonin's chin shot up. "Oh, now I understand, Ms. Bernard. You're telling me you wish to have a continuance so you can *woodshed* your witness?"

Tom penned an exclamation point on my legal pad. I added a smiley face.

"No, sir." Sarah wasn't flustered. "My client has given me details of his childhood that reveal significant mitigation evidence. *Adverse Childhood Experience*, the psychologists call it, known to them as ACE. My client may or may not take the stand in his defense—the decision is his constitutional prerogative—but his sister is a critical, indispensable witness to bring evidence of his childhood before the jury. A defendant has a right to a defense. I need my client's sister."

Judge Bonin's mouth stretched wide—a smirk.

"And if you have an opportunity to talk to the defendant's sister, and she tells you about his difficult childhood, you will no doubt file another motion saying you need *further* time to bring expert witnesses to tell us how these childhood events warped his psyche. Correct?" Judge Bonin slapped down the pen he held in his hand. "There will be no end to your motions. Yes, you would like to speak to your client's sister before trial, but that, counselor, is your desire, not your right. Unless you point out some power I do not know I have, I cannot force her to speak to the attorney for her brother."

Judge Bonin leaned back in his chair, freed of the initial irritation that had been rooted in the possibility Sarah might actually have good reason for her motion. An easy call.

"Motion denied. The court will be in recess for fifteen minutes."

Next to me, Tom smiled. I had no wish to leave the courtroom for a cup of the battery acid coffee they brewed in the lawyers' lounge.

"So tell me about Richard's mom, Tom. I saw a reference to a visit near the beginning of Deuce's investigation notebook. He said the mom didn't know where her son Remmy might be."

"Ah, ha! Buddy told me the story. He can ham it up when he gets going."

I could believe that, and that he could be mean.

"When Richard was released after serving time with us on the drug charge, he listed his mother, Sylvia Tolbert, as next of kin. He gave her address as Rocksy Courts on West Main."

"I know the place. Circa 1950 yellow brick, detached units that have seen better days."

"You got it. Buddy said they found the manager in a lawn chair facing the traffic on West Main, sunning his bare chest, chewing tobacco, aiming his spittle into the gutter."

"Yuk!"

"The guy told the detectives the lady had moved into the Housing Authority complex across the tracks. Buddy told Deuce to take off his starched white shirt, the T-shirt he had on underneath being more appropriate garb for a visit to the projects. I guess Buddy was already properly dressed for the call."

Always.

"The detectives parked their unit close to the building marked *Office* and set a club on the wheel. They flashed their ID, and the manager said Sylvia Tolbert lived in Unit 54, on the ground floor, over on the left. They knocked; no answer. They knocked louder and heard scuffling. The rubber tip of a walking stick parted a tattered curtain hanging in a window. Buddy identified himself to the pale rheumy eye peeking through the dirty glass. More scuffling and the sound of a bolt sliding across the door. The door opened in, revealing a small grey-headed figure hunched in a wheelchair, one spindly leg in a cotton stocking protruding from below the hem of a flowery housedress. Just one leg, Buddy said, demonstrating by imitating a flamingo. Wisps of greasy grey hair sprang from the bare spot on top of her head, 'looking like they didn't want to stay any longer than they had to on that speckled brown egg,' as he put it. They stepped into ripe air."

"Yuk," I said again.

"Buddy explained they were trying to locate her son, Remmy. The woman raised her eyes; her blue-white lips stretched wide. 'Remmy, Remmy, I remember Remmy. I haven't seen him in ages. How's he doin'? You didn't happen to bring me any cigarettes, did you?' The old lady wheezed her question without the usual pause that comes with a change of topic. 'The doctor says I can't have no more, but what the hell do I care.'"

Tom found this story hilariously funny. I didn't. Poor woman.

"Since an ashtray overflowing with butts sat on a table next to the greasy plaid sofa, Buddy figured he wouldn't be leading the woman into any bad habits she didn't have already. He took a pack from his rolled sleeve, pulled out a cigarette, and gave it to her. With the lit cigarette quivering in her bony fingers, Mrs. Tolbert said she hadn't seen Remmy in ages. When asked about his friends or other family, the old lady just shook her head. Buddy asked about Remmy's father. The old lady gazed off into the middle distance before answering. 'Maybe that was Tolbert. I'm not too sure. No, Tuffy. Tuffy Johnson. Tuffy was Remmy's father. He's dead now.'"

Adverse Childhood Experience for sure. Mom wasn't even sure who fathered her son.

"Buddy asked where the family had lived, but she wouldn't answer until she'd dragged the cigarette down to a stub. Belle River, she said. On the water. Other children? Yeah. A daughter Bev. She took care of the paperwork so the front office probably knew how to get hold of her. 'I once had some more kids, but the State took 'em away long ago,' she said."

Remmy didn't get much of a start in life.

"Without any warning, Buddy said, she dropped her head, slipped low in her wheelchair, and curved her spine into a question mark, her one leg poking out until it touched his shoe. Her chin hit her chest and bounced, startling her awake. 'Holy shit!' she cried. She raised one hand and flipped them the middle finger. 'Guys,' she said, 'the big nurse'll be comin' to make me breathe into the fuckin' machine. I gotta get rest.' Her head dropped again. Down for the count.

"Buddy said Deuce totally panicked. He thought they'd killed her with the cigarette! 'Are you OK?' he shouted. Face close, he just about choked on her stink. The old lady opened one eye and cackled like the Wicked Witch of the West. 'Shee-it, man. I'm just fuckin' wonderful. Fuck off, nigger.' She turned to Buddy and told him he could come back sometime with more cigarettes, and she passed out again."

Now I laughed along with Tom. I couldn't help it. I could just imagine Deuce in a cold sweat, sweetheart that he seemed to be, scared to death they'd killed the woman. Sarah would have a hell of a problem putting this witness on the stand. Maybe they could roll her wheelchair into the courtroom to show Remmy had one relative willing to claim him, and hope to hell she didn't open her mouth.

"Buddy said they got Bev's address from the super—a trailer park in Anse Noire, in the Basin—but no one came to the door. At this point in the investigation they got the anonymous phone call telling them Richard was in Birmingham. They took off."

* * *

I stayed at Tom's side in the courtroom for the rest of the day. At one point he leaned toward me and pointed out Mr. Strait sitting in the back. The big DA, our boss, had come to watch.

The next rulings went better for Sarah. Judge Bonin agreed with her that requiring a "stun belt" under the defendant's shirt to control his behavior during trial wouldn't be warranted. He had no criminal history of violence and had given no trouble during his incarceration. And Sarah persuaded Judge Bonin to exclude from the jury's view both a poster-sized photograph of PawPaw's body on the Delcambre dock and a grossly enlarged picture of Mrs. Falgout's face taken in the emergency room the day of the attack. Unduly gruesome, the judge ruled. Not a major defeat for the prosecution. The jury would get to hold and examine smaller photographs, and these would give them an up-close-and-personal look at the lopsided reconstruction of her face, including the flap of withered skin covering her left eye socket.

Then came the *Daubert* hearings, the pretrial screening of expert witnesses required to protect a jury from being unduly influenced by so-called *junk science* presented just to hoodwink lay jurors. I'd done a lot of work studying the reports Sarah had to give us before trial. Now she succeeded in getting the judge to accept a couple of her proposed expert witnesses—a clinical psychologist and a sociologist. The Judge also ruled that expert testimony about post-traumatic stress disorder and the after-effects of head trauma would be permitted. He was persuaded by a faded newspaper clipping about a car-train collision in which Tuffy Johnson, the man Remmy's mother thought was his father, had been killed, and the testimony of a neighbor from Belle River who had visited three-year-old Remmy in the hospital after the accident. Remmy might well have suffered PTSD from the experience, he ruled.

"No sweat, Mandy," Tom said. "The defense has to be allowed some expert testimony. I'm saving up to go after the pharmacologist. Anyway, Mrs. Falgout on the stand will knock all this out of the jurors' minds."

I thought better of once more telling Tom about my concern. Lydia Falgout couldn't help us one bit until the penalty phase.

After lunch, Sarah put on Dr. Jesus Martino, the expert Tom had in his sights. Dark hair streaked with gray, a ready smile, strong features, and enough lines in his face for maturity without looking like an old geezer. He had jury appeal. Sarah took him through his education and his present positions. Just hearing the titles of his publications impressed me.

Tom stood to begin the cross-examination.

"Dr. Martino, defense counsel has introduced you to this

court as an expert on the effects of the use of cocaine in combination with consumption of alcohol. Correct?"

"Yes, sir."

"In particular, the effects of cocaethylene, which you say is a third compound formed by use of the two drugs together, more lethal than either one of them individually. Right?"

"Yes, sir."

"And I understand you are asking the judge to accept you as an expert qualified to give opinion evidence during the penalty phase of the trial, after they have found the defendant guilty of first degree murder of Pierre Boudreaux in the first or guilt phase. Right?"

"Perhaps the better way to phrase that, sir, is *if* they have found him guilty."

Score one for the expert. Tom had an experienced witness on his hands.

"You propose to opine to the jury that alcohol and cocaine, in combination, induced Mr. Richard to acts of violence. Correct?"

"Yes."

"I have several questions to ask you because, of course, I do not believe the judge should allow you to do so. Do you understand?"

"Of course I do. You do your job and I do mine."

Tom stood at the podium holding my outline of the topics he needed to cover. I hadn't written out every question word for word but made a list of just a few on each of the requirements for qualification of an expert. Once Tom heard the response given by the witness, he'd follow his instincts.

"Dr. Martino, are you a medical doctor?" Tom asked.

"No, sir. I am not."

"You just have a PhD." Tom gave the word *just* a tad of emphasis. "Pharmacology, I understand."

"Yes, sir."

"And from a prestigious university, it appears?"

"I think so. The University of Miami."

"And you have completed the many detailed drug studies that Ms. Bernard has so carefully recited to the court?"

"Yes, sir."

Good job, Tom. Begin with a compliment to give the witness a false feeling of comfort, then go in for the kill. I remembered learning the strategy in Trial Advocacy.

"Have you been admitted as an expert in courts of law, sir?"

"Yes, I have."

"In what field have you been admitted as an expert?"

"In pharmacology."

"The study of drugs?"

"Yes, sir."

"But you are not a neurologist, nor a medical doctor in any specialty that deals with the effects of alcohol, cocaine or other drugs on the human brain, correct?"

"I am not a medical doctor."

"So all of your conclusions are based upon the *qualities* of known drugs and *observations* of behaviors that result from the use of these drugs rather than medical studies of the brain itself. Correct?"

"I wouldn't say that, sir. The scientific knowledge of a pharmacologist is gained from knowledge about the drugs themselves and their effects, including their effects on the brain."

"But you determine those effects by looking at human behaviors, not from studies of the brain itself. Not from medical studies. Correct?"

"I wouldn't say that. I am familiar with the studies."

"Ah. Familiar with the studies of others, but not yours. You are not presenting yourself to this court as an expert in that field. You are not attempting to be qualified in neurology. Correct?

"Right, sir. You could say that."

"So we are in agreement that you are an expert in drugs. Is cocaethylene generally recognized as a distinct drug that has certain effects on the human brain?"

"Cocaethylene is the compound formed by cocaine and alcohol taken together and this compound has effects on the human brain. Cocaethylene is not itself a drug."

"So-o, the answer to the question is *no?*"

"You could say that."

"I do."

Sarah started to rise to make an objection, but she sat back down.

Tom looked at my memo before asking his next question. Good. He was making use of my outline.

"Let me ask you, sir, is your opinion about the properties and effects of cocaethylene a generally recognized scientific finding that has been reviewed in the scholarly journals, tested by peer review, presented and accepted in courts of law?"

"I would have to answer that question by saying my group has been conducting the cutting edge research in the field. We are the pioneers in this area of study."

"Ah, yes. Again, your answer is no. Cocaethylene has not been the subject of peer-reviewed scholarly studies. This is a new science."

"You could say that."

"I do. And one not yet universally accepted in courts of law."

Tom looked up at Judge Bonin for perhaps only the second time in his examination of the witness. Knowing his judge, he had moved quickly through his questions.

"Turning to another area of your qualifications, Dr. Martino, your report describes the quantities of alcohol and cocaine you say were consumed by the defendant prior to the events that bring us to his trial for the murder of Pierre Boudreaux. How did you come by this information, sir? About the quantities of drugs the defendant consumed?"

"From the defendant himself."

"So all you know about what the defendant consumed you learned from him?"

"Yes, sir. I can't think of a better source. The defendant is in the best position to know what he consumed that day."

"Ah. Unless it was in his interests to shade the information to his benefit. Wouldn't you agree with me that the information did not come from what we might call an unbiased and impartial source?"

"Objection." Sarah stood. "Your honor, counsel is arguing with the witness."

"Overruled. Continue, Mr. Barnett."

We had the judge with us.

"Thank you, your honor. Dr. Martino, let me ask you this. If the defendant's brain was so impaired by this special compound —cocaethylene you call it—would he still be an accurate reporter of his consumption of alcohol and drugs during that period? Or, in view of what you consider considerable impairment, would he be somewhat confused about such details?"

"I think Mr. Richard was an accurate reporter of his condition."

"You do? And on what do you base that opinion, Dr. Martino?"

"Mr. Richard was cooperative throughout my examination. He appeared to be giving full effort. As a check on my observations, I administered Green's Word Memory Test."

"Ah, yes. Green's Word Memory." A drip of sarcasm. "Even if the defendant was cooperative and forthcoming, was he necessarily accurate? He reported on events occurring many months ago, correct? Events occurring when he was, as you say, seriously impaired."

Tom had checked off all the bullet points I had noted for him to use.

"I do a great deal of interviewing in my scientific work. I believe Mr. Richard had accurate recall."

"You believe." Tom allowed another hint of sarcasm into his response, but just a hint. He knew Judge Bonin had no use for theatrics. From anyone but himself, that is.

"In your report, Doctor, you state that the defendant was probably first exposed to alcohol *in utero*, then consumed alcohol starting at age eight, and consumed alcohol for substantial periods of time throughout his life. How did you come by this information, sir?"

"The information was provided to me by the defendant and by his attorney."

"Were you able to verify the information from any direct or impartial sources?"

"No sir. I was not."

"Not even from his family?"

"No. I did not have the benefit of talking with his family. I understand his mother is not competent and his sister—well, I guess you need to ask Ms. Bernard about her client's sister. Let me just say I have not spoken with her."

"How about from friends? From records of hospitalizations, alcohol or drug treatment?"

Tom came up with that question. I hadn't thought of it.

"No, sir."

"Let me ask you this. You have just told me the only information you have about the defendant's drug use comes from him or his attorney. Does any of this information indicate to you that someone forced the defendant to drink alcohol at the time of the events in question?"

"No, sir."

"To sniff cocaine?"

"No, sir."

"So, he *chose* to drink and he *chose* to take drugs. Right?"

"Not entirely. When he drank at an early age, he was no doubt influenced by his environment. And once he used alcohol as a coping mechanism, the use of alcohol and of illegal drugs increased."

"Should we perhaps say *if* he used alcohol at an early age, since we have no independent verification of that information?"

The doctor smiled at this reply. "Perhaps, sir."

A glance at the judge's relaxed expression told me Tom was pulling this off. He was good. I felt pride just being with him.

"If you are able to do so in a few words, Doctor, could you tell me the opinion on this subject you believe would be valuable for the jury to hear—the opinion you plan to give at trial."

Dr. Martino took a deep breath. To have any chance of being accepted by Judge Bonin, his opinion needed to be concise yet clear. Could Dr. Martino do that?

"It is my opinion the defendant suffered from an addiction to alcohol and cocaine. Chronic cocaine use produces marked violence, impulsivity, unpredictability, and grossly impaired judgment. Addiction is a chronic relapsing disorder characterized by compulsive intake followed by loss of control and impairment in social and occupational function. Mr. Richard's addictions had advanced to severe dependence. Chronic use of alcohol and drugs in combination produce the substance of which I spoke earlier, cocaethylene, and this substance causes additional impairment."

Tom smiled. Too long.

"We are in Iberia Parish, in south Louisiana, doctor. Do you think the good jurors of this parish do not know the effects of alcohol and drug use? That they need an expert on the subject?"

Judge Bonin didn't bother to hide his smile, and I couldn't hide mine. Sarah's out-of-state expert had just been home-towned.

"I do not believe the average lay person knows the seriousness of the effects of alcohol and drug dependence, nor of the additional effects of the drugs in combination."

Still absorbing the humor in Tom's remark, the judge wasn't paying attention. Tom went into summary and conclusion.

"Dr. Martino, based upon unverified facts and no medical training, it is your opinion that Remuald Richard's use of alcohol and cocaine, which was *not* forced on him by anyone, caused a severe and grossly abnormal behavioral state that should mitigate or lessen his responsibility for the crime he committed. Is that your opinion?"

"No, sir. I know only in extreme cases does alcohol and drug abuse affect criminal intent. This is not one of those cases. My opinion is to be presented in the mitigation phase of a trial."

"Ah, I see. So, what you're saying is that because the defendant used alcohol and drugs, the jurors should cut him some slack?"

Sarah Bernard sprang to her feet.

"I have been very patient, your honor. I understand Mr. Barnett's duty to probe the qualifications of Dr. Martino, but the prosecutor has now strayed into disagreeing with his opinion. The weight of the opinion will be for the jury to determine."

"Your honor," Tom responded, "*Daubert* tells us that someone who gives an opinion to the jury needs more than an education in his field. *Daubert* requires the court to keep from the jury an expert opinion if the expert had insufficient facts on which to base his opinion, or if the expert has misapplied the facts. I submit that a pharmacologist may be qualified to discuss the effect of each drug, but not a new compound formed by the two in combination—a compound not yet tested by reliable scientific methods subject to peer review. I submit further that the doctor's opinion is based on insufficient, tainted, self-serving facts coming only from the defendant himself."

Judge Bonin leaned back in his chair and tented his fingers.

"Counselors, I have read Dr. Martino's *vita* as well as his reports, and your briefs, which are both excellent, by the way. I have heard your examination and cross-examination. I am prepared to rule." He took a sip of water from the paper cup at his right hand. "I will exclude from the jury the testimony of Dr. Martino. I will prepare written reasons for my ruling if the defense requests. We will now be in recess." The judge smiled. "No, after a full day of these motions, I am ready for adjournment." He turned and left the courtroom through the back door.

"Good job, Tom," I whispered. I turned and saw Mr. Strait stand up in the back row. He raised his thumb to Tom.

"You nailed the weakness, Mandy. All the facts on which this doctor based his opinion came from the defendant himself. I'd say we're a pretty good team."

Once again, the compliment and the smile gave me a flush. At the other counsel table, defeat had drained the usual animation from Sarah's face. She even looked close to her age.

"Family meeting next, Mandy. Let's go give them an update on today's events."

"No, Tom. Not me. I'll leave you to handle my family."

"Mandy, right now is my chance to get Sarah to consider a deal. She has a social worker and a psychologist, but she's seen her best expert witness go down the drain. It's too late to find another. And she has no one to cry for the jurors. If I had a green light, I could explore—"

I may have been in the middle of a swoon over this guy but I still had some reason left.

"No, Tom."

"Please?"

This time his smile didn't work.

"No. You know what I think. Your mission with my family is doomed. There's no way Ti Pierre will go for less than the death penalty, and Bub and Mazie will be with him. Even 'Tienne and J. Allen, who probably wouldn't vote for death if they were on a jury, will want to leave the decision to those twelve good citizens of the parish. Mom, Aunt Tut and Dora will stand alone. You're just going to tick everybody off."

And tick me off, as well. Didn't Tom see he was asking me to get in the middle? I stood up, ready to head out before I had a chance to say anything I might regret.

"I'll be having dinner with Mom and Dad tonight."

Tom put his hand on my arm. "Easy there. I'll be only a half hour or so. I know there's little chance they'll go for the plea, but I have to try, and I have to leave the door open in case they change their minds once the trial begins. Wait for me in the office. Please."

I did. The whole time fuming at myself for being spineless. Was I losing my principles because of my feelings? Damn.

A half hour later, Tom came back.

"You called it, Mandy. Your Mom made her pitch. Your Aunt Tut and Dora joined her. Dora is afraid down the road it might turn out Remmy was innocent. I assured them we know for sure he's guilty, but I didn't want to argue against myself by calling him a monster. Then came Ti Pierre, and I was cooked. Your uncles went with him." Tom packed his papers into the big red file. "Full speed ahead. No turning aside."

My cell phone jangled. The display read MOM.

"Mandy." Mom had her high squeaky voice again, the one she gets under stress. I felt a stab in my gut. "Get on home as soon as you can."

"What is it, Mom?"

I could barely hear her answer. "Taddy thinks he saw *the man* watching him."

Mom stopped talking, her words stuck in her throat.

COUSIN DUD

"Tom." My voice was as thin as my mom's. "Taddy saw the man..."

Tom read my distress. He dropped his papers on the desk and pulled his car keys out of his pocket. "Come on. I'm driving you home. I'll call the sheriff's office on the way."

He took my arm, transmitting to me the strength I needed to walk to the back stairs and down to the parking lot. His touch erased the worries about our relationship that had plagued me for the last hour. Dad was already home when we got there. Detective Aymond and FBI Agent Robert Taylor pulled up ten minutes later.

"But where's Detective Washington?" Mom asked. She figured they'd be questioning Taddy and knew he felt more comfortable talking to Deuce.

"Out of town for a few days, ma'am." A crisp response from Agent Taylor.

"'On leave' is what's written on the board," said Detective Buddy Aymond with a knowing look I couldn't interpret. I never knew what that guy was thinking.

Tom had dialed Deuce's direct number right after he called dispatch, but his call had gone straight to voicemail. *Out of the office for two weeks. If you need immediate assistance, contact the sheriff's switchboard.*

My best guess? As good as his word, Deuce had turned his attention to cracking the case of his informant's death, to the exclusion of everything else. *On leave* meant Sheriff Landry had not agreed to let Deuce pursue the investigation on company time. A Lafayette case, he probably said. Deuce was out there walking the wire without a net.

"You'll tell Deuce about this development, right?" I asked Buddy. "This is important."

I didn't want to say in front of Mom what I now believed: the two cases—the death of PawPaw and that of the informant—were connected.

"Already done, Mandy."

I'd called it correctly. Deuce was on his own time, but Buddy had stayed on the home-front to keep preparations for the trial of Remmy Richard simmering. Deuce and Buddy may not have been physically together on these assignments, but they were in contact and in tune. Since the guy who killed his informant had threatened Taddy, I liked having Deuce on my priority.

Agent Taylor spoke to my parents with a cool professional tone. Additional manpower had been assigned to keep Taddy in sight. A dragnet for *the man* had been set up in the neighboring parishes. Not totally reassuring. His quick glance to Buddy Aymond betrayed his concern; he no longer believed Taddy to be safe.

Taddy tried to give Agent Taylor a slightly better description of his stalker, but all he could add to his prior report was clothing: jeans and a dark ball cap.

With the looks and gestures a family develops over the years, I let my Dad know I had something I wanted to discuss with Agent Taylor and Buddy without my little brother in the room. I think Dad told Taddy he needed a hand for a chore, but I don't quite remember. When the pair vanished into the kitchen, Mom had the first question for Agent Taylor.

"Tell, me, are you going to question Taddy some more? Please say no."

"Not today, ma'am."

"Thank God."

Agent Taylor had picked up the family signals. He turned to me and asked if I had something on my mind.

"I haven't told you what's nagging at me right now, but I may have seen the guy we're talking about."

Tom just about jumped from his chair. "What? What are you saying, Mandy? You never told me about seeing him."

"Well, I wasn't sure it was him."

"When? Where? You're supposed to come across with information like that," he snapped. Ouch.

"I think I've seen a small white pickup truck hanging around a couple times."

Buddy interrupted with a dismissive snicker. "Look, Mandy. We got five thousand white trucks riding around in Iberia Parish."

"I know. And that's why I haven't spoken before. I didn't want to seem paranoid."

Agent Taylor now. "Go ahead, Mandy. Where? When? What caught your eye about this truck in particular?"

"The first time was before PawPaw went missing, actually the Sunday before, at the lake, when I went over to call Taddy in for supper. The day the storm was coming and those pelicans flew in from the Gulf. I noticed a white pickup truck parked on the shell turn-around across the lake and a guy leaning on the front bumper smoking a joint. That same afternoon, Taddy told us he'd seen a man on the Alexanders' dock even though PawPaw was certain the house was empty and the Alexanders had gone north. It occurred to me then to wonder if maybe Taddy had seen the same person I did, but it was just a passing thought."

Mom had a hand over her face. I hated to have to scare her like this.

Agent Taylor prodded. "Continue, Ms. Aguillard, if you will. Any other times?"

"Tom, remember the day you buried Taddy's Great Egret? I think that Sunday afternoon the pickup truck was in the same place, across the lake on the shell turn-around."

"You never said—"

"Yeah, I know. I wasn't sure. I only thought so later on."

I didn't confess the whole of it. For me, troublesome dreams always followed emotional days, whether good emotions or bad. Come morning, I'd never be quite sure whether an image from my dream was an actual scene coming back into memory, or just meaningless mental garbage best tossed away as soon as possible.

"But I'm quite sure about the truck following us the day Deuce and I went to interview Mrs. Falgout. Deuce treated it all as a joke. He yanked his unit off the road and into a driveway. A minute later the truck came back and zoomed on by. Just someone with nothing better to do than following what he heard on police radio, Deuce said. No matter, we couldn't see in the window anyway."

The pad Buddy had in his hand dropped onto the table. "That's it?"

"Yeah. Not much. I'm sorry. But I thought I should tell you."

"You should. Thank you," said Agent Taylor.

"And remember, Uncle J. Allen saw someone coming out of the Jefferson House drive way before..."

"Yeah. We got that one. Ok. First *the man*. Tell us, Ms. Aguillard, what do you recall about him?"

"The only time I got any look at him was from PawPaw's dock, and that was from way away. White man, thin, youngish, shrimpers' boots. By his movements, he seemed to be smoking weed like a pro, rolling the joint with one hand. The other times he was in the truck and I couldn't see him well at all. White, thin face—couldn't say much more than that."

"OK. What about the truck? Can you give a description?"

"A small truck. Not new. I didn't see a brand, and I looked. No ram's head hood ornament, big H or Toyota swirls. Made me wonder if someone took the insignia off. When the truck followed us, Deuce and me, we tried to get the plate number but couldn't read through the dirt. Funny, though, there wasn't any dirt on the truck itself, just on the license and the side window. Maybe Deuce can do better. Sorry, guys."

I was looking at two worried faces—Mom's and Tom's—and I didn't feel so good myself. Agent Taylor wore his professional mask. Buddy looked disgusted with my pitiful contribution to their investigation.

Agent Taylor turned down Mom's invitation to join us for a gumbo supper. He had work to do, he said, but he appreciated the offer. Tom stayed for dinner but not dessert. He said he needed to return to the office. He forgot my car was still at the courthouse, but I didn't mention it. I'd ask Mom to give me a ride to work in the morning.

* * *

With just ten days until 350 people would report for jury selection, Tom cleared his calendar. The other assistant district attorneys had taken over his routine duties now so he could work without distractions. On Wednesday, Thursday, and Friday, I spent long hours at the office doing research and preparing exhibits. Taddy's safety never left my thoughts. I kept my cell phone in view all day, every day, and frequently checked in with my mom. She had set aside all her usual routines to bird-dog Taddy.

Everywhere I went I looked hard at each white pickup I saw. God, there were a lot of them, but now not a one seemed interested in me. I felt just a hint of what it might have been like to have been a European Jew before the Second World War. You never knew who might be the enemy, or what they might do to you if they were.

Tom kept total focus on the trial, and his requests to me came faster and louder. He ordered me to prepare poster-sized exhibits: a map showing the route PawPaw probably took the last morning of his life; several blown-up photographs of PawPaw's recovered body; a silhouette drawing with blood-red marks indicating the location of the fatal stab wounds. Without waiting the hour for Kinko's to create the exhibits, he ordered me to check and see if they were ready.

"Sure, Tom." I wasn't about to admit that just looking at those pictures roiled my gut. Or that his tone of voice tempted me to snap a salute and answer *aye, aye, sir.*

"I want twenty copies of Deuce's plat of the ground floor of *The Southern Wave,* enough for the jurors and the judge, with a few extras. Not poster-size for those drawings. We don't want to emphasize the considerable distance between Skipper Domingue's location and the two men he overheard arguing."

I was not at all happy with the orders, but I worked at keeping my cool. At this point I was totally invested in the trial myself. I wanted to do anything I could to help Tom succeed.

"I want a very large blow-up of an excerpt, with emphasis supplied, from the incriminating statement Remmy made in the hospital in Birmingham: *Two dead on my watch.*"

I talked back about this request. "Tom, that's *other crime* evidence the jury can't hear."

"I know that. The blow-up is just to show to Judge Bonin. He's going to have to figure out how I can explain what sent the detectives off to Birmingham, and I want to point out our very large problem. He'll probably want to edit Deputy Hamilton's testimony to say Remmy talked about *one* dead on his watch. We'll need a new poster when we have the judge's solution."

Tom had even more requests for exhibits for the penalty phase of the trial. He wanted me to create a poster-sized drawing of the Boudreaux family tree, to locate the eightieth birthday party photograph we had made for PawPaw's Celebration of Life, and to mount a collage of photographs taken of Mrs. Falgout lying in the pile of leaves at the site of the fire on Captain Cade Road. Of course we weren't counting on pictures alone to impress the jury with that scene. The sight of Mrs. Falgout herself, up close and personal, would be our very best exhibit. That missing eye!

Tom asked me to make a trial book with 8 by 11 inch copies of all the exhibits for each juror, for the alternate jurors, for the judge, and for the defense as well. "Stop," Tom corrected his instruction. "Make that two books, one for each phase. I can't be showing them the Falgout stuff right off the bat. But then, Sarah might even agree to allow me to give the exhibit books to the jury; she wouldn't want to appear to be withholding evidence from their eyes. Jurors hate it when they suspect something is happening they aren't permitted to know."

Tom had even more instructions for me. "Stick around. Richie is on his way over for our final sessions with guilt phase witnesses. He'll be handling some of them on direct."

I knew next to nothing about Richie Castille. In the months I'd been hanging around the office, we'd exchanged no more than good morning and goodbye. His huge drug caseload required him to spend every criminal cycle in the courtroom arranging pleas and trying cases. Also, he had a lot to do with managing the confidential informants the narcs used out in the field.

I was beginning to appreciate the complexity of his assignment. Rumor had it he'd been furious when Mr. Strait bypassed him to promote Tom to first assistant. I hoped that was water under the bridge. Having Richie on hand for this trial relieved me of a major worry. Tom needed experience and skill next to him in the second chair.

I knew the last two weeks before a capital trial would be tense, but Tom's tunnel vision was gettin' to me. Another order and I might explode. I felt like saying, "Tom, it's me. Mandy. How about easing off a bit on the commands?" I knew part of my irritation came from worry about Taddy's safety. I was looking around for someone to blame for my unease. When five o'clock rolled around, I was glad to go home alone, leaving Tom closed in his office with Richie.

Mom's antennae were up again, and she brought up the topic of me and Tom.

"You don't seem to be spending as much time with Tom, and I thought maybe he was a bit short with you the other night. Is everything OK?"

"I'm getting a lot of orders about prep for the trial, that's all."

I didn't want to get into this with Mom, or let Aunt Mazie's remarks about Tom's serial girlfriends find any room in my head. I left the room quickly.

The next morning Richie Castille met us in the library. Big guy, cool dude. He shaved his head and wore blue jeans and cowboy boots. He was given to theatrical gestures and pauses for emphasis. I could believe he enjoyed doing his imitation of Mr.

Strait at the annual Christmas party, and that he could give his drug-case juries a show.

Richie rubbed one palm against the other." Who's up first, Tom?"

"I'd like Deuce to be the detective who walks the jury through the initial investigation," Tom responded. "He kept the investigation notebook so he'll be less likely to get caught in any of Sarah's machinations as she works through her cross. But today Deuce is out of town. We'll talk with him as soon as he returns. We have Skipper Domingue waiting right now."

"You have his statements for me?" Richie asked.

I'd pulled Domingue's initial affidavit and a typed version of our first interview. Tom held out his hand to me as if he were summoning an operating nurse to give him a scalpel. I slapped the papers on his palm. "Yes, doctor," I said. He didn't even notice my attitude, just passed the papers to Richie.

Richie speed-read four sheets in less than a minute. When he'd finished, he dropped them on the table and raised his hand. "Bring him on!"

With the help of Deuce's drawing of the ground floor of *The Southern Wave*, Richie grilled Skipper Domingue about every detail in his testimony. Tom listened intently but didn't interrupt. After Skipper left, I commented that our witness now seemed a good bit more certain of the details, not only about everyone's location at the time he overheard the conversation, but also about what had been said.

Richie smiled. "There's an art to getting good testimony out of your witnesses. We don't take 'em out to the woodshed to beat what we want into their heads, but we do question them so many times the answers we like get more forceful and more specific. We can't get carried away and have the witness alter anything that's in the initial account. Sarah would chew Skipper to bits over any discrepancies between what he said in his first affidavit and what he says in court."

An art, yes. Does the artist distort reality?

The process of witness preparation fascinated me. I didn't know if Tom and Richie were better at it than other prosecutors with ten years of experience, but at the time I thought so. I felt fortunate to be on the inside.

Damn. I was star-gazing again.

Mark Hamilton, the Birmingham, Alabama, officer who'd located Remmy in the hospital and overheard his incriminating statement, had come to Louisiana two weeks earlier to testify at Sarah's motion hearing when she'd argued that Remmy's words were the product of delirium, or failing that argument, coerced, and should be excluded from the trial. Tom had won the motion; Remmy's statements would come in as excited utterances, totally voluntary. Tom didn't want to require Hamilton to make a second trip to Louisiana only to have him come a third time for the trial itself, but Richie thought they should bolster up a few details to reinforce the absence of any coercion on the part of the Alabama officers. They agreed to give Mark a phone call to go over his testimony one more time.

Tom and Richie worked together smoothly. Richie appeared to have buried past grudges, but maybe he just loved working with witnesses. I could see Tom respected Richie's trial experience. They really were a good team.

Then the two of them got into what to do about the *unknown* caller who had tipped off the officers about Remmy being in the Birmingham hospital. Buddy and Deuce had been pretty sure the caller was Remmy's cousin, Dudley LeBlanc, but they had no confirmation of that fact.

Tom had a suggestion. "Buddy's downstairs in the sheriff's office. I'm going to call him up here for some creative thinking about how to approach cousin Dud."

"I was just on my way up to see you guys," Buddy said. "First thing, before it slips my mind, Deuce just called in from the Harris County Jail in Houston. He's always a cool cat, but I could hear the excitement in his voice. He says he's onto something important about the death of his informant."

"Wait a minute, Buddy. Let me put you on speaker. I want Richie to hear this." Tom punched a button on the phone. "OK. Keep going."

"Deuce wants a meeting with you as soon as possible, Tom.

He asked me to see if Mr. Strait might be available also. Friday, if he's back in town, but Monday, at the latest. OK?"

"Any time, Buddy. Mr. Strait stays nearby when we have a big fire burning. What does Deuce want to talk to him about?"

"He's pretty close with the details, but apparently there's a connection to our trial. An important tie, he says. He didn't elaborate. Just said he needs Mr. Strait. I'm up in five."

"Hey." Richie stuck in a thought. "If drugs were involved in the murder of Deuce's informant, we might have another capital case on our hands. What trumps? Murder or drugs? Would it be your prosecution, Tom, or would it be mine?"

Tom knew better than to rank the cases and activate Richie's resentment. "Strait's call. We have job security, that's for sure."

When Buddy joined our meeting, a broad smile had smoothed the wrinkles from his bulldog face.

"You're looking triumphant," Tom said.

"Guys, I do believe I've found a wedge to get the cooperation we need from Remmy's cousin Dudley."

"Shoot."

"First, I'll go back a bit."

Tom's lips tightened. Trying to get Buddy quickly to the point worked on his last nerve. This time, if Buddy didn't get there soon enough, I'd go out and get what worked last time—fresh coffee.

"Back when we were looking for Remmy, we picked up Dudley's name from the list of kin in Remmy's five-year-old probation report, same list where we got the name of his mom, Sylvia Tolbert. And from the same probation report, we picked up a prior arrest—assault at the Tiger Lounge in Jeanerette in a fracas over a poker game. Victim: one Dudley LeBlanc. One and one make two—yoo hoo! We went looking for Mr. LeBlanc to see if he knew where we could find his drinkin' buddy, Remmy Richard. Maybe druggin' buddy as well."

Buddy smiled—no, smirked—as he watched Tom's pen twirl through his fingers like a miniature drum major's baton. Buddy enjoyed dragging out his reports just to get Tom's goat. I was right. A jerk.

"Deuce and I found Dudley working the counter at a local

plumbing supply store. He flat denied knowing Remmy's whereabouts, but something about the way his eyes kept slipping sideways didn't pass the smell test. That's why, when the anonymous call came in tipping us off to find Remmy in a Birmingham hospital, we suspected cousin Dudley was the caller. Who else could Remmy ask for help in his time of need? Remmy had no family, and we'd never found any friends except the Falgouts. No friends for good reason. Look what he did to them.

"So I ran Dudley's record. He's got five pending charges, disturbing the peace up to assault. No convictions. The witnesses listed on the affidavits of arrest were probably all criminals themselves so the charges would no doubt just sit there until the defense figured out the DA would never put them on the stand. But Dudley might not know that." Buddy wore his leer again, which he passed from Tom to Richie, skipping me. "I got to thinking. I could tell cousin Dud I'd make those charges disappear in return for a little 'cooperation.'"

"Go for it, Buddy." Buddy left and Tom turned back to Richie.

"Here's a bonus. If we get Dudley under the tent, I could use him as a witness in the penalty phase to testify about the fight at the Tiger Lounge. Then we'd have some evidence about Remmy's propensity for violence."

* * *

Buddy went to work. The following day he came back to our witness preparation session with good news. *"Blind hog found an acorn*, as my bourrée buddies like to say about an unexpected lucky hand. I think I've got Dudley on our team."

Maybe we had an example of good luck, but it looked to me more like an example of the DA's advantage. Being part of the victim's family, I was grateful to have the prosecutor's hand to play.

We called Dudley, and he came in. Buddy had figured it right; Dudley admitted he was the caller. After an hour of back and forth, Dudley agreed to testify, voluntarily, that Remmy had asked for money to make a getaway. And Richie extracted an important bonus, actually a very tasty acorn for the blind hog. Dudley would quote Remmy as saying he needed the money to skip town because he had *done in two.*

We now had corroboration of the incriminating statement Remmy had made in Birmingham a week later.

But Tom wasn't going to be able to just slip the statement in. The law had built in balance. Tom had a continuing obligation to disclose to the defense, and Sarah would surely go to work on suppressing Dudley's testimony. A prosecutor has power and resources, and can use a few tricks, but he has to share the rewards of his edge.

I watched Tom make two notes on his legal pad. "Statement for Judge: edit." "Disclosure?"

Now I felt more sure of Remmy's guilt, and about Tom's ability to prove it.

Richie looked at his watch. "It's dark outside. Are you walking out?"

I thought Richie was asking me, but Tom answered.

"We've got hours to go yet, but I'll see you in the morning."

"Watch out for Honoré's ghost!" Richie said, and left.

I told Tom I felt a lot better about his chances.

"I know we don't have a sure thing, Mandy, but I owe it to your family to give this trial everything I've got. I'm convinced Remmy killed your grandfather. I represent the victim's family, your family. Full speed ahead."

I couldn't ask for anything more. Although I had a nagging worry about the Bar Exam results due Monday, and was just a bit miffed Tom didn't mention them, I felt pretty good.

"But what's this business about Honoré's ghost?" I asked. "I heard Buddy say the same thing?"

"Remind me to get Richie to tell you the story. Local legend, and he's best at that. I'm just a north Louisiana boy. Short version: the ghost is supposed to haunt people who work too late."

I now had backdoor privileges to the DA's office, so I no longer came and went by the courthouse steps. But that night when I left, I drove around to look at the building from the front. I perched on Iberia Street and took in the scene. There she stood,

Lady Justice, stunningly illuminated against the gleaming white facade of the building.

Do your job, Lady, I told her.

SISTER BEV

Tom beckoned me into the library. Sarah sat at the end of the table, her right hand flat against her temple. No fancy briefcase in sight today. Tom had *what the hell is she going to come up with next* all over his face.

"Why the gloom and doom, Sarah? Did somebody die?"

"I'm about to piss you off and piss the judge off even more. I'm filing another motion for continuance."

"Jesus! You must have a death wish. We're ten days before trial. It's Friday afternoon. Judge Bonin is long gone from the courthouse and probably already out at his camp a few inches into Jim Beam. You gotta be kidding."

Continuance? Now? We were geared up to begin picking a jury. For sure SOB would show Sarah why his initials made an appropriate nickname. What earthly reason was she going to give him?

Sarah squeezed her eyelids together. When they opened, those incredible emerald pools were as lifeless as swamp water.

"I've lost my client's sister," Sarah said. I could barely hear her words.

Tom shook his head in exasperation. "Bev Dubois is lost? I suppose you're telling me St. Anthony is no help."

Sarah didn't appreciate Tom's attempt at levity. She frowned, straightened up in her chair, physically gathering strength to explain her situation.

How could she look so damn good when she appeared to be in major distress?

"I thought I had a chance to get Bev Dubois on board to testify for her brother. Where there's life, there's hope, as they say. Well, when there's death, there's no hope."

So Tom called it. Somebody did die.

"She died? Too bad, but look, this business is our job, not our life," Tom said.

I didn't get it either. Why on earth was Sarah crying over her client's sister?

Sarah pulled in enough breath to be able to get out two words. "My fault."

"What? Your fault?" Tom had the frown now. "So tell me."

Sarah ran her tongue over her top lip and swallowed hard before she could speak.

"Mike, our investigator, located Remmy's sister in a trailer park in Anse Noire, on the levee. Well, you know where she lives; your detectives found her place when they were looking for Remmy. My guess is she gave them no help."

"That's what they reported to me at the time. She said she didn't know where Remmy was, and didn't care either."

"You know what it's like out there. Everything's temporary. The wheels never come off the trailers 'cause you gotta be able to make tracks whenever there's a threat of a bad storm coming or a report of too much rain falling upriver." Sarah could paint a picture with just a few words.

Sarah said Mike drove over there three times trying to catch Bev at home. No luck. Each time he wrote *Please call* on a card, which he left in a tilted mailbox with DUBOIS hand-lettered on the side. Bev didn't call. On a fourth blank trip, when he turned his truck around to leave, he caught a glimpse of a face in the window of the trailer next door. He knocked. A shriveled-up woman with a dark shadow over her upper lip, hair screwed up in pink sponge curlers, raised the window and asked him what he wanted. When he said he was looking to talk with her next-door neighbor, the lady suggested he come back some day around five-thirty, the time when Bev and her husband—the lady called him Spike—came home from work. But, she warned Mike, they kept mostly to themselves, didn't have much to do with people.

Sarah had a grip on her emotions now and calmly continued her story. I took my cue from Tom and sat absolutely still.

"Something told me I should take over for Mike and try to see Bev myself. I arrived one day around five-fifteen and parked thirty feet up the road, around a left-hand curve so I could watch the driveway in my rearview mirror. My little ragtop would set off alarms if I perched her in that neighborhood."

Right on, Sarah. I'd heard she called her baby blue MG "my melancholy baby."

"Just after five-thirty, a pickup so beat-up I couldn't tell what color it once was, pulled in and parked on a patch of shells under a big pecan tree at the far end of the Dubois trailer. A man and a woman got out of the truck. I stepped up quickly and intercepted them as they reached the concrete steps leading up to the door. I called Bev by name and asked if I could speak to her a few moments. She stopped, but her husband kept walking right around her like he hadn't heard me. He shrugged his shoulders, turned his key in the lock, and went inside."

I bet Sarah knew a few techniques about questioning a reluctant witness. I thought I might learn something here. Sarah's extra weapon—being drop-dead gorgeous—wasn't going to help her any with these folks. She continued.

"I told Bev I represented her brother and wanted to talk to her. She froze—you'd think she'd seen a ghost or something—and then she let me have it. She said she hadn't seen her brother in years and didn't want anything to do with him now or ever. She already had one foot on the bottom step so I slipped around her and sat down on the step above. She was going to have to walk right over me to get to the door. 'But your pants,' she blurted out, watching my off-white slacks pick up two black eyes from the good inch of leaves and trash on the step. I smiled and said not a problem. I figured I could cough up for an extra dry cleaning if a woman's natural abhorrence for dirt helped soften her up."

Well over her shaky start, Sarah now warmed to telling her story. She was proud of how she handled a reluctant witness. She told Bev her brother was in a shit-load of trouble, charged with a capital crime. She was going to have to explain him to a jury, tell them who he was. She said Bev just stared at her for a good thirty seconds. 'You want to know who my brother is? Remuald Richard, that's who. That's the son-of-a-bitch's name.' Then Bev snorted out a bitter laugh. 'Fuck! That's a good one. Son of a *real* bitch,' she said. I knew I had a challenge on my hands."

I thought back to the story of the detectives' trip to the projects to visit Sylvia Tolbert, Remmy's mother. Mommy Dearest hadn't been at all sure which of her gentlemen friends was his father.

Sarah continued. "I kept going, asking about growing up in her family. Bev put a hand over her eyes and got philosophical on me. 'Family, family. You can't ever seem to get free of your fuckin' family. When you need 'em, they lie hidden under a rock. Just when you *don't* need 'em, out they crawl.' She said many times she prayed she'd never have to hear from a single one of 'em ever again. With that last statement Bev kind of collapsed onto the step, next to me."

Sarah said she gave the interrogation her best shot. She looked Bev straight in the eye and said she had to convince a jury that if her brother did what the DA said he did, he must have had some cause, some reason, some explanation or motivation. She needed to know enough about him to pick men and women for his jury who could relate, who might care about what would happen if he lost his case. She needed jurors who realized that if they'd been dealt his hand, this might have happened to them. She said she told Bev straight out she wanted to save her brother's life. Silence.

"Then you know what came back to me in return for all my eloquence?" Sarah asked. "'You want to save my brother's life? Lady, I'm not sure I do.'"

Egad!

Sarah said she told Bev their investigator had found an old

address and was working on locating Remmy's school records. The family seemed to have moved around a lot. "You know that expression eyes wide as saucers?" Sarah asked. "Make that dinner plates. A shudder rippled Bev's shoulders. 'Investigator? You people have an investigator? An investigator will be diggin' into all our shit?' I had to think quickly how to handle this. Bev was not just slow to cooperate; she seemed genuinely afraid. I told her there'd be no 'diggin' if she would just speak to us. Our investigator would leave her family alone and go on to talk to the defendants on the hundred other cases we had."

Sarah said Bev came through with an explanation for why they'd moved so much when they were young—to keep one step ahead of the State welfare lady who might take them away from their mom.

Areas for inquiry were mounting up. Sarah next got to the issue of addictions.

"I told Bev Remmy said he had a substance abuse problem, and that substance abuse may have been in the family. Bev yelped, tossed back her head, and laughed like the Joker. 'Substance abuse? My God, lady. We're *all* fuckin' drunks!'"

Tom seemed to be enjoying Sarah's story, but I didn't doubt for a minute his brain cells were clicking away. We weren't taping, but he'd made a few notes and a few times looked over at me to indicate I should be doing the same. I had written a heading on my yellow pad: *Family shit for mitigation.* Then I listed quotes under several categories: *unstable home, unknown father, family alcohol, previous removal of children (Mom's info).* And I wrote a question. *Why is Bev afraid?*

Sarah continued.

"Then Bev gave me some really good stuff, serious *adverse childhood experience,* ACE as we call it. I asked when her brother first started drinking. Must have been when he was around six, she thought. Their mom gave him drinks just so she and her boyfriend of the moment could get a laugh watching him stagger. 'Poor fucker never had a chance,' Bev said. Bev was three or four years older than Remmy so she must have been about ten when that happened. Bev said her mom had another reason for wanting her to be loaded around the mom's boyfriends—to stay still for what the men did to her. Nice family, right? I asked Bev if she also had a drinking problem. She set her lips hard and said she'd had eleven months of sobriety and wasn't going to risk everything she'd accomplished by getting involved with her brother's shit. Bev stood up and stepped onto the top step, turned and confronted me, her eyes glinting. 'In the name of God, lady. Will you please lay off?'"

"Very few of the murderers I prosecute come from the sunny side of the street," Tom said. Fortunately, no one needed me to say anything at this point. I couldn't have.

Sarah said she figured she'd done all she could for the day. She thanked Bev again and told her she was going to find an expert witness who would explain to the jury how a lifetime of alcohol abuse could make a person do things he wouldn't ordinarily do. She told Bev she wanted to come see her again and asked if perhaps she knew other people who would remember her family when she and Remmy were young—other family members, neighbors, friends. Bev didn't offer anyone. Sarah said she held out her hand to say good-bye. After a moment, Bev took it. Upset as she was, Bev couldn't be rude. Her hand felt cold and limp. She turned and opened the door to go inside.

"Then something interesting. Just before the door closed behind her, Bev looked back and spoke to me. 'You could tell my brother for me I'm sorry about everything.' The door slammed shut. Tom, that last comment gave me hope. Bev cared about her little brother. With a few more conversations, I thought she'd agree to help." Sarah paused. "That was the last time I saw her."

Sarah reached for a bottle of water on the library table, twisted off the cap, and swallowed a third of it. Tom and I waited for her to be able to continue.

Sarah said she got back in her car and used the driveway to turn around. The next door neighbor's face—the neighbor Mike had told her about—peered out of the little window in her front door. Wide face, a shadow of a mustache over the top lip, but no curlers this time. Sarah flashed a smile and waved. An investment in the future. Sarah had a premonition she might need to talk to the neighbor-lady again. Once out on the highway, Sarah said she slapped the dashboard in excitement. For the first time since she'd met Remmy Richard she thought she had something to go on, a witness who could corroborate early drinking and testify that his mother got him started. Not a defense to the charges, of course— she knew the intoxication defense was just about impossible unless a defendant fell down drunk and accidentally set a gun off on the way to the ground—but at least something to talk about in the penalty phase, should she have to go there. ACE and lifetime alcohol abuse could be the basis for an effective argument in mitigation. Bev seemed intelligent and spoke well. With training, Sarah thought Bev could be a good witness for her.

I wondered why Sarah was spilling out for us all the ammunition she had for the penalty phase. Trying to get Tom's sympathy? I was really puzzled.

Sarah said she left Bev's home with her mind spinning so fast she lost concentration on her driving. Whomp. She felt warning bumps at the edge of the pavement just in time.

"Bev was telling me to get out of her life, but I know I saw feeling in those dark eyes."

Sarah sighed and took another long drink of water. "But then everything turned to shit." Her voice cracked.

A couple weeks later, Sarah said, picking her head up from routine trials, she realized she'd let time slide by. She asked Mike to go check on Bev. He reported he sat outside the trailer three different times and found no one. Sarah asked him if he'd checked with the neighbors. No one seemed to be around there either. Three wasted days. Sarah said she screamed at Mike in frustration, regrouped, and said she'd go check it out herself.

"I told the judge I needed a bit of extra time at lunch for a personal matter. I tore over to Anse Noire on the break, slamming to a stop beside Bev's front steps. I didn't try to hide my car this time. No truck in the driveway. A flyer from Domino's Pizza hung on the doorknob. No answer to my knock. I went to the trailer next door—home of the sponge-roller lady. The door creaked open on the third knock. She appeared. No curlers but the same furry upper lip."

Sarah managed a weak smile at her own attempt at levity.

"I told the neighbor I was looking for Bev Dubois and she didn't seem to be home. She wasn't home and she wouldn't be, the neighbor snapped. I asked about Bev's husband. He'd gone to see his sister for a few days but was due back the next day. 'But, lady, I can tell you right now,' the neighbor said, 'he's not going to be overjoyed to see you. You better forget about him.' The neighbor slammed the door in my face.

"I went again Wednesday. Still no luck. On the following day, yesterday, I found Spike Dubois at home. He answered the door, called me a few choice names, and actually tried to push me down the steps! I stood my ground. 'OK,' he said. 'I'll tell you what happened. You oughta know what you did.' Then he let me have it, with both barrels.

"After my visit, Spike said, his wife got moody. She referred to me as that damn fancy lawyer-lady who asked her cool as you please to talk about family, just like she was askin' what did you do in school today. Spike said his wife couldn't rest at night. She told him she had 'monkey brain'—couldn't keep crazy thoughts from jumping around in her head, from tree to tree like a monkey. And then nightmares. She told Spike about some of them. She'd be a young girl, sleeping in the sun after a swim in Lake Palourde. Z-z-z. She'd wake with a start. A big woolly beast would come crashing out of the underbrush. He'd fall on top of her, wide neck pinning her face. She'd twist and turn, struggling to get free. The beast's paw would close over her mouth. She'd wake with a scream stuck in her throat. Stuff like that. I'm no shrink, Tom, but those are PTSD nightmares. The kind of stuff that haunts someone who's been through major distress."

I could agree with Sarah on that. Tom showed no sign of impatience with Sarah's long story. After a moment to compose herself, Sarah continued her account of the visit with Spike.

"Spike said his wife told him none of her dreams actually happened. She never swam in Lake Palourde. There was plenty she *could* have dreamed about: the men, the music, the pain, the shame. By God, one time her dear mom pimped her to some guy in exchange for a used washing machine! Instead of recalling actual horrors, Bev had these floating, crazy images she tried to catch in her hands and crush out of existence.

"Spike said about ten days ago his wife didn't get up to go to her job at the donut shop. She just moaned and dug deeper into her covers. Later he found out why. The evening before, she'd walked down the road to her AA meeting, but she didn't stop. She kept on walking until she reached the corner store. She bought a bottle of Jack Daniels, came home, and hid it in the shed. In the night, when Spike was snoring, she got up and went for it. A few pulls on the bottle and the soothing syrup sent her back to bed to merciful sleep. She slept all the next day. She confessed to Spike that she'd slipped, but she said it wouldn't happen again. That night she went to her meeting and came home still sober.

"Spike said his wife had two good days and two good nights. That's all. Apparently, when Spike said he told his wife the guy from the lawyer's office called again and said he wanted to talk to her, she cracked. She took money from his wallet, which he didn't notice. A couple of days later she said she didn't feel too good and stayed in bed.

"About four afternoons later, Spike wasn't sure exactly how many, he pulled his truck into the driveway after work. Up ahead he noticed something in the big pecan tree at the end of the trailer, next to the shed. Two bare feet, swingin' free. Bev had propped a ladder against the side of the shed, climbed up on the roof, thrown a rope over a branch, tied the other end around her own neck, and stepped off into oblivion. That's how Spike found her, hanging there, wide eyes bulging, face swollen and grey, her dirty tennis shoes below her on the ground."

Tears came back to Sarah's eyes. Anger? Regret? Shame? Guilt? Maybe all of the above. I couldn't put one label on what she was feeling. Tom took in her condition and left the room, returning in a few minutes with three cups of coffee and a plate of donuts on a tray.

"I'm sorry, Sarah." Tom spoke softly. He was feeling for her and offered the only solace he could think of. "I'm open to talking to the Boudreaux family about a plea to life for Remmy. No promises, but I could try."

Wrong thing to say. Sarah's chin shot up. She spoke more in anger than any other emotion.

"No, and hell no! My client is adamant. He denies he was ever around when Pierre Blanchard took the knife. I'm a mess right now, I know it, but believe me I'll get control of myself and do my job. Remmy knows the risks, but knows what he wants. I'll fight like hell for not guilty in the guilt/innocence phase."

"So he's still claiming another dude did it? Isn't that just the defense of last resort?" Tom seemed incredulous.

Sarah had now totally regained her professional self. "I know you have evidence a jury might buy, Tom, but I think I've a damn good shot. Of course," Sarah's lips smiled but not her eyes, "I have to be ready for a bad result."

"And if you get a bad result?"

"I'm not done. I've lost Bev as my witness in mitigation, and Spike may know stuff but isn't going to do me any favors because he thinks I'm responsible for his wife's death. 'For two cents I'd string you up on the same tree,' is what he told me. But there's got to be someone out there who knows their story. I've spoken to John Clark, my boss, the chief PD for the district, and he's opened the purse strings. I've some major private investigator talent digging. There were two older children in that family who were taken away by the state of Illinois. I haven't found them yet, but I will. I know I lost the motion to qualify my guy on cocaethylene, but with time I think I can find an expert who will pass the preliminary qualification, now that I know how important the evidence is. But I've got to have some time. Tom, I need a continuance."

Tom shook his head. "You're going to lose your motion for a continuance, Sarah, and I won't have to say a word against it. SOB will do the job for me. Just like last time."

"Not if you join me, Tom."

"What? I've already told you—"

"Think about this, Tom. If you get a conviction, and we have to go to the penalty phase, I'll have pitiful evidence to offer. You'll be on a fast track to getting the jury to give Remmy the death penalty. However, within a few more months, you'll be on just as fast a track to a reversal for incompetent counsel. Incompetent Sarah Bernard didn't put on any defense, some appeal court will say. If not the State appeal courts, the federal habeas. Think on that for a few minutes. Do you want to retry this case down the road? When I've had time to locate witnesses and you may have lost yours? You want to put your victim's family through this again?"

Sarah looked at me when she asked that last question.

Now I understood what Sarah had done and why she'd done it. She'd given us a reasonably good line of evidence in mitigation. If we didn't allow her the chance to develop it, we'd have denied the defendant a possible defense. Damn clever.

I almost opened my mouth. Tom's raised eyebrows told me he also got it, and he probably saw even more than I did. I kept still.

"I'm asking you again, Tom. Will you join me in the motion to continue?" Sarah asked.

"I can't join in your motion, Sarah. The Boudreaux family would eat my lunch. You know these hot potato cases are victim driven. But I have to say, you've got one of the better 'po me' stories I've ever heard. Old SOB might even go for it."

I'd never seen Sarah's face so hard. "I've got to give it a good shot. What about we try Richard for the Falgout matter first? He admits the visit to her house, but he denies he did the bad stuff. If you brought a lower charge I might be able to get him to take a plea on that one."

"No." Tom said only that one word.

After Sarah left, Tom turned to me. "Quite a story."

I looked for a bottle of water. I'd been quiet so long my tongue felt like sandpaper.

"Tough. I feel for her. To be the cause of someone's death!"

"Not that. I mean about the possibility of reversal and remand if she puts on very little evidence in mitigation. Could you do a little research for me on that issue?"

Was that all Tom took away from Sarah's story? How it might affect his trial result?

"Sure," I said. "Interesting issue."

Tom stood up. "Sarah isn't going into the penalty phase totally bare, you know. She could always put Richard on to tell his story. It's unusual for a defendant to take the stand, but on this one Sarah just might try. Remmy could be a good witness, now that he's clean and sober. Sarah has some other witnesses—one person who knew the family long ago, her two experts, and she just might turn up the siblings from Illinois. She's a powerful advocate. She'll have a case. I need to look at the reversals—see how her evidence compares to other cases that have been sent down for retrial because 'incompetent counsel' didn't muster enough mitigation. Could you do a little research on cases reversed because the defendant didn't have much mitigation?"

A new assignment. "Today is Friday, Tom. I hope next week is time enough."

"Get on it as soon as you can," Tom said. "State reversals only. I don't worry much about federal habeas any more. With the new restrictions on post-conviction relief, the burden of proof shifts completely once the state system has been exhausted. If we're good enough for the State of Louisiana to have confidence in the outcome, we're home free."

Just hearing reference to the new federal law we call AEDPA, the Antiterrorism and Death Penalty Act, gave me a chill. Thank God Tom hadn't asked me to study that one. If he had, I wouldn't see daylight for days. I had enough to do researching State reversals.

Tom glanced toward the library door to see if anyone was about. He tipped up my chin. A very sweet kiss.

Then he delivered a sock in the gut.

"I've got to make a run up to north Louisiana this weekend to see my parents, Mandy. I haven't been in six weeks. With what's ahead, I may not get loose for awhile."

Pow! Truly a kiss off. Our preoccupation with trial prep had crowded out time with one another. I'd been counting on some catch-up this weekend. My Dad planned to take Taddy out to the marsh Saturday afternoon to repair wood duck houses on his lease. I'd hoped Tom and I could go too. Taddy needed to get out from under Mom's constant watch, and I needed distraction from thinking about the Bar results due Monday.

Another downer hit me. Tom hadn't invited me to meet his parents.

KEY WITNESSES

Knowing the Bar Association website would be jammed on Monday morning, I logged on fifteen minutes before nine. The screen refreshed shortly after the hour. Second on the list, the name Amanda Aguillard leapt from the screen. Tears streamed down my cheeks. I raced around the office with the news.

The whooping and hollering brought Mr. Strait out from his office. "Congratulations. And Mandy, I have a matter I want to discuss with you. Check with Bonnie later this morning. She'll figure out a good time for us to talk."

For a second, I wondered what he needed to talk about, but emotion swallowed my question. At last, sixteen years of study and tests, three years of super hard work and serial anxiety over semester exams, then the big one—the Bar Exam—all history. Life provided few enough of these super highs and fresh starts. For now, I would enjoy, enjoy.

Tom's response—a hug like to a co-worker—pricked, but when I got to my office, a spectacular bouquet of *alstroemeria*, my favorite flower, left no room on my desk for me to drop my purse. *Congratulations and love, Tom.* This gift took thought. Tom must have consulted with my mom and had faith I'd pass.

Or maybe not. He might have thought I'd need consolation

for a disappointment. Damnit. This guy could yank me.

The next morning I remembered Mr. Strait had asked me to come to see him. I encountered Bonnie in a major fluster.

"Oh, Mandy," she stammered, "Mr. Strait just called to say he'd be here in fifteen minutes. I thought I'd deliver a couple of fresh bottles of water to his desk and freshen things up a bit." Her pursed lips, short steps, and fussy mannerisms told me she not only enjoyed service to her boss, she fantasized about making attention to his needs more than a day job.

"He's not going to be a happy camper, I'm afraid," Bonnie buzzed on. "See that man sitting out there on the bench? Whoops, no. He's not sitting on the bench. Now he's pacing up and down the hall. Mr. Andry. Do you know him? He's an architect by training, and quite an artist. He and his wife Evelyn have the little restaurant on Main Street. *Lagniappe*, they call it. A little something extra. There's a basket at the desk for you to pick up a piece of homemade chocolate when you pay your bill."

"I know, and I love the place. Especially the banana mango cake! I've been for lunch a few times, and Tom and I went to dinner the night Brother Andry unveiled the caricature he did of Mr. Strait. What's the problem?"

"Wait. I can't tell you now. I just heard the boss coming in the back. I've got to warn him about what's waiting." She disappeared into Mr. Strait's office.

When Bonnie came back she beckoned me to go on through, giving me a knowing wink as I passed her desk. Did she know everything that spun around in the office?

Unlike my first solo meeting with the boss, this time I had Mr. Strait's full attention. With a welcoming gesture, he invited me to sit down across his desk. He removed his round glasses and laid them carefully on the surface. And he smiled—a rarity in itself. But still no small talk. He tented his hands and looked me in the eye.

"Ms. Aguillard, Mandy, I have been impressed with your work. I'd like to offer you a permanent job as one of my assistants."

A jumble of thoughts fought each other for space in my

brain. I should have realized my internship would soon come to an end, and passing the Bar Exam put a deadline in play, but I'd been distracted by the coming trial. What about the new information Deuce had dug up about the man following Taddy? The guy was still out there. Did I need to quit everything else and concentrate on my little brother's safety? How would working in this office affect my relationship with Tom, and where was that going anyway? Way too much to deal with. I hope my face showed proper appreciation of his offer as I stalled.

"Mr. Strait, thank you very much for your consideration, but —"

He sweetened the deal. "You'd be a real Assistant DA, Mandy. Not Tom's *girl.*"

He'd seen that professional relationship for what it was.

"I'd start you off in St. Martin Parish handling misdemeanors —the crash course in how to conduct prosecutions. You'd screen cases and file the bills, handle all the misdemeanor defendants who come in looking for a deal. On trial day, you'd pick up a file, put your witnesses on the stand, cross-examine the defense witnesses, and argue your cases, one after another. Felonies would be down the road, when you might feel ready."

I think I told Mr. Strait I needed time to think. I hope I did, anyway. He smiled again.

"I'll give you some time to consider. We have three weeks until you get sworn in as a lawyer."

Three weeks! I had a three-week deadline to decide how I'd spend the rest of my working life. For at least two of those three weeks I'd be occupied being backup for a capital murder trial.

Mr. Strait was not finished. "I know I have the reputation for being unapproachable, Mandy, and I find that position useful for me and beneficial for those who work here, but I'm always available for my assistants when there are serious matters to decide. Tom, Ritchie, and you are deep into this Richard case, and a death penalty trial stretches us all to the limit. Feel free to come to me with any problems you might be having."

He'd already categorized me as one of his assistants.

"In the meanwhile, do you have a few moments to talk to

Brother Andry out there? He's giving Bonnie fits about wanting to see me and I absolutely have to get on the road to Baton Rouge for a legislative hearing. Andry can't understand why we're declining prosecution of some woman he found in his house. You just have to listen to his story—actually it's one of our better ones —and give him a chance to vent. Bonnie!" Mr. Strait called out. Bonnie appeared in a nanosecond. "Give Mandy the police report on the Andry investigation." Bonnie scurried off to do her boss' bidding. "Bottom line, there's no criminal intent. Give me a few moments to slip out the back."

I returned to my office, picking up the police report and a cup of coffee on the way, straight caffeine being my medicine of choice for the headache taking up residence behind my eyes. Talking to a victim was going to be a new experience, and it scared me. I still hadn't had lunch. Not a problem. I couldn't have digested anything.

First I called home to check on Taddy. All OK there. I closed my eyes to block everything out and tried relaxation from tip to toe. Then I went to the front to greet Mr. Andry and show him in —not to my cubbyhole but to the library. I figured I deserved decent space for this duty.

Andry swept his arm out to invite me to sit first—as if I were a guest in his restaurant.

"So what can we do for you, Mr. Andry?"

I could tell from the skeptical look on his face, that he was well aware he'd been shunted down to the lowest person on the staff.

"Well..." I could also tell he couldn't resist telling his story to a fresh pair of ears. He began—and then stood up to enhance his performance. "It was a week ago Wednesday. Evelyn and I went back to the house after we finished cleaning up from lunch. You know where we live? Out Highway 182 on the way to Lafayette. Cypress house, well screened from the road by a jungle of bushes. Must have been about three in the afternoon when we got there. To be accurate, I went home first, Evelyn came about a half hour later."

I'd heard about that routine. Most people thought Mr.

Andry's contribution to *Lagniappe* was limited to being host *extraordinaire*, putting on his natty tweed sport coat, meeting and seating the customers, mixing a drink or two, then wiping off the bar when the day was done. Not so, Tom had told me. He shopped, supervised the maintenance, and kept the books. And let's face it, he made *Lagniappe* a fun place to be.

"The front door of our house seemed to be bolted from the inside. Puzzling—we never do that—so I waited for Evelyn in my studio. She had a key to the back. We went on inside together. Well, we knew right away something was amiss." He flipped his left hand out in a gesture of disgust. "Pillows disturbed in the den, a picture off the wall. And then, in the bedroom, we saw... Well, let's just say we knew someone had been there." He pantomimed someone throwing back the covers. "Dis-gusting! Then we heard a woman's voice, humming at the top of her lungs. We opened the bathroom door. A vision to behold! A dome of bright orange hair in a pool of bubbles."

Mr. Andry told his story with the panache of a Saturday night British comedy on PBS.

"I know I shouted, probably screamed like a banshee. 'What the hell are you doing in my house?' A woman stood up, turned around, one hand on her fat hip, stark naked. In her pelt, as my grandmother liked to say. *Enormement!* That woman had boo-boos down to her knee caps. She could've nursed an elephant!"

I know a smile broke out of my face. I couldn't help it. *My* grandmother would have said, *C'est une valentine.*

"Look, Ms. Aguillard. This isn't funny. You know what she said to me? 'Your house? This isn't *your* house.' A sassy shake of her head. 'This is Stephen's house.'"

"Who's Stephen," I asked.

"Hell, I don't know." Mr. Andry sat down. "I was in full rage, but Evelyn had her wits about her and called 911. You know what the woman told the deputy who came? She'd met this guy named Stephen at the E&L Lounge, and he invited her to come to *his* place. He left her there, in *my* house, and went out for beer. Ms. Aguillard, that woman was in our house, in our bathroom. She'd been in my bed—and probably not alone!"

I struggled to keep hold of some sort of professional demeanor. "I have the sheriff's report right here, Mr. Andry. They arrested her, right?"

"Yes, they arrested her, and they took her down to the station —after she'd put on some clothes, thank God. They kept her for just a few hours and let her go."

I had a grip on my funny bone now and could think like a lawyer. "I'm looking at the report, Mr. Andry. Apparently the bartender at the E&L remembered her, that she'd had a drink with some guy and left with him, but the bartender didn't know either one of 'em. On follow-up, not the bartender, not the woman, no one, knew the man's last name or ever saw him again."

"So that's it? That woman was in my house, damnit!"

"Yes. I understand. She claims she was invited—"

"That's absurd. She must have known it wasn't some Stephen's house."

My mind ran through the possible charges. Burglary? The woman didn't enter to steal anything. Nothing taken except a couple inches of bubble bath. Unauthorized entry? She thought Stephen had asked her in. Criminal trespass? Implied authority. She said Stephen just opened the back door. I felt like I was answering a law school exam question, but I couldn't think of a single charge for a woman invited to have a romp.

"Sir, the District Attorney has a problem bringing a charge. Think about this for a moment. Suppose the DA took the case to trial. Two witnesses, you and the woman. No Stephen. She says Stephen—boyfriend as of the previous couple of hours—invited her to come to *his* house. What do you think would be the verdict?"

Mr. Andry stood up again, paced around the table, muttering. "A three-hundred-pound woman in a bathtub of bubbles, in my house, in my bed, and the law isn't going to do thing about it. Dickens was right."

"Dickens?"

"Yeah. Charles Dickens. The law is an ass."

We talked it out together. Mr. Andry understood the concept of criminal intent. None here. I learned a good lesson. What people need most is a willing ear. He left thanking me. At least not every case coming into the office involved a capital murder.

I kept checking with Bonnie, but Tom still hadn't returned.

I picked up the Falgout/Boudreaux material, now no longer contained in one red file or even two, but packed onto a rolling cart. For the rest of the day, and the day following, I poured over the record. I listened to tapes and reread every word by and about our three key witnesses for the guilt/innocence phase of the trial —Dudley LeBlanc, Skipper Domingue, Deputy Mark Hamilton. I reviewed my taped interview with our penalty phase star, Lydia Falgout.

The tape of the Falgout interview puffed me up a bit. I'd done a good job. Lydia Falgout clearly stated she'd seen no one other than Remmy Richard. But, and a big *but* at that, would she have seen another person if he'd been there? She had no clear answer one way or the other. When Remmy came to her door, Mrs. Falgout had not looked inside the truck he came in. She'd been hit from behind as soon as she came out of the back of her house with her money.

I could see no value in talking to Lydia Falgout another time. Her testimony was good for us as it stood; I'd be shooting myself in the foot to muddy the water. We had given Sarah everything we had. And anyway, Mrs. Falgout would be a penalty phase witness at least a couple weeks down the road. I checked her testimony off my list of concerns and turned to the material on the key witnesses for the guilt phase of the trial.

Dudley LeBlanc seemed to know quite a bit about his cousin Remmy Richard, but what did he know about Remmy's buddies? About his drug suppliers? Did any of them have an accent? Rereading Dudley's statements, I found no indication anyone had asked him the critical question. Dudley's knowledge about Remmy's friends might well bolster Sarah's *other dude* defense, and we wouldn't want what he knew to come out for the first time in Sarah's cross examination. We needed to ask cousin Dud if he'd ever had contact with someone who had a Tennessee accent, and we needed to ask him ASAP.

Then I looked at all the material concerning Skipper

Domingue. Skipper had described the scene of two men he overheard talking in *The Southern Wave*, the bunkhouse down the highway toward Intracoastal City. And he overheard what they said. Incredibly, here, too, I could find no mention anyone asked Skipper about their voices. Did one of them, by any chance, have a Tennessee accent? We needed to run that down right away.

I felt good about the testimony of our third key witness. As an experienced officer, Mark Hamilton would know how to handle himself on the stand. We could leave him alone.

My conclusion? We didn't have all the information necessary to go to trial. I walked over to Tom's office, talking to myself all the way. Bonnie stopped me in the reception area.

"Tom left for an appointment with the jury consultant, Mandy. He asked me to tell you he'd see you in the morning."

Damn.

"Is Ritchie around?"

"I think he's just about to leave. I'll see if I can catch him."

She couldn't. He'd gone to be with Tom. Frustration fired my gut.

Bonnie read me and threw out a lifeline. Distraction, really. "See the guy out there in the hall leaning on the his supply cart? Ti-Pop's his name. I need to get him to change a couple of burned out bulbs. I heard you were asking about the courthouse ghost. Ti-Pop's a believer. Wanna come?"

"Sure." Anything to whip my foul mood.

We stepped out into the hall and Bonnie introduced me to an old white man with rheumy eyes and a drop of spittle in the corner of his mouth. Bonnie tended to her light bulb request and moved on to ask about the courthouse ghost. Ti-Pop's eyes dropped to the floor.

"Miss Bonnie, you t'ink me a crazy ol' man."

"No, I don't think that."

Ti-Pop shuffled his feet, placed the light bulb he had in his hand back on the cart, and slanted a look in my direction. "Well..."

"Mandy's cool, Ti-Pop. You can talk in front of her. Tell me."

He did, glancing around to make sure no one could overhear.

He spoke directly to Bonnie, his face showing a shadow of suspicion each time he glanced in my direction.

"I hadn't heard him for months. But one night, about a week ago, I'm moppin' the floor in the sheriff's office. I know I'd left the door open. In fact, I'd propped my bucket right there. I don't like to get shut up in places. I heard him. A swoosh, two doors slammin' shut."

"So you think Honoré's ghost was there, in the sheriff's office?" Bonnie asked.

"I know it. Yeah, I do. Sometimes he's other places, but dats where I hears him swooshin' by, in the sheriff's office. You know why in the sheriff's office? 'Cause dat's right under where they had the trap door. They shouldn't a done that up there, you know, strung Honoré up over the trap door like dat."

"Honoré Migues did a bad thing, Ti-Pop. Putting a bullet into that lady after she turned him down and married Mr. Crawford. And smack in front of the whole lunch crowd at Coleman's Cafe."

"Yeah, I know. My daddy was out on the lawn the day they did the hangin'. I was still a kid in short pants, but I can't forget when Daddy came home and tol' me. A hangin?' Bad business. And no one knows where Honoré got buried. I don't t'ink he *was* buried, and dat's why his ghost just can't res', can't go on to the beyond."

"Do you ever hear the ghost say anything?" Bonnie asked.

"Just moanin'. In the beginnin' he scared me, but I'm kind of used of him now. I talk to him a lot, even if he don't answer. Makes the time pass quick. And, you know, if you don't make friends with a ghos', watch out. Heaven help you if you ever get lost up there on the third floor. 'Go-oo ho-o-o-me.' That's what the moaning says to me. Don't go up dere, Miss Bonnie."

"They made a maze of the place when they did all that renovating. Covered up the trap door. Next time they remodel, I bet they'll find it," Bonnie said.

I hoped they'd never uncover the spot, but the story sure was a convenient urban legend for people who didn't want to work after dark. Bonnie thanked Ti-Pop for talking to us, and I did too. Patience to wait for Tom had been restored.

Back in the office, Bonnie gave me a nice compliment. "You have the right vibes for this job, Mandy. Mr. Andry left here smiling, and Ti-Pop doesn't tell most people about what he hears." Bonnie also had me on board already.

"Tell me, does Ti-Pop share with you because you also believe?"

Bonnie flushed. "To be honest, I kinda do."

* * *

The next morning, Wednesday, mid-point in the last week before trial, Tom bounced into my office with his charm in full display.

"We called your Mom and Bub to come in this morning to talk about their testimony. I'm hoping you'll join us and give me a hand."

We called must have meant Tom had someone else extend the invitation, not telephoned himself. Add that to the number of things about Tom I seemed to find aggravating these days. And I still hadn't had an opportunity to discuss my concern about our key witnesses.

I agreed to meet with my mom and Bub. Why was I so reluctant to stand my ground? Maybe because once you let a man get on top of you, it's hard to take back control. Damn.

As it turned out, Ti Pierre had gotten word of the invitation. He came also, his obnoxiousness in full display.

"Look here, Mr. Barnett. I'm now the head of this family. I'm the one who should tell the jury about what happened. You want someone to let them know what the loss means to us? I should do it. The oldest."

"I appreciate your willingness to testify. I really do. But—"

Ti Pierre cut him off. "And putting Bub on the witness stand to talk about the death of his father is one shitty idea, man. How could you ask him to do that? He's suffered the most."

Tom needed me. "Uncle Ti. Let me explain a bit about what we have to do for the first phase of the trial. Right at the start, we have to tell the jury how we came to know PawPaw was missing.

Remember how it came down? Bub went over to the house for his usual coffee and biscuits. PawPaw didn't answer the door so he went to get Mom. She called everywhere. So just the two of them were there at the beginning. After that, law enforcement can take up the story, but for the first part, we need Mom and Bub. You weren't there."

Pierre banged his big fist on the library table. "*I* know all that stuff. *I* can do it."

"Anything you'd have to say would be hearsay, just repeating what someone else said. The judge won't allow that. Mom could tell the story without Bub, that's true, but we'd like the jury to meet Bub right off."

Yes, and see him. I hoped my smile in Bub's direction told him love motivated my willingness to display his handicaps to the jury. "If you feel you can't do it, Uncle Bub, Mom can carry the ball."

Bub sat up as straight as his curved spine would allow. "Of course I can do it. For PawPaw, I could do anything."

I turned to Tom with a suggestion. "Why don't we see about Uncle Ti testifying in the penalty phase? You know, a bit about how much the family has been devastated. He'd be real good at that."

Tom clouded up. When it came time to consider the capital issues, Tom didn't want some rant from Ti Pierre turning off the jury. I gave Tom a slight lowering of one eyelid, almost but not quite a wink. I was saying, *just trust me Tom. When that time comes, I can get Ti Pierre out of the picture.*

Tom's expression eased as he got my drift.

"Good idea, Mandy. The penalty phase." He turned back to Ti. "We'll see about doing that. But now, let me go over the details of the first day with your sister and brother. We're a couple of weeks away from the penalty phase of the trial. I'll be calling you to come in and meet with me when we're close. I like to review testimony with witnesses near the time they take the stand. Works better that way. We'll see about having you testify at that time."

Tom hadn't promised Uncle Ti he could testify, just agreed

he'd see. I smiled, thinking about how my parents handled my brother, me, and now Taddy, when one of us had a request they had absolutely no intention of granting. *We'll see* meant NO. Uncle Ti wasn't aware of our little family translation, but Tom had picked up on it. He turned back to his original plan—Mom and Bub in the first phase of the trial.

Ti Pierre swallowed the hook. "All right, Mr. Barnett. Let me get back on my run." He left.

Tom had thank you to me all over his face.

When we finished working with Mom and Bub about their testimony, I tried again to talk to Tom about my witness concerns. No luck. But he did bring up something I hadn't thought of.

"Ritchie has a new worry, Mandy. He's wondering if there's any possibility our two cases—the death of your grandfather and the death of the CI—could be related. Was it possible a Tennessee man with a connection to the local drug trade could have figured in the Richard events?"

The same idea had been lurking around in my head. In fact, I believed it was likely.

Tom continued. "But frankly, I just can't face thinking about that right now. Anyway, Ritchie and Buddy are in my office waiting to go over the questionnaires returned by our prospective jurors. They're the locals who know where all the bodies are buried. We'll be tied up the rest of the day, and again tomorrow. But tonight we can relax. How about dinner?"

"OK. But I do want to talk to you about our key witnesses."

"Tomorrow. We can talk tomorrow. Tonight for dinner the trial will absolutely be off the table. I hear Gino Delafosse is at *La Pousierre* in Breaux Bridge. Wanna dance?"

"You bet."

Putty in his hands, I didn't press. My heart wanted to put my relationship with Tom front and center. And like him, I wanted to forget this damn trial, just for a little while.

Tom did relax. But somehow, when he'd fallen asleep at my side, and I lay awake unsatisfied, I had the feeling I'd been used— solely for his distraction and release.

PART IV

REVELATIONS

I took my seat next to Tom at the counsel table in the courtroom. Across the aisle, Sarah fidgeted with her papers. She was really going to do it—make her motion to continue the trial because of the death of Remmy's sister. Tom leaned toward me and whispered a question.

"How about the issue of reversal for incompetent counsel if Sarah offers no evidence of the defendant's dreadful childhood? Did you prepare something for me?"

Damnit again! I'd been so pissed at Tom for not being around when I needed him, and then so high with my Bar results, I'd forgotten to print out the memo I'd spent Saturday putting together. I'd wing it and tell him my conclusion.

"Sorry, Tom. I did the research, but the assignment totally slipped my mind. I found no cases on point. By analogy, appeal court remand solely because counsel offered no direct testimony about a troubled childhood would be quite unlikely. Sarah's planned defense, even without anyone from the family to take the stand, will most likely meet the minimum standard for competence, at least as the law is now. We don't know what the Supremes may say down the road."

Could Tom say my competence met the minimum standard

for an intern? Hardly. I couldn't think of the name of a single case in support of what I'd just told him.

"That's all I need to know," Tom said without looking up from his papers. He didn't exhibit a bit of disappointment in me, or much interest either. He'd focused only on the business at hand—Sarah's latest motion.

Richie joined us. He stuck close to Tom these days, thank goodness, but for motion days he rarely got involved. This morning he tipped back his chair and raised his eyes to the one silver art deco ball decorating what used to be the balcony of the courtroom before the latest renovation stuffed the area with air conditioning ducts. Tom needed someone like Richie at his side. He was such an old hand at trial work not even a death penalty case raced his motor. Ritchie mused.

"Did you ever stop to realize how little a judge knows about what's really going on? In a minute His Honor will sit up there looking omniscient and wise. Not! An empty head, body hidden in a dress. After months of in and out, up and down, we lawyers will produce a spare drama to spread out on the stage before him. He'll have a few tough decisions to make; I'll give him that. We'll let him know a bit more of the background to help with those, but for the most part, the guy's clueless."

Tom loved it. "Ah-ha! Richie's our philosopher this morning."

I appreciated Richie's ability to ease the tension.

Sarah took the podium to make her motion. While she spoke, Judge Bonin struggled to wear an appropriately impassive judicial demeanor, but he didn't succeed. Faced with a choice between disbelief and anger, he picked the first option. His tight mouth and raised eyebrows broadcast his disdain for Sarah's eleventh hour plea.

"Mo-tion de-nied." Two words sounded like four. Judge Bonin gave each syllable the same hard emphasis, and he illustrated his ruling with a sarcastic smile. "Next case," he bellowed.

Several attorneys jumped up from their seats and rushed forward to replace us at the counsel tables. Poor guys. They'd inherit SOB's ill humor.

We packed up quickly and headed for the exit. Outside the double doors, two men in serious suits flanked a somber-faced, out-of-uniform Deuce. Agent Robert Taylor wore pinstripes and shiny black FBI shoes, not the fatigues and boots I'd seen on him in the field. The other man wore black. Deuce introduced him as Raul Menendez of Drug Enforcement, the DEA. Tom led the group into the DA's office. On the way, Deuce and Tom had a short exchange I couldn't follow—something about Buddy being missing in action. I'd ask Tom about that later, if I got a chance!

We settled down in the library. Deuce placed a notebook, similar to the one he had for the Falgout/Boudreaux investigation, minus the label, on the conference table. He directed his first comment to me.

"Let me tell you right off, Mandy, we've made significant progress identifying the man who threatened your brother. We've pulled in more reinforcements from Lafayette, and your house is the center point of maximum security. Nobody can get close to him."

I wish I could say Deuce made me feel better. If I closed my eyes, I saw the stunned look on Taddy's face after he'd stumbled on the body.

Deuce turned to Tom. "I understand your main concern right now is the trial of Remmy Richard whereas I'm out there working on the death of my CI. But bear with me. You'll see where I'm going in a minute."

Tom looked skeptical. He kept the Richard file under his right hand and from time to time checked his watch. I had a foot in both projects. Deuce's investigation would be critical to finding out who was threatening Taddy, but my family also chomped at the bit to get on with the trial they expected to bring justice for the death of PawPaw.

Deuce gave us an account of his activities during the past ten days. First, he made a trip to Nashville, Tennessee, to meet with Jack Alexander. Deuce had two goals in mind: the owner's permission to search Jefferson House, and finding out if Alexander could give him any help figuring out why odd events kept happening at our lake.

Tom interrupted. "Traveling on whose dime, Deuce? I heard you were on leave from the sheriff's department."

"Right. My boss refused to fund my investigation into Mitchell's death because he's still pissed the FBI has taken the case out from under him. I did better with the Lafayette sheriff. Remember, I'd been on loan to him for the aborted drug bust, and he felt pretty bad about what happened. Guilty even. As follow-up, he gave me cover, and a good chunk of change. I took a leave from Iberia."

Tom apologized for the interruption. Deuce went on with his report.

"Mr. Alexander seemed really affected by what happened to your grandfather, Mandy, and he wanted to cooperate any way he could. You know, I guess, he has Jefferson House on the market."

I did know, and I knew who I hoped would buy the place—the man who'd done such a fantastic job recreating the plant nursery destroyed in the catastrophe. Many of the original plants couldn't be replaced—they'd been gathered from all over the world—but a lot could be done.

Deuce continued. "Alexander quickly signed off on permission for us to search his house, the grounds, and the dock, the search to be conducted in cooperation with any law enforcement agencies we chose, with or without the drug dogs. Then he helped me think through possible explanations for the events that kept taking place out there. We explored a lot of ideas, but came back to the most common reason for criminal activity —drugs. Either the trade or pursuit for money to buy the stuff. We figured that while the house stood empty, someone familiar with the area had been using the place. I asked Alexander to tell me about every family member and every guest who had occasion to visit Jefferson House in the past year."

At this point Deuce patted his notebook. Alexander had given him a long list of names and supplied good information on most of them, but until Deuce asked, Alexander didn't include his troublesome nephew on his list. To Alexander's knowledge, Mickey Brown hadn't been in Louisiana for over a year, but he'd reached for the phone and called his sister for verification. He got through to her right away.

Deuce spoke more quickly now, and his eyes sparkled. A couple times his words stacked up in his mouth until he had breath enough to get them out. We caught his excitement.

"Alexander's sister, half sister, actually, said a while back her son briefly had a job in Louisiana—night work for some warehouse. Smooth talker, he had no trouble getting jobs, but they never lasted long. He just couldn't stay away from drugs. But the sister didn't give up on her son. Over this past Christmas she got him to go to a farm in Minnesota for aftercare from his most recent treatment program."

Deuce now had an address for the farm and vital stats on Mickey Brown, enough information to run him down.

"Are you with me so far?" Deuce asked Tom.

"I'm with you."

Not totally. Tom checked his watch again. Deuce looked at me, inviting my reaction.

"Mickey Brown would have a Tennessee accent, I suppose."

"Bingo, Mandy." Deuce took a breath, visibly trying to calm himself. "I knew I was onto something, could almost taste it, but I didn't want to head for Minnesota on my own. I checked back with the Lafayette sheriff. With his OK, I brought the FBI and DEA into the investigation. These guys." Deuce gave Agent Taylor and Agent Menendez a nod and a smile.

"Together, we three conducted a thorough search of Jefferson House. The dogs didn't light on anything inside, but they went crazy in a couple of the outbuildings and under the dock. No solid drugs, but they must've picked up on residue. Your story from here, Agent Taylor."

FBI Special Agent Robert Taylor took over.

"You've heard how we put together Operation Rough Romaine?" he asked Tom.

"Not in detail. Go over it for me." Tom still had his hand on the Richard file.

"Last winter, in a joint investigation with our counterparts south of the border, our agents witnessed cocaine being loaded onto an airplane in the mountains of Columbia. In northern

Mexico, they watched the cocaine being repackaged, then strapped to the underside of pallets of lettuce and loaded onto eighteen-wheelers for the trip to the U.S. Our agents in Texas picked up the same rigs being checked at a trucking company in Houston where the rigs were rerouted to grocery warehouses all over the south. You know, the cartels that run these operations make billions. They can start with a kilo of cocaine that cost $2000 in Columbia; when the same kilo finally hits the US streets at retail, it could net $200,000. The ultimate user pays through the nose—literally—for the risks taken by everyone along the way."

And we think we're going to stop the flow of drugs? For a cut of that kind of money, people will continue to take risks no matter how many agents we put on the payroll, how many walls we build, or how high we build them.

"So how did we pull off Operation Rough Romaine? We identified bit players in northern Mexico and in Houston, put them under pressure, and offered them incentives to cooperate. They gave up bigger fish. At this end, at the produce warehouses all over the south, we set up undercover agents to meet the special pallets of lettuce and accompany them to the area distributors. When we got our ducks all in a row, we had cooperating individuals in place all along the route.

"On the day of Operation Rough Romaine, we closed in. We followed the drugs and made arrests. All in all, the operation netted over fifty perps, some for offenses carrying lifetime penalties. A very good job, if I do say so myself."

"We'd all second that," Tom said.

"But as you know, we lost Lafayette. Deuce's CI had gotten himself assigned to take the wheel of one of the trucks so we could nail the retail distributors in Acadiana, but someone tipped off the driver of the rig headed this way. The driver bypassed Lafayette, kept right on going, probably to Alabama."

"Damn shame," Tom mumbled.

"Right. We've learned to live with less than one hundred percent success, and this operation was more productive than most, but we don't sit still for retaliation." Agent Taylor looked over at Deuce. "Our man inside the Lafayette warehouse, Deuce's informant, turned up with a bullet in his brain."

Agent Taylor looked at me now. "That's the body your brother stumbled on, Ms. Aguillard. Tough on the kid, but his observation turned out to be key to cracking the case. Even in shock, your brother paid attention to details. Remember what he said? The man who threatened him didn't talk like someone from around here. Southern accent. 'Baw-die,' I think he put it. Cool kid."

"Thank you," I said, swallowing hard to keep tears at bay. What is it about women and tears? We cry when we're sad, yes, but sometimes when we're over the top with any emotion—anger, fear, relief, even joy, pride, you name it. My God, I cried when I got the Bar results.

Agent Taylor continued.

"And now for the rest of the story. Deuce was determined to get whoever hit his CI. He persuaded us to work the same system, in reverse. In Operation Rough Romaine, the little guys had given up bigger fish. Now we went looking for a big fish we'd nailed in the operation to give us a smaller one—namely, the Houston trucker who sent produce to the Lafayette area. I studied the list of all those who were arrested over there and came up with a candidate to turn—Ramon Romero, the owner of a trucking firm who'd been passing the lettuce through his shop and on to Acadiana. Son of the founder of the company, silver spoon, inherited his job, lived high, we figured Ramon was accustomed to much more luxurious accommodations than the Harris County Jail. Are you with me?"

"I'm with you," Tom said. And he was. He took his hand off his own papers and picked up a legal pad. Ever the prosecutor, he perked up at facts indicating the possibility of a connection that might end up on a local DA's desk. Maybe on his.

"The three of us—Deuce, Agent Menendez, and I—tried to visit Ramon Romero at the jail. He refused to see us. Talk to the cops? No way. And get a bullet in the forehead? Better to gamble on first offender leniency, get a short sentence, and have his life to live. But we didn't strike out totally with the visit. The jail gave us the name of Ramon Romero's lawyer."

Deuce interrupted Agent Taylor. "Tom, could we get Mr. Strait in here? We're getting to the local angle."

Tom declined the request. He would hear it first. Mr. Strait's staff protected his time.

Agent Taylor continued.

"The trip to see the lawyer, that was a kick. A chrome and glass office in a high-rise overlooking downtown Houston. Pony-tail, two pinky rings, eight hundred dollar silk suit, the guy made a good living handling defendants with serious drug charges. He also turned us down. No way he'd ask his client to give State's evidence, he said. Then Deuce here went to work, carefully laying out a plan that would give us what we needed at minimum risk to the guy's client. Deuce may be the new kid on the block, but he's pretty good at making a deal."

I had the same thought. Deuce was not destined to spend his career like Buddy Aymond, still doing sheriff's patrol when he was on the verge of retirement. Would Deuce go to the FBI? Would he follow his father's footsteps to the State Police? I wondered.

"Deuce told the lawyer we needed info about the Lafayette drug scene for a different investigation, one for which Ramon Romero had no legal responsibility. In return for something verifiable that would take us farther down the trail in our case, and wouldn't require public testimony from his client, we'd put in a good word with our agencies. They'd see about getting Romero some favorable consideration in return. You know, the possible drug sentences today are horrendous. Romero's lawyer was looking for a deal, but one that wasn't going to put his client in line for a cartel bullet. Took some time, but eventually the lawyer agreed to set up a meeting. I'll pass the baton back to you, Deuce. It's your story."

"Not really. Romero had no charges in my jurisdiction I could use for chips, but I'll tell this part. We met with Romero and his lawyer in the lawyers' consultation room at the Harris County Jail. We made our offer. Bottom line: Romero agreed to tell about the routine he used to send the special pallets of lettuce to the produce distribution centers across the south."

Deuce and Agent Taylor had Tom's full attention now. "This is great work, guys."

"Romero told us he made his delivery arrangements on the telephone, using code words, speaking to people he couldn't identify, and then didn't have any further contact. But once, when one of his trucks had an accident just outside Lafayette, he had to make a follow-up call. Romero called the contact and reported the breakdown. The familiar voice told him to contact a number with a 337 prefix to arrange an emergency offload of his cargo. Romero didn't have a name of the person in 337, but the man he talked to—and here's the zinger—had a strong southern accent. Texas accent, I asked? Definitely not. North Carolina? Maybe. Somewhere southeast for sure. Yes, he said. Could be Tennessee."

Reflexively, my hands clapped together. An enormous grin covered the bottom half of Deuce's face.

Tom pinned down the obvious conclusion. "You're thinking the 337 area code guy was Alexander's nephew, Mickey Brown. Right?"

"Right. Mickey Brown had a drug history. He'd been around here. He had the accent. Take over, Raul. Your shop, the DEA, worked the next step."

"This was Thursday, last Thursday. Seems like a month ago," Raul said.

I had to pay close attention to understand Menendez. Heavy Latino accent. His tongue pinned his words behind his front teeth before letting them go. Agent Menendez told us the DEA ran background on Mickey Brown, real name Michael, and found a criminal record in Nashville, Tennessee. Brown got on the books as a juvenile and continued to add new charges through last year. He had a bunch of arrests for possession of drugs and petty theft, but only one conviction—three years ago for a misdemeanor simple battery. Nashville PD faxed Menendez the police report for the original charge in what looked like a drug deal. Brown had ended up with only a simple battery conviction after having been arrested for aggravated assault after a knifing. Wow!

"Da guy musta had amigos to get off with a misdemeanor," Menendez said.

Or important family. The Alexanders have clout around here so they probably had even more back home in Nashville.

Menendez said he made contact with the drug treatment facility in Minnesota—*the farm*. Mickey had spent the months of last December and January in their program, but he'd been gone since then. Disappeared. Left no forwarding address. *The farm* wouldn't tell much about him. Privacy and all that patients' rights crap, Menendez said. But he was sure they were talking about the same guy. Same date of birth.

Deuce interrupted. "While Raul is talking to *the farm,* I pick up that one Michael Brown, same DOB, had a job as a night clerk in the warehouse at the Lafayette grocery distributor where my guy, Glen Mitchell, worked. Bingo!"

Deuce leaned back in his chair and again gave us his big smile. "So Tom, do you think we've got enough to get a judge to sign a warrant for the arrest of Mickey Brown? We can start with a charge for conspiracy to distribute cocaine. Then, after we do some more work to ferret out the dirty hand of the drug cartel that just saw the demise of one of their lucrative distribution routes, we move on to the next charge—principal for the murder of Glen Mitchell. I'm damn sure Mickey Brown fingered Mitchell for the hit by the cartel's assassin."

Tom stood up. "I know you're not going to stop until you make that next link, Deuce. Let's go see Mr. Strait."

I hung back, and Tom didn't look for me to join them.

I waited with Bonnie while the men went into Mr. Strait's office. They came out an hour later. Mr. Strait had approved the facts for an arrest warrant, and Tom, Deuce, Agents Taylor and Menendez left to find a judge. They planned to celebrate over a late lunch. I didn't get an invitation for that either. I went to my little office, and, I'll admit it, sulked.

Mid afternoon my phone rang. A call from Mom cut into my funk.

"Mandy, we have a problem." She had her high squeaky voice again.

"What, Mom? What is it?"

"Taddy—I don't know where he is."

"What? Tell me. You went to pick him up at school, right?" Mom had taken the week off to deliver him to school, pick him up at three, and keep him in sight until his head hit the pillow at night.

"I was a few minutes late. When I pulled up to the usual place in the car line, he wasn't there. The duty teacher couldn't tell me if he went with anyone else, nor could the principal."

"Oh, my God, Mom. Hang tight. I'm on my way home."

I called out to Bonnie as I tore out of the office. "Tell Mr. Strait Taddy's gone missing."

I didn't care to leave word for Tom.

I hope I never have another period of time like the hour that followed. Ever.

Mom had called Dad at the same time she called me. He stood in the doorway when I pulled up in front of the house. The three of us clung to each other. We cried. We prayed. The whole neighborhood soon crawled with cops; Mom had called 911 from school. Memories of the search for PawPaw came tumbling back in all their horror.

And then I heard that voice.

"What on earth is going on here? What on earth is going on? Oh, my goodness me. Everything is topsy-turvy. Yes, topsy-turvy, that's what everything is."

My God! Aunt Mazie. She'd pulled up in her little Toyota, wheels on the neutral ground, pointed the wrong way. She rolled down her window and called out to us as the back door of the car popped open and Taddy and Jay tumbled out. The boys stood shell-shocked at our emotional meltdown. Mom went tearing down the walk to grab Taddy.

I screamed at Aunt Mazie. "Where the hell did you find them?"

"What do you mean where did I find them?" Aunt Mazie asked. "What are you saying? Whatever are you saying? At school, of course. I found them at school."

"You picked up Taddy at school?" I shrieked.

"Of course. I was visiting 'Thilde, just visiting, you know. Drinking a cup of coffee. I offered to go pick up Jay. Yes, pick up

Jay. When I got to the school, Taddy stood there with Jay. You know, right there with Jay. I told them both to get in the car, and we'd go get a sno-cone. Yes, we'd go get a sno-cone. They both love cherry, yes they do. Then I brought Taddy home. What on earth is going on around here? What's going on? What are the cops doing all over the place?"

I looked at Mom and Taddy and wept. I cried out of utter relief. Then I went to the first cop I could find and sheepishly told him to call off the alarm. Taddy had been found.

I recalled Deuce's words of advice when we thought a white pick-up truck was following us. In a critical investigation, when the tension is high, you have to watch out for paranoia.

But, by God, the truck we saw that day did turn out to be part of this drama.

I closed my eyes and silently prayed. *Please, God. Find that damn Mickey Brown and put him in jail. Maybe then my family will be safe and we can go back to work putting Remmy Richard away for the death of PawPaw. The family can't take any more of this.*

THE LAKE ROAD

The words on my calendar grabbed my eye. MONDAY - *Jury Selection - State v. Richard.* I had to talk to Tom. Today was already Thursday. One more workday, then the weekend. Not that I looked forward to pointing out any potholes in the road to the Richard trial. Not to Tom or to my family. Whatever opinion they had about the appropriate penalty for Remmy Richard, every single one of them counted the days until the ordeal of the trial would be history.

I stood before Bonnie's desk and made my pitch. She shook her head slowly, right to left and back again.

"No. Not a good idea. Tom, Richie and Buddy took the packet of jury questionnaires and closed themselves behind the door at nine o'clock this morning. They gave me clear instructions. Do not disturb!"

So Buddy had reappeared. I never got a chance to ask what that was all about.

I had to respect what Tom was doing. I remember hearing the selection of a prosecution-minded jury is as important to the outcome of a trial as the evidence, especially in a capital case. Some say even more important. Tom, from north Louisiana, was at a disadvantage. He needed input from the locals.

"OK, Bonnie. I'll wait, but let me know the minute Tom comes out of there, even to go to the bathroom."

Once again, Bonnie's kind smile made me accept the situation—but not for long. We'd be taking a monstrous risk to start this trial. What if, after swearing in the first witness, new information from Skipper Domingue or Cousin Dudley triggered the need for further investigation? Stop the trial? Double jeopardy. We might never again be able to try Remmy for the murder of PawPaw.

Mr. Strait had told me to bring him my problems. Did I dare? No. My underlying instruction had been to follow Tom's direction. And I had another concern about talking to the big boss. What would I say if he brought up his job offer? I hadn't made up my stupid mind. I cooled my heels until afternoon. At two o'clock, impatience conquered caution.

I walked past Bonnie's desk, watched her body stiffen with disapproval, and rapped on the door of Tom's office.

"Yes?" Tom's voice through the door. Far from an invitation to enter, but I did.

"Tom..."

He looked in my direction but kept a finger of his left hand marking his place in a packet of jury questionnaires. His right hand held a pen. "I'm going to get to you, Mandy."

Buddy leaned back in his chair, his feet on the desk, big fat feet in black brogans with worn down heels. Both of Richie's hands held stacks of questionnaires. This wasn't going to be easy. At that moment, all three of those guys annoyed the hell out of me.

Words caught in my throat, then sputtered out like water broken free from a fire hydrant.

"We've *got* to ask our key witnesses some more questions, and we're running damn short of time. The detectives could do it, I know, but I don't have the authority to ask them to. Do you think you could...?"

Tom dropped his pen on the table. His words slowed to a crawl. "We're going to be seeing every damn witness in the next few days." The *esses* hissed.

Richie's eyes widened as he picked up the chill between us, but he got my point—and agreed. "Maybe we should address the issue now, Tom. I think I mentioned to you my concern that if or when we learn anything that could possibly tie the two crimes—"

"One thing at a time. We finish with the jury first."

Anger bit my gut. Tom hadn't given my concern a speck of respect. Nor Richie's either. If Richie had the thought there could be a connection between the two cases, I could be damn sure Sarah would also. We could look forward to her jumping on Mickey Brown as the mysterious *other dude* she claimed did the deeds for which Remmy had been charged.

"OK, Tom. I'm *so* sorry for bothering you." I spit out the words, and headed out the door.

Tom called out to my back. "If you want to, go talk to Mr. Strait."

I paused, and answered him without turning around. "Thank you. That's just what I'll do."

Yes, but only after I got my emotions under control. I flew back to my little office, sat down and tried to get air down my throat.

Something else popped into my brain. I punched the number on my phone to call Mom.

"Months ago, when PawPaw was still missing, you told Detective D'Aquin you knew something about a difference of opinion PawPaw once had with Jack Alexander. Something to do with Mr. Alexander's nephew who went fishing with Uncle Bub when they were boys. Can you tell me anything more about that?"

"There was some incident way back when, but I never heard the details. Your dad might know more. Is it important? I could probably reach him through the fire station."

"Yes, Mom. Very important."

Almost an hour passed before she called back.

"Took me a while to run down your dad, but he gave me an earful. Way back, when PawPaw had Alexander's visiting kids over to fish, he caught the nephew doing some really bad stuff to a litter of kittens. I shudder just thinking about it. The boy picked up each kitten, swung him round and round, and then threw him like a shot putt out over the lake. He launched three of 'em before PawPaw could get down to the lake to put a stop to it."

I swallowed hard. Cruelty to animals is a standard red flag in any mental evaluation.

"So, what happened about that? How did PawPaw handle it with Mr. Alexander?"

"Your dad says PawPaw stormed over to Jefferson House and told Mr. Alexander he never wanted to have that boy in the yard again. Actually, Mr. Alexander was as upset as PawPaw. That was the last time he ever had the boy at the lake. If you want to know more you could call Dad. He's still at the station. I have to go pick up Taddy and don't want to be late. Even though Taddy knows for sure he's not supposed to leave with anyone, not even family, I don't take any chances. I'll talk to you tonight."

Click. Mom ended the call.

My God. Early delinquency, a charmer who could get jobs but not hold them, addictions, and now cruelty to animals. The symptoms raced through my mind to a possible diagnosis. We could be dealing with a sociopath. Now I had the courage to go directly to Mr. Strait.

Bonnie showed me right into his office. His intense eyes peered at me through the round glasses, and his hands tented before him on the desk. He listened in silence to what I had to say about the urgency of talking to our witnesses again, about the possibility we had received evidence we were obligated to disclose to the defense, and about time ticking down to the beginning of the trial.

"Tom is totally focused on moving forward, Mr. Strait. For two solid days he's been closeted with Detective Aymond and Mr. Castille going over the jury questionnaires. He says he'll get to me later, but I'm concerned."

His eyes fixed on mine, Mr. Strait tapped his forefinger on the desktop. Fifteen seconds crawled by before he spoke.

"I agree with you about the need to talk to those witnesses. Soon. We can defer consideration of the exculpatory evidence issue until we know what else Skipper Domingue and Cousin

Dudley might have to say." His expression softened. "I've seen this kind of obsessive preoccupation with pre-trial preparation before. Serious trials, especially capital cases, suck the life out of us. No doubt I was guilty of the same tunnel vision when I was on the front line, but that's what the support of the office is here for—keeping perspective. We've got to get a conviction the right way or not at all."

Mr. Strait picked up the telephone and called downstairs for the detectives. Elnora reported that Buddy had left Tom's office and didn't say where he was going, but she reached Deuce in the Lafayette Sheriff's Office fine-tuning the dragnet for Mickey Brown. Mr. Strait handed me the phone. I laid out the issue for Deuce, and he saw the urgency right away.

"Let's tackle Skipper first," Deuce said. "I could shake loose from here and get to *The Southern Wave* by around 6:30 tonight. Could you see what you can do about setting up a meeting? Call me back to confirm?"

"I'll do it."

"I know you could talk to those guys by yourself—I learned that when I saw you with Mrs. Falgout—but I wouldn't want you to go into that bunkhouse alone, unless maybe you get turned on by sweaty men decorated with tattoos."

Thanks, Deuce. I needed the levity.

With just a wave of his hand, Mr. Strait indicated the phone on a side table. Thank God I'd thought to bring the number with me. Skipper Domingue agreed to the 6:30 meeting.

"I'll see you there," Deuce said when I called him back. "I'll keep checking around to try to find Buddy. He's AWOL, I'm afraid."

Mr. Strait and I talked a little more about the issue of exculpatory evidence, and I could tell he took seriously the possible need for disclosure to the defense. He was sure Tom would finish jury prep by tomorrow and be ready to make the crucial decision.

"His case, you know. It's his call."

Back in my office, I settled in my chair and willed tension to drain away. No doubt about it, I could be looking at a very satisfying career if I went to work for Mr. Strait. If I wanted to be a prosecutor, that is. *Amanda Aguillard appearing for the State of Louisiana.* I liked how that rang.

But my mind swirled in confusion about my future with Tom. One argument couldn't erase the closeness I'd felt during the past six months, especially when everything seemed to be going south during the tense run-up to a capital trial, but had I been a blind and infatuated idiot?

Even worse, was Tom even thinking about a future with me? Damn the poison thoughts my Aunt Mazie had put into my head.

* * *

That night, I left the house at 5:30, giving myself an hour for the thirty-minute ride to meet Deuce for our interview with Skipper. I didn't know the exact location of *The Southern Wave,* but I figured someone at a gas station in Delcambre would give me directions. Only one road led from Delcambre to Intracoastal City. Had to be along there.

A police car blocked the right turn out of our driveway so I turned left, opting for the back way around the lake, past the turn-off to the Jefferson House, the site of the old salt mine, and onto the cane field road through to the swamp area on the far side of the lake. Front way or back, the distance from my house to Delcambre would be about the same. Fewer cars traveled the back way, but the route was perfectly safe. At the tail end of winter standard time I could count on at least another hour of daylight. Plenty of time to get around the lake.

I hadn't been this way in years. Past Jefferson House, I went by half-a-dozen modest frame houses nestled into the lakeshore. I had no idea where I'd live one day when I had a real job, but I hoped I could be in the country, with all its imperfections, and not a developer's perfect dream, the houses all built according to the latest architectural fad—French Provincial, southwest, New England Colonial, whatever, the St. Augustine grass lawns fertilized and watered to a deep green, trimmed weekly to a perfect carpet. No soul.

My hands on the steering wheel sensed a slight shimmy, the vibration increasing when I reached the rougher surface near the site of the old salt mine. I wasn't concerned. Cane trucks rattling these roads during grinding take a toll on the blacktop. Come spring, no doubt this route would be on the parish short-list for asphalt patches. I slowed a bit, but kept moving. Another quarter mile and I couldn't blow off the sensation of a drag to the right. I had a problem.

I pulled over to the side of the road, stopped the car, and stepped down. I came around to the front and took a look at the suspected source of trouble—the front passenger-side tire. Yup. Almost flat. I must've picked up a nail or something sharp. Damn.

I could change a tire—I'd done so a few times in college when I drove a beat-up truck J. Allen had retired from life on PawPaw's farm—but calling Dad to come out to give me a hand would be quicker. Then I made a more careful inspection of the offending tire—and gasped. No sharp object lying innocently in the road had caused my problem. Someone had sliced a deep and ugly gash into the outside wall. I clamped my jaws to still a shudder of fear.

I opened the passenger side door, and reached for my phone. My brand-new, graduation present iPhone sat in my purse, dead as a doornail. Keeping the charge had not crossed my mind during my hell of a day. OK. I could just roll on the flat.

Then I noticed steam coming out of the hood. Damn. Someone had also drained the radiator. My car was a goner.

What was plan B? Run home? Just a couple miles. I looked down at my stupid work shoes. No. I couldn't run in three-inch heels.

I could walk home. No. Not enough time.

When did someone get to my car? Perhaps while I changed clothes after work. What about the high security the detectives assured me would keep everyone away? Apparently worthless. This was crazy. Who would do such a thing? Why? The hell with Deuce's warning to beware of paranoia. I had a full-blown, gigantic case of it. I couldn't get enough air into my lungs to stop shuddering. Someone was after me, and he was probably that sociopath, Mickey Brown. I scrambled into the car, locked all the doors, and succumbed to panic.

Five minutes or fifteen, I couldn't say. Enough, already. Rational thought returned. Forget trying to make the meeting with Deuce. Get the hell out of there. I got out of the car, went around to the back and reached for the latch to open the trunk. Maybe I had an old pair of running shoes in there I could put on my feet.

Everything went black.

* * *

Consciousness returned slowly, expanding in concentric circles from a center point in my brain like ripples on the surface of the lake. Where was I? On my way to meet Deuce for an interview with Skipper Domingue. Someone had another plan.

I cautiously raised my eyelids and saw nothing. Night had swallowed the day. Spread-eagle, flat out on my belly, my right cheek scraped the coarse surface of the blacktop. OK, I was on the road behind my disabled car on the back way around Lake Peigneur.

I struggled to sit, the effort causing a shot of pain at the base of my skull. I reached up and touched my hair. Sticky and wet. I smelled my fingers. Blood. I closed my eyes to let a wave of dizziness pass. No slip and fall had put me in this position. I'd been hit.

I didn't know if I'd been out cold for minutes or hours. I remembered that my phone, my only timepiece, lay dead in the car. Did the moon high overhead mean it was close to midnight? I should have paid more attention to that kind of science when I was in high school.

But what damn difference did it make what time it was? Holding the back bumper, I pulled myself to my feet. Wait. Whoever did this might still be somewhere around. I shrank back down behind the trunk of the car.

Idiot. What makes you think the person is somewhere up

front? He could be anywhere—up front, on the side, next to your ear, right behind you. I raised my head for a cautious look around. Nothing but the night.

Clouds scudding across the sky intermittently allowed the moon to cast a pale light on the scene. Dense trees walled both sides of the road. I knew the area; there would be no houses or any possible source of help for at least a mile in the direction I'd come, and ahead, only swamp and sugarcane fields until the road around the back of the lake emerged at the Delcambre Canal. No wonder Uncle Jay thought Ti was crazy to think he could find landmarks for pirate treasure out here in this jungle. Worst of all, no one would know I was missing. Deuce would wonder what had happened to me, but he'd just go on to the bunkhouse because I'd told him the interview with Skipper could *not* be delayed. People at home wouldn't expect me to return for hours. If and when they set out to find me, they wouldn't come this way on the first try. Tom? Damn Tom. I wasn't even on his radar.

The clouds blew off, the night sky opened, and for just a moment the moon cast a brighter light on the road ahead. Nothing. Just as well. At this point I trusted no one but myself. I pulled up to a standing position. The clouds again covered the moon, and all light disappeared. The reality of my isolation overwhelmed me. I fell against the car and gave way to sobs.

For how long? I don't know. I needed to think. Should I get back in the car and stay there until dawn, hoping someone might come by? No. I wouldn't trust anyone who did come. Cicadas buzzed. An owl hooted his mournful call. I felt I'd been dropped onto the surface of the moon.

I had to think that the person who slashed my tire was the same person who threatened Taddy. Mickey Brown? Yes. But what was his game? Threats and vandalism were doing a good job of frightening the hell out of us, but if he were really dangerous, wouldn't he have done something worse by now? But then maybe if he were Sarah's mythical other dude, he'd already done worse—killed PawPaw and maimed Mrs. Falgout.

Why did he hang around? He could've gone to Mexico or Canada months ago. Then I thought of all those indicia of socio-pathology. No one could predict what someone like that had in mind.

Home. That's where I wanted to be. I stood up, straightened my shoulders and resolved to walk the way I'd come.

But I had only one shoe. I pushed in the latch on the trunk, dug out my flashlight, and searched the ground. No shoe around where I fell, or up under the car. I walked around the car, covering every foot of pavement on either side and a good twenty feet behind and ahead. The guy must have pitched my right shoe into the bushes on the side of the road. I'd never find it in the dark.

I felt more than heard a low rumble. Vehicle headlights appeared ahead. I snapped off my flashlight, dashed for the side of the road, and threw myself down into the growth. Blackberry-bush stickers and poison ivy seemed minor risks under the circumstances. I crouched in the thicket until the car sped past. No. It was a truck. Light color. Damn. I watched the taillights swerve again to avoid my car. Uncontrollable shudders returned.

Insects buzzed and pricked my face and neck. No mosquito at Lake Peigneur would have to seek out another blood meal for at least a week. I wanted to go home. OK. Get up and go.

I had only one shoe. Oh, I remembered, I had been going to the trunk to look for an old pair of running shoes.

No such luck, but I found a towel and created a makeshift boot for my bare right foot. I started to walk. Diddle, diddle dumpling. As each layer of cloth wore through, I retied the material to construct a new sole. Underneath the cloth, my foot scraped raw and bled.

Strange shapes emerging in the intermittent moonlight set my imagination into overdrive. What lurked behind the trees pillowing up close to the road? Croaking frogs, buzzing cicadas, the hoot of an owl were enchanting background noise from the screened porch at my house, but even those familiar sounds seem menacing when you're completely alone in a pitch black southern night. The closer you listen to the sounds in our lowlands, the more you hear the abundant life that calls south Louisiana home.

A rat ran across the road; a soft flutter of wings and a puff of air had to be a bat flying within an inch of my face; a limb recoiled as some denizen of the night found a new perch. An owl perhaps? I could have handled each of these events alone, but together they tipped over the boat. I dissolved into tears and sank down on the tarmac.

But for just a few moments. Get up you wimp. You want that nut to come back and give you more of what he's already done? I resumed my hobbling walk.

A break in the trees at the drive to Jefferson House sent my spirits soaring. I was close to home. I could feel gravel embedded in the cuts on my foot, but if I just made a few hundred yards more, put one foot down and then the other, I could get there. I rounded a corner, and a small glow appeared ahead. No sailor sighting safe harbor rejoiced more than I did at the sight of a light on my own front porch.

Then disaster. Taking my eyes from the pavement for just that moment, I tripped and fell. Pain shot through my right ankle, above my shoeless foot. My flashlight had fallen with me, smashed and gone dark.

The glow of light from my house taunted me from a distance. How could I get there?

First: get out of the middle of the road, ninny. If someone did come by, they'd run me down before I could get out of the way. Keeping my ankle immobile, I dragged myself to the shoulder, shredding my left pant leg on the rough asphalt. Next: assess the damage. My ankle and my toes wiggled. I hadn't broken anything. I flexed my foot. Painful, but working. Now to see if I could get up. No, not without something to get hold of. The clouds broke and I made out the shape of a road sign on the shoulder just ahead.

I dragged myself toward the sign, each pull leaving cloth of my pants on the pavement. Then I was leaving behind my own skin. I reached the sign, grabbed the post, and pulled myself upright. My ankle held. I grasped the signpost until a wave of dizziness faded. Then somehow, some way, with my porch light as a beacon marking safe harbor, I made it home.

"Mom," I called out as I fell on the steps. She heard my

pounding and came to the door, holding the telephone.

"Deuce is calling for you—my God, what happened? You're all torn apart!"

Mom dropped the phone on the floor and reached out her arms to pull me inside.

"I'm OK," I said. I picked up the phone and sat bleeding on the carpet to talk to Deuce.

"Skipper's not sure one way or the other," Deuce reported, "but he thinks one of the guys he overheard had an accent. Maybe you would've done better at getting him to recall the voices. Wait a minute. You sound funny. Is something wrong?"

"I'm home now, Deuce. Can you come on over here?"

Deuce didn't get it. "Not right now, Mandy. My buddies are calling. We have sightings of white trucks all over the parish, and I've got a few dozen to run down."

"Well, Deuce, I have one to add to your list." I told him my story.

"You stay locked inside your house, hear me? I'm calling Tom right now. I'm telling him to forget the damn trial and get over there to be with you."

When Deuce hung up I told Mom I needed a bath, first aid, and a cold beer! Did I need Tom? I really didn't know.

THE WHISKEY RIVER BRIDGE

Dad took one look at the bottom of my feet, set his lips hard together, and shook his head at Mom.

"The ankle looks OK to me, but someone has to pick each piece of gravel out of those cuts on the bottom of her foot and she'll probably need a shot or two. Tetanus, antibiotic, serious pain medication. Our girl is way beyond my First Aid, Mimi. We need to get her to the emergency room."

All I wanted was to hit the bed but I was too weak to protest. Dad's arms lifted me into the car, and I faded out hearing Mom giving an order to one of the officers on duty. "Go with them," she said. "Nobody leaves this house without someone who has a gun on his hip."

I surrendered to the caregivers.

Two hours later, Dad and I returned home. Weak as a kitten, I let Dad carry me up the front steps. The sight of Tom coming to me from the living room made me even weaker. He looked like hell. He reached out his arms and encircled my shoulders. I let myself lean on his chest but kept my fingers gripped tight on the bars of the crutches. I felt his lips brush the side of my face.

"Thank God you're safe." He whispered the words as a prayer.

Yes, I was glad to see him, but I couldn't get past the past week—or past thinking about what a doormat I'd been for months. I'd be keeping my distance until I had a chance to figure out where we were headed.

"I'm a bit worse for the evening's adventure, Tom, but nothing's broken. I'm going straight to the bath. Maneuvering the tub is going to be *another* adventure. Mom says she has a plan."

And you're not part of it!

He spoke softly into my ear. "When Deuce called me and said you hadn't shown up in Delcambre, I—I—" His voice cracked.

On one level, I was mad as hell. But underneath the hurt, Tom Barnett still had me. Damn. My tears welled up again. I managed to get out three words.

"Not now, Tom."

Mom came to my rescue. "I'm afraid we need to steal Mandy and get her cleaned up a bit before those meds kick in and she passes out cold."

I hesitated at the door to the hall and looked back at Tom. His arms hung at his sides as limp as two wet towels.

"We'll talk tomorrow," I said.

* * *

I woke up in the morning to the sound of Mom tiptoeing into my bedroom. The bedside clock read almost ten. I couldn't remember when I'd slept so late.

"Hello there, my girl. How're you feeling?"

"Stiff and sore, and I can't say I had sweet dreams." I stretched and felt one monster cramp seize my left calf.

"They sent you home with pain pills in case you might need 'em. Can I get you one?"

"No, thanks. But a good strong cup of coffee would be very welcome. And water. I feel I've been crossing the Sahara."

"I'll leave you yesterday's *The Daily Iberian*, Hon. I just got around to looking at it. There's an article about the jury selection beginning on Monday. Tom was here earlier, but he had to leave for a meeting with Mr. Strait. He wanted to come into your room to see you, but I only let him take a peek. I assured him you were going to be fine. The poor guy is pretty upset. He said he'd be back as soon as the meeting finished." Mom glanced at her watch. "Long meeting. That was over two hours ago."

Mom's strong coffee helped clear my fuzzy head. I felt better.

I read the article in the newspaper but didn't like it much. When called by the reporter, Tom had refused to comment, which left the field to the defense. Sarah took full advantage. Tom would have a lot of work to do when he questioned potential jurors for Remmy's trial. Many of them would have read the article and considered the possibility there could have been *another dude*. Damn. Maybe there was.

Even after all I'd been through, the case stayed in my mind.

Mom had a different take. "You don't have to worry about the article. I find it amazing how few people read the paper, or read anything, these days."

Mom helped me dress and look a little more presentable, which I wanted to do before seeing Tom. I got settled on the living room sofa to wait. Dad kept asking me what was going on, but I couldn't tell him. I didn't know.

As it turned out, I had plenty of time. Tom didn't arrive until after one. And right out of the box he had surprising news.

"The trial is being continued."

"What?" Mom and I said at the same time.

"Well, first off, Deuce gave us a report about his meeting with Skipper Domingue. When pressed to remember the conversation he overheard in the bunkhouse, Domingue thought one of the men might have had a drawl, as he called it. In view of what Taddy told us about the man he ran into on the path to Jefferson House, that puts us in possession of investigatory evidence we'll be needing to disclose to the defense. Then another shoe dropped. Yesterday a tool pusher coming in from seven days offshore couldn't find his vehicle on the Diamond Offshore remote lot. When the sheriff's men did a thorough search of the premises, and ran the info on the twenty-some white trucks parked there, they found a five-year-old Toyota pickup with a Tennessee plate registered to one Michael Brown. Their conclusion? Sometime in the past week someone stole the worker's truck, another white pickup of course, left the Toyota in its place, and headed out. Best guess? Mickey Brown. Unfortunately, with fresh wheels, now he could be anywhere.

"If that wasn't enough big news for one day, Buddy surfaced —you know he's been missing for 48 hours—and went out to ask cousin Dudley what he knew of Remmy Richard's pals. Dudley babbled a bunch of nonsense, but in the process spilled out a good dozen names we'll have to run down. With all that, and the possibility of triggering double jeopardy if we go forward with the trial and then have to stop, I had to accept the situation. Continuance."

"So you made the call?" I asked.

Tom shrugged his shoulders, and smiled. "I guess you could say I did, but when Mr. Strait listed the considerations, I knew what I had to do."

I had the picture. Smart man, that Mr. Strait.

Tom continued. "I called Sarah and she came right in. She was ecstatic. Together we informed Judge Bonin we'd be filing a joint motion to continue the trial. I won't repeat the words the judge used in reaction to that news."

"How about Buddy and Deuce. How are they taking it?" I asked.

"The detectives understood right away, but it took a good hour for Mr. Strait to get the sheriff to calm down. He was all gassed up and ready to roll for Monday's performance before the jurors. Damn guy. He actually said he'd already had his dress uniform cleaned! I had a little more than that invested in proceeding."

Tom turned to Mom. "And now to our victims. Mr. Strait is going to call all your family members to come to a meeting at five o'clock this afternoon. He and Sheriff Landry will appear together, and I'll be there as well. I expect your brothers and sisters will be very disappointed, but we really have no alternative. There are enough questions about this case to require any ethically responsible prosecutor to blow the whistle. We need to get to the bottom of any new information before we can go to trial."

Dad shook his head. "One thing you certainly got right, Tom.

This whole business is going to be a long haul. I get what you're saying about continuing the trial—too many questions—but the man scaring the dickens out of Taddy, and responsible for what happened to Mandy yesterday evening, is still at large."

I didn't want to tell Dad my thought. Sarah may have been right all along. The man was out there, all right, and he wasn't just trying to scare us. He was a real killer.

Tom read my mind. "Every member of your family is going to have security now. Every one."

Yeah. Lot of good that does.

Mom left to call Dora and tell her not to get on a plane to Louisiana. Tom had more information to give us.

"I didn't know about this until this morning, but for some time Agent Taylor has had an FBI profiler working on the search for Mickey Brown."

"Really? The FBI has the resources, don't they? So what does he think?" I asked.

"*She*. A PhD psychologist. She thinks Mickey Brown is a sociopath."

"Bingo! That's what I thought. Delinquency, animal torture, charmer who gets but can't keep jobs. But the way I understand it, a sociopath isn't necessarily a killer."

"Right. Not necessarily, but there's a lot to know about this guy and little of it good."

Dad had the next question for Tom. "Does the profiler think he's really dangerous, or is he just trying to scare the wits out of us?"

"I wish I knew."

Tom was stalling. If Mickey Brown really did kill PawPaw and beat the hell out of Mrs. Falgout, even if it happened months ago in one drug-induced interval, we had reason to be scared. This guy had nothing to lose. My turn for a question. "One thing makes no sense to me, Tom. Why does Mickey Brown stick around? He must know everyone's looking for him. If he has a car and access to money from his drug business, I'd think he'd just head for the hills."

"Agent Taylor tackled that. He says Mickey Brown is not

some poor schmuck who sells on a corner outside the projects or on the strip in Lafayette. His theory is that Brown is the drug cartel's *go-to* man in this area, and they aren't going to *let* him leave. You can't fool around with the guys who control the life. Remember what happened to Deuce's confidential informant? And the FBI also has an alternate theory; this area is where Brown has access to drugs. He doesn't want to leave his supply."

Maybe I suffered from the after-effects of yesterday's ordeal, but I had trouble seeing the picture. Was it because we had Remmy Richard on the eve of trial for the murder of PawPaw but he really hadn't done it?

"Dora's happy to waste her plane ticket," Mom announced when she returned. "So what about Remuald Richard, Tom? Do you think he's just someone who got caught up in something much bigger than he could understand? Is his so-called confession no more than an admission that he supplied information, and maybe a car, to Mickey Brown and then felt responsible for what happened afterwards?"

"He's no angel, Mrs. Aguillard. He was there for Mrs. Falgout, set her up and either beat her himself or watched her get beaten up time after time. He's going to have to answer for that. As for what happened to your father, he was involved in some way. We have to get to the bottom of all this before we proceed to trial. That's a prosecutor's professional responsibility."

"OK, so where do you go from here?"

"Priority one is finding Mickey Brown. The profiler believes he's probably still in the area. After that we tackle the legal consequences."

Good old Mom turned us away from these worries. "So Mandy, do you want to come with me to the meeting this afternoon and witness your Uncle Ti have the tantrum of the decade?"

"Not on your life. Surely I'm entitled to be excused."

Tom leaned forward on the sofa. I could tell he had more to say, but his sideways glance at Mom gave away his reluctance to talk to me with her in the room. Mom picked up on this right away.

"I'm going to fix a sandwich for Mandy, Tom. Is your name in the pot?"

"Thank you, but no. I need to get back to the office to dictate the motion to continue. I'll be seeing you later on this afternoon."

Mom disappeared into the kitchen. Tom didn't get up. He stayed seated, holding my hand.

"Mandy, I've been a total fool, and I know it. I've never been so scared for anyone as I was for you when Deuce called me last night. If anything had happened to you..."

I squeezed Tom's hand. "Go do what you have to do, Tom. We can talk later. Maybe tomorrow."

He brushed his lips across the top of my hand and left.

* * *

Saturday morning I awoke to a buzz of conversation on the other side of my bedroom wall. I started to swing my feet over the side of the bed. A wave of nausea hit me. I had a way to go before being OK. I ached all the way down my back.

"Mom," I called. "Can you give me a hand?"

No response. My robe lay on the foot of the bed where she had placed it after supper. Wobbling on the crutches, I made it to the bathroom, then out the bedroom door to see what was going on. I found Dad, Mom, Uncle Bub, and Aunt Tut staring at the TV screen.

"What's so riveting about *The Price is Right*, guys?" I asked.

Dad jumped up to help me. "We were just about to get you up." He made a place for me on the sofa. "Detective Washington sent word the TV had cameras on someone threatening to jump off the Whiskey River Bridge. He said we should tune in. Wait! Here it comes."

The television screen showed a live feed, the camera playing on a large concrete structure. I watched a roadway take shape in the picture. Green metal struts crossed underneath. On one strut, I could make out the figure of a man balanced on his left foot, his right hand grasping another metal strut over his head. A gaping void opened beneath him.

The voice of the announcer came through.

> *This is Martin Newman signing off from the Whiskey River Bridge in the Atchafalaya Basin. We now return to regular programming. We will have our next live update at the top of the hour.*

Dad slapped his hand on his thigh. "Damn. We missed it."

"Tell me what's going on."

"We don't know, dear. Elnora from the sheriff's office called and told us to turn on the TV to channel 10, Eyewitness News. They had a camera on a jumper on the Whiskey River Bridge, and Detective Washington thought the guy might be Mickey Brown. She said Detective Aymond was on his way out there also."

Mickey Brown? Maybe he might just drop into the treacherous current, into the swift waterway that led straight to the Gulf. If he did, he'd never be heard from again. Now that would be a fine solution.

"Has anyone heard from Tom this morning?" I asked.

"Yes, sorry. Slipped my mind. He called and said he's running down some information and would be by later."

I pulled my phone out of the pocket of my robe and called him. He didn't pick up.

Mom got up and looked out the front door. She reported we still had our officers on duty. We sat staring at the screen for the next hour. At last the live feed came on again.

> *Martin Newman, Eyewitness News, on location on I-10, at the Whiskey River Bridge. We are live on the scene. As you can see, the situation here is as it was an hour ago. To recap for those of you who have just tuned in, before eight o'clock this morning, our camera crew was returning from assignment in Baton Rouge. They spotted a man—now identified by law enforcement officers as Michael Brown of Nashville, Tennessee—clinging to a girder beneath the bridge that crosses the Whiskey River branch of the Atchafalaya River.*

*We have remained at the scene, bringing you
hourly live reports.*

A shudder ran through me. "Mom. Who is that I see there? Is
it Tom?"

Mom stood up and peered more closely at the screen. "Tom?
I think it is."

The announcer continued.

*Westbound travel has been reduced to one lane,
backing up traffic from Baton Rouge all the way to
Highway 415. Here at the bridge, we see various
vehicles positioned to facilitate a rescue of the
individual perched below. Rescue vessels from the
Iberville Parish Sheriff's Office have taken up
positions below us, on the right bank of the river,
poised to head out into the fast moving current.
Wait. Now I see a deputy of the Iberia Parish
Sheriff's Office lying on the roadway of the bridge,
directly over the location of the man beneath him.
The deputy is on his stomach, hanging over the
edge, tethered by ropes to prevent him from
slipping. He's talking to the individual below.*

I stood up and moved closer to the screen, and gasped.
"That's Deuce, Mom."

"God, yes. It's Deuce."

"And that's Tom standing next to him," I said.

"I think so. Hush. Let's hear this."

I felt seasick just peering at the figure below the roadway. "Is
the guy—Mickey Brown, I guess—swaying like that? He's gonna
fall."

Dad corrected us. "It's mostly the camera swaying. From the
angle of the picture, I figure the camera is on a boom hanging
over the water."

I sat down so I wouldn't lose my balance. "My God. Look at
Deuce! He's gesturing with both hands. God I hope those ropes
are secure. Wait, he's backing off. The deputies seem to be

lowering some kind of contraption over the edge, down to where the man is."

> *It appears that the deputies are trying to convince the man under the bridge to take hold of a basket-like device so they can raise him back up to the roadway. The man is waving them off. Apparently he has refused the effort at rescue. Deputy Washington is placing an instrument on his belt and returning to his position on the roadway, leaning over the edge.*

We saw the reporter consult with another individual at his side.

> *We have just been informed that Deputy Washington is going over the edge. He has asked for a recording device so he can preserve whatever this man has to say.*

The announcer tipped his head, apparently listening to the bug in his ear.

> *We appear to be settling in for a long wait, ladies and gentlemen. We will return to our regular programming, but stay tuned. We will interrupt at any time we have developments from the scene.*

"Damnit! Why can't they just let us watch? Even if you aren't a part of this, it's surely better theater than *All My Children!*" Dad got up and went to the kitchen for a glass of water. I felt hot. Sweat gathered under my arms.

"Speaking of children, where's Taddy?" Mom asked.

Dad answered. "It's OK. He's in his room playing a video game. I shouldn't feel this way, I know, and I wouldn't want Taddy to hear me say this, but I'd be perfectly happy if they'd back off and let the guy fall into the river. It isn't as if the deputies took a Hippocratic oath, or anything."

My read, it was only a matter of time before that happened anyway. If the guy wouldn't take help, the way he was hanging, he was gonna drop. The Whiskey River had the deepest channel in the whole basin. The current was incredible.

Fifteen minutes later, the live feed came on again.

> *Ladies and gentlemen. We are again on the scene at the Whiskey River Bridge. A man tentatively identified as Mickey Brown of Nashville, Tennessee, is hanging beneath the roadway, a good hundred and fifty feet above the swiftly moving river below. Detective Deuce Washington of the Iberia Parish Sheriff's Office has been trying to persuade the man to accept help—to grasp a basket hanging just a few inches from his free hand. The man has apparently refused to do so. But we have a new development, a new situation developing. Another Iberia Parish deputy sheriff has arrived on the scene. He is speaking with Deputy Washington in what appears to be a heated discussion.*

"My God! Look at that!" An Iberville Parish deputy was fitting a harness of some kind around the newly-arrived deputy's waist. Deuce was gesturing, trying to grab the harness from him. The newly arrived deputy was clearly Buddy Aymond.

> *Ladies and gentlemen, it appears the newly arrived deputy is taking the harness from Deputy Washington and going over the edge attempting to rescue the man below. He is insisting that Detective Washington think of his family. Yes, the second Iberia Parish deputy, tentatively identified as Buddy Aymond, intends to go after Michael Brown himself.*

The reporter kept talking, but we weren't listening. In stunned silence we watched everything change. Buddy gave up trying to get into the harness. He grabbed a rope tied onto a pillar on the roadway and swung himself over the edge, dangled for a few moments, and then found footing on the same strut as

Mickey Brown, two feet from him.

Dad stood up and grabbed the sides of his head. "What on Earth? Is Buddy crazy? He isn't tied. He could fall."

Up on the roadway three men rushed forward. Tom, an Iberville Parish deputy, and Deuce. They were shouting to Buddy, who stood on the strut below, next to Mickey Brown.

Dad shook his fist at the screen. "Grab him, Buddy!"

"Oh, my God!" I shrieked. " Buddy, are you crazy? Trying to be some kind of goddamned hero?" Ice crept up my spine.

In horror, we watched Mickey Brown grab onto Buddy's rope and the two of them began to wrestle. Something turned the whole scene to slow motion.

And then the strut was empty.

"Wait!" Dad yelled. "Are they out of the range of the camera?"

No.

> *Ladies and gentlemen, the two men have lost footing on the strut. The rope is swinging free. The men are no longer visible.*

A long silence. The report resumed.

> *It would appear that the two men who were on the strut have plunged down into the Whiskey River. They have disappeared beneath the surface of the water.*

Silence again. The screen showed the reporter moving among the crowd, speaking to one person and another. After what seemed like an eternity of dead air, the sound came back on.

> *We have just witnessed a tragic event, and a heroic event as well. Deputy Buddy Aymond took the place of a young Iberia Parish deputy who was attempting to rescue the man on the strut under the bridge. He insisted he be the one to pull the man back up. Both men, Mickey Brown and Deputy Buddy Aymond, have fallen to the water below. A rescue boat has been launched from the shore, but—*

"They're gone." Mom stuck her fist in her mouth. I squeezed my eyes shut. Aunt Tut covered her eyes with her hands and started to pray the rosary. Of course. Dad cleared his throat and went to the kitchen to get a drink of water.

"Buddy did that on purpose," I whispered.

The camera found Deuce and Tom in the crowd on the roadway. Safe.

* * *

Two days later, Tom and I went together to talk to Father Martin at Our Lady of the Sea. Buddy Aymond had no family to plead his case, and he couldn't by any stretch of the Canon Law be said to be a Catholic in good standing, but Father Martin got it. Although bedeviled by demons, Buddy had been a human being in good standing with the loving God of our faith.

Deuce and his family sat with us at the service. On my knees, I asked God to be with Tom as he prosecuted Remmy Richard as a principal to murder, death penalty off the table. The recording of Mickey Brown's confession would appear to make the case a synch, but *it ain't over 'til it's over.* My most fervent prayer: be with Tom and me as we work through the possibility of a future together.

ACKNOWLEDGEMENTS

The author acknowledges with gratitude the counsel of Ann Dobie, Diane Moore, Vickie Sullivan, Stephanie Judice, and her more than daughter-in-law Margaret Simon, accomplished writers all, who patiently guided the development of the writing abilities of someone from another field. Without their encouragement, this work would have vanished long ago.

ABOUT THE AUTHOR

Anne L. Simon was born in the East, educated at Wellesley, Yale and Louisiana State University Law Schools, and moved to South Louisiana fifty years ago. She practiced law with her husband, raised a family, and became the first female judge in the area. Now retired, she travels, enjoys family near and far, takes long walks with her dog Petey, and writes stories based on experiences in her adopted home.